PRAISE FOR ROBERT BAILEY

The Mediator

"Relentlessly suspenseful and full of heart, *The Mediator* is fresh, surprising, and packed with twists—and with fallible but gutsy characters to pull for. I couldn't put it down."

—Meg Gardiner, #1 *New York Times* bestselling author of *Shadowheart*

"Bailey delivers another winner. Relentless tension, razor-sharp legal maneuvering, and a protagonist whose determination burns through every page, this addictive thriller proves that a mother's love is the deadliest weapon of all."

—Robert Dugoni, *New York Times* bestselling author of the Tracy Crosswhite series

"Max Ringo, disgraced lawyer turned mediator, is a heroine worth rooting for in this race-to-the-last-page thriller about a scheme driven by billionaire greed. But it's Stephanie, whose quiet redemption as she takes back the reins on her life, that levels up this tale of two women pitted against forces conspiring to take them both down in different ways, bringing the story to its powerhouse conclusion and provoking cheers along the way."

—Jenny Milchman, Mary Higgins Clark Award–winning author of the Arles Shepherd thrillers

The Boomerang

"Breathtaking! A brilliant concept, brilliantly told. *The Boomerang* sets the standard for big, palm-sweating thrillers, with the added extra that it positively brims with that element often missing in such books: heart. Word of warning: before you start, clear your calendar—I guarantee you won't want to stop until the very last page. Bravo!"

—Jeffery Deaver, *New York Times* bestselling author and creator of Colter Shaw, from CBS's *Tracker*

"The stakes couldn't be higher in this compelling and character-rich political thriller. As much about the shocking secret truths buried deep in the annals of power as it is about fatherhood, friendship, and the things we'll do for the people we love most, *The Boomerang* is thought provoking, riveting, and action packed. Don't miss it."

—Lisa Unger, *New York Times* bestselling author of *Close Your Eyes and Count to 10*

"*The Boomerang* is much more than a fast-moving thriller with a unique premise. It is a powerful story of family and friendship that will touch the heart of anyone who has had a loved one with cancer."

—Phillip Margolin, *New York Times* bestselling author of *An Insignificant Case*

Rich Justice

"Sturdy legal thrills for readers willing to go the distance with a flawed hero in an even more flawed world."

—*Kirkus Reviews*

Rich Waters

"Small town, big story—*Rich Waters* works like magic as a mystery and a legal thriller, but what I loved best was Robert Bailey's attention to the details of character and place. I'd ride with Jason Rich to a courthouse anywhere!"

—Michael Connelly, #1 *New York Times* bestselling author

"A compelling dive into the life of a lawyer out way past his depth."

—*Kirkus Reviews*

Rich Blood

"*Rich Blood* is a deliciously clever legal thriller that keeps you turning pages fast and furious. Robert Bailey's latest is wildly entertaining."

—Patricia Cornwell, #1 *New York Times* bestselling author

"Well-drawn characters match the surprise-filled plot. Phillip Margolin fans will be enthralled."

—*Publishers Weekly* (starred review)

The Wrong Side

"Bailey expertly ratchets up the suspense as the plot builds to a surprise punch ending. Readers will impatiently await the next in the series."

—*Publishers Weekly* (starred review)

"Social tensions redoubled by race intensify a workmanlike mystery."

—*Kirkus Reviews*

Previous Praise for Robert Bailey

"*The Professor* is that rare combination of thrills, chills, and heart. Gripping from the first page to the last."

—Winston Groom, author of *Forrest Gump*

"Robert Bailey is a thriller writer to reckon with. His debut novel has a tight and twisty plot, vivid characters, and a pleasantly down-home sensibility that will remind some readers of adventures in Grisham-land. Luckily, Robert Bailey is an original, and his skill as a writer makes the Alabama setting all his own. *The Professor* marks the beginning of a very promising career."

—Mark Childress, author of *Georgia Bottoms* and *Crazy in Alabama*

"Taut, page turning, and smart, *The Professor* is a legal thriller that will keep readers up late as the twists and turns keep coming. Set in Alabama, it also includes that state's greatest icon, one Coach Bear Bryant. In fact, the Bear gets things going with the energy of an Alabama kickoff to Auburn. Robert Bailey knows his state, and he knows his law. He also knows how to write characters that are real, sympathetic, and surprising. If he keeps writing novels this good, he's got quite a literary career before him."

—Homer Hickam, author of *Rocket Boys / October Sky*, a *New York Times* #1 bestseller

"Bailey's solid second McMurtrie and Drake legal thriller (after 2014's *The Professor*) . . . provides enough twists and surprises to keep readers turning the pages."

—*Publishers Weekly*

"A gripping legal suspense thriller of the first order, *Between Black and White* clearly displays author Robert Bailey's impressive talents as a novelist. An absorbing and riveting read from beginning to end."

—*Midwest Book Review*

"Take a murder, a damaged woman, and a desperate daughter, and you have the recipe for *The Last Trial*, a complex and fast-paced legal thriller. Highly recommended."

—D. P. Lyle, award-winning author

"*The Final Reckoning* is explosive and displays every element of a classic thriller: fast pacing, strong narrative, fear, misery, and transcendence. Bailey proves once more that he is a fine writer with an instinct for powerful white-knuckle narrative."

—*Southern Literary Review*

"A stunning discovery, a triple twist, and dramatic courtroom scenes all make for a riveting, satisfying read in what might well be Bailey's best book to date . . . *Legacy of Lies* is a grand story with a morality-tale vibe, gripping and thrilling throughout. It showcases Bailey once more as a writer who knows how to keep the suspense high, the pacing fast, the narrative strong, the characters compellingly complex, and his plot full of white-knuckle tension and twists."

—*Southern Literary Review*

"Inspiring . . . Sharp in its dialogue, real with its relationships, and fascinating in details of the game, *The Golfer's Carol* is that rarest of books—one you will read and keep for yourself while purchasing multiple copies for friends."

—Andy Andrews, *New York Times* bestselling author of *The Noticer* and *The Traveler's Gift*

THE MEDIATOR

ALSO BY ROBERT BAILEY

JASON RICH SERIES

Rich Justice

Rich Waters

Rich Blood

BOCEPHUS HAYNES SERIES

The Wrong Side

Legacy of Lies

MCMURTRIE AND DRAKE LEGAL THRILLERS

The Final Reckoning

The Last Trial

Between Black and White

The Professor

OTHER BOOKS

The Boomerang

The Golfer's Carol

THE MEDIATOR

ROBERT BAILEY

THOMAS & MERCER

This is a work of fiction. Names, characters, organizations, places, events, and incidents are either products of the author's imagination or are used fictitiously. Otherwise, any resemblance to actual persons, living or dead, is purely coincidental.

Published by Thomas & Mercer, Seattle

www.apub.com

EU product safety contact:
Amazon Media EU S. à r.l.
38, avenue John F. Kennedy, L-1855 Luxembourg
amazonpublishing-gpsr@amazon.com

ISBN-13: 9781662534133 (paperback)
ISBN-13: 9781662534126 (digital)

Cover design by Brian Lemus
Cover images: © John D Sirlin / Shutterstock; © xijian / Getty

Printed in the United States of America

For Mark Wittschen

DAY ONE

1

Kidnapping the boy turned out to be easy.

It would have been harder if he'd gone to school. The plan was to nab him at Lowe Mill that afternoon. He was in a play that rehearsed at the art center, and they could have detained him in the parking lot while he smoked a joint.

As luck would have it, though, Nathan Ringo decided to skip his first class.

They got him at a gas station in Five Points. Hicks had followed the kid inside the convenience store and picked out a soda from the cooler while the teenager asked for the strongest thing they had. When the clerk went to the back, Nathan grabbed a HEATH bar and a CELSIUS energy drink.

Breakfast of champions, Hicks thought, watching from the window as two of his associates slid into the back seat of the kid's unlocked car.

A minute later, after showing his fake ID and paying for the items with cash, Nathan Ringo emerged from the store carrying a brown paper sack. He stood in front of his vehicle and took out the green package of delta-9 gummies, which looked for all the world like candy. The kid popped two in his mouth and then opened the door to his sedan.

After he plopped down in the driver's seat and shut the door, they took him. A chloroform handkerchief over his mouth and nose and he was out just like Wonder Woman in the old TV show.

One of the men drove the kid's car while Hicks followed in the truck. The farm was a little less than half an hour away, and they pulled into the barn at 9:17 a.m. Exactly forty-three minutes before the start of mediation.

Ahead of schedule, Hicks thought, calling his boss while his men set up the video camera.

2

On the top floor of the Regions Center, the highest structure in downtown Huntsville, Perry Strassburg ended the call and gazed out the window of his office. Fifteen years ago, he would have had a near-perfect view of Big Spring International Park. Now, it was hard to see the pond around the hotels and businesses that had popped up in every direction. In the past decade, Huntsville had surpassed Birmingham as the largest city in the state of Alabama, and Perry relished the explosion of growth and his role in it. But while the spoils of the area's success could be seen downtown, the driving force behind Huntsville's upward climb was miles to the west.

Redstone Arsenal, the US Army's premier missile defense base, and the government contracting industry that had grown up around it, would always be the economic engine of the "Rocket City."

And I'm about to control the whole thing.

Perry closed his eyes and concentrated on his breathing. It was less than a five-minute drive to the mediation, and he'd just gotten some good news. He tapped the phone against his pant leg and then stuck it in his pocket.

Very . . . good news.

Still . . . he was anxious. Everything he'd worked for over the past twenty years was coming to fruition. Each decision. Every move on the chessboard of life. It all came down to this.

His marriage to Stephanie Richardson had always been about this day. Not love or even lust. It was a business partnership. And, as Perry knew all too well, sometimes to move forward in business you had to leave partners behind. Even if that meant stretching, bending, or breaking the rules.

The irony was that Stephanie's own father had taught Perry these truths.

"*The rules are what we make them,*" Dagger once said. "*Money talks and bullshit walks. And in this town, no one talks louder than us.*"

Perry rubbed his face with his hands, trying to ward off the nerves. Had he gone too far? Crossed some invisible line in the sand?

No. I'm doing what I have to do.

He felt his phone vibrate, indicating a text. He snatched the device and glanced at the screen. It was a message from his personal assistant.

Sir, your car is ready. The mediation is supposed to begin in twenty minutes.

Perry Strassburg went over the plan again in his mind. It was crazy and yet it was also . . .

. . . *perfect.*

And the most bizarre thing . . . the part that he couldn't quite believe himself . . . was that he couldn't even take full credit for the idea. Someone else had planted the seed.

And made the first domino fall.

"It'll work," he whispered, tapping his knuckles against the glass. Then he responded to the text.

On my way.

3

The leather on the ancient steering wheel was coming undone, wearing thin on both sides.

Frayed.

Like me, Max thought, frowning at her reflection in the rearview mirror of the truck. For over two decades, since she was thirteen years old, she'd religiously straightened her brown locks. But after the accident, she'd let the curls take over. "*The way God intended,*" her father liked to say. He'd loved her wavy hair when she was a kid, but Max had always been embarrassed by it. Her mom and her best friend, Caroline, both had beautiful straight hair, and Max wanted to be like them. Alas, nature or God or both had never cooperated, and now she didn't have the energy to fight the frizz anymore.

Max sighed and grabbed her phone from the passenger seat. She was stopped at the red light in Hampton Cove. If she turned right, she would head toward the Robert Trent Jones Golf Trail course. Left was over the hill to Jones Valley. During her former life, if she was coming home from Anniston or Gadsden or Guntersville in the evening, she'd turn left to go home and might get a take-out pizza from the Mellow Mushroom. And maybe an IPA to drink while she waited on the pie.

She'd had a husband then. A thirteen-year-old son. Memberships in the Gothic and Symphony Guilds. Her young family attended the First United Methodist Church almost every Sunday. She and Caroline taught a women's class on balancing the challenges of career, family, and faith. Life had been good . . .

Max gripped tight to the withered wheel and took a deep breath. Still, even now, she could make out the faint scent of her dad in the cab of the pickup. He'd put 250,000 miles on the Tundra before he passed of a heart attack last spring. Max felt her eyes begin to water, and she ground her teeth. *No. Don't go there.*

She glanced down at the passenger side floorboard and saw the empty Styrofoam coffee cup from McDonald's that she'd picked up on the way. She'd taken a short detour so that she could meet her mentor in the Alabama Lawyer Assistance Program for an early breakfast. She could hear his words in her ear.

"You can do this," Max whispered, glancing at the phone in her hand as the stoplight turned green. The mediation was supposed to start at 10:00 a.m., and it was already 9:47. *I'm gonna be late,* she thought, gritting her teeth and pressing her foot to the accelerator. She'd sent Nathan a text this morning before she left the cabin in Mentone, asking him to wish her luck and telling him that she'd meet him for dinner.

That was a couple hours ago, and her son had yet to respond. Max took another deep breath and exhaled, letting the air out slowly. She was trying, and so was he. Not replying to a text meant nothing other than that he was busy or that he was simply a teenager who was into his own world.

As the Tundra began the slog up Governors Drive, Max could feel her heart racing. She'd been out of rehab for eight months.

Too soon, she thought. *This is all happening too soon.*

It was her mentor who had recommended mediation work, and she could still remember all the pros he'd identified: "*You don't need an office, don't even need a law license. All that's required is some common sense and the ability to read people, Max. And if you don't settle the case, nobody loses. You go home and the parties march on to trial. But if you succeed, everyone wins. The parties control the result, and you've helped both sides reach a compromise.*"

The only con was something she'd face regardless of what she tried: "*You have to get out there. See people in the world you used to know. And they may not hire you because of your history. But you'll have to deal with that regardless.*"

As Max moved into the city limits, passing Huntsville Hospital, where Nathan was born some sixteen and a half years ago, and the First Baptist Church with its "eggbeater Jesus" mural, she felt an overpowering wave of nostalgia. Then, getting off Memorial Parkway on Clinton Avenue, she saw her old building come into view.

Beasley Rogers, LLP

When was the last time she'd been here?

Images popped into her mind. Knox Rogers and Paul Beasley in her office, asking her questions about client funds missing from the firm's trust account. Informing her that there was a bar complaint against her and that the firm could not, in good conscience, renew her contract. Max put her left-turn blinker on and turned into the parking lot.

As if on autopilot, she parked in the second row, third place on the right side. The same spot she'd chosen almost every day for twelve years. She glanced at her phone. It was 10:03 a.m. Her heart was pounding, and she felt sweat under her arms.

She gritted her teeth and opened the door of the Tundra. It was warm for late October. Pushing seventy degrees with very little breeze. At least fifteen degrees warmer than it had been when she'd woken four and a half hours earlier in the cabin in Mentone. She stared up at the beige-colored building with its floor-to-ceiling windows on each level. Then she opened the driver's side rear door of the truck and grabbed her briefcase. Still not quite believing this was real, she unfastened the bag and pulled out the order.

It had been entered two weeks earlier by the Circuit Court of Madison County, Alabama, in the case of *Strassburg v. Strassburg.*

> This case has been ordered to mediation. Based on the lists of potential candidates submitted by the parties, and, after a hearing was conducted to discuss same, the Court appoints Maxine Ringo as the mediator with the consent of both the plaintiff and the defendant.

The directive was signed on the eighth day of October 2025 by the Honorable Caroline Parker.

Max clipped the case shut but held tight to the order. She'd mediated four matters in the last three months. Two car wrecks, one divorce, and one contract dispute. All had been referred to her by Judge Parker.

I don't deserve this, Max thought for at least the hundredth time since being emailed the order. She closed the door and gazed around the lot. Most of the lawyers for her old firm had likely already started their day. Depositions for the litigators on the first and second floors. Real estate closings on three and four. She let out a ragged breath and stared up at the top of the building. Mediations on five. Several of the older lawyers in the firm were mediators, and there was enough business to devote an entire floor to it. As Max didn't have her own office, she'd asked Knox if she could use the firm's space, and he'd surprised her by agreeing. Now, she was rethinking that decision.

On shaky legs, Max took a step forward. And then another. She stuck out her chest and remembered something her momma used to say. "Shoulders back, boobs out."

Her mom had been a free-spirited, fun-loving soul, and Max wished so badly she could talk to her now. Or her dad. But they were gone. All she had in the world was Nathan, and she'd almost destroyed that relationship.

"It wasn't your fault, Max." Her mentor's confident voice in her mind. *"You didn't sign up for addiction. It took you like a thief in the night."*

"Whatever," Max whispered as the double doors opened, and she entered the building for the first time in almost two years. She approached the reception desk and was relieved that the person behind it was a stranger. A young woman with brown hair, holding a phone to her ear. As Max got closer, the receptionist pressed a button and gave her a fake smile.

"Can I help you?"

"Yes. I'm here for the mediation."

"Are you with one of the parties?"

"No," Max said, forcing her voice not to waver. "I'm the mediator."

4

Nathan Ringo was high as a kite. Hicks could see it in the boy's eyes. The adrenaline rush of being kidnapped was gone, and the THC had kicked in. Hicks had checked the boy's pockets. Nathan had bought a pack of one-hundred-milligram delta-9 gummies at the gas station in Five Points and had taken two of them before they detained him. That was a strong dose. Hicks sometimes took a five-milligram gummy to help him sleep. He could only imagine how out of it the kid was. Killing the pain of life.

Hicks adjusted the camera. Making sure the screen framed the boy's face.

"What's going on?" Nathan asked, slurring his words. "Wh-wh-why am I here?" he stuttered, then coughed.

Hicks ignored him and put a piece of Big Red in his mouth, relishing the cinnamon-sugar hit.

"H-h-hey?" Nathan whimpered.

"How good is your momma at handling stress?" Hicks asked, squinting at the boy.

Nathan wrinkled his face up. His eyes carried a dead look in them. Hicks could see the wheels slowly trying to churn. To process what was happening. Hicks finally answered his own question.

"You better hope she's on her game."

5

The longer Max waited, the more her heart pounded in her chest. She'd hoped to be whisked right up to the fifth floor, but that hadn't happened. Instead, for the past several minutes, she'd sat in the reception area of her old office. She hadn't seen any of her former partners yet, but it was only a matter of time. Worse, she was now ten minutes late for the mediation. Not exactly the ideal beginning.

She stared at the television screen, which was set to a national news channel, and then studied her nails. She'd cracked the index fingernail of her left hand this morning, and her filing job had been a tad shabby. Which was a perfect word for how she felt. *Shabby* . . . Sitting out in the waiting area of a firm she used to be a force in.

The doors flung open, and a young attorney strode through them. He had a file jacket tucked under his arm and was suited up. *Travis Starnes,* Max thought. Travis had just joined the firm when she'd been fired. He blinked at her and then walked past without saying a word. Did his face blush a tad? Had he experienced that awkward sensation of recognizing someone you have no interest in talking to? Or maybe he'd wanted to say hello, but was afraid to? Or perhaps he was so into what he was doing he hadn't even registered that she was there? Max felt a tiny tickle of dread in her brain. Had she done or said something inappropriate around Travis before her termination? Was that why he'd blushed?

How many times would Max see some version of his reaction today?

She'd straightened her pant legs and stood, about to tell the receptionist that she really needed to get upstairs, when someone else entered the area.

"Max?"

Max turned and saw a tiny woman with blond curls standing just inside the door. She wore a red sweater and black pants. "Leigh Ann?" Max's voice cracked just a tad on the last word.

"Hey, I'm sorry to keep you waiting. Are you ready?" Her voice was no nonsense and contained a twinge of anxiety. *Probably doesn't want to be seen with me . . .*

Max nodded and gathered herself. "Yes."

"OK, follow me."

Max did as she was told, feeling an odd mixture of fear and relief. Leigh Ann Norris had been her paralegal throughout her time at Beasley Rogers. They'd worked closely on hundreds of files. In the world of medical malpractice defense, the attorneys leaned hard on their staff, and Max was no different. Written discovery, medical record summaries, deposition and trial exhibit preparation, et cetera. You name it, Leigh Ann could do it. She'd worked with Knox for years before Max joined the firm, and she hadn't been too keen on taking on an extra assignment. But, after a few tense moments in the early going, they'd become great teammates. *And friends,* Max thought. Leigh Ann had been the only member of the firm who'd sent her a card after her parents' deaths, and she'd also shipped a goody bag to the Florida Recovery Center during Max's lengthy rehabilitation. As they stepped inside the elevator, Max was having a hard time making eye contact with Leigh Ann. Her face was hot, and her heartbeat was thudding. *If I don't calm down, I'm going to hyperventilate.*

But as soon as the elevator doors closed, she felt her hand being grasped tight. "It is so good to see you," Leigh Ann said in a loud whisper. Max looked up and saw that her old colleague's eyes were warm and friendly. Wide with curiosity.

"Thank you," Max managed. She tried to say something else, but the lump in her throat made it hard. "Thank you for—"

"I'm just glad you're OK," Leigh Ann interrupted. "And I'm proud of you for starting your new venture. Mediation? That's awesome."

"Yeah, I'm excited too. And nervous. Not sure how good I'll be at it."

Leigh Ann snorted. "Girl, you've been good at anything you've ever done."

"I hope you're right."

Before either woman could say anything else, the elevator buzzed.

"Oh, shoot," Leigh Ann said, still talking in a loud whisper. "I forgot to push the button." The doors opened up, and they were still on the lobby floor. A crowd of people was waiting to get in.

Max's stomach clenched, and she backed up against the wall as three people entered the enclosure. She recognized each one. Liz Wynn, an estate lawyer, blinked at her but then said, "Well, hi, Max, how are you?" Liz wore a sweater and a khaki blouse, and Max remembered that Liz had drafted Max's will some ten years ago. She was a quiet, reserved woman who Max had always admired.

"I'm fine, Liz. How are you?"

"Oh, same old," she said. Max almost laughed. She'd had this exact same interaction with Liz hundreds of times when she still worked here. The only difference today was the surprise in her old partner's voice.

"It's good to see you," Max said, meaning it. Then she glanced at the older man next to Liz. George Vann was a silver-haired employment lawyer with wire-rimmed glasses. "Hey, George."

"Max," he said, giving a small smile but saying nothing else. Again, not that much different from their prior interactions. George was a stoic attorney who could get so focused that he might walk right by you in the hall and not speak or even look at you. That wasn't a knock on the other person. It was just George. Max had learned that a lot of effective attorneys had quirks. The fact that he'd noticed and spoken to her at all was a pleasant surprise. She turned to the third attorney, but before she could speak, he started talking, and it clearly wasn't to her.

"Look, I've been listening, but that doesn't mean my client is ever going to pay 500K. Your lady was texting at the time of the accident." J.R. Ford was one of the best litigators in North Alabama, handling a variety of civil litigation from the defense side. He had thick gray hair parted to the side, and Max remembered how Knox had always ribbed J.R. about his perfectly coiffed locks. *And a hundred other things . . .* Max smiled at the memory, looking down at her feet. From the looks of it, J.R. was playing hard-ass to a plaintiff's lawyer wanting to settle some type of wheels case. Then, as the elevator opened on the third floor, he strode out the door, still reading the lawyer on the other end the riot act. "You're in fantasyland, Allen. We'll never go that high. Ever." Then, Max heard him yell down the hallway, still on the phone, "Louise, where are we on that Jenkins summary judgment motion?"

Max couldn't help but chuckle, though she wondered if J.R. either hadn't seen her or had chosen to ignore her. *Probably the former,* she thought. J.R. Ford didn't just practice law. He lived it every second of the day.

"As you can see," Liz said, "not much has changed around here."

Max smiled, realizing that George Vann had also exited the elevator without a word.

"It's kind of comforting," Max said, glancing at Leigh Ann, who rolled her eyes.

"I'm still not sure if George even knows who I am," Leigh Ann said. "And I've been here as long as him."

"He does," Liz offered. "I think." They all laughed, but it didn't do much to break the tension.

Liz got off the elevator on the fourth floor with a wave. "Good luck today, Max."

Max blinked, not realizing that anyone besides Knox and Leigh Ann would know her business at the firm. "Thank you."

As if reading her thoughts, Leigh Ann said, "Knox sent out a firm email, saying you'd be here mediating a case this week and . . ." She paused.

"And?" Max pressed.

". . . and that he'd granted you permission to use the firm's facilities with the full support of the executive committee."

Max felt a ripple of pain in her ribs, as if she'd been sucker punched.

"I'm sorry, Max. Because of the circumstances of how you left, Knox just—"

"Wanted to let everyone know that a thief would be in the building."

"That's not how he or I would have put it. Everyone knows what you were going through then. That wasn't you."

The elevator opened onto the fifth floor, and Leigh Ann stepped out into the hallway. Max tried to move, but her feet felt like bricks. *That was me,* she thought.

"Come on," Leigh Ann said. "Let me show you your quarters."

Max felt like a prisoner, which she guessed she kinda was for the next two days. She forced her legs to move, not realizing that she was holding her breath.

"Restrooms on either side of the hallway," Leigh Ann said, waving her arms to the left and then the right. Max remembered that each floor had a bathroom area off the elevators and then another door leading into the offices. She watched as Leigh Ann opened that door now and held it wide for Max to enter. She did, seeing a long hallway.

"This floor is a circle like the others. The only difference is the conference rooms are on the ends. The plaintiff is down the hall to the left and the defendant and her attorneys are to the right. I believe everyone is here." Leigh Ann gestured to a small office sparsely decorated with a circular table and three chairs. The window looked out over Memorial Parkway, and Max wished she was in any of the cars passing by in either direction. She felt sick to her stomach. "This is where our mediators camp out while the parties are considering their next move, and it's also a good spot for a lawyers-only caucus."

Max let out a ragged breath. "OK," she said, cursing the weakness in her tone.

"There's a kitchen across the hall with a drink cooler full of bottled water and sodas and a coffee bar. There are snacks in the cabinets." She paused. "Knox wants to be as helpful as he can be."

"Tell him I said thank you," Max said.

"He's in a deposition in Athens, but he'll be back this afternoon and should be in for a few hours tomorrow. I know he wants to see you."

Max forced a smile. "That would be great. I miss him. And you."

Leigh Ann leaned in for a hug. "Miss you, too, girl." She hesitated. "Are you OK?"

"Fine," Max lied.

"Good luck," Leigh Ann said.

Before Max could respond, the paralegal was hustling out the door to the elevator. There was work to be done, and this interlude had probably cost Leigh Ann precious time she could have been billing on files. Max remembered the pressure of the billable hour. How every day was broken into 0.2 billing events. Preparing emails. Reviewing files. Drafting discovery. *Capture the time* was a common phrase in their department.

That programming was hard to shake off after the accident. She'd thought the oxycodone would allow her to keep working through the pain from her injuries, and, for a while, it did. Eventually, though, her need for oxy eclipsed her desire for anything else.

And she'd lost everything.

Max took another deep breath and slowly exhaled, knowing these thoughts weren't serving her. *The only way to get back . . . is to get back,* she reminded herself as she forced her legs to move down the hallway.

6

The conference room for the defendant was packed.

Three suited-up lawyers sat on the far side of the table, each with their laptop out. Two men, one woman, none older than thirty, if Max had to guess. Max had knocked gently before entering, but it appeared that they had yet to notice her. The lawyers continued to peck away at their laptops.

A woman was standing behind the three young attorneys, talking on her cell phone with her back to Max. Behind her, a window looked out over south Huntsville. Max stared past the woman, focusing on the top of Lowe Mill, the ancient redbrick structure that used to be a textile mill but now served as an entire district for aspiring actors, painters, writers, and other artists in Huntsville. She was supposed to meet Nathan at a café over there when the workday was over. Though things with her son were still awkward, she knew they couldn't be any clumsier than this scene. She felt invisible. If she'd come in bringing coffee or to dust the table, she figured she'd be getting the same reaction as she was right now.

"It's about time."

The cold, familiar voice sent a shiver through Max's chest, and she turned toward it. Douglas Julian "Dagger" Richardson sat at the head of the table, farthest from Max. His chair was pushed back, his hands clasped across his stomach. He wore a charcoal pinstripe suit, but the jacket was already off. Sleeves rolled up. *Ready to fight,* Max thought.

"How are you, Dagger?" Max asked, taking a step forward. "It's been a long time."

"Yes, it has," he said, making no move to get up and not answering her question. He had short white hair that was thinning at the temples but still looked robust and healthy for a man well north of seventy. "You're late."

"I know, and I'm sorry. I misjudged the time it would take to get here from Mentone."

"Mentone? Why the hell . . ." He shook his head and trailed off. "Whatever. Do you have anything for us? I'd like to get on with this mess."

Max felt her stomach tighten. But before she could respond, the woman on the cell phone ended her call and wheeled toward her.

Amy Dance had been a personal injury plaintiff's attorney the last time Max had dealt with her, her star on the rise. In the time that Max had been away, Amy had shifted her focus to domestic relations and was now regarded as one of the best divorce lawyers in town. When Max had seen Amy's name on the pleadings, she'd been pleased. The two had been involved in a number of tense depositions over the years, and Max certainly wouldn't have called Amy a friend. But there was mutual respect. Or at least Max thought there was.

She saw no evidence of that feeling in Amy's face, which was tight and drawn. "Hello, Max."

Max walked around the table and extended her hand, which the other lawyer quickly shook. "Looks like you have an army with you today," Max said, trying to lighten the mood as she glanced down at the three younger attorneys. They all stood, and introductions were made.

Relieved to have broken the ice, Max saw that the Beasley Rogers folks had set out a coffeepot on a burner and a plate of muffins. Making the setting as comfortable as possible was something she'd learned in mediation training, and she was glad to see that Knox had made sure her wishes were carried out.

She made a show of grabbing a muffin and napkin and then sat down next to Dagger. Another recommendation was to avoid sitting at the head of the table, as it sent the wrong message. She wasn't a decision-maker today. She wasn't the boss. She was merely a facilitator of resolution. As she took another bite of the muffin, which wasn't half bad, she noticed that there was one other person in the room. Max winced with the realization. The most important person . . .

Max blinked at the woman, who was wearing a baggy gray sweater over what appeared to be black leggings. A denim baseball cap with "30-A" stenciled in yellow on the top covered her head. The woman had her arms crossed tight across her chest and was staring at the table.

"Mrs. Strassburg?" Max asked.

The defendant raised her eyes, which were red. Max figured the woman either hadn't slept well or had been crying. "Hi," she said. "Please call me Stephanie."

Max knew of Stephanie Richardson Strassburg, but she had never met the woman. Their closest connection was in the Gothic Guild, but that organization was huge, and Max had not been diligent in her attendance.

"OK," Max said. "Stephanie."

"So what's the plan, Max?" Dagger barked. "Are we just going to sit in here and hold hands? Maybe say a prayer? How about the Twenty-Third Psalm? That's one of my favorites."

"Dagger?" Amy, who was still standing, scowled at the old man, whose face had turned red.

"Well, Max?" he continued, crossing his right leg over his left and holding his palms out wide. "Do you have the foggiest clue what you are doing?"

Max ignored Dagger's question and focused on his daughter instead. "Stephanie, Judge Parker appointed me to mediate this case. As a mediator, I'm completely neutral and have no authority to make any decisions or rulings. My only role is to help you and Perry settle the case. If you want my opinion, I'll give it, but my sole objective is to facilitate a resolution. I'll be going back and forth between this room and Perry's, communicating offers and counters in the hopes that we can reach an agreement. The beauty of mediation is that you have control over the outcome, which is not the case at trial, where a judge will hear all the evidence and make a ruling. Today . . . and tomorrow if need be . . . you and Perry are steering the ship. You have the power to bring closure to this case and to your marriage." Max paused. "I'm here to help you reach a resolution of this divorce."

"Like hell," Dagger said. "You're here to draw a fee. A crumb from your old pal Caroline Parker. This case has absolutely no chance of settling, and your buddy the judge knows it. I'm sure that's why she appointed you. If there was even a snowball in hell's chance of a compromise, why in the world would she select you to negotiate the peace?" He glared at her. "How long have you been out of rehab? A month?"

"Eight months," Max snapped.

"Are you even licensed to practice law anymore?" Dagger fired back.

Max blinked and forced the anger out of her tone. "My suspension expires next month, but we both know that a law license isn't necessary to be a mediator. As for my experience, I've mediated several cases, settling all of them. I was appointed by Judge Parker to mediate this case from, according to the order, a list submitted by each party." Max held Dagger's glare. She could feel the disgust coming off him. Then she turned to Stephanie. "Most civil cases these days, including divorce matters, are at some point either ordered to mediation by the court or the parties will choose to mediate before the court enters an order. The mediator is typically either appointed by the judge or voluntarily selected by agreement of the parties. In this case, I was appointed by the judge from lists of potential candidates submitted by the parties . . . and, at least according to Judge Parker's order, both parties have consented to me."

"You weren't on our list," Amy Dance chimed in. She had stuffed her hands in her pockets, standing to the side of Dagger. "But . . . in all fairness, the other candidates identified by Perry were definite nos, and he wouldn't agree to any of ours. Personally, I would have preferred Knox Rogers."

"Me too," Dagger said.

Max blinked down at the table. "I'm surprised that Perry wouldn't agree to Knox," she said. What she didn't say was *Why in the hell would he want me?* She looked up and saw the same question in Amy Dance's expression. "I'm just as surprised as you that I'd be on anyone's list, much less Perry Strassburg's."

Amy studied Max and shrugged. "Truth is, there aren't that many domestic relations mediators in North Alabama. Normally, our cases are assigned to Page or Joan-Marie."

Max nodded. Page Conlon and Joan-Marie Stephens were two highly experienced divorce attorneys who now specialized in mediating divorce cases. "Did either of you ask for one of them?" Max asked, genuinely curious.

"Yes," Amy said, crossing her arms. "We did, but Perry wouldn't agree. Nor would he consent to Knox. The other lawyers on his list were Burgess Cloud and Roland Lusk."

"Lusk?" Max asked, feeling a shiver of fear run through her. Roland Lusk had been Thayer's divorce lawyer, and the name alone made her queasy. "Is he mediating now?"

"He's done a handful, and Cloud mediates a few on the side as well, but both are primarily hard-nosed divorce lawyers." Amy cracked a tiny smile. "Like me. We didn't feel like they were right for this dispute."

Max stood and brushed her palms down her pants as if to wipe something off, though her slacks were clean. She thought through what she'd just heard. "So, what was I? The lesser of several evils?"

"You were a wild card," Amy corrected.

"Well . . . you consented to me, correct?"

"We did," Amy said.

"Dagger?" Max challenged.

He frowned and then nodded.

"Then let's stop wasting time, shall we?" Max walked toward the door. "I'm going to introduce myself to the plaintiff and I'll be back in a few minutes. Have there been any negotiations up to this point?"

"No, there haven't," Dagger said.

"No," Amy said, shooting Dagger a disapproving glance.

"All right then. Since Mr. Strassburg filed this petition and is the plaintiff in this lawsuit, I'll encourage him to make the first offer." Max grabbed the doorknob.

"Encourage that no-good thief to kiss my ass," Dagger said.

Max started to open the door, but Amy's voice, higher and with more urgency, stopped her. "Mrs. Strassburg is here in good faith, Max," she said, walking around the table and standing behind Stephanie, a subtle reminder to Max and perhaps Dagger about who the actual client was in this dispute.

"I appreciate that," Max said. "I hope we can get it done."

Halfway down the hallway, Max stopped and checked her phone. She'd put it on silent before entering the defendant's conference room, and she'd missed two calls and a text from her ex-husband. She clicked on the message.

> Hey, just checking in. Cell coverage here is spotty. Making sure you've got Nathan tonight, tomorrow, and through the weekend. I'll be back on Monday.

Max ground her teeth with irritation. Thayer was a pharmacist, and he was in the Caymans for a continuing education seminar. Max thought he might have taken his new girlfriend, but Thayer hadn't said one way or the other. Regardless, he'd been planning the trip for a while, and this was the first time that Thayer had trusted Max with Nathan for several days in a row since the divorce. It shouldn't surprise her that he was "checking in." *I would be too.*

Yes, Max replied. He'll stay with me at the hotel tonight and tomorrow and I'm taking him to Mentone for the weekend.

She pressed send and put the phone in her pocket. Her heart was beating fast, and she tried to bring herself back to the present.

Too much too soon, she thought again. A high-stakes mediation. Keeping Nathan for five whole days. She had planned to take him hiking on the mountain Saturday and then perhaps a Sunday drive to Chattanooga for lunch. Nathan loved rock climbing, and they'd been texting about going to High Point Climbing and Fitness after lunch Sunday afternoon. Chattanooga had a great facility, but . . .

Is he going to be up for hanging out with me that long? She sighed. *Am I up for it?*

For a split second, she started to type out a text to her son but then deleted it. *He's in school. He isn't going to respond.*

Max took a deep breath and again wiped her clean pants with her palms. The encounter in the defendant's room was volatile but typical of a mediation. Dagger Richardson, quite predictably, had been a hard-ass and acted as if there was no chance for settlement, but Max was given hope by those last few seconds with Amy and Stephanie. The client was Stephanie Strassburg, and Dagger . . .

. . . is a problem.

Max knew from experience and training that sometimes the client was the challenge. Other mediations hinged on the lawyer's expectations or need for a result. And there were occasions where outside influences could dictate the outcome.

Dagger Richardson was an outside influence. Not a party, but a presence that would have to be dealt with. Would Stephanie do anything contrary to her father's wishes? *Not likely,* Max thought.

She reached the door to the plaintiff's conference room and gazed behind her down the hallway. She was amazed at how quiet it was. The only people on this floor today were the human beings in these two rooms . . . *and me.*

This was her show, for better or worse. And if the case didn't settle, no one lost anything. They could still fight it out in court. Another beauty of mediation.

That's why I'm here, she told herself, trying to relax.

Then she opened the door.

7

The scene inside the plaintiff's quarters was the polar opposite of that in the defendant's. As Max shut the door behind her, she saw one lone person standing in the far corner of the room.

"Hello, Perry," she said, taking a long stride and stopping when her thighs pressed against the table.

Perry Strassburg was peering out over North Parkway. "Max Ringo," he said, not looking at her. "It's been a minute."

"As I recall, our last encounter was also a mediation," Max said, walking along the far side of the table from him.

"That's right. Ben Hedden was the mediator. A stockholder dispute with a medical group that you and Knox represented. And Ben got it done."

"Yep. We didn't do much corporate litigation, but the client requested that Knox handle that one." She paused. "Has Ben officially retired?"

"Last year," Perry said, still not looking at her. "He was the best."

"He was," Max said, taking a seat. "I'm sure you wish he was handling this one . . . and not me."

Perry turned around. His eyes were a stark violet that went well with his navy suit, white shirt, and baby blue tie. He had jet-black hair slicked back in kind of a Gordon Gekko do, and his custom suit was tailored in a slim fit. *Sleek* was how Max would describe him. Like a fast animal. *Or a snake . . .*

"On the contrary," he said. "I'm looking forward to working with you."

Max couldn't tell if he was being serious or just polite. "Likewise," she said.

He continued to stand but now began to pace with his hands in his pockets. "That case we had together was one of my last in private practice. A few months later, Dagger asked me to join Richardson Concepts, and . . ." He clapped his hands. "Here we are."

"Here we are," Max echoed.

He ran a hand through his hair. "Let me guess. The old man is running the show in the other room."

Max said nothing. Silence as acquiescence.

"And . . ." Perry continued. "He told you to tell me to kiss his ass."

"He encouraged me to do so."

Perry had now made his way around to Max's side of the table. "I bet."

"It is a challenging set of circumstances," she said, watching him approach, again thinking of a snake.

He took the seat next to her and leaned his elbows on the table. "So, you've had some time to look at the position statements, the pleadings, and you know the players pretty well from your prior life." He looked at her sideways, as if he were a coconspirator. "What do you think?"

Such a different vibe, Max couldn't help but think. She'd barely gotten through the introductions in the defendant's room. But here, Perry was diving right in.

"I think you need a lawyer," Max said, offering one of her first observances after reading through all the materials. "Unless, during my years away, you also became a divorce specialist. And even then—"

"'A lawyer who represents himself has a fool for a client,'" Perry interrupted, pushing his hands off the table and turning his chair to face her. They were only a couple feet apart, and Max could smell his aftershave. She'd been in depositions before when male lawyers and sometimes even female attorneys would invade her personal space, trying to intimidate her. Perry wasn't quite there yet, but he was toeing the line.

It's his shtick, she thought. *The smooth operator. Now he's trying to sell me on his position.*

Max kept her mouth shut and waited for more.

"I don't trust anyone else with my business." He scoffed. "Besides, can you think of any lawyer in this county you'd rather have trying your case than me?"

The arrogance in his tone was palpable, and Max bit her lip, trying to stay neutral. The truth was that she could think of several attorneys she'd rather utilize than Perry, and a lot of it boiled down to specialty. Perry was a corporate lawyer trained in mergers and acquisitions and also skilled enough to handle business litigation. A good attorney? Absolutely. Max's first choice for a divorce case or personal injury matter? Hell no. Not even close. She cleared her throat and forced a smile. "My opinion on that really doesn't matter, does it?"

"No," he said. He leaned forward, and Max felt her whole body tense. He was invading her space now. "I guess it doesn't."

Max pushed her chair back and stood. She took a few tentative steps backward.

"Are you afraid of me?"

"Should I be?" Max asked.

Perry didn't answer the question. He crossed his legs and made a tent with his hands over his stomach. It wasn't that different from Dagger Richardson's body language a few minutes earlier. Max was already growing tired of the power tactics on both sides. "What's your first offer, Perry?"

"Not until you size the case up for me. What are we dealing with?" He lowered his voice. "Show me that Max Ringo intelligence. That's one of the reasons I chose you."

Max crossed her arms. "All right."

"Please," Perry said, gesturing at the chair that Max had just vacated. "Sit."

"I prefer to stand." She paced a few feet to the head of the table, as if she were about to begin an opening statement in court.

"You and Stephanie have been married for ten and a half years. No children through the marriage, though you both have kids from prior relationships. She has two girls, both in college, and you have a son who lives in Park City, Utah. Stephanie is the sole heir of the Richardson family, which owns over eighty thousand acres of land in Madison, Morgan, and Limestone Counties. The property is valued at approximately $175 million. You are the chief executive officer of Richardson Concepts, drawing a salary of over three million a year with stock options worth twenty-five million. You own thirty percent of Richardson Concepts; Dagger owns thirty and Stephanie forty." Max had been staring out the window as she recited the facts, but now lowered her gaze to Perry. "How am I doing so far?"

"Spot on," he said. "Pretty much. All the Richardson land is now in an LLC."

"I was getting to that," Max said. "The members of the LLC are Stephanie, Dagger, and you, and the ownership interests are identical to those of the company. Stephanie owns forty percent, with you and Dagger both at thirty."

"They cut me in five years ago when Dagger couldn't pay the property tax. He was . . . overleveraged, and I bailed him out."

"I was wondering," Max said, not quite through with her summary. "You and Stephanie also own three homes. One here in downtown Huntsville. Another five-bedroom bungalow a few blocks from the beach in Watercolor, and a condo in Canyons Village at Park City, where your son lives rent-free." She licked her lips. "And a French bulldog."

"Fredo," Perry said, grimacing. "Little menace. She can have him." He rubbed his hands together. "All right then, Max, what should my first offer be?"

"What do you want?"

"What do you think I want?"

Max leaned her left hip against the edge of the table. "I'm not a mind reader."

"Humor me."

"OK." Max started to pace again. "You want to keep the condo in Utah for your son. Otherwise, Stephanie can have the remaining houses here and at the beach. You want Stephanie's interest in Richardson Concepts, because that gives you the majority stake in the company, and you feel you deserve that since you've taken Richardson Concepts to new heights in the past decade. And, in a perfect world, you would want her to buy you out of your interest in the family partnership that owns all the real property. You will agree to a reasonable alimony amount, perhaps even more than reasonable, provided that there's a cutoff date in the near future." She stopped moving and scrutinized him. "Close?"

He cocked his head to one side, as if he were thinking, but didn't answer.

"The problem you have," Max continued, "is that Stephanie alleges infidelity, which, if proven at trial, could significantly affect the property settlement and alimony awards. She also claims that you sexually assaulted her."

"False," he said. "A complete lie."

"The affair or the abuse?"

"Both."

"How do you think Judge Parker will see that?"

"She won't. As soon as this mediation fails, Caroline will recuse herself, and an out-of-county judge will be brought in."

Max knew it shouldn't surprise her to hear him reference the judge as "Caroline." Lawyers did that all the time, especially with contemporaries, and Caroline Parker was the same age as Max, which meant she was younger than Perry by a few years. Still, hearing her old friend's first name out loud rattled her. It helped her to think of Caroline as "Judge Parker." That made things easier. Their relationship now was strictly professional. There was no Caroline. Only Judge Parker. "Well, how do you think the judge appointed to try the case will see it?" Max asked.

"This case will never see the light of a courtroom."

"How can you be—?"

"Because you are going to settle it. I have confidence in you, Max." Before she could respond, he got up out of his seat and walked to the wall nearest him. There was a built-in cabinet with old editions of *The Southern Reporter* tucked in its shelves. Perry had placed a laptop on the counter of the cabinet, and he snatched it and set the computer on the table, clicking the power button. "Come here. I want to show you something."

"I've read everything you and Amy have sent me," Max said, holding her ground.

"This is new information," Perry said. "Come. Sit. I think you'll find this of particular interest."

Max took a cautious step forward and sat in the chair that she'd vacated a few minutes earlier. Perry leaned over her and pulled up a link on the screen. It was a video, and Max saw the screen change to the grainy image of a room.

"If this is a clip of Stephanie having her own tryst . . ." She stopped talking when she saw the camera angle change. Max blinked as she processed the scene. A large room. A boy sitting in a chair. His arms were tied behind his back. A piece of duct tape covered his mouth.

Max tried to talk, but the words wouldn't form. She blinked again and focused on the screen. The same image met her gaze.

Nathan. Her son. Bound and gagged. And, from the looks of his eyes, drugged.

Max felt the scream in her gut first. Rising up through her chest to her windpipe and then her lips. But before any sound could be released, strong fingers gripped her neck and a rough hand covered her mouth.

All that came out was a muffled whimper.

8

Stephanie Strassburg had to get out of there. She took the elevator to the lobby and walked out as fast as she could. She wanted a breath of fresh air, but the first gust that came through her lungs was a cigarette smoke cloud from a heavyset lawyer out for his midmorning nicotine hit. Stephanie gagged and walked down the sidewalk until she was clear of the smoke. Then, whispering "screw it" to herself, she strode to her car. She unlocked the front door to her silver Range Rover and climbed into the front seat. Then she clicked on the radio and turned the volume as high as it would go.

Luke Combs's "Hurricane" blared out of the speakers so loud it hurt her ears, but she didn't adjust the knob. Anything was better than being stuck in that stuffy room with those lawyers and her dad. She checked her voicemail. There was a message from CCI. Her next round of scans was scheduled for tomorrow morning. They'd been set for today, but she'd moved them in order to get the first day of mediation over with. She was still planning to get fluids this evening.

Stephanie closed her eyes. She might postpone the imaging studies again. She wasn't sure she wanted to know. It had been five days since she'd rung the bell after her last chemo treatment. She was beginning to feel a tad better. The awful side effects had lessened. She'd puked this morning, but she thought that was due more to nerves over the mediation than to the god-awful poison that was presumably killing the cancer.

She glanced at the clock on her dash. It was 11:07 a.m. The mediator had been in with Perry for at least thirty minutes, and Stephanie was growing sick of her dad's tough talk and Amy Dance's qualified opinions while they waited. "*If we can prove the affair, we might be able to . . . If the judge believes that Perry abused you, then . . . All the travel might constitute abandonment . . .*"

It was bullshit, Stephanie thought. She knew Perry was cheating on her. She'd just never caught him in the act, and the investigator her dad hired had been unable to obtain anything but circumstantial evidence. As for the abuse . . .

I never called the police. I never filed a report. Never even told a friend.

According to Amy, without some independent proof of the affair or abuse, the judge would likely split everything down the middle.

I don't even care, Stephanie thought. *I just want to be free of him.*

Stephanie gritted her teeth, thinking of her girls. They were all that mattered to her anymore. Mem was a junior at Alabama and Ella a freshman. Both Chi O's, just like Stephanie. They'd been nonplussed by the dissolution of the marriage. After their father had passed, all they'd wanted was their mother's happiness. And, at least for a few years, she'd been content with Perry.

But Stephanie had eventually seen the marriage for what it was. A business merger. And Perry for who he was.

A monster . . .

Stephanie peered at her phone, but there were no messages. Amy had said she would text when the mediator came back. She knew she needed to get back up there before her father blew everything up.

He's more upset than I am . . .

Dagger, like Stephanie, had been seduced by Perry. Perry had promised to deliver big profits for the company when Dagger named him CEO, and he had delivered. He'd bailed Dagger out on the property tax fiasco a few years back. He'd been the best thing to happen to the Richardson family and the company in years.

Stephanie had been willing to look past the cheating. She'd even endured Perry's disturbing sexual kinks and his loss of interest in her.

She'd stayed quiet. Been the team player. Done what was best for her family.

And where did that lead me?

Stephanie stared at the law office building with disgust. The divorce petition had hit her like a left hook. Combined with the cancer diagnosis a week later, it had made her life a wreck. And while everyone in town knew about her failed marriage, she'd told no one about her health.

After the scans tomorrow, if things got any worse, she might tell her family.

Then again . . . *what good would it do?* She didn't want to hurt Mem or Ella or ruin a second of their college experience. If they were still living at home, she'd have to tell them. But they were mercifully gone, having the time of their lives in Tuscaloosa, and Stephanie was determined not to be a burden.

Stephanie let out a ragged breath and opened the door. As she walked toward the entrance, relieved that the smoker was finished with his break, she again looked at her phone, which still showed no new message.

What is taking so long?

9

Max tasted iron in her throat. After Perry's hand had clasped over her mouth, she'd bit her tongue, and it must be bleeding. She struggled to breathe through her nose as she stared at her son on the screen. Nathan's eyes were glazed over. Sweat beads glistened on his forehead. He had on a plaid flannel button-down and a black undershirt.

"If you make a scene, your son will die." Perry's instructions were firm, deliberate, and matter of fact, and they snapped Max back into the present. Blood rushed to her face and her heart rate surged. Her ears were ringing. She squeezed her fists together and then elbowed Perry as hard as she could in the stomach, hearing the air escape his mouth as he staggered backward. Max jumped out of her seat and lunged toward him, but he held up his index finger and spoke in a mangled whisper. "If you run out of this room and tell someone, he's dead. If you scream, dead. Call the police? Dead. You're going . . . to listen . . . to what I have to say, do you understand?"

Max moved her eyes from the screen to Perry and then back. *"What have you done with my son?"* Max's breath came out in ragged hiccups, and her heartbeat was sprinting. She was on the verge of hyperventilating.

"He's fine. And he will stay fine as long as you do what I say."

"You kidnapped him?"

Perry had regained his wind, and he was now standing in a fighter's stance, one foot in front of the other, about three feet away from her.

"Max, we set aside two days for this mediation, and that ought to be plenty of time for you to settle this case on my terms."

Max opened her mouth to say something, but the words wouldn't come. She coughed, trying to find her voice as Perry took a few steps backward.

"I want the company, Max. They can have the land. I'd prefer they buy me out of the family partnership, but I'll waive that as long as Stephanie gives me her forty percent of the company and Dagger sells me his interest. Stephanie can obviously keep the house in town and the beach cabin." He hesitated. "And I don't give a damn about the condo in Park City. I can find somewhere else for my son to live. *All I want is the company.*"

Max forced herself not to look at the video that still played on the laptop. "You kidnapped my son to blackmail me into helping you obtain Richardson Concepts for yourself?"

"Yes."

Max's nostrils flared. *"Who do you think you are?"*

"Perry Matthew Strassburg. One of the most powerful humans in this state and about to be even more so once you entice my wife and father-in-law to part with their share of the family business."

"Why would you need Nathan for that?"

"For security, Max. Like when the bank places a mortgage on your house to guarantee payment of their loan." He paused. "I can't lose what I've built. I've worked too hard for it."

"I understand your motivations, *but that's my son.*" Max looked at the screen and choked back a sob. "I'm going to the police."

"If you do, he'll die." He gave a dramatic sigh. "Another high school drug addict OD's. How sad . . ." He trailed off.

"I'll tell them what you did, and you can't erase what's on your computer."

"Sure I can. By the time you get the HPD or the sheriff's office interested, your boy will be dead, my laptop will be destroyed, and there'll be no evidence of this kidnapping at all except in your tortured mind. It'll be your word against mine. You, a drug addict yourself some eight months out of rehab, still on suspension from the practice of law for stealing money from your former law firm's trust account, and me, one of the most respected citizens in this town. Who do you think anyone will believe? Especially when the cause of death will be the lethal dose of fentanyl that Nathan got from God knows where."

"You're a lunatic," Max said, glaring at him as he circled the room like a shark, inching closer to her.

"I have a very strong position here, Max. No one in this town will be predisposed to believe a word you say. Did you hear any whispers when you arrived today? Did you feel them? Weren't you giving blow jobs to doctors in return for oxycodone when you hit rock bottom? Once you couldn't steal any more money, you traded sex for drugs, didn't you? That's what I heard."

Max closed her eyes and bit her lip. Flashes . . . images . . . awful scents came back to her. She thought of the recurring nightmare that she used to have every night. Of sitting in the front seat of a familiar car. Wrung out, unable to be still and needing her next fix. Being guided to do the unthinkable . . .

"How has your reception been so far?" Perry whispered. He must be right next to her now. She could feel his breath on her neck. "Did Amy Dance welcome you with open arms in the other room? I heard your old buddy Knox Rogers had to send out an email alert that Max Ringo, the disgraced attorney that this very firm fired for embezzling money from clients, was back in the building. That true? Or just another nasty rumor attached to—"

Max's eyes shot open, and her right fist fired up at his chin like a piston. Then she kicked him in the shin with the toe of her heel. "You sonofabitch," she hissed, pointing a shaking finger at him. "You can't do this."

Perry limped around to the other side of the table, chuckling to himself and rubbing his chin. "I knew you were a fighter, Max. That's another reason why I handpicked you to mediate this case." He pointed at the laptop. "The big reason, though, is that I knew I could lean on you. I hope you are feeling a . . . *heightened* . . . sense of urgency."

Max looked at the screen again, forcing herself to focus and block out the panic that engulfed her. "Is he OK?"

"He's fine, Max. High. But fine. Coincidentally, my guys had nothing to do with his mental state. Nathan stopped by a gas station for delta-9 gummies on the way to school, and that's where we detained him."

Max could hardly believe her ears. *Is this really happening?* During the first few days of detox, she'd had a number of hallucinations. That was what this situation felt like. The beginning of some type of pressure-driven schizophrenia. She'd known that the Strassburg assignment was a lot to take on. The location of the mediation. The stakes. Everything.

Too much too soon.

She closed her eyes tight and then opened them again. Nothing had changed. Perry Strassburg was leaning over and massaging his lower leg. She glanced at the laptop. The image of Nathan on the screen was still there, and her right wrist was now throbbing in pain from punching Perry.

Max gathered herself and concentrated on her breathing. It was something she did when the urge for an oxy fix came on. *Just . . . breathe.* After several seconds, Max crossed her arms and peered at the man pulling all the strings. "You picked me so that you could blackmail me," she said.

"Obviously," Perry fired back.

"You put me on a list with other candidates you knew that Amy would balk at. And you expected that if I was the only mediator left—"

"Your old pal, Caroline Parker, would have no problem appointing you," Perry finished. "But don't look so glum, Max. At the end of the day, what I want is incredibly fair. I've built Richardson Concepts into a giant. Dagger didn't have the vision for expansion. It was mine, and the fruits should belong to me. The land is his family's legacy, and I'm not touching that." He took a step toward Max. "And I'll let you in on a little secret." He lowered his voice. "Dagger needs the money. He's gotten himself into another mess, and, once again, I'm here to bail him out. But this time . . . it's going to cost more." He licked his lips. "The bottom line is that all you have to do to save your boy . . . *is your job*."

"If it's all so reasonable, then why didn't you just let me do my job without threatening to harm my son?"

"Because I don't like to take unnecessary chances."

"Bullshit," Max fired back. "There's got to be more to it."

His mouth opened a sliver, and she saw him grit his teeth ever so slightly. A tell. Max was no poker player, but he'd just shown her a card.

"What's really going on here, Perry?"

"I've already told you." He gestured to the laptop and turned his back on her. "Do your job, Max, and everybody wins. Your son sees the light of another day. Your mediation career gets a huge boost. Stephanie keeps her family's property, and Dagger doesn't lose his fortune." He held out his palms. "Justice is done."

"Justice?" Max asked.

"Indeed," Perry said.

"By kidnapping my son."

"Sometimes justice needs a kick in the pants."

Max rubbed her right wrist, noticing that it had begun to swell. "What about an opening offer?"

"I've told you what I want," Perry said. "How you get there is up to you." He strode toward her, and Max held her ground. When he got within a few feet, he pointed his index finger at her and then back at the laptop. "It's simple, Max. Either settle this case on my terms . . . or your son dies." He licked his lips. "And if you breathe a word of this to the police, the press, or another living soul—" He snapped his fingers and narrowed his gaze. "Do you understand?"

Max managed to nod.

Perry Strassburg continued to stare at her, eyes cold and dead. "Try not to forget what's at stake."

10

As if on autopilot, Max walked into the kitchen off the hallway. She reached into the ice maker, pulled out a couple of cubes, and rubbed them over her tender wrist.

This can't be happening . . .

She pictured Nathan as she'd seen him on the screen. Drugged. Bound. Gagged. Her wrist continued to throb despite the cold being applied to it.

"Everything OK, Max?"

She wheeled around and saw Leigh Ann Norris standing in the opening between the kitchen and hallway. Max cleared her throat and became conscious of the ice in her hand. "Yes, fine." Her voice was breathless, and she swallowed, trying to calm herself. She could still taste blood in her mouth from when she'd bitten her tongue. "I slammed my hand down on the kitchen counter after spilling some orange juice this morning, and it's been hurting ever since."

Leigh Ann grimaced. "I've got a compression sling I use sometimes for my arthritis. Want to borrow it?"

Max shrugged. "Maybe? I'll buzz you if it starts feeling any worse."

"Please do." Leigh Ann pursed her lips.

"Anything else?"

"The defendant's lawyer, Ms. Dance, called the reception desk wondering where you were. Then Candace buzzed me, and I talked to

Ms. Dance, who said it had been almost an hour, and they hadn't seen you. She . . . sounded pretty impatient."

"It's a slow process sometimes. Perry Strassburg is . . ." Max trailed off, still not quite believing her impossible predicament.

"Don't say any more," Leigh Ann said. "I've heard Knox talk about him. I just wanted to check on you . . . and I'm glad I did. I'll go down and get that sleeve. It'll be on your desk in a few."

"Thank you."

As the trusty paralegal walked away, Max tossed the melting ice cubes in the sink with her good hand. "Do my job." She whispered Perry's words, forcing her feet to move and feeling a wave of white-hot fear run through her as she strode down the hallway.

This can't be happening . . .

11

Max took the vacant seat at the head of the table. She was breaking several rules in her mediator's playbook, the least of which was where she sat, but it was the only spot where Amy, Dagger, and most importantly, Stephanie could see her. Dagger's three associates took up the other chairs.

In her training, she'd also been warned to avoid situations where a party provided his authority up front and asked the mediator to figure out how to get there, which was exactly what Perry had done. *Rife with potential land mines,* Ben Hedden had said. Finally, and worst of all, a mediator should never have a personal stake in a mediation. Max was committing an egregious ethical violation by continuing.

But what choice do I have?

"Well?" Dagger asked.

Max knew she needed to be patient. Despite the urgency and panic that flooded her veins, she couldn't force things. A case never settled at mediation on the first offer. She moved her eyes around the stuffy conference room, sensing both dread and irritation. They all knew what was coming, and Max could tell that Dagger and Amy were ready to pounce. The defendant's frustrated reaction to the plaintiff's opening offer at mediation was as inevitable as the sun rising in the east.

Max tried to focus on her training. To be a good mediator, you needed to be more than a message toter. You had to bring something intangible into the room. Experience. Knowledge. A grasp of the issues. Something that would get the parties to move off their strongholds and positions. You had to know when to push and when to be gentle. And you couldn't be afraid to send a jolt through the room if the parties needed to hear it. Max breathed out through her nose. She trained her eyes on Stephanie and cleared her throat. "I'm . . . sorry for the delay. Perry was adamant that the cheating and abuse allegations in your counterclaim are slanderous, and he's tempted to take you to trial. I . . . had to talk him into making an offer at all."

Stephanie's eyes were fierce as she stared back, and her lip trembled. The silence in the room was now palpable, but Max forced herself to watch only Stephanie.

"*He's a monster,*" Stephanie finally said. She slammed her fist on the table, and Max winced, feeling the blow in her own injured right hand. Max glanced at Dagger. The old man's face had darkened. He was staring at the table, arms crossed tight over his chest, fists clenched.

Max tried to read the room. She looked at Amy Dance, but her old rival was peering down at the carpet. Max cleared her throat, sensing the tension in the air. If she'd wanted to send a jolt, she'd accomplished the objective. She thought about her own encounter with Perry. The entitlement and eccentric arrogance that oozed from him. She licked her lips and chose her words carefully, trusting her instincts. "Perry says he's never laid an *unwelcome* hand on you. That everything was . . . consensual."

Before Stephanie could respond, Dagger held up his palm at her and spoke through clenched teeth. "What's his offer?"

Max studied Stephanie, who was gazing at the far wall. Max wanted to probe the abuse allegations further but thought better of it when she saw Amy Dance staring at her. Amy gave a quick, almost indiscernible shake of her head.

"We're wasting time," Dagger continued.

"All right then," Max said, snatching her legal pad and turning the page, holding it up so only she could see the blank space. "Keep in mind that this is a starting point and not at all where I think he will end up." She paused, trying to come up with an appropriate beginning. Something slanted Perry's way but not so ridiculous that they would all want to leave. She thought back to her preparation for the mediation. The expectations she'd had going in as to where the parties would be. "With respect to the homes, Perry wants to keep the condo in Park City for his son, but he's willing to give Stephanie the house in town and the cottage at the beach." Max looked up, saw Amy nodding, and continued. "He is also not claiming any rights to your dog."

Stephanie snorted. "I bet not. Fredo has bitten him twice. He is an excellent judge of character."

"Get on with it," Dagger growled.

Max cleared her throat. "He'll agree to pay $10,000 a month in alimony for two years or until Mrs. Strassburg remarries, whichever is sooner, and he'll sell his interest in the family partnership that owns all the real property for fair market value." She looked up from the pad and studied Dagger. "In return, he wants Stephanie to give him her interest in Richardson Concepts."

"Not on your life." Dagger spat the words and was up out of his chair. He smoothed back his hair with a shaking right hand. "You tell that sonofabitch that we'll see him in court."

Max kept her voice calm. "It's a first offer, Dagger. A beginning point. Nothing more. Nothing less." She thought back to the secret Perry had disclosed. That Dagger was in financial trouble. If that was true, Dagger was doing a good job of disguising it. Max hadn't mentioned the potential for Dagger's interest in the company being bought out, and she was glad she hadn't. Still, it was a card she'd have to play at some point.

"The offer is ridiculous," Amy snapped, her tone one of resignation, not surprise. A *here we go* sound that Max knew she'd probably used herself when the plaintiff in a soft tissue case would come in with a seven-figure initial demand. Many of those cases . . . *most of them* . . . still settled for much less than the starting offer.

"I agree," Max said. "So now it's your turn. My advice is to work toward where you want to go. Trust the process and make a reasonable move."

"Is that what Perry did?" Dagger asked.

"No," Max said. "I've already told you the hang-up I had with Perry. But two wrongs don't make a right." She paused. "And two stupids don't make a smart."

Dagger blinked and stuffed his hands in his pockets. Perhaps the saying, one of her mother's favorites, impressed him. *Or maybe he's just tired of the bullshit . . .*

"Give us a minute, will you, Max?" Amy asked, taking a seat next to Dagger.

"Of course," Max said, snatching her notebook and pen and pushing herself to her feet. "I'll be right down the hall."

When Max returned to her office, she saw Leigh Ann's compression sleeve lying in a chair. She rubbed her swollen wrist and slipped the device on. Underneath it was a sticky note in Leigh Ann's sharp cursive.

"Give 'em hell," the note said. Max smiled and felt her eyes watering. It was something Knox always said to her before she'd present an opening statement or just prior to a big deposition that he'd assigned her to take or defend. Max rubbed her thumb over the letters and put the note in her pocket.

"Have you tried ice?"

Max wheeled toward the voice, realizing that she hadn't shut the door. Perry Strassburg stood in the hallway.

She'd managed to get control of herself while communicating the first offer to Stephanie's team, but now she struggled to maintain her composure. Grainy flashes of Nathan played in her mind. Holding him in the hospital. Pushing up his little blue cap and touching his nose and smelling and kissing her son for the first time. Walking him to kindergarten at Jones Valley Elementary. Seeing him turn to wave before he walked into his first class. His red shorts and orange socks hadn't matched, but he was determined to wear them, and Max had eventually relented. And then her own goodbye. Pulling out of the driveway the day before rehab and seeing him standing by the garage. She'd blown him a kiss, but he'd done nothing. The accusation might as well have been plastered on his face. *Why are you leaving me?* Max squeezed her eyes shut tight and then opened them. Perry was still there.

"A little cold might help with the swelling," he added.

"What do you want?" Max asked.

"I have to use the bathroom. That's allowed, isn't it?" The nonchalance in his tone was unsettling.

She ignored the question. "They're mulling over your first offer. I'll be in to see you as soon as I hear their counter."

"Well, I hope you made it a doozy."

Max took a step toward him. "Perry . . . I can sett—"

"In due time, Max," he said, turning away from her and walking out the doors to the elevator without looking back.

Damnit, Max thought, pacing the small confines of the office until she felt dizzy. She didn't want to be here when he returned from the call of nature, so she slid out of the room and exited the double doors. Not wanting to wait for the elevator, she took the stairs, remembering that the only exercise she got on some days was walking up and down the four flights after hours. She used to bring a pair of tennis shoes for that purpose.

The memory made her smile but didn't make her happy. She'd worked so hard back then. Twelve-hour days. Long nights. Weekends. She'd missed so much of Nathan's childhood, and so had Thayer. Nathan had spent his early years in day care, mother's morning out, and preschool. Max remembered the impossible guilt she used to feel. When she was at work, she felt she should be at home. When she was having a quiet evening with her family, the pressure of the job was always on her. Emails. Texts. Calls. And when the phone wasn't dinging or ringing, she felt guilty she wasn't billing hours. It had been a vicious cycle that she'd had trouble balancing. And then the accident changed everything . . .

Max took the stairs slowly, keeping her head down, knowing that she needed to focus on the present. Trips down memory lane weren't going to serve her and, if anything, would drain precious energy. Neither could she think too much about Nathan, though his drugged-out, pale face kept flashing in her mind. *Is he OK? Is he hungry? Have they hurt him?* She sucked in her breath. *Will they?* As she reached the third floor landing, she stopped and sat down. She knew she needed to compartmentalize. To get in a mental cave with only the facts of the case. She'd been good at that in her law practice. Whether she was prepping for a big deposition or in the throes of a two-week trial, she'd once been able to erase the external world and work the case.

Now, she tried to do the same with the Strassburg divorce.

Time is of the essence. Max nodded, thinking of Perry's tell. In some respects, time was always a factor in litigation, but Max figured that Perry needed control of Richardson Concepts, and he needed it fast. She'd seen him grit his teeth. Sensed the urgency behind his confident blue eyes. Max didn't know what was driving it, but she knew it was there. *What can I do with that?* She needed to probe. To ask questions of Amy, Dagger, and Stephanie. *To do my job,* Max thought, cursing herself for having not inquired about the state of the company. *No,* she thought. *I had to convey Perry's offer and absorb the reaction. And also ask about the abuse.*

Had her approach differed any because of the crazy circumstances? Max pictured Nathan with his mouth taped shut. How scared he must be. Her eyes watered over, and she wiped them hard. She wanted to scream.

When she heard footsteps coming her way, she was a tad surprised, as most folks that walked would only go up a couple flights. That was why she'd perched on the third floor landing. But when she saw the woman approaching, her stomach tightened. The lawyer was deep in thought and didn't stop until she'd almost run into Max.

"Oh, sorry," the woman said, starting to brush by.

"Hey, Lori," Max said, peering up at her former associate.

"Max?"

Lori Cannon was now in her early thirties. She had thick auburn hair tied up in a bun and wore a stylish brown pantsuit. During Lori's first few years in the firm, Max had acted as a mentor to her. Lori had shadowed Max, going to depositions with her, helping Max prepare and respond to written discovery and . . . *witnessing my complete collapse.*

"It's me," Max said, rising off the concrete with a grimace. The sleeve was helping, but her right hand was still in a lot of pain.

"I heard you were going to be here today. Mediation, right?" Lori's voice was tentative. Max could hear the fear in it.

"Yep."

"What are you doing in the stairwell?"

Max shrugged. *What am I doing indeed?* "Wanted to get some exercise and had some epiphanies on the case I'm working and decided to sit for a moment. I know, it's weird."

At this, Lori smiled. "It's good to see you. I . . ." She fumbled for words. "I've missed you."

"Same here, Lori. And, for what it's worth, I'm sorry. I was a terrible person for you to work under."

"No," Lori said. "That's not true. It hasn't been the same without you."

Max peered past her to the cinder block wall, thinking about the last time she'd seen Lori. They'd gone to meet with a doctor in Tuscumbia. A treating physician who had performed a subsequent surgery on the plaintiff in their case. Max had been out of it for most of the trip there and had been silent while Lori conducted the interview, only chiming in with a couple of questions near the end. On the way back to the office, Max passed out. "I'm sure you've heard awful things about me."

"You became dependent on oxycodone after suffering injuries in a gruesome car accident," Lori said. "It wasn't your fault."

Max felt tears sting her eyes as she looked away. That likely wasn't the company line. Lori was giving her the benefit of the doubt. She wiped her eyes and gazed at her former associate. "Thank you."

"You were a legend around here."

Max snorted. "I doubt that."

"You were. To me . . . to a lot of women . . . and men in the firm." Lori's eyes widened. "I'll never forget your cross of Dr. Goodman in the *Rainwater* case. The plaintiff's lawyer paid a thousand dollars for that deposition."

"Old Ronnie Higgs," Max said, chuckling and shaking her head, remembering the deposition like it was yesterday. "Ronnie was convinced that Goodman was going to link the fall at the hospital to all his client's back pain and surgeries."

Lori whistled through her teeth. "By the time you were through crossing the doctor, you'd turned Goodman into our expert. No link at all. Case over."

Max couldn't help but smile. "One of my finer moments."

"Ronnie is still pissed about that," Lori said.

"He's still practicing?" Max raised an eyebrow.

"Had a depo with him last week. We actually shared a laugh about it, and he said he missed you but that he was also glad you were gone. That you were the best lawyer he's ever seen on cross-examination, and he hated it when you were opposing counsel. That you just had a way of wading into the hard questions . . . and getting a witness to say exactly what you wanted."

"We had good clients, and usually the facts were on our side."

"Don't be so modest, Max. Until your accident, you were the best litigator in the firm." She paused. "Knox says he's never had a more talented protégé, and I don't even take offense, because I saw you in action. You were the best."

Max blinked the tears out of her eyes and focused on the concrete floor. The words were nice to hear. They reminded her of who she used to be. *And how far I've fallen . . .*

Lori patted Max's shoulder. "Good luck with the mediation." She started to walk up the stairs.

"Hey, Lori."

The young woman turned around. Her eyes radiated intensity and confidence.

"I'm proud of you," Max said.

"Thanks."

"By the way, I told you what I was doing in the stairwell. How about you?"

Lori grinned. "A really smart, kick-ass lawyer in this firm once told me that the only way to keep your figure around here was to walk the stairs." Lori gave a curtsy. "Bye, Max."

"Bye," Max said. Then, again brushing the imaginary dust off her pants, she began to climb the stairs herself. When she reached the hallway on five, Amy Dance was waiting.

"We have a problem," Amy said.

12

Dagger Richardson was tired of wasting time, and he had precious little to spare. He didn't like any of the counterproposals that came from Amy Dance, the attorney he'd handpicked to represent his daughter. They were all much too generous. He told Amy he had a lunch appointment and that he might be back later that afternoon, storming out before either of the two women could protest. He also dismissed his three associates, who'd only been there for show.

Five minutes after leaving the offices of Beasley Rogers, Dagger turned left off Oakwood Avenue into the entrance of Huntsville Country Club. As he expected, there were already six carts lined up at the first tee box. The Big Team, the club's high-dollar gambling group, teed off every Tuesday through Sunday at twelve noon. If this were a normal Wednesday, Dagger would be joining them.

But there was nothing *normal* about Dagger's life these days. Dagger parked in the back lot near the eighteenth green and tried to calm down. *That sonofabitch,* he thought. *After all I did to set him up in law and in business. After I gave him my daughter too . . .* Dagger clenched his teeth, knowing that Perry Strassburg wouldn't be taking any guilt trips reserved for him. The prick was incapable of guilt.

He's a dead man, Dagger thought, remembering Stephanie's broken voice as she'd called Perry a monster just minutes earlier. He got out of his Lincoln sedan and strode down the steps toward the nineteenth-hole lounge.

His banker was already waiting for him. Eric Busby had a short, military-style haircut and wore a golf shirt and slacks. They shook hands, and Eric got right to it.

"How's the mediation going?"

"Slow," Dagger said. "But we have two days, so I'm not going to lose hope yet."

"Dagger, the bank has given you several extensions on your outstanding loans. We are going to have to call Friday. I've told you this multiple times."

"I know that, Eric, and I appreciate the bank's patience."

"If you'd just sell some of the land . . ."

Dagger gazed down at his menu as a waitress came by.

"Your usual, Mr. Richardson?"

Dagger typically ordered a cheeseburger club sandwich and fries, one of his favorite cheat meals, and would wash it down with a cold beer. But that wasn't in the cards today. "No, Sally. Just a chef salad and unsweet tea."

"All right. Mr. Busby, yours will be right out."

"Thank you," the banker said, still looking at Dagger. "A move by you to sell some of the more valuable pieces would be a change in circumstances. You could buy some more time."

"No," Dagger said. "What about the class action suit I told you about?"

"Not enough. So many people lost fortunes in that same cryptocurrency play, and any payouts will be years down the road and only cents on the dollar. Dagger, you know we can't wait for that." He paused. "What about asking Perry to buy you out?"

Dagger gazed out the window, where an older couple were teeing off on the tenth hole, a par three. The man topped one just a few feet off the box.

"Dagger, surely he's floated the idea? With the divorce and your . . . age."

"What's that supposed to mean?"

Busby squinted at him. "It means that you've put a lot of work into making Richardson Concepts a global power in government contracting and were smart enough to hand the reins to a star like Perry Strassburg. No one would fault you for cashing out, especially under these circumstances. Even if you didn't owe the bank almost $25 million, would you still want to work with Perry in light of his divorce from your daughter?"

Dagger continued to gawk out the window. The woman was now on the tee, and she hit a nice shot that appeared to land on the front of the green. "What if I buy him out?"

Busby was taking a sip of tea and almost spat it out. "How is that possible? You can't even pay us off right now."

Dagger gritted his teeth. "What if, as a by-product of this mediation, Stephanie ends up with Perry's interest in Richardson Concepts?"

Busby cocked his head. "Is Stephanie going to pay off the loans?"

Dagger didn't answer.

"Even if that happened, where would the cash flow come from to satisfy what you owe? Is the company about to merge or be bought out?"

Dagger blinked his eyes as the waitress set his glass of tea down. He took a sip.

"Is there something you're not telling me?" Busby asked.

"Eric, I know what I'm doing, OK?" Dagger winked at the banker. "I need you to believe in me."

Busby leaned forward. "Dagger, we've loaned you $25 million. What more belief do you need?"

"Can you give me another two weeks?"

"I'm sorry, but I can't. I'm going to ask you again. Is there something you're not telling me?"

Dagger looked at his watch. "Eric, I've got to run. I'm sorry. I'll get Sally to wrap up my salad to go." He stood and held up his index finger, willing it not to shake. "I just . . . need you and the bank to show a little faith." He started to walk away but Eric's voice carried after him.

"I've done all I can do, sir. You've got until close of business Friday."

13

It wasn't until Max turned right onto Clinton Avenue that she let out the scream.

For the second time in the past two hours, she felt like she was trapped in one of her hallucinations from detox. She squeezed the tattered wheel of the Tundra and screamed again. And then again. She glanced to her left and another truck was driving parallel to hers. An old man was behind the wheel, looking at her like she might be an alien.

She shot him the bird.

He recoiled as if she'd punched him. Then he returned the gesture and sped off.

Max blinked back tears as her truck limped past the downtown post office and then the north side of the Von Braun Center. She knew she couldn't afford to panic. She also didn't have time for a break.

And yet here she was, in the Tundra, turning left onto Church Street and passing the Regions Center. It was fifteen minutes after noon, and she'd already blown the morning.

And what if it's already over?

Amy Dance had been frustrated and apologetic, but she'd said there was nothing she could do. Dagger had left the building, and Stephanie was unwilling to make a counteroffer that her father hadn't approved.

"OK, let's break for lunch and come back at one thirty. I trust you'll tell Dagger the plan."

"And I'll try to get him back," Amy said. "But if he won't come . . ."

Max didn't need Amy to clarify the consequences. She'd pulled herself together enough to fill Perry in, and he just shook his head before warning her not to do anything stupid. Then he gave her another glimpse of Nathan on his laptop. Still tied up but now either asleep or drugged to the point of passing out.

"You better hope the old man comes back."

Max had held the scream as long as she could, but now she couldn't seem to control herself. She yelled again and then released a sob, struggling to catch her breath. She knew that many mediations broke up after only a couple hours and upon the first round of unreasonable offers, but Max took no solace in this reality. Not when her son was God knows where, tied up, probably scared to death. She almost hoped he was high. At least the THC would dull the anxiety. Maybe that was what had led to him passing out.

Max drove the truck without thinking, turning right onto Pratt Avenue and then, a couple hundred yards up, left into the Dallas Mill Deli.

How can I eat? Max thought, as guilt and fear permeated her being. Still, she needed a reset. She parked, grabbed her legal pad, and strode toward the entrance of the iconic Huntsville establishment.

The last time she'd been to Dallas Mill was over two years ago. She and Caroline would meet here for lunch at least once a week. It was her old friend's favorite spot, and she and Max always ordered the same thing.

"Chicken salad on wheat," Max said as she reached the counter, grabbing a bag of Lay's and a strawberry pretzel salad from the fridge. After paying, she sat down at a two-seater table by the window and waited for her sandwich. She opened the bag of chips and popped one in her mouth. Then she began jotting down notes.

A settlement on Perry's terms hinged on the answer to two simple but daunting questions. First, was there any universe where Stephanie would forfeit her rights to the company her father had founded? And second, would Dagger, the mastermind behind Richardson Concepts, patriarch of the family and living legend in Huntsville legal and business circles, sell out?

There's no way in hell . . . she thought, looking at the two questions on her pad.

Max wasn't Ben Hedden. She'd only mediated four other cases. She hadn't built up years of trust mediating with Amy Dance. She hadn't handled any divorce cases, nor had she mediated a property or business dispute. And even if she was Ben . . . *some cases can't be resolved.* With the personalities and egos involved here . . .

Max chewed the top of the pen, a nervous habit. *Dagger is having financial problems . . .* If that was true, he was doing a good job bluffing. Leaving the mediation was the ultimate power play. *But is that why he did it?*

When her sandwich was ready, Max stood to meet the server halfway and saw something outside the window that made her throat go dry.

Judge Caroline Parker was climbing out of a Lexus GX 460 SUV. She wore a red sweater dress with cream-colored pantyhose. She waved at someone in front of her, and Max saw that she was meeting a man wearing green scrubs and a jacket. Caroline's husband, Dr. Bruce Parker, had the same salt-and-pepper hair and beard that Max remembered. He kissed his wife on the cheek, and they began to walk toward the front door.

Max wheeled toward the bathroom. She went inside it, locked the door, and paced the tiny confines, which smelled like Lysol. Her heart was racing, and she couldn't seem to slow it down.

I was bound to see her at some point, Max told herself, trying and failing to control her breathing. Max scrutinized her reflection in the mirror. *Is that why I came? Hoping she'd be here so I could beg for help?* Max splashed water on her face.

Or am I just a glutton for punishment?

Max dried her hands and heard someone twisting the knob of the locked bathroom door. She couldn't stay here forever. Without thinking any more, Max unlatched and opened the door. She walked with her head down toward her table and grabbed her notebook, leaving the chips and pretzel salad. Dallas Mill had an outside patio, and Max made a beeline for it with her head still lowered. Behind her, she heard the clerk's voice yelling "Ringo?" and she cringed.

She figured Caroline and Bruce were still ordering. *Did they hear my name? Did she see me?*

Once on the porch, Max walked through a door to the parking lot and hustled to her truck. She unlocked her door, flung the notebook on the passenger seat, and cranked the ignition.

"Damnit!" she hissed. She felt naked. Vulnerable. She thought of Nathan and let out an audible sob. *I'm failing him . . . like always.*

Max hit the steering wheel with her sleeved right hand and yelped in pain. She'd forgotten about her injured wrist, and now it throbbed. Hot tears filled her eyes, and she swiped at them. She straightened in her seat, still afraid to look into the restaurant.

"I can't do this," she whispered, gritting her teeth. As she put the Tundra in reverse, she sneaked a peek through her windshield into the deli. She'd meant only to glance inside and use the backup camera to get out of there. But what she saw held her gaze in place and brought a cold chill into the cab.

Caroline was standing next to the window with her arms folded.

Staring right at Max.

14

Perry Strassburg peered across the table at his investment banker. They were seated in a corner booth at J. Alexander's, in the heart of Town Madison. Outside the window was a view of Toyota Field, home to the Rocket City Trash Pandas, Huntsville's double-A baseball franchise.

"Perry, this merger has to go through. The Syndicate is hearing that a request for proposal from the government is imminent."

"I know," Perry managed. "I just need until Friday."

"We may not have that long. Even if the merger happens, we'll still have to file an HSR report to obtain approval of the deal, and that process could take another thirty days. What if the government issues the RFP before the deal is approved? We're running out of time, man."

Perry forced his voice to remain calm. "I have the pieces in place to obtain almost immediate government approval after filing the HSR. All I need is control of the company to be able to close the deal with the Syndicate, and I will get that during this mediation. I promise you. It's going to happen." He paused. "You're just going to have to trust me."

"I have. And so has the Syndicate." He paused. "But it's nut-cutting time, buddy."

"I'm well aware of the urgency," Perry said.

"*Are you?* Because I'm not getting that vibe from you."

Perry eyed the banker but said nothing. Andrew Wick had been a friend for years. They'd been in the Pinnacle Club together right out of graduate school, which was law for Perry and business for Wick.

Pinnacle was advertised as a club for young male professionals in Huntsville to network and develop relationships that could help them in business. In reality, it was more of an adult fraternity, and some of the events bordered on complete debauchery.

Wick wore a plaid blazer over a white golf shirt. Gray slacks. Black loafers with no socks. He had thick black hair. His family had moved to Huntsville from Shanghai in the late '90s. He'd graduated from Grissom High, got his undergrad in finance from the University of Alabama and his MBA from Emory in Atlanta. Wick was one of the smartest people Perry knew, and his knowledge of the market, through both legitimate trends and illegitimate insider information, had padded Perry's bank account. Wick was also well connected in the government contracting world, and he'd brought Richardson Concepts a number of new clients and opportunities.

Three months ago, Wick had presented an opportunity so big that Perry still couldn't quite believe it.

"How's the mediation going?" Wick asked, grabbing a fry from the plate in front of them. They'd both ordered salads with protein, but Wick couldn't resist J. Alexander's incredible french fries.

"Not well," Perry said. "Dagger left after my first offer, but I think he's bluffing. *I know he's bluffing.*"

"Why don't you just tell him about the merger?"

"You know we can't do that," Perry said. He thought of saying more and then decided against it.

Wick took a sip of Diet Coke. "Perry, we're talking about over a billion dollars. We could cut him in. Dagger is no saint. There are rumors swirling about the Syndicate. What if the government doesn't approve? With Dagger's contacts, especially General—"

"No," Perry said. "We can't do that. We're also talking about something that goes far beyond money, and you know damn well what it is." Perry grabbed a fry and turned it over in his fingers. He lowered his voice to a whisper. "Do I need to say it out loud?"

Wick looked away. Then he shook his head.

"Good. We can't cut anyone else in. I'm either able to close the deal or I'm not. But I have to acquire full ownership of the company to close. You know that."

"I do. But what if you fail? What if the merger doesn't go through . . . or if the government doesn't approve?" He bit his lip. "Do I need to say what will happen to us out loud?"

"I won't fail," Perry said, ignoring the question. "The deal will close, and the government will approve." Perry ate the fry in his hand as the waitress set down their salads.

"They've been following me," Wick said. For the first time, his voice betrayed his nerves, the last word coming out a whispery whine.

"You're being paranoid."

"No. I'm not. My wife too. My son, Jacob, said he thought he saw a couple of men in dark suits watching his soccer practice yesterday."

Perry took a bite of salad. "Are you sure?"

"Do me a favor. Go to the bathroom. When you're done, look out the window in the back. Tell me if there's a black Yukon with tinted windows in the front row of cars."

"You're crazy."

"Humor me."

Perry flung his napkin down and walked around the bar to the restroom. He didn't have to go, so he washed his hands. As he exited the restroom, he glanced to his right.

Sure enough, there it was. A black Yukon. Tinted windows.

He strode back to the booth. "OK, it's there. So what?"

Wick leaned forward. "The same SUV followed me to the office this morning. Jacob said it was a black Yukon that he saw at practice." He paused. "Have you been paying attention to who might be following you?"

"Wick, this is ridiculous."

"No, Perry. This is the Syndicate. And we're in way too deep *not* to follow through. If we don't, we're going to lose a lot more than money."

Wick's words hung in the air between them, and Perry forced himself to stay calm. "That's why we can't cut Dagger or anyone else in," he said. He took another bite of his salad and washed it down with Diet Coke. "Don't worry, brother." Perry winked at him. "We'll get it done. I have a plan."

"I hope you do," Wick said. "By the way, when was the last time you checked on your son?"

Perry felt his stomach clench as if he'd been punched. "Why do you ask?"

"Have you not been listening to me? They know everything about us, Perry. All the soft spots. I've got a lot more than you do, but Tru is yours." He nudged Perry's hand with his fist. "If I know it . . . you can bet your ass the Syndicate does too."

Perry leaned his back against the booth and stretched his arms over his head, feigning confidence. "Tru is fine. Great."

"Glad to hear it," Wick said. Then, dropping his voice even lower to a whisper, he added, "Do you really think Max Ringo can settle your divorce? You remember the stories floating around about her?" Wick smiled, showing his teeth. There was no humor or even mischief in his eyes. *He's cracking up,* Perry thought. "Well?" Wick pressed.

"I do remember . . . and I believe that Max can find middle ground," Perry said, thinking about Nathan Ringo's current whereabouts and forcing self-assurance into his tone. "In fact . . . I think Max is the perfect mediator for this case."

On the way back into Huntsville, Perry made a call he'd been dreading.

"It's not working," he said when the person on the other end of the line answered.

"It will."

"How can you be so sure?"

"I just am. Give it time."

"I don't have time."

"Yes, you do. You have two days for the mediation, right?"

Perry didn't respond. He leaned forward and glanced into the rearview mirror. There was a black Yukon three cars back.

"Perry?"

"I'm here. I'm just—"

"You're going to have to trust me."

"I don't trust anyone or anything."

"You're going to have to this time."

Before he could respond, the line clicked dead. Perry stuck the phone back in his pocket. For the first time, he felt chinks in his emotional armor. The lunch encounter with Wick had rattled him.

And I lied to him.

Perry hadn't spoken with his son in weeks. He pulled up Tru's number and clicked on it. After five rings and no answer, Perry ended the call. Again, he leaned forward and peered through the rearview.

The Yukon was still there.

15

When Max entered the defendant's conference room at 1:28 p.m., Amy Dance was the only person she saw. "Are they—?"

"On the way," Amy interrupted. "Caught in traffic."

"Right," Max said, trying hard to control her breathing. "Dagger too?"

"Yes. I got him on the phone, and he's coming back. Word of warning. The abuse allegations are very upsetting to him. I'd steer clear of that stuff for purposes of mediation."

Max cringed, knowing she'd made a rookie mistake. "I'm sorry."

"It's OK," Amy said. "You were in with Perry a long time, and if that's his hang-up, then you needed to tell us. There would never have been a good time." She leaned forward and spoke out of the corner of her mouth. "Confidentially, I think the assault claims are weak, as we don't have any independent evidence beyond Stephanie's word."

Max said nothing. *I still have a chance,* she thought, scanning the two questions on her legal pad. She thought of just putting it out there. *Will Stephanie and Dagger ever give up their interests in the company?*

But she held her tongue. Instead, she pivoted to another important topic. "Tell me about Stephanie. I didn't know her very well before . . ." Max hesitated but then decided *fuck it.* ". . . before I blew up my life."

Amy blinked and looked away for a second. "She's been through hell."

"She's barely said a word today."

"I think she might be in shock."

"She wasn't expecting the divorce?" Max was surprised by this nugget. "But the abuse and the affair. I'm surprised she didn't file."

"She felt like she was taking one for the team. She didn't think Perry could afford to divorce her."

"Why is he?" Max asked, surprising herself with the obvious question. "He's benefited by having the power and assets of the Richardson family name behind him. Why break that up? Why now?"

"I have a theory," Amy said, crossing her arms. But before she could say anything else, the door swung open and Dagger stepped inside.

"I'm sorry for walking out," he said, striding to the end of the table. "It's just . . . she's my daughter and . . ." He trailed off, and, for the first time, Max thought she saw the real Dagger Richardson. The pain emanating from the man was palpable.

"I understand," Max said. As she was about to say more, Stephanie Strassburg stepped through the still-open door. Her cap was pulled down so low that Max could barely see her eyes.

Max stood and shut the door. Then she turned and rubbed her hands together. "Let's get to work."

The afternoon passed in a blur.

By 4:50 p.m., the parties had reached an agreement on the homes. Stephanie would keep the mansion on Echols Avenue and the beach house in Watercolor. Meanwhile, Perry would buy out Stephanie's interest in the Park City condo for $2 million. They had also moved to within $10,000 on the alimony figure, with Perry offering $15,000 a month and Stephanie coming down to $25,000. But that was where the progress ended.

No headway was made on the land or the company. As for a lump sum cash award, Max hadn't offered anything on Perry's behalf, while Amy insisted that her client receive a minimum of ten million.

Hence, on the only issues that mattered to her blackmailer, Max had failed. She was also disappointed in her efforts to learn any more about Stephanie Strassburg. Indeed, the defendant had barely said a word all day since calling Perry a monster. It was like she had shut down or, more likely, submitted to her father's command.

Max had her exit meeting with Perry first. "I need to know if my son is all right."

"You've seen the video."

"Show me again."

"I'm tired and late for a meeting, Max. Trust me. He's fine."

"Not good enough," Max said, blocking his path to the door.

"You don't have any leverage, Max. Now get out of my way." When he brushed past her, she closed her eyes.

"You must be in a fix worse than me," Max said, speaking toward the window. It was still light outside, daylight saving time a week or two off. "What are you afraid of, Perry? Did you write a check that your ego can't cash?"

"I'm not the one with the problem ego in this mediation."

She wheeled toward him. "Your actions reek of desperation. I should call your bluff."

"I'd think twice on that. It was nothing to me to kidnap your son, and I won't hesitate to end his miserable life." He creased his eyebrows. "Someone is bluffing today, but it's not me. To settle this case, you have to push Dagger . . . or convince Stephanie to lean on him."

"Please, Perry." Max hated the weakness in her voice.

He approached her, and she tensed. "I hope tomorrow goes better than today. For your sake. And for Nathan's."

Five minutes later, Max presided over a much different scene in the defendant's conference room. "I really think we're headed in the right direction," she said, hating how lame she felt and knew she sounded. "Just need to keep chipping away and trust the process."

Stephanie stood and crossed the room toward Max. "Thank you," she said, her voice barely audible, hat still pulled low over her brow.

"Yes, thank you, Max," Amy said, and her tone at least wasn't dismissive. *Perhaps I've made up a little ground . . .*

"Go ahead, Amy," Dagger said. "I'd like a word with Max alone."

Amy's gaze held on him, but he didn't budge, and she made her way around Max. "See y'all tomorrow."

Seconds later, Max stood at one end of the long table and Dagger sat at the other. Sensing that he was about to share something important and grateful for the opportunity to speak with him alone, she made the first move, circling around and taking the seat next to him. Dagger had both of his elbows on the table and rested his chin on his folded hands. His gray eyes looked tired and red. "Long day," he said.

"Yes," Max agreed.

"You have children?"

A vision of Nathan tied up in the chair, eyes closed, came to her. She placed her hands on the table and noticed the sleeve. The pain hadn't been too bad this afternoon, but she knew she should probably have it x-rayed. "Yes. A son. His name is Nathan."

"Nathan Ringo," Dagger said. "Good name. I knew a judge once who said that, when naming a son, you had to make sure that the name sounded good when being blared by the public address announcer at Bryant–Denny Stadium." He chuckled. "The tackle is made by number thirty-two, *Nathan Ringo*." He winked at her. "Mission accomplished."

"Thank you," she said, wondering if Nathan's name had ever been introduced in a sporting event. Her son had always been drawn to the arts. Theater. There were a few soccer games early on and the obligatory Little League coach's pitch season at Mayfair Park, but that was it for Nathan with sports. "I know you're worried about your daughter."

"I am." He sighed. "Her mother and I had prayed for more kids, but God only blessed us with Stephanie. I had hoped for a son to carry on the Richardson name."

Max said nothing, knowing it was important to let him talk.

"When she married Perry . . ." He leaned back in his chair and chuckled. ". . . at least in those first few years, I felt like he was the son I'd never had. I know that sounds cliché, but it's the truth. Perry was smart. Savvy. An excellent lawyer. A corporate litigator, just like I'd been. Confident. Arrogant. An asshole when needed." Dagger again winked at Max. "Just like me."

Max winked back.

"Anyway, Richardson Concepts was my baby. I inherited the land from my parents, and that's important to me. It's the family's legacy." He paused. "But *my legacy* is Richardson Concepts. I founded it in the early 2000s when government contracting in Huntsville was taking off. We went from a struggling start-up to being the largest family-owned business in the state of Alabama. It took almost fifteen years, but by the time Perry and Stephanie married, the company was worth north of $50 million."

"And since Perry's arrival?" Max nudged, her voice soft.

Dagger snorted. "Truth? Perry has been a terrific CEO. He's almost tripled the value of the company in a decade and made us one of the strongest independent government contractors in the Southeast and in the top twenty of the nation. I'd be lying if I said I wasn't a little jealous of his business prowess." Dagger hesitated, rubbing the back of his left hand with the fingers of his right. "It's my fault that I gave him too much power." He turned to Max. "Stephanie's been thrown to the wolves. Everyone in this case is a predator. Perry. Me. Hell, I bet Amy Dance hunts her food with her bare hands. She's an animal in the courtroom, as you well know. That's why I hired her." He looked down at the carpeted floor. "But not you. You're neutral."

"I'm doing the best I can," Max said. "It's a tough case. A lot of moving parts."

Dagger squinted at her. "You've kept the parties negotiating, and that's more than some mediators could have done." He licked his lips. "*Tenacious.* That's how Knox described you."

Max raised her eyebrows.

"I always do my homework, Max. Knox Rogers and I go back thirty years. He said you were an exceptional trial lawyer. Detail oriented. Unafraid of confrontation. And smart as almighty hell." Dagger crossed his arms. "Knox felt you'd bring the same qualities to mediation that you did to trial work. He said that firing you was the hardest thing he'd ever had to do in his legal career."

"He was right to fire me," Max said, peering down at the table.

"He didn't say he was wrong. Only that it was difficult to terminate his prize pupil. So much . . . 'unfulfilled potential,' is how he put it."

Max raised her eyes to meet Dagger's. Was he bullshitting her? Buttering her up to make a play? *Probably,* she thought, but the words, at least the ones the old warhorse was attributing to Knox, rang of some truth. They were similar to what Lori had said in the stairwell.

I was a tenacious litigator . . . Feeling a momentary rush of pride, Max sat up straighter in her chair. Then, releasing a breath, she shifted her thoughts to Nathan. Was he hungry? Tired? She swallowed. Her throat had tightened. She coughed as the last terrible question popped into her mind.

Is he alive?

Max was glad to have made an impression on Dagger, but at the end of the day, none of that mattered. She bit her tongue, hesitated, and finally broached the topic she knew she had to ask him about. "Dagger, Perry told me about your financial problems. Are you interested in selling your stake in Richardson Concepts?"

Dagger's face paled in the glow of the fluorescent light above. "My interest in the company is *not* a part of this mediation."

"It can be," Max said. "I think Perry would be amenable."

"You think I'd sell out to that sonofabitch?"

Max said nothing, holding his glare.

Dagger shook his head. "You don't know me very well, Max. I'm not the one that's going to jump out of the way in this game of chicken. You hear?"

Again, Max stayed quiet, absorbing the predictable reaction. *I had to put it out there.*

After a few tense seconds, Dagger grabbed his briefcase and rose from his seat. "If you are able to settle this case on terms that I deem favorable to my daughter, I promise I won't forget it."

"What's that supposed to mean?" Max asked.

"Exactly what you think it means," he said, looking down at her with a twinkle in his gray eyes. "Good night."

16

On the heels of being blackmailed all day, bribery was a nice change of pace.

Max would have laughed at Dagger's not-so-subtle attempt to sway the mediation if she wasn't so tired. If she also wasn't scared to death. Max took the stairs because she knew the elevators would be packed with her former colleagues. As she reached the bottom landing and entered the lobby, she braced herself for several more awkward greetings, but the ground floor was empty as she hustled through to the outside.

Once Max was inside the cab of the Tundra, she let her shoulders slump. She was tired, but she knew she wouldn't be able to sleep tonight. Max checked her phone and saw two texts. One from Thayer. The other from a number she didn't recognize.

Her ex-husband's message was short and predictable. Just making sure you have Nathan. He hasn't responded to any of my texts or calls.

Max gripped the phone tight. *What should I say?* Her eyes watered over, and she swiped at them with the back of her left hand. She knew she needed to stay strong and focused. She also knew she'd have to lie. Stalling, Max stared out the window and saw Stephanie Strassburg exit the building. The woman's cap was pulled low over her eyes, and she was walking with her head down and her arms crossed. *Weird,* she thought. Stephanie should have been long gone. Max had spoken with her father for at least fifteen minutes, so Stephanie had plenty of time to make her departure. *She should be home by now . . .* Blinking and forcing her mind back to the present, Max thumbed something she knew Thayer would accept. He's fine. Studying with friends at Lowe Mill, probably has his phone on silent. We're meeting for dinner later.

She sent the text and gritted her teeth. She needed to move. To do something to keep her mind from racing to what might be happening to Nathan. She took a deep breath and forced herself to check her other message, which had come in at 4:37 p.m.

You should have never come back.

Max's hands felt numb as she read and reread the message. "What in the hell is happening to me?" she wondered. The area code was 256, meaning the sender was local. She didn't think the texter could be Perry, as he had said earlier that he'd handpicked her for this mediation. If anything, he'd wanted her to come back.

Who, then?

She remembered seeing Caroline at Dallas Mill. Her old friend had been staring at her through the window. Had she imagined it?

No. Caroline had been staring, but was it a mean look? Or just shock? Max wasn't sure about anything anymore. *But Caroline referred this mediation to me. She signed the order. Without her, I wouldn't be here. And this wasn't the first mediation she's given to me. She's trying . . . In her own way, she's still trying to help me.*

Max squeezed her eyes closed and then forced them open. She glared at the text that still shone on her iPhone screen. It was probably one of her old colleagues. Some bitter lawyer still pissed about Max's exit from the firm. Max slammed the phone down into her drink console and then winced with pain. She needed to go to the emergency room.

Max put the truck in gear and eased out of the parking lot. As she was about to turn right out and head toward the hospital, she saw a Range Rover in front of her turning left. She noticed the woman behind the wheel was wearing a cap pulled low over her head.

"Where are you going, Stephanie?" Max asked out loud. Stephanie Strassburg lived in a seven-thousand-square-foot mansion on Echols Avenue, in the exclusive Twickenham area.

But the Twickenham district was right, and Stephanie was turning left. *And what caused her to delay leaving the office?* Feeling a tingle in her brain, Max flicked her left-turn blinker on. *I don't know anything about her . . .*

Seconds later, Max was on Clinton Avenue, heading west.

17

Stephanie Strassburg pulled into CCI at ten minutes after five o'clock. She trudged toward the entrance on shaky legs, still reeling from the vomiting episode she'd had just before leaving the mediation office. That was how it was for her with chemo. She'd be fine, and then, all of a sudden, the nausea would hit her like a ton of bricks. This time, the attack came on the elevator, and she barely made it to the bathroom on the lobby level before emptying out her stomach. She sighed, tasting the bile in her mouth as she approached the entrance. It was after hours now, but a tech was waiting on her. Tasha was her favorite chemotherapy technician. A Black woman with blond braids in her hair, Tasha had three daughters and two cats, and she and Stephanie had bonded over the travails of raising daughters in the digital age. Stephanie followed Tasha through the lobby to the back. Several patients were still receiving treatment or fluids, and Stephanie waved at a man she recognized.

"Coming in for the late shift?" he asked.

"Hey, Mr. Baynes," Stephanie said. "How's the golf game?"

"I'm down thirty bucks this quarter, but I had two sandies yesterday and birdied the last hole to break even. Not bad for someone who's lost forty pounds in six months." He patted his belly. "I swear they're saving my life by trying to kill me."

Stephanie smiled at the old man. Gene Baynes wore a light-blue sweater with an emblem of a mountain over the heart. He was always talking to the technicians and nurses about his golf group and how much money he'd won or lost that week. Stephanie remembered seeing Gene hustling to the driving range while she was on her way into a Gothic Guild luncheon several years ago. Ships in the same harbor chasing different rainbows. *Now look at us . . .* Gene's sweater was open at the neck, and Stephanie blinked at the tube carrying the chemo into his port. *Poison to kill poison,* she thought, as Tasha gestured for her to take a seat.

Two minutes later, Tasha had hooked up the bolus of fluids, and Stephanie saw the saline traversing down a windy tube to her port.

"Long day?" Tasha asked.

"Very," she said. "Thank you for letting me in. I don't feel good."

"It takes a while for the side effects to wear off. The fluids will help."

"So you say," Stephanie said, but there was a tease in her voice. "Have you been on any more dates with that new man? The one from the gym?" Stephanie's favorite thing about receiving chemo or fluids was listening to Tasha's adventures as a single mother.

For a moment, there was silence, and Stephanie almost opened her eyes. Then, in a low whisper, Tasha started in. "He took me to Char last night, and afterward, we went to his apartment. We had a drink, and . . ." She paused to giggle. ". . . he ended up making me breakfast in the morning."

Stephanie smiled, happy to be lost in someone else's drama.

18

Max sat in the Tundra and stared at the words across the top of the glass fortress.

CLEARVIEW CANCER INSTITUTE

Is Stephanie a patient? Visiting someone? Volunteering?

Max glanced at the clock on the ancient dashboard. 5:14 p.m. She googled CCI and saw that it was now after hours. *Meeting a doctor? Having an affair?*

Max was curious and thought about going inside, but she'd seen a woman let Stephanie in and figured the door to the entrance was locked. Max rolled down the window and breathed in the cool fall air. Then she let her eyes dart around the massive parking lot, which was still at least half full with cars.

She wondered how many of these patients had been prescribed oxycodone for pain. Max had known the risks of opioids, but she couldn't handle the constant, chronic pain after her surgeries. Once she'd taken oxy for two weeks . . .

"It's no one's fault, Max." That was the overriding theme at the Florida Recovery Center. A blameless situation. Perhaps they thought it was easier for people to get over addiction if they felt some higher power had manipulated everything. Relinquishing control was, after all, the first step of AA. And despite the fact that Max's addiction was a treatment-induced dependence on oxy and not the pleasure- or escape-driven quest for a buzz that so many of her co-dependents at the FRC had been on, none of that mattered to the doctors, nurses, and counselors in Gainesville.

They were all treated the same. *An addict is an addict is an addict.*

Max didn't have time to wait for Stephanie. Besides, what would Max say to her? And wouldn't that look creepy? The mediator following one of the parties to the doctor's office.

It is creepy . . .

Max put the truck in gear, leaving the window down and relishing the now-chilly air as it flooded the cab. She forced an image of Nathan out of her mind and turned right out of the facility, then left onto Governors Drive. Headed toward town.

"Keep moving," she whispered.

19

Dagger Richardson finished the glass of Scotch in two long swallows. Then he poured himself another. He glared at his reflection in the mirror above the bar, feeling hate well within him. Then he walked around the first floor of the farmhouse, gazing at the photographs that counted the generations. His grandmother and grandfather. Isaac and Regna Richardson. They'd been farmers, but Isaac had wanted more for his son. Next, he saw the portrait of his father and namesake. Douglas Julian Richardson. Big Doug or B.D. to those that knew him well. Isaac had sent Big Doug to law school, and the boy had come back with ideas about expansion. Four hundred acres became four thousand in two decades of buying and selling land. Thirty years after that, when Dagger was graduating law school, the property empire had grown to over fifty thousand acres.

Dagger lowered his eyes to a framed photograph of him and B.D. taken on the steps of the state capitol building in Montgomery. The old man had his hand clasped behind Dagger's neck, and Dagger was holding up his law license certificate. Even now and through a damn picture frame, Dagger had the odd thought that B.D. might choke him at any second. After graduating in the top 10 percent of his class, Dagger joined the blue-blooded firm of Jones & Butler, where he became the head of the commercial litigation department and eventually the managing partner of the Huntsville office. Twenty-five years into his practice, he'd handled cases throughout the state and federal courts of Alabama and was at the absolute top of his game.

He also wasn't satisfied.

B.D. had told him he needed to make his own mark. That he couldn't just live out his life sucking on the family tit. He'd increased the family's land holdings little by little over the years, but he hadn't made so much as a ripple compared to his own father.

That was why, at fifty-one years old and in his zenith prime as a lawyer with one of the most profitable business litigation practices in the state, Dagger went out on his own, founding Richardson Concepts after an all-night drinking binge with his old friend, General Micah Zorn, the commander of Redstone Arsenal. With the general's help and Dagger's own vast pool of connections, the company exploded onto the local, state, and, eventually, regional scenes. Richardson Concepts had a pivotal role in assisting Boeing with upgrading the design of the Apache helicopter. They were also groundbreakers in technology that the US Army was utilizing in espionage efforts overseas. By the late 2000s, Richardson Concepts had over a thousand employees and had made *Forbes Magazine*'s list of fastest-growing businesses in the United States.

And it still wasn't good enough for Dad. Dagger scoffed and took another drink of Johnnie Walker.

B.D. had been a volatile man. Prone to drink too much and speak his mind, not unlike Dagger himself. Big Doug slapped Dagger's mother quite often, and corporal punishment was a rite of passage in the house. The worst fight Dagger had ever been in was with his own father. B.D. had been sixty-seven, and he'd backhanded Dagger after Dagger's legal advice concluded that the family was stuck with the contract his father had foolishly renewed with the sharecropper that leased the land.

Dagger had fired back on B.D. with a left-right combination of his own, which led to a full-on fistfight in the front yard of the farmhouse that Dagger stood in now.

Dagger peeked through the blinds to the dying grass, focusing on the spot where he'd gone toe-to-toe with his father, ending the fight with a kick to the knee that had taken Big Doug down for good. They'd never fought again after that.

I proved myself, Dagger thought. But he'd never received any praise from his father. Not even after Richardson Concepts was rolling. Big Doug was incapable of showing that kind of affection. When the old man had died in 2005, Dagger hadn't cried at his funeral. He'd tossed dirt over the casket and walked away with a sense of relief.

He'd never wanted those types of childhood memories for his own children. He'd wanted them to know he loved them. He'd promised himself that he'd be a good and loving father.

Dagger finished his second glass of Johnnie Walker and poured himself a third. His hand shook as he refilled his glass, but he paid it no mind. It sucked getting old. He had more to do. But the clock seemed to be ticking faster. Robbing him of everything he cared about. He peered across the room to the wedding portrait of his wife. White dress. Straps over her shoulders. Toothy smile. Judy had been so beautiful.

They'd wanted three kids. Two boys and a girl had been Judy's dream, and that would have been just fine with Dagger. But by the time Stephanie came in the spring of 1983, Judy had already miscarried three babies. The lost children weighed on his wife, who became more and more religious, seeking answers from Jesus about why her children had died. Judy's path wasn't the one Dagger wanted to walk. He distrusted preachers and organized religion. Every time he got near a church, someone asked him for money. His isolation from Judy was replaced by adoration for their only child.

There had never been a question about spoiling Stephanie. While Judy treated their daughter like a fragile antique that might break at any moment, Dagger had taken the young girl everywhere. To the office and court, to breakfast, where she drank Coke in a coffee cup to mimic her father, and, finally, to her favorite activity: riding the farm on horseback any chance they could get. At first, Stephanie rode on the same stallion as Dagger, but she quickly learned to handle a horse herself. Dagger lavished gifts and experiences on the young girl, and she returned his attention by being a star. She won the Huntsville High Beauty Walk as a freshman. Was cheerleader captain her junior and senior years. A

4.0 grade point average and valedictorian of Huntsville High School. Full ride to anywhere she wanted to go, and she chose Alabama. She met her first husband, Paul, during a mission trip her junior year at the Capstone. He was eight years older than her, but the gap didn't bother Stephanie or Dagger. He welcomed her being with a mature, stable man. They married a year later, and all was right with the world.

Paul Weaver was a commercial pilot and good provider. He treated Stephanie with love and respect. He wasn't wealthy or flashy, and he was quick to say he'd "outkicked his coverage," which of course he had. But by 2009, they'd had two girls, and Dagger was sure that a grandson would be on the way soon.

Then, on February 3, 2009, while he was giving a flying lesson, Paul's twin-engine craft hit a bird during takeoff and crashed into a tree on the third hole of Sunset Landing Golf Course. The airport's dispatcher had called Dagger with the news, and he had to somehow tell his baby girl that her husband and the father of her children was gone.

Sometimes, late at night and lost in sleep, Dagger could still hear Stephanie's screams. The wailing. And then the sobs.

She was never the same.

For three years, Dagger watched her disappear into a haze of vodka and Xanax. She kept up appearances. Symphony Guild. Gothic Guild. Every damn high-society club in town. The church. But Dagger saw through the act. His daughter was dying on the inside.

He took a long sip of Scotch and opened the back door. He clicked the gas fireplace on and sat in a rocker beside the flames, staring into them. Then past the covered porch to the rows upon rows of cotton. Above the fields, the sun was setting a magnificent orangish red. Dagger sipped the liquor, taking it in, trying to think.

Though Dagger and Judy had a house on Adams Street downtown, this was home. *And it always will be.*

When Dagger was feeling bad or needed to clear his mind, the farm was where he came. The original homestead, where his grandparents first settled over a hundred years ago, was in Toney,

Alabama. A good twenty-five minutes from town. Still in Madison County, but very much "in the country," as Judy liked to say.

He remembered the first dove hunt of the season, which was always in mid-September. For almost a century, the Richardsons had been hosting a dove hunt on this land, and Dagger had continued the tradition a month earlier, shooting his limit at seventy-seven years old.

Not bad.

He drank from the glass and closed his eyes, cursing his poor judgment. He'd introduced Stephanie to Perry at a Christmas party that a local plaintiff's firm threw every year at the Roundhouse downtown, a huge warehouse-like building that numerous groups used for events.

Then, Perry Strassburg had been a rising force in the Huntsville legal community. A partner at Jones & Butler focusing on corporate and business litigation. Fierce. Aggressive. Arrogant. When Dagger looked at Perry, it was like peering in the mirror. He'd hired Perry to represent Richardson Concepts in a contract case, and, after the attorney had successfully resolved the dispute, Dagger put him on retainer to handle all legal matters for the company. A few weeks later, Dagger made the ill-fated introduction to Stephanie.

Dagger drank his Scotch and still felt cold despite the heat of the liquor and the fire. He'd misread Perry. Or perhaps he'd read him perfectly and just didn't like the inevitable result. Perry was a young lion, and Dagger was an old one.

And lions aren't meant to grow old.

Dagger gritted his teeth and finished off the glass of Johnnie Walker, rattling the ice in the glass. He'd made mistakes. Been reckless. Kept taking risks when he should have been conservative. And now, like five years ago when he'd become cash strapped after a series of poor investments, he'd put himself behind the eight ball again.

He pulled out his phone. Checked his email. Three more messages from the bank.

The sharks are circling, Dagger thought. The irony wasn't lost on him. He'd been a predator his whole career in law and business. He'd eaten off the carcasses of competitors for as long as he could remember. But now it was his blood in the water, and the one person he'd trusted to take the reins of both his family and the company had stabbed him in the back.

"I let a wolf into my house, and he's taken everything," Dagger whispered. *Just like Judy said he would . . .*

God, he missed his wife. She'd been so good at reading people, and she'd never trusted Perry or his motives. Judy had passed almost three years ago from uterine cancer. It had been a painful and unmerciful end, the disease stripping her of her weight and then her dignity. *Cruel and unfair,* Dagger thought.

Like her life with me . . .

He again scrutinized his phone. He glared at the two missed calls from his banker and then sifted through his contacts, stopping on the one he wanted.

Dagger Richardson was a lot of things. But a quitter wasn't one of them. He clicked the name, and the phone began to ring.

The man answered on the second ring. "Hey, old boy."

"General."

"What's up?"

Dagger closed his eyes. "I think it's time."

20

The emergency room was packed. There wasn't a single empty seat, and Max didn't have the luxury of waiting. She knew that a sprained or even a broken wrist was low on the totem pole of priority. She went to the desk, checked herself out, and signed the form that allowed for discharge without medical authorization.

Once back in the Tundra, Max glared at the clock. It was now 6:35 p.m. The benefits of the compression sleeve were wearing off, and the pain was increasing. She removed the device and clicked the interior light on. Her wrist was swollen, and the third finger of her right hand was crooked. *Grin and bear it,* she thought, pulling the sleeve back on and turning off the inside light. *Think.*

Max drove down Clinton Avenue, glaring up at the glass windows of the Beasley Rogers building. Then she hooked a left on Seminole Drive and saw Lowe Mill in the distance. A few minutes later, she pulled into the parking lot and hopped out of the truck, not exactly sure what she was looking for. She knew Nathan was supposed to be here tonight, practicing for the play *Jesus Christ Superstar*. She went inside and walked around the maze of art galleries until she reached the makeshift theater. She peeked inside, noticed four teenagers sitting in plastic chairs, and walked toward them.

"Have any of you seen or heard from Nathan Ringo?"

A boy looked up at Max with glazed eyes, clearly high on something. "No, dude. Where's Nathan at?"

"That's what I'm asking you," Max said, not hiding her irritation. "Have any of you heard from him?"

A girl leaned her elbows on her knees and thumbed the side of her face. "He texted me this morning."

Max felt a tingle of hope. "What time?"

The girl took out her phone, clicking the screen. "Eight thirty-two."

"What did he say?"

She glanced up at Max. Unlike the boy's, her eyes were alert. Fearful. "I don't want to get him in any trouble."

"I'm his mother," Max said. "I've been trying to reach him. He was supposed to be here for rehearsal."

"That was a couple hours ago," the boy said. "We've been finished for a while. Just chilling now. Probably about to head to Gold Sprint. Have you checked there?"

Max shook her head. The Gold Sprint coffee shop was where she had been supposed to meet Nathan. "That's my next stop." She studied the girl. "What's your name?"

"Betty," she said.

Max leaned toward her. "Betty, I'm worried about my son. I'm not interested in punishing him. I just want to find him. What did his text say this morning?"

Betty clicked on her phone again and spoke while looking at the screen. "'Hey, B.J. Grabbing some gummies at Sleazy's. Get you something?'" She looked up. "B.J. is short for Betty Jean. A lot of people call me that." Her face flushed red, and Max heard snickering in the background. "It's embarrassing . . . for obvious reasons."

Max sighed. "Did you respond?"

"I said, 'That'd be great.'"

"Did he say anything else?"

"No. That was it. I didn't see him in school, and he missed practice."

Max straightened and scratched her back with her good hand. "What and where is Sleazy's?"

"It's a gas station in Five Points. I'm not even sure of the real name."

That has to be where Nathan was kidnapped, Max thought, feeling her heart flutter. "Have you been there before?"

"A few times."

"Can you take me there, or could I follow you? I'm worried about Nathan. He's not answering his phone."

"Doesn't he live with his dad? Have you called him?"

Max's stomach tightened. "His father is out of town. I'm keeping Nathan for the next couple of days."

"Nathan told us you were an opioid addict," said the boy who was stoned. "What's that buzz like?"

Max ignored the question. "Please, can someone help me here?"

"Ma'am, tell us. What was it like?" the stoner pressed. "The oxy fix?"

Max turned and walked as fast as she could out of the theater. She felt heat behind her eyes and gritted her teeth, knowing she needed to keep it together.

Once back in the parking lot, she stopped, wondering if she'd been too hasty. Maybe there were some more questions she could ask those kids. Then she turned and saw Betty running out the door. "Hey, Ms. Ringo?"

Max waited for her. When she got within a few feet, Max crossed her arms. "What?"

"I'll show you where Sleazy's is . . . if . . ."

"If what?"

Betty stared at Max with dead eyes. "They have the strongest gummies in town."

The girl couldn't have been more than fifteen.

"Come on," Max said.

21

"Sleazy's" turned out to be a CITGO a quarter mile past Star Market in Five Points. Max darted her eyes around the relatively small gas station with its four pumps. Finally, she glanced at her phone and the text she'd just received.

Please don't forget about our deal. Loose lips sink ships.

She didn't recognize the number, but she knew it had to be from Perry Strassburg. *Am I being followed?* she wondered, not for the first time. She felt skittish and knew she had every right to feel that way. The day had been surreal.

And it's not even close to over . . .

"What do I ask for?" Max said.

Betty gave a sheepish grin. "The strongest thing they have."

Max snorted. *What in the hell am I doing?* She was losing steam and knew she should probably eat something. But her stomach was twisted into knots and her mind was slow, her thoughts scrambled. *Move,* she told herself, and she eased out of the Tundra. Just before slamming the door, she squinted at her teenage passenger. "This could take a few minutes."

Betty shrugged as if she didn't care.

Max walked toward the entrance with purpose, stepping inside and going straight to the drink cooler. She snatched a Monster energy drink and a SNICKERS bar and put her items on the counter. "I'd also like some delta-9 gummies." She hesitated. "The strongest thing you've got."

The clerk, a thirtysomething Indian man, turned and walked into a storage area. Seconds later, he was back with a small pouch with no label. "These are a hundred milligrams."

"Is that a lot?" Max asked.

"If Snoop Dogg or Willie Nelson were in here and asked for a strong gummy, this is what I'd give them."

"Well . . . that's instant credibility."

"That'll be thirty-seven dollars even." As the clerk rang her up, Max took out her phone and pulled up a recent picture of Nathan.

"Have you ever seen this kid in here?"

The man squinted at the screen and shook his head. "No."

Max opened her pocketbook. She took out three twenty-dollar bills and placed them on the counter. "You can keep the change if you give me any information about this boy. He's my son. I haven't been able to reach him all day, and he was last heard from on his way to this store."

"Never seen him," the clerk said. "My dad works the morning shift, and he's home now."

Max glanced around the store, seeing the surveillance cameras above the doors. "Do you still have footage from this morning?"

He blinked at her. "Ma'am, I can't let you see our recording."

"Why not? The police would sure see it if I reported my son missing and that he was last seen here buying these gummies." She held up the pouch. "In fact, I suspect you might have some exposure selling delta-9 gummies to minors. Did you know the kids at Huntsville High refer to this place as Sleazy's and say it's the only store in town they can buy beer and THC without being carded?" She stared at him until he looked behind his shoulder to the storage area.

"What time did you say he was here?" he asked.

"I'd like to see everything from eight thirty a.m. to nine thirty."

He turned without another word and walked into the back. "Come on," he said.

Max followed him, feeling her heartbeat pounding. Technically, this wasn't breaking Perry's rules, but she was getting perilously close. Especially in light of the warning text she'd just received.

I'm too far along to go back now.

"Here, sit," the clerk said, gesturing to a carpeted stool.

Max sat and looked at the dusty laptop screen, which was much bigger than hers or Perry Strassburg's from earlier today. Clearly an older model.

"Here you go. This picks up at eight twenty-nine a.m. The split screen shows the inside of the store in front of the register and just outside the doors." He reached around and clicked the mouse on the keyboard, and the recording started. Max could smell the stale scent of cigarettes on the man's breath.

"Thank you," she said.

For the next fifteen minutes, Max focused on the video, watching at least ten different people enter the store and buy everything from junk food to sodas to beer. Several times, she saw the clerk, who appeared to be an older version of the young man helping her, go to the back and return with a small bag.

At 8:46 a.m., Nathan walked through the front doors. He wore a long-sleeved T-shirt and faded jeans. Max's hands shook and her heart pounded as she watched her son on the screen, but she managed to bring up her phone and snap a picture of him. Twenty seconds after Nathan walked inside, a nondescript middle-aged man entered the store. He wore a black sweater, dark jeans, and a gray cap and perused the aisles. He looked around, picking up and examining several items, including a can of soda. When Nathan approached the counter, the clerk went to the back and returned with a pouch of what appeared to be exactly what Max had just purchased. Nathan paid with cash at 8:49 a.m. and exited the doors. The man in black, who bought nothing, followed behind him a few steps. Max watched until both her son and the man in pursuit were both out of the camera's view. Then she rewound the tape and zoomed in on the man in black. He had a high and tight haircut on the sides, but the hat covered the top of his head. Max snapped several photographs of the man and sighed. *It's something,* she thought. Not much, but at least she had a visual on her son's potential kidnapper.

Was it just him or a team? Max wondered, standing and stretching her arms. *Has to be at least one more person.* Unfortunately, the video cameras didn't stretch to the pumps. *It might not be him at all . . .*

Max walked out of the storage room and tapped the clerk on the shoulder. "Thank you."

"See him?"

"No," Max lied, sick to her stomach. "Can you do one more thing for me?"

"Sure."

"Get me another pack of the strong stuff."

Five minutes later, Max dropped Betty off at her home, just south of Oakwood Avenue. The girl had thanked her, and they'd exchanged phone numbers in case Nathan reached out to her before calling Max. "I hope he's OK," Betty said.

"Be careful with those gummies," Max said.

"You too," Betty fired back, winking at Max. She must have seen the extra bag.

Max sighed. She pulled out of Betty's driveway, and once back on Oakwood, she saw a gymnasium coming up on her right. "Optimist Park," Max whispered, turning into the parking lot, which was half full. The lights were on inside the recreation center, and she figured there were basketball games or practices taking place. Max pulled to a stop behind the center field fence of the adjacent baseball field. She cracked open the Monster and took a swig, burping as the caffeine filled her system. She tore the top off the SNICKERS bar and tasted chocolate-peanuty goodness. Then she took out the pouch of gummies and rolled the small bag over in her left hand.

She could take a small bite to dull the pain in her injured right hand. That might help her relax.

Max flinched when she heard the ding of the cell phone announcing a new text message. She closed her eyes but then forced them open. She glanced at the screen and breathed a sigh of relief as she read the message.

How'd it go?

Her mentor. In all the craziness of the day, she'd forgotten about him. They'd had breakfast just twelve hours earlier. Max had been a nervous wreck then, so anxious that she barely touched her biscuit.

Now, she was on the absolute ledge. She took a deep breath, exhaled. Then she threw the pouch of gummies in the back of the truck. Instead of texting back, she decided to call.

He picked up on the first ring. "Hey."

Max closed her eyes tight, trying not to cry.

"Max?"

She gritted her teeth. "I need your help."

22

Jason Rich was once the billboard king of Alabama. Brash, cocky and tacky, Jason's highway posters played off his last name.

IN AN ACCIDENT? GET RICH.

Simple. Catchy. Effective. Jason had been wildly successful settling personal injury claims all over the Southeast. Little did anyone know, however, that his personal life was a train wreck. He hailed from Guntersville, and a call from his sister brought him home. "I was about to fall off the wagon in a big way, but Jana called, saying she'd been arrested for the murder of her husband." Jason had told Max his whole story during their meeting after Max's discharge from the Florida Recovery Center. "I was lost in every way a person could be. I told myself I was going home to save Jana, but in actuality, I was saving myself."

Jason's exploits over the last few years had become the stuff of legend. He'd successfully handled three murder trials, including his own, and had gone toe-to-toe with the Sand Mountain meth ring. He'd lost a lot along the way, but, in the end, he'd found himself. He gave up the billboards but had no trouble maintaining an active and successful practice.

It was Knox who'd recommended Jason to be Max's mentor. Despite being his rival in the courtroom, Knox had grown to respect and even admire Jason's resilience.

Max smiled as she thought of the strange circumstances that had led her path to cross with that of Jason Rich. She was now sitting on a couch in front of a massive fireplace. She held a warm mug of coffee in her hand, though she hadn't consumed much of it. She was still wired from the energy drink.

Jason took a seat in a chair by the fire. He leaned forward with his elbows on his knees. "So, you said on the phone that you almost relapsed tonight."

"I bought some delta-9 gummies, but I didn't take any." She paused. "I wanted to."

"Why?"

Max felt her eyes growing hot. She wiped at them with her right hand, immediately wincing as her wrist throbbed with pain.

"Do you want some ice for your hand?"

"No," Max said.

"How'd you hurt it?"

"I punched Perry Strassburg in the face."

Jason chuckled. "I'm sure plenty of mediators and lawyers have wanted to do that."

"I did," Max said, throwing a shadow punch. "Right in the jaw."

"Max, what—"

"Jason, I didn't come out here so that you could talk me out of drinking or doing drugs. I came because I need advice . . . and help . . . and I didn't know where else to turn."

Jason leaned back in his chair, squinting at her. "OK. Legal advice?"

"I need to talk with you confidentially."

"Max, you're scaring me. What have you gotten into?"

"A mess." She took out her pocketbook from her purse. She still had a few one-dollar bills. She grabbed a few of them and gave a sheepish smile. "You good with a four-dollar retainer?"

Jason didn't smile. "Make it one."

Max passed the cash over to Jason and sat back down. Again, she studied the flames.

"All right then," Jason said. "Tell me."

23

The farm was in New Market, Alabama. There were about eighty acres. A barn. A two-story brick house with a wraparound porch. Nothing special. There were a dozen or so spreads just like it in the area.

Best of all, the place had no connection to Perry Strassburg.

"My colleague says the mediator is in Guntersville at the home of Jason Rich."

Perry grimaced, taking a sip of bourbon. They were sitting in a couple of lawn chairs by the barn. No lights. The whiskey warmed Perry's body against the chill. "Rich is her mentor in the state bar's recovery program. She texted me that she was going to see him. Trying not to fall off the wagon."

"I'd be tempted," Hicks said.

"Me too," Perry agreed.

"Mill Creek Road is a dead-end street with about ten houses on it. My agent can't get close without arousing suspicion. She's going to camp out on Highway 79 at an abandoned convenience store and will pick up her surveillance on Ringo's way back. There's a GPS bug on the truck, so we're in good shape."

"Sounds good," Perry said, sipping the bourbon. "I guess."

"You worried she's going to spill the beans to Rich? Going to that CITGO where we picked up the boy was close to crossing the line."

"I agree, but Max knows what's at stake if she talks." Perry rubbed his neck and took another sip of whiskey. "Let me see the boy."

Hicks opened the barn door, and Perry followed him to a stall in the back.

Nathan Ringo was lying on his side on a cot. His hands were cuffed in front of him. His feet tied in back. The duct tape no longer covered his mouth. Truth be known, the tape had just been for show. No one could hear his screams out here.

"How long's he been asleep?" Perry asked a man sitting on a stool in the corner.

"About thirty minutes."

Perry rubbed his chin and smelled the bourbon. "Has he eaten anything today?"

"Not much. Half a cheeseburger and a few fries for lunch, and he didn't touch the chicken fingers we got him for dinner."

Perry said nothing and began to walk out of the barn with Hicks close behind.

"Has my visitor arrived?"

"A few minutes ago," Hicks said.

"All right then, I'm going in for a minute." Perry headed for the porch, but Hicks's voice stopped him.

"Hey, boss."

"Yeah."

"What happens to the kid if his mom can't close the deal tomorrow?"

Perry didn't stutter. "You know what happens."

24

By the time Max finished describing the mess she was in, Jason Rich had begun to pace around the top floor of his house. Now, they were both standing in his kitchen. Behind Jason, Max could see the dark waters of Lake Guntersville. "Max, this would test anyone's devotion to recovery. Good grief."

"I know."

"I just can't believe . . . *the audacity of the man*. Kidnapping a kid to control ownership of a company? I've seen God complexes, especially sometimes from judges, but how does he think he can get away with this?" He squinted at her. "Max, the sheriff of Marshall County is a close personal friend of mine. The district attorney is too. Let me reach out to them. Surely, they'll have an angle."

Max was shaking her head before he even finished. "Perry said he'd kill Nathan if I went to the police. I can't involve the law."

"What if he doesn't know? I'll call Sheriff Daniels. Hatty is smart, knows people in Huntsville."

"Perry has connections in the sheriff's office and the police department. He'll find out . . . and he'll kill Nathan. I told you what he said he'd do. He'll give him a lethal dose of fentanyl, Nathan will overdose, and no one will give a rat's ass because Nathan is a stoner and his mother is a disgraced addict."

"Max, that's not—"

"*It's true.* And we both know he could get away with it. I'm the perfect foil for his plan."

Jason said nothing, scratching his neck. For a long moment, the cabin was silent. Max turned and walked back to the couch, plopping down and pulling her knees up under her chin.

"I'm sorry," Jason said, taking a seat next to her. "My advice to you as an attorney . . . and as a person who's been in a few scrapes outside the bounds of the law . . . is to focus on what you can control. You said it yourself. What Perry wants, while his methods are detestable, is not unreasonable. Stephanie's interest in the company has a value, and you can have Perry match what she'd be giving up in land and cash. There also appears to be strong motivation for Dagger to sell his interest, and it makes sense for him to do so in light of the divorce. It sounds like you have set the table for a dramatic move where Perry throws the kitchen sink at them in return for the company."

Max nodded. "What if it doesn't work?"

"You can't control the outcome," Jason said.

"I have to do more. This is my son."

Jason pushed himself off the couch and took a couple steps toward the front door. "Max, sometimes all you can do . . . is your job. Believe me, I know."

"What if I mediate the case successfully and they kill Nathan anyway? What if they kill me too?"

Jason turned, frustration etched on his face. "I'm sorry, Max. I don't have the answers."

For several seconds, silence filled the room. *It was foolish to come here,* she thought. *All I've done is put Jason in danger too.* Max stood and approached him, touching his shoulder with her left hand. "Thank you. I appreciate you listening, and I'm sorry to involve you." Before he could respond, she opened the door and closed it behind her. By the time she reached the bottom step, tears filled her eyes.

"Max?" Jason had come outside and was standing on the stoop.

"It's OK," Max said, wiping her eyes and then her nose. "You gave me good advice. I appreciate it."

"It's not near enough."

Max shrugged and heard his footsteps coming closer. When he didn't say anything, she looked up and saw that Jason was staring across the street, an odd grin playing on his lips. Max followed his gaze and spotted a one-story rancher. A couple of lights were on.

To the side of the house, a plume of smoke rose above the roof.

"Jason, what is it? Why are you smiling?"

"Because I just had an idea," he said, rubbing his chin. "I can't help you."

"I know, it's O—"

"But I'm pretty sure I know someone who can."

Before Max could respond, Jason started walking toward the road.

25

The flames raged high.

Max and Jason stood twenty feet away, admiring the height and intensity of the spectacle. "Odd night for a bonfire," Max said.

"No," Jason said, chuckling. "He's just taking out the trash."

Max looked at Jason and then back at the fire. A man was leaning forward in a lawn chair, throwing what looked to be a garbage sack into the blaze. There was a bottle of Jack Daniel's on the ground next to him, and the man leaned back in his chair and gripped the fifth, placing it in his lap but not taking a drink. Max heard the faint sound of music in the background. A country song, the singer's voice twangy and melancholy. "Who is he?" Max asked.

"Come on," Jason said. "Let me introduce you."

Max followed Jason's lead, noticing that there were two other chairs set out, empty.

"Colonel?" Jason asked, his voice firm.

The man squinted up at him, then moved his eyes to Max. He wore a gray sweatshirt, jeans, and cowboy boots and had a scraggly salt-and-pepper beard. A black cap covered his head, with the emblem of a shield and a bald eagle in profile. The man grunted but said nothing.

"This is my friend, Max Ringo," Jason continued.

The man set the bottle on the ground. Then he pressed his huge hands on the sides of the chair and began to stand.

"Please don't get up," Max said.

But he already was. Now at his full height, Max saw that he was a huge man. At least six feet, four inches tall and a shade over two hundred pounds, if Max had to guess. Keeping his posture, he took a step toward her. The fire lit up his face, and his eyes were bloodshot red. He took off his cap, revealing a mop of curly brown hair, and extended his hand. Before he could say anything, Jason said it for him.

"Max, this is Colonel Satchel Shames Tonidandel."

"Excuse me," Max said, leaning closer to Jason. "What—"

"Satch Tonidandel," the old man growled, putting his cap back on. "The last name is like saying three first names fast. Tony. Dan. Del." He paused. "Tonidandel."

"Got it," Max said. "Pleased to meet you."

"Colonel, Max has a problem that I can't help her with. It's not unlike the kind of scrape I got into a few years back."

"You're going to have to be more specific, boy. I lost count of your scrapes."

Jason chuckled. "All of them. Cade. Dean. The Sand Mountain meth ring. Max is dealing with . . . folks like that."

The colonel took a step toward the fire. He leaned down, grabbed the bottle, and unscrewed the top. He took a sip of Jack Daniel's and then placed the fifth back on the grass. When he turned around, Max thought she saw a tiny spark in his eyes. She also noticed that he had a perpetual snakelike squint to his expression. She shuddered beneath his gaze.

"And so . . ." the colonel said, glancing at Jason. "She needs a person like me."

"Yes, sir."

"And what kind of person is that?" Max asked.

The colonel studied her. "An ornery one."

Twenty minutes later, Satch stoked the fire, rubbing his chin. He hadn't said a word while Max broke down her predicament. Jason had been quiet as well, occasionally clarifying something with a question but otherwise keeping his mouth shut. The only sound was the melancholy music in the background, the same song on repeat.

"Well," Max said, peering at the colonel and sticking her hands in her pockets, wincing as her right wrist bent to go in the pouch. "What do you think? And what is this song?"

"It's called 'Spotless,' by Zach Bryan and the Lumineers. It reminds me of my brother Mickey. Let me see that picture again."

She pulled up her phone camera and showed him the photographs from Sleazy's surveillance tape. First of Nathan. Then of the man in black.

"Hold it on that bastard and zoom in."

Max did as she was told.

"He followed your boy out?"

Max nodded.

"Didn't buy anything?"

"No. He grabbed a soda out of the drink cooler but put it back before leaving."

Satch threw the stick he'd been using in the fire. "He has the look of an operative. Maybe a cop." He scratched his neck. "Maybe something worse. Hard to tell from just a few photographs."

"I did the best I could."

"You did good," Satch said. "Real good. Talking that clerk into letting you see the tape was ballsy." He grimaced. "No offense."

"None taken." Max gave a sheepish smile.

For a long moment, the only sound other than Zach Bryan's twang was the crackling of the embers. The fire was beginning to die out. "I need to think on it," Satch said.

Max waited for him to say more. When he didn't, she crossed her arms and stood from the lawn chair. "With all due respect, Colonel, I don't have time for you to think. Will you help me?"

He kicked at a stray limb on the ground. "You'll hear from me tomorrow."

Anger and desperation rose within Max. "*Tomorrow?* When? The mediation ends tomorrow. I need to know when. The morning. Before lunch?"

But the colonel was looking at the fire again. "Been a long time since I came up with a battle plan." He looked past Max to Jason. "There could be casualties."

"There always are," Jason said.

The two men considered each other. Max could tell they were communicating in some way, without words. A shared history that she didn't know or understand. *And don't have time for.*

"Colonel, please," Max said.

He rubbed the back of his neck and trudged toward the house. He seemed to be carrying some kind of hidden weight, and he stooped a little bit.

"Colonel?" Max yelled after him, her voice not quite a shriek but almost.

He stopped and spoke without looking at her. "Like I said . . . I'll think on it."

As they walked back across the street, Jason broke the uneasy silence. "Five years ago, I went to war with the leaders of the Sand Mountain meth organization. They were trying to kill me."

"For what?"

He sighed. "It's a long story. The important thing for you to know is that I'd be dead if it wasn't for that ornery SOB you just met. He was a full colonel in the 101st Airborne. The Screaming Eagles. His younger brothers, Chuck and Mickey, were captains under him. They became . . . like my family when I moved home." He nodded and Max heard emotion in his voice. "Like my brothers."

"What happened in that war?"

"We won," Jason said. "But Mickey was killed, and the colonel blames himself. Chuck, the middle brother, is a deeply religious man who's found his own path through God and nature. He's on a trip with his church to Israel right now and has traveled a lot since Mickey died. But the colonel hasn't. He blames himself for . . . the decisions he made. It's crazy. Satch beat the terrorists in Afghanistan. He beat Tyson Cade and Matty Dean, the two meth czars over here. Hell, he even beat cancer." Now, Jason's voice shook. "But he hasn't been able to get over the guilt over Mickey." Jason wiped his eyes. "I guess it's like the colonel says." He peered at Max, his eyes blazing with intensity. "It's tough being brothers."

Max stared at the concrete driveway. Then back across the road. The fire was out. The house now pitch dark.

Beaten by guilt, Max thought. *Sounds familiar.* "Do you think he'll help me?" she asked as they reached the Tundra.

Jason grabbed her good hand and gave it a squeeze. Again, his gaze was fierce. "There's not a doubt in my mind."

Max opened the door to the truck and climbed inside the cab. She should've been exhausted, but she wasn't. She felt oddly energized. When she started the Tundra, she saw that Jason was still standing beside the vehicle. She rolled down her window. "What?"

"I hated litigating against you," Jason said, rubbing the stubble on his chin. "That malpractice case we had. The facts were favorable to my client's side, but you worked it like a dog. You had my client doubting her memory of conversations with the doctor, and you chewed my expert up during his deposition."

Max shook her head. "You remember that?"

"Hell yes I do. Knox was the revered attorney, the old guard, but you were the one that made me earn everything I got. If we'd gone to trial . . . I'm not sure we would have won."

"You're trying to make me feel good. Stop."

"No. That's not what I'm doing. A successful trial attorney has to have a bit of an edge to them. They have to be real. I know . . . because

I struggled with that. I was quirky. Tacky. I wasn't like my father, who was a well-respected lawyer. When I came out of rehab, I thought I would lose my edge."

"Did you?"

He shook his head. "Far from it. Sobriety was like a superpower. I know your situation is different from my own." He put his hands on the sill. "But I also know that you had that edge . . . and you need to get it back. You need it for what you're going through."

"How?" Max asked, frustrated by the ambiguity of his words. "What the hell are you talking about, Jason? I was just a lawyer doing my job. Now I'm a mediator trying to do the same thing."

"No," Jason said. "You were a badass, Max. Mean. Ruthless. Unafraid to hurt feelings." He lowered his voice. "I didn't trust you . . . and I was a tad scared of you."

Max looked away from him. "I made a lot of enemies being that way. Besides, how in the world can those qualities help me get my son back?"

Jason tapped her on the shoulder with his knuckles, and she looked at him.

"Like I told you earlier, Max. Control what you can control. Starting with *you*. Think of this mediation the same way you would a trial. Victory is a settlement on Perry Strassburg's terms. When you were a trial lawyer, what would you do to win?"

Max felt her stomach tighten. "Anything it took."

"That's right." Jason's eyes were wide. Excited. "Anything it took," he repeated. "Now . . . do you want to win?"

"Quit patronizing me," Max snapped.

"I'm not. Answer the question."

Max gritted her teeth. "I have to win."

Jason took a step back. "Then you know what you have to do."

26

What's my edge? Max thought as the Tundra hurtled down the mostly barren highway. It was 11:15 p.m. By the time she got to her hotel, it would be midnight. She was tired, but in a good way. She'd avoided a relapse. She was in an impossible situation and yet she hadn't lost her senses. She'd investigated. Sought help. The trip to Jason Rich's house hadn't produced the results she'd hoped, but she was better off for it. Hopefully, Colonel Tonidandel would help her. But even if he couldn't offer assistance, Jason was right.

I was a good trial lawyer.

She glanced up at her reflection in the rearview mirror. There had been a time, not that long ago, when she had exuded self-confidence and even arrogance in carrying out her role as a litigator. You needed a little moxie to handle the grind of the job and the constant stress of dealing with the egos and expectations of doctor clients that never, at least in their own minds, made a mistake and plaintiff's lawyers who pushed the envelope at every turn. Some people hated confrontation. Caroline had never enjoyed it. That was probably why her path had bent toward being a judge.

But Max had thrived on the adversarial process. She'd hated aspects of being a civil defense litigator. Keeping up with billable hours sucked. Written discovery was tedious, and depositions were a grind.

But the drama of battling it out with other lawyers? Arguing a motion at a hearing? Cross-examining difficult witnesses? Max loved every bit of it, and instead of being drained by the drama, she'd thrived.

"*That's a gift, Max,*" Knox had told her once, after watching her handle another lawyer's objections during a deposition and a threat to call the judge without breaking a sweat or showing the slightest bit of panic or submission.

In the last almost three years of accident, addiction, and recovery, had she lost her gift?

As Max passed through New Hope, glancing at the Dollar General on the left and the Hardee's on the right, she wasn't sure. She'd never burned out. Even when she was hooked on oxycodone, she'd never lost her ability to handle confrontation. How else had she been able to sweet-talk and threaten some of her doctors and friends to give her more of the drug?

Max bristled at the memory, not wanting to go there. *How can I get my edge back?*

Jason's words reverberated in her mind. "*You were a badass, Max. Mean. Ruthless. Unafraid to hurt feelings . . . I didn't trust you . . . and I was a tad scared of you.*" Max couldn't help but smile. The fact that she was a woman in a male-dominated profession always amped up her adrenaline. She did whatever it took to win. And by and large . . . *I always won.*

She'd been bulletproof before the accident. But she was a different person now. Humble. Grateful for a second chance. She gritted her teeth as she thought of her encounters with Perry Strassburg.

Weak.

The whole day, she'd walked around with her tail between her legs. Even before Perry dropped his bombshell.

As she passed through Hampton Cove, Max sighed and turned on the radio. She was tired of thinking. The song playing on the classic rock station was "The Stroke" by Billy Squier, and Max rolled all the windows down and turned it up full blast. In law school in Tuscaloosa, she and Caroline loved to blast '80s hair metal on nights when they needed to blow off steam. They'd go to Jackie's Lounge or Innisfree, drink a few beers, and then hit Taco Casa on the way home.

Max felt a tickle of adrenaline. There was one song in particular that amped her up when she was getting ready for something big. She'd play it before an expert's deposition. Or in the car before trial when she was handling the opening statement or closing argument. She grabbed her phone and clicked on the music app. When was the last time she'd listened to her playlist?

Before rehab? She couldn't remember. At some point, she'd become so numb she didn't care about music anymore. Since her discharge, she listened to the radio but hadn't given much thought to choosing a specific tune.

She thumbed through the songs at the next stoplight and found the one she wanted. Max clicked on it and tensed when she heard the eerie whistle sound beginning.

As the engine of her dad's old Tundra revved going up the hill on Governors Drive, the first guitar chord blasted out of the speakers. Once. Then twice.

And Max felt it. The adrenaline spike that she experienced every time she played the song.

Max's favorite movie as a kid was *Vision Quest* with Matthew Modine. The ending scene when Louden Swain comes into the gym, jumps rope to warm up, and then runs out into the arena to take on Shute, the wrestling champion, always gave her goose bumps. The acting and setup were awesome, but it was the song that made the scene.

"Lunatic Fringe" by Red Rider.

A one-hit wonder from a forgotten band. To Max, the lyrics meant chasing what you wanted right up to the edge of crazy. The fringe of losing your mind. A perfect song for Louden Swain.

And for me . . .

As Max Ringo moved into the city limits of Huntsville for the second time in the last fourteen hours, she ground her teeth together, blasting the '80s anthem and singing along. She knew she'd have to embrace her inner crazy if she was going to settle the Strassburg divorce and save her son.

I always win.

DAY TWO

27

By 6:15 a.m., the Blue Plate Cafe was hopping. As Dagger Richardson walked through the doors, the blended scents of coffee, bacon, and pancakes were overpowering. As was the crowd. He shook hands with several regulars as he made his way to the booth near the back of the restaurant.

His breakfast companion was already seated, with a steaming cup of java and a glass of ice water in front of him. As Dagger took his seat across from him, neither man spoke.

A waitress came over and took Dagger's order. "Coffee and toast," he said. When she turned to his guest, he waved her off.

Dagger Richardson stared at the man. "Well?" Dagger asked, after the waitress set a cup of coffee in front of him. "What do you think?"

For seventeen years, General Micah Winfield Zorn had been the commanding officer of Redstone Arsenal, retiring just eight months ago. Before that, he'd led troops in the Gulf War, and he'd spent most of the '80s in the Middle East. He'd joined the army at the tail end of Vietnam and had seen action there after the fall of Saigon. General Zorn was a short man at five feet, seven inches tall, but he had a barrel chest, thick forearms like Popeye, and a scar under his left eye, a permanent reminder of his three weeks as a hostage in a prison camp in Ho Chi Minh.

In 2008, a year after his term began as head of the base, the general came to Dagger for legal advice. Zorn was having an affair with his secretary, a woman two decades his junior, and the mistress was making threats. She'd tired of the tryst and wanted more. She was also pregnant. Or so she said. General Zorn was fifty-four at the time and figured he shot blanks, but he didn't want a paternity test. He also didn't want to lose his marriage or his reputation.

He needed the problem to go away.

Dagger was the county attorney back then. He knew people in the sheriff's office and at the jail. He said there wasn't much legally he could do about the situation, but . . . if the general was willing to go outside the rule book, there were several options.

A week later, the woman was stopped for a DUI driving home after having drinks with Zorn after hours. She was put in a holding cell for the night, and guards found her the next day hanging from a ceiling pipe.

The coroner ruled her death a suicide, hard to know for sure. The video cameras in that particular cell hadn't been working for days.

That was at the apex of Dagger's power. General Zorn was, to put it mildly, grateful and impressed.

Since then, the two had helped each other out from time to time, and it was the general's assistance and backing that really pushed Richardson Concepts off the ground in the early years of the company. When you are an upstart government contractor, having the support of a three-star general in charge of the largest military base in the region is quite helpful.

But the general's assistance over the years hadn't quite measured up to what Dagger had done for him.

And both men knew it.

"I think that we've been friends for a long time," Zorn said. He had a Midwestern accent, having grown up in Gary, Indiana, the son of a plumber and a schoolteacher. "And I owe you." He took a sip of his coffee. "I believe I've repaid some of that debt over the years by supporting Richardson Concepts and feeding you . . . *information* that you shouldn't have received. Including about the merger talks your son-in-law has been having." He raised his eyebrows at Dagger.

"You have, and I appreciate your help very much."

"I'm a bit surprised that you haven't had a come-to-Jesus with Perry. My sources tell me that this conglomerate . . . the Syndicate is what they call themselves . . . is backed by private equity, and their motives involve a bit more than just making a splash in the government contracting world." He creased his eyebrows. "A lot more."

"Spit it out," Dagger said.

"My people are worried that the muscle and money behind the Syndicate is a group of foreign operatives with loose ties to the Chinese and the Russians." He gazed at his cup and then back up at Dagger. "Both countries have a common interest in having eyes on the Arsenal. With Richardson Concepts owning several valuable IDIQs and an RFP for engineering the receptors intended to take down hypersonic missiles launched toward our country imminent . . ." He glared at Dagger. "You can fill in the rest."

"*What?*" Dagger asked, feigning surprise "You can't be serious."

Zorn frowned. "I am. Dagger, are you aware that there are more foreign operatives in Huntsville, Alabama, than any other city or town in this country other than Washington, DC?"

Dagger rubbed the back of his neck. "I assumed that we had our fair share of international spies due to the defense contracting industry and the presence of the base . . . but not at that level. I don't believe it." But Dagger was bullshitting the general. He knew damn well what was going on. As president of the company before Perry, Dagger had bid on and won as many indefinite delivery, indefinite quantity contracts as he could. Possession of IDIQs gave Richardson Concepts the veritable "license to hunt" when the government sent out a request for proposal, which made the company much more powerful. *And valuable,* Dagger knew. *Especially to a foreign country wanting to not just spy but also interfere with operations at the most important missile defense base in this country . . .*

The general smirked at Dagger, sipping his coffee. "I think you're a bit more tuned in on all this than you're letting on. But regardless, if what I'm hearing is true, this merger is an espionage play disguised as a lucrative buyout. And the Syndicate isn't going anywhere. If your son-in-law doesn't deliver what they want, other companies with IDIQs that own land or buildings near military bases will be targeted. Perry is playing a dangerous game."

Dagger held his eye. "You said the value of the deal to Richardson Concepts would be in the billions."

Zorn nodded, but, if anything, his eyes were colder. "A hell of a payday . . . for committing treason."

"You're upset," Dagger said.

"You're damn right I am. Why do you think I'm here? Waiting for you to ask me to do something that you don't have the stomach to do yourself." He gritted his teeth. "The truth is I'm glad to do it. I just wish there was some other way." He took another sip of his coffee. "You don't think you can talk Perry out of the merger?"

"Not a chance," Dagger fired back. "And I don't want to. Not after what he's done to my daughter. With him gone, you and I can deal with the Syndicate."

"Deal with them?" Zorn spat. "I want you to tell them to kiss your ass."

"We can discuss the best way to play them after we take care of Perry."

"If he doesn't close on the merger soon, the Syndicate will probably take care of him for us. Couldn't we just wait for the other shoe to drop?"

"No," Dagger said. "I can't wait. Not with the money I owe. Busby's calling the loans tomorrow." He sighed. "The only way to get an extension . . . is a change in circumstances. I'm sorry, but I need you, man."

The general tapped his fist once on the table and held his index finger up. "'I'm sorry' is something you never have to say to me. What happens if you don't pay off the loans tomorrow?"

"The bank forecloses, and we lose over a third of my family's land. And I open myself up to a lawsuit by Perry for breach of fiduciary duty, since I took out these mortgages as president of the family partnership and haven't disclosed to him or Stephanie that I'm behind on them." Dagger looked at his drink. "I'm ruined. No different than you would have been destroyed if that secretary had lived to give birth to your child." Dagger slowly raised his eyes, and General Zorn was glaring at him. "It's exactly the same as your situation, Micah. I'm not going to die if the bank takes me out, just like you weren't going to keel over if that little cunt had told your wife about you impregnating her. But everything I've worked for my whole life . . . my reputation . . . my name . . . turns to shit in an instant."

General Zorn gulped the last swallow of his coffee. "Dagger, I've had a crew watching your son-in-law for weeks, and he is not an easy target."

"He will be today," Dagger said, raising his eyebrows. "He's at Beasley Rogers for the mediation."

"That building is crawling with video cameras."

"You're exaggerating. I'm sure there is surveillance at all the entrances and exits. But in the parking lot? Easy pickings for one of your marksmen."

Zorn glanced at his Rolex. "How long will he be there?"

"Hard to say with a mediation, but my bet is all day. Ten a.m. to five. How many folks do you have watching him?"

Zorn sighed and took a long sip of water. He smacked his lips. "Enough."

For a moment, the table was silent. Then General Zorn leaned a beefy forearm on the table and spoke in a low growl. "OK," he said.

"OK, what?"

"I'll do it." The general stood as the waitress put a plate of toast in front of Dagger. When she walked away, Zorn leaned forward and spoke in a harsh whisper. "After I take care of this problem for you . . . we're even."

Dagger Richardson sat in the booth for a long time after the general departed. Lost in thought. Almost hypnotized by what had just transpired.

Behind and around him, the sounds of the Blue Plate Cafe continued on.

Laughter. Coughing. The sizzle of bacon from the kitchen. The steady hum of conversations. The jingle of the front door opening and closing.

But Dagger felt like he was hearing it all on a television or radio far away. He was numb. Both in body and in spirit. For the second time in his life, he'd put a hit on another human being. He wouldn't be pulling the trigger today, but, by the time the sun set over his farm in Toney, Alabama, this evening, his son-in-law would be dead.

Because of me.

The thought ought to make him shudder with fear, but it didn't. Was that because he thought himself noble? Dagger almost laughed at such a ridiculous notion. He wasn't killing Perry because he wanted to prevent treason against the United States of America. Though General Zorn didn't know it yet, Dagger had his own plans for the Syndicate. He just needed to remove his son-in-law from the equation, obtain an extension on the bank loans, and perform the same kind of magic he'd worked his whole life.

My final act, he thought, moving his gaze from the now-cold mug to the plate of toast he'd yet to touch. *From the cusp of financial ruin . . . to multibillionaire.*

A comeback even Big Doug might have appreciated.

He threw a twenty-dollar bill on the table and headed for the door. Once outside, Dagger breathed in the crisp fall air. To his right, he could see the Saturn V replica at the Space & Rocket Center. To his left, the Beasley Rogers building, and past it, downtown Huntsville.

This is my town.

28

At 7:25 a.m., Stephanie Strassburg pulled into the side parking lot of the Clearview Cancer Institute. That gave her the shortest walk to the imaging area.

It had been a long night, and she'd barely slept at all. The nausea had been awful, but around ten o'clock, it had finally subsided. Then, it was Stephanie's mind that wouldn't turn off. *Has the cancer spread? Is it treatable? Will the divorce settle? Will Dad let his vendetta with Perry go?*

At 3:00 a.m., she'd given up and gone out to the couch. She'd spent the rest of the night watching reels on Instagram and holding tight to Fredo.

Now, as she opened the door and trudged toward the entrance, she knew that the time had arrived. The folks pulling the strings on her life would have answers today.

About damn time, she thought as she opened the door.

Max watched Stephanie from inside the cab of the Tundra. In the drink console of the truck was a steaming cup of black coffee. In her lap, a half-eaten breakfast bagel. She'd checked into the Courtyard by Marriott on University Drive last night at a few minutes past midnight. She'd risen this morning at 6:00 a.m. and gone straight to the fitness center of the hotel, knocking out thirty minutes on the treadmill and a quick weight circuit. The workout did her good, and she felt energized and motivated. The physical activity also prompted several ideas.

One of which had led her here. If she was going to convince Stephanie to give up her interest in Richardson Concepts, then she had to know more about the woman. After grabbing a to-go breakfast on the run, Max had parked a few houses down from Stephanie's mansion on Echols Avenue, thinking through her next play. She could just knock on the door, but that would likely freak Stephanie out. And wouldn't Amy Dance be angry if the mediator was having private conversations with her client? Max didn't have time for such ethical considerations, and a mediator's duty wasn't as clear as opposing counsel's. If Perry had a lawyer, that attorney couldn't talk with Stephanie without Amy's presence or consent. But for the mediator, things were murkier.

What if Stephanie doesn't have any plans this morning? Max had resolved to wait fifteen minutes and then knock.

Seven minutes in, Stephanie backed her Range Rover out of the driveway.

Max followed her, quickly realizing that Stephanie was going right back to where she was last night. Max wasn't surprised. Perhaps, in some way, she expected it.

Now, sipping from the coffee, she watched Stephanie enter the building and go into the imaging department. Max set the drink back in the console and opened the door to the truck. She strode toward the entrance and then inside the double doors. She peeked through the window to the imaging area and saw Stephanie signing in.

She's a patient.

Max decided to wait in the hallway. She took out her phone and decided to play offense. She pulled up her text exchange with Perry last night and thumbed out a quick message.

Call me.

While she waited to see if he would do as she asked, she blinked at the cryptic text she'd gotten late yesterday afternoon. She read the words again.

You should have never come back.

Then, thinking of how the old Max would have responded, she typed a two-word reply.

FUCK YOU.

Max nodded to herself, and then the phone began to buzz in her hand. It was Perry.

"Hey."

"What do you want?" he asked. "I hope you have heeded my instructions."

"I have, but I need you to do something for me."

There was no response, so Max continued.

"Can one of your goons take out my son's cell phone and respond to Nathan's father's texts? He's been lighting me up, because Nathan is being unresponsive to his messages. I'm afraid that Thayer doesn't trust me all that much. You know, because I'm a druggie, lost custody of Nathan, went to rehab, yada, yada, yada. Now, I'm happy to tell him the reason for Nathan's unresponsiveness, but I suspect—"

"One of my people will respond," Perry said, his tone impatient. "What should they say?"

"'I'm good, Dad, but I'm having issues with my phone. Gonna take it to the Verizon store after school.'"

"All right," Perry said. "Mediation starts at ten again, right?"

"Yes."

"Are you prepared to settle the case on my terms?"

"You bet your ass."

"I hope so, Max. It makes me nervous with you following my wife."

Max's blood turned cold, but she'd assumed he'd been watching her. "Is Stephanie sick?"

"I'm worried, Max. I'm hoping your little journey to Guntersville last night kept you sober. But now you seem to be wasting more time."

"Don't worry about me, you sonofabitch," Max fired back. "You just make sure my son is unharmed."

"Or what?"

Before she could respond, the line went dead.

Damnit, Max thought. Why had she warned Perry about Thayer? Had that done Nathan any favors? What if Thayer did call the police? Max might not be credible, but Thayer was. The police would certainly take him seriously.

Doesn't matter, Max thought. *If Thayer calls the police, Nathan is dead.*

Max was still turning these questions over in her mind when Stephanie Strassburg exited the imaging lobby and walked down the hall toward her. Max started to get up but then saw that Stephanie was moving with her head down. The woman strode right past Max, lost in her own misery.

Worried about the scan results . . . which she may be about to receive.

Max followed about twenty paces behind. Each of the oncologists had their own waiting area, and Stephanie sat in the one for Dr. Maples and Dr. Conroy. Max took a seat in the area for Drs. Carter and Davis.

Fifteen minutes later, Max saw a nurse come out of the back and announce in a loud voice, "Strassburg."

Stephanie stood and followed the nurse to the door, and then it shut behind her.

Max felt sick to her stomach. *Jesus,* she thought. Stephanie was dealing with a divorce and cancer at the same time.

Alone . . .

Max knew there were other things she could be doing, but her instincts told her to wait.

Whatever Dr. Maples or Conroy told Stephanie back there was going to have a dramatic impact on Stephanie Strassburg's life.

And affect every decision she makes from this point forward . . . including the settlement terms of her divorce.

Max clasped her hands together and said a silent prayer. For Stephanie and Nathan. And herself.

She took out her phone and texted Jason.

Any word from the colonel?

Seconds later, his response came through. Nothing other than asking the name of your hotel. Where are you staying?

Max texted back the answer. Then, tapping her feet on the tile floor, she thumbed out another message. Jason, is he going to come through?

He responded in seconds with the same thing he'd said last night.

There's not a doubt in my mind.

Max sighed and closed her eyes. *Please, God. Help me.*

29

Stephanie stared at the painting on the wall. It was of a house in the country. Fire drifted out of the chimney. The sun set over farmland and a small pond. She guessed the image was meant to be calming. To set a person's mind at ease. Unfortunately, Stephanie had seen the picture so many times in this very room that her stomach tightened now when she saw it. It clenched worse when Dr. Maples entered the room. Usually, the big, burly physician would barge in and bellow "Looks good," or something reassuring, but this time he was quiet. His assistant, Reba, was with him. Reba went to the same church as Stephanie. She was a tall woman with dark-brown hair and a kind smile.

But she wasn't smiling now. She patted Stephanie's shoulder and stood next to her.

Dr. Maples sat on his stool and clicked a few keys on the computer in front of him. Then he turned to Stephanie. "The MRI of the uterus shows that the tumor hasn't shrunk any. It's actually a little bigger."

Stephanie bit her lip. "And the PET?"

Maples grimaced. "You have more hot spots in the liver, and now you have a number of them in the spine. Have you been having back pain?"

"Yes," Stephanie said. "I haven't thought much about it, because the side effects of the chemo have been so bad. I was up all night vomiting again."

"Does the Zofran work?"

"A little, but it doesn't stop it."

Maples rubbed his chin. "We need to get an MRI of the spine and liver to see what we're dealing with."

"What do you think we're dealing with?"

"Aggressive metastatic uterine cancer that's spread to the bladder, liver, and bone." Maples said the words fast, holding her eye. "Unfortunately, the options are limited for such an advanced stage. I'd like to try another round of radiation and a different type of chemotherapy."

Stephanie peered up at Reba, who was looking away. *A death sentence,* she thought. Then, she stood. "No."

"What do you mean?" Maples said.

"I mean no more tests. No more radiation. No chemo. I'm done."

"Stephanie, please think about—"

"What's there to think about? I'm dying, right?"

He looked at the floor. Stephanie glanced at Reba, who was still staring at the wall. Probably at the damn painting. "Right?" she repeated.

Maples finally nodded. "Your condition is terminal."

"So, what? Eight to twelve months? Two years? How long?"

Maples rubbed his hands together. "It varies. Could be three months. Could be two years."

"And that's regardless of treatment, right?"

"I think the studies show that radiation and chemotherapy will prolong your life."

"But what kind of life will I have? I spent three hours on the tile floor of my bathroom last night. I'm not sure I want to prolong any more nights like that."

Maples pushed his stool back and scratched the stubble on his cheek. "We could see if you qualify for one of the new immunotherapy drugs."

"Is there any guarantee that one of those will do anything more than the chemo and radiation?"

"It's really hard to say, Stephanie."

Stephanie put her hands on her hips and studied Maples. "I'll think about it."

"Sounds good," Maples said, his tone more energetic as he clicked keys on his computer. "Let's see you back here in two weeks for follow-up."

"Do you want me to walk you to scheduling?" Reba asked.

Stephanie shook her head. She plopped down in the plastic chair and stared again at the painting of the farmhouse. "I just want to be alone for a second, OK?"

"I'm sorry, Stephanie."

Stephanie closed her eyes. She hated that farmhouse portrait. "Me too."

30

Max caught up to Stephanie in the parking lot. For a second, she almost didn't say anything, but she willed herself to make a move. *Now or never.*

"Stephanie?" Max's voice was dry, and she wondered if the woman had heard her. She'd started to repeat herself when Stephanie turned around.

"Oh . . . hi. What are you doing here?"

Max decided to tell the truth. "I wanted to talk with you. When I got to your house, you were pulling out of the driveway, so I followed you here."

Stephanie squinted at her. "You *followed* me? And you've been here the whole time?"

Max nodded. When Stephanie just stood there, Max asked, "Why are you here?"

"Sitting with a friend receiving chemo."

Max wasn't exactly surprised by the lie. If her instincts were correct, Stephanie had been doing a lot of that lately. "I saw you. A nurse called out your name, and then you went to the back."

Stephanie's eyes narrowed and then she pushed past Max. "It's none of your business."

Max followed close behind. "Does your father know?"

Stephanie ignored the question and unlocked her SUV.

"How about Amy Dance?"

Stephanie climbed inside the vehicle. While the door was still open, Max hurled another question. "Does anyone?"

Stephanie glared at her with the door half open. "Leave it be."

Max took a step closer. Stephanie couldn't shut the door without hitting her.

"You can't go through this alone, Stephanie. You shouldn't. No one should."

Stephanie opened her mouth, but the words wouldn't come.

"I'm going to Gold Sprint Coffee right now," Max said. "Meet me there. I don't have a dog in this hunt. I just want to help you." Max creased her eyebrows. "Please. Don't do this by yourself."

Stephanie gazed off into space. "I have to."

"Why?"

Stephanie looked at Max with dead eyes. "Because I don't want to hurt the people I love. I don't want them to see me . . ." She trailed off, wiping a tear that had slid down her cheek.

"What would talking with me hurt?" Max asked. "I'm a mediator. I can't disclose anything you tell me to Perry or anyone else unless you give me consent."

She crossed her arms. "Shouldn't my lawyer be present for any conversation between the two of us?"

"Probably."

"Then why are you talking to me without Amy?"

"Because I want to settle your case, Stephanie. And I can't get anywhere unless I know what *you* want. Not Dagger. Not Richardson Concepts. Not the Richardson family partnership. Not even Amy Dance." She licked her lips. "*You,*" she repeated.

"I want what's best for my girls and my family."

"Your daughters are in college. You and Perry have no children together. Your girls shouldn't be affected much by the divorce. As for your family . . . we both know who you're really talking about."

Stephanie gripped the steering wheel, her knuckles white. "My father is very important to me."

“As I’m sure you are to him. But, at the end of the day, the only question that really matters . . . *is what do you want?*” Max took a step back. “And did whatever just happened in there . . .” Max cocked her head at the CCI building. “. . . change or affect *your* desires.”

Stephanie peered down at the asphalt.

“What legacy do you want to leave Mem and Ella?” Max asked. When she saw the tears begin to creep out of the corners of Stephanie’s eyes again, Max started to walk away. When she reached the Tundra, she climbed inside and cranked the ignition. Then she looked out the windshield toward where Stephanie was parked.

She was still there. Door open. Staring off into space.

31

At 9:30 a.m., Max pulled up in front of Gold Sprint and hustled inside. She wanted to give Stephanie a chance to meet her, and the coffee shop was less than a half mile from Beasley Rogers. As she was paying for her latte, she saw a familiar face entering the door, but it wasn't Stephanie. The girl wore jeans with holes in the knees, a long-sleeved T-shirt cut low to show her cleavage, and a nose ring. Max approached her, and when their eyes met, the girl opened her mouth in surprise.

"Well, hello, Betty. Shouldn't you be at school?" Max asked.

"Nope," Betty said. "This is a free period, and I always come here. Usually, Nathan meets me. Have you heard from him?"

Max thought about lying to ease her concerns but decided against it. She could use a person to commiserate with. She shook her head. "No."

"I'm worried, Ms. Ringo. I know Nathan's been having a hard time lately. He's not crazy about his dad's new girlfriend, and he's been . . ."

"What?" Max asked, feeling a sinking sensation. She was Nathan's mother. She should know if something was wrong before Nathan was kidnapped.

"I shouldn't say. He would never want you and especially not his dad to know."

"Know what?"

Betty blinked. "Do you mind if I get a coffee?"

"Not at all. I'll even buy it for you. But you have to tell me what's been bothering my son first."

"I don't have to do nothing." Betty started to walk past her, but Max moved to block the path.

"I'm going to—"

"Please." Max hated the weakness in her voice. She'd been strong so far this morning, but now she sounded desperate. "Please," she repeated. "Nathan thinks he might be gay."

Two minutes later, Betty sat down next to Max at a couch by the front door. "Did I just rock your world?" the girl asked.

"A little," Max said, setting her latte down on the coffee table in front of them. She wasn't upset at the revelation per se. She was angry with herself for not being present in Nathan's life. He was a teenager. Having all kinds of questions about his sexuality and life. Now he was driving a car and doing gummies and God knows what else.

And I haven't been around. I checked out.

She felt a hand on her shoulder. "You all right?" Betty's voice was soft. Kind.

Max felt tears welling in her eyes.

"He's a really great guy, Ms. Ringo. I don't care if he's gay. For selfish reasons, I kinda hope he's not." She blushed and drank a sip of her drink.

"It doesn't matter to me either," Max said, meaning every word. "I just wish that I would have been here these last few months."

"Yeah, he said you were kind of a train wreck." She covered her mouth once the words were out. "Oops. Sorry."

"No. It's OK. He was right to say that. I was a train wreck."

Still am, Max thought, and then gritted her teeth. "Betty, what has he said . . . or done that makes you think he's struggling with his sexuality?"

She took another sip of espresso. "We've been hanging out for a while, and I've maybe tried to send some signals that I'm interested, and he hasn't acted on them."

"Maybe he misinterpreted them. Teenage boys—"

"I took my shirt off in the dressing room and put his hand on my boob."

Max smiled. "Ah, OK."

"Sorry. It was stupid. The theater is like that. We're always changing clothes around each other and there's a good bit of downtime and I'd had a couple gummies and . . . I like him." She shrugged. "I'm weird. As I'm sure you've figured out by now."

"I like you," Max said, again meaning every word. "I can see why Nathan does."

"There's another guy in our acting troupe who's gay, and two of the girls are too. It's not uncommon in our world, and it's almost kinda expected for you to at least be bi. When I came on to Nathan, he got upset and told me that he wasn't sure he was into girls." She hesitated and spoke in a lower voice. "He may just not be into me."

"I doubt that," Max said. "You're beautiful."

"You're just saying that."

"Nope," Max said, finding herself talking more like the young girl in her presence. "I'm not. You're gorgeous. Great hair. Cute figure. Fun personality."

"Thank you," Betty said. For a moment, they sat in silence, drinking their coffee.

"There's something else," Betty said. "Something . . . that's bothering me." She paused as if she didn't want to say the rest.

"Go on. Spit it out."

"Look, I'm no angel when it comes to drugs. I drink, take gummies, and smoke the occasional joint. But Nathan's been scaring me lately."

Max swallowed. "How so?"

The girl took a sip of her drink and stirred it. Stalling.

"Betty?" Max felt uneasy as the silence deepened. She touched her hand. "Why are you afraid?"

Finally, Betty peered up from her coffee. "Nathan is hooked on meth."

32

Max pulled into the Beasley Rogers building at 9:55 a.m. She'd waited at Gold Sprint for another ten minutes, but Stephanie never came. In truth, she'd been relieved to have a few moments at the coffee shop by herself.

Max was still reeling from Betty's revelations. She felt grateful to know this information about her son. But also so guilty for not being a better mother. For abandoning her son and their prior life as a family. For being a druggie herself . . .

At the end, after losing her job but before going to rehab, Max had tried methamphetamine. It was cheap, and easy to find in North Alabama. Max closed her eyes, hating herself. Hating the addiction that had consumed her and turned her into a shell of herself. She'd paid her dues. She'd gone to rehab, but she couldn't erase the things she'd done. The people she'd hurt. *I hurt my son . . . He saw me at my absolute worst.*

It was overwhelming, and she thought of what Jason had said about Colonel Satch Tonidandel.

He couldn't beat the guilt.

Finally, like Betty, she was afraid. If Nathan was addicted to methamphetamine . . .

When was his last hit? Are they giving him meth wherever he's been held? Is that how they'll kill him? What if he goes into withdrawal?

Max bristled, knowing that she needed to flip the switch. She didn't have time to feel sorry for herself or to be afraid.

I always win, she thought to herself as she opened the door to the Tundra and strode toward the entrance.

Always.

The players in the defendant's conference room were the same. Amy Dance was now seated at the head of the long table, wearing a navy suit dress. To Amy's right was Stephanie Strassburg. She was still in the mesh workout clothes that she'd worn to CCI. Behind the two of them, standing and pacing, was Dagger.

"Good morning," Max said.

"What's good about it?" Dagger snapped.

Max glanced at Amy, who rolled her eyes. It was a conspiratorial gesture, and Max felt like maybe she was beginning to make some headway with her old rival.

"It's our move," Max said. She'd learned in training to frame things in each room in terms of "we" and "our." *I'm on both teams,* Max thought.

"We'll go down to 20K a month on alimony, but that's it," Amy said. "The ten million lump sum is nonnegotiable."

"What about the land and the company?" Max asked. "I think we can make a deal on the alimony and cash just as we did on the houses. But with respect to the real property owned by the family partnership and the business . . . we are at an impasse."

"Thanks for telling us something we don't know," Dagger said.

Max studied the old man, observing the red around his pupils. The stooped shoulders. He didn't look well.

"Just want to make sure we're all on the same page as to the starting point," Max said.

"We are," Amy chimed in before Dagger could say anything else sarcastic. "Max, do you have any thoughts or suggestions?"

Max crossed her legs, grateful for the opening. Again, she felt the slightest tinge of kinship forming with Amy, and she remembered Ben Hedden's wise counsel. *An effective mediator builds relationships . . .*

"I'll start with a question for Stephanie." Max gazed at the defendant, who was staring at the table. "Between the company and the land, what means the most to you?"

"He shouldn't even have an interest in the land," Dagger spat. "And like I told you yesterday, Max, Richardson Concepts is my legacy. I built it from nothing and made it one of the strongest government contractors in North Alabama."

"And Perry Strassburg has taken it national and even international," Max said, keeping her voice matter of fact. "It's gone from a value of fifty million in 2015, when he became CEO, to over a one hundred fifty million today. He's increased the value threefold."

"*I gave him that opportunity,*" Dagger hissed.

"You sent him to the plate, and he hit a grand slam home run. You should be commended, Dagger. And so should Perry. But I'm not talking about who gets the credit for the success of Richardson Concepts, LLC, or who started the Richardson land empire. I'm talking about *this case*. A divorce between Stephanie and Perry Strassburg. There are assets on the table. Marital property that must be divided in an equitable manner. Today, the parties have control over who gets what." She turned to Stephanie. "That means you get to choose what you want today. You may not get everything you covet. You may have to make some difficult choices. But you and Perry get to make those choices today. If the case doesn't settle, then Caroline Parker is going to recuse, and this case will be reassigned to an out-of-county judge. Then that stranger, likely a person that neither you nor Perry nor Dagger has ever dealt with before, is going to make those choices for you." Max gestured toward Amy. "I'm sure your lawyer has told you that control over the outcome is one of the primary benefits, if not the most significant benefit, of mediation. *You*, Stephanie, get to say how this story is going to end today."

When Max stopped, the room went silent. *Good,* she thought. *Maybe some of this is getting through.*

Eventually, Dagger sighed. "Well, Max, you never answered Amy's question. What do you think?"

Max cleared her throat. "The Richardson dynasty is the land. What is the name of that country song that's popular now about land?" Max had developed a taste for country at the FRC. She snapped her fingers. "Come on. Does somebody—?"

"'Buy Dirt,'" Amy offered. "It's a Jordan Davis and Luke Bryan duet."

"That's it," Max said. "Well, you don't have to do that, Stephanie, because you already own half of North Alabama. Dagger is right. Perry should have never been part of your family's partnership. So, if I were you, I'd try to posture yourself so that Perry will willingly give up his thirty percent interest in the family partnership, whose assets are valued at $175 million. That would be $52.5 million that he'd be giving you. Then, just to keep it clean, if you relinquish your forty percent of the $150 million company, that provides him a value of $60 million, leaving the delta at a little less than $8 million, which is made up for and even exceeded by the lump sum cash award that Amy has made a part of your package. Finally, and I'll mention this only because you are here, Dagger . . ." Max could feel her heart pounding. "Dagger, you could also sell your thirty percent interest in Richardson Concepts to Perry for the fair market value of $45 million, and you both would have a clean break from the bastard."

A hush settled over the room as Max finished. She had thrown in "the bastard" because she knew that was how everyone in here thought of Perry. Again, making it seem like she was on their team, professionalism be damned.

Amy broke the silence. "Assuming we agreed to all that . . . and I'm not saying we would . . . do you think Perry would go for it?"

"She knows he would," Dagger said, glaring at Max. "Don't you?"

Max felt her stomach clench. "No, sir, I don't."

"Bullshit," Dagger said. "The prick's got something cooking, and he's about to pull the rug out from underneath us."

Max kept her tone neutral. "I don't know if Perry would go for it or not, Dagger, but I will say this. The proposal seems equitable to me. Perry obtains full ownership of the company he's almost tripled in value. You and Stephanie both obtain a financial windfall that appears to be fair and equitable. *And* . . . you both keep the land, which is clearly the more stable asset. The company may go belly up. Isn't government contracting volatile? Not land. There's no better investment . . . or legacy you could give your daughters. I'm not sure I can come up with anything closer in terms of a fair division of assets."

Again, silence filled the room. Stephanie looked at Dagger. "What do you think, Dad?"

Max felt a wave of giddy excitement roll through her, moving her eyes from Stephanie to Amy. *Almost sold,* Max thought.

"I think it's too good of a deal for that sonofabitch," Dagger finally said, crushing Max's optimism in one fell swoop. "Much too good."

"OK, what do you have in mind?" Max asked. "You asked me what I thought. I've told you."

"All right then, I will—"

"Max, can we have a moment?" Amy asked, standing and holding her palm up at Dagger as if she were a school crossing guard. "I'd like to discuss your proposal with my client and her father."

"Of course," Max said, picking up her legal pad. "You know where I am."

33

Max was greeted by an unwelcome sight when she entered her mediator's quarters.

Perry was sitting in one of the chairs, with his feet on the small table. He was talking on the phone and ushered Max in, as if he was in his own office.

"Shut the door," he said.

Max crossed her arms. "If you want to talk, let's go to your conference room."

He put his hand over the phone. "You don't tell me what to do. It works the other way around. Now shut the door."

Max gritted her teeth but then did as he asked, using her foot to close the door.

"What's the code to your son's phone?" Perry asked.

"I don't know. You'll have to ask Nathan."

"He's not being cooperative."

Max actually smiled.

"Do you find that funny? My agent can't send a text to Nathan's father saying everything is fine and dandy if he isn't able to get into the boy's phone."

Max checked her own phone. Thayer had not sent any texts that morning.

"Just leave it be for now."

Perry scrutinized her. "I don't like having my time wasted. Do you have an offer for me?"

"No, but it shouldn't be long."

"I'm beginning to doubt my decision. Perhaps the drugs have dulled your talents." He stood and stepped around her toward the door. "You better hope not."

"Perry, is Nathan—"

"Haven't you wondered something, Max?" He kept his back to her.

"What?"

"Whether I might just kill him anyway."

Before she could answer, he opened the door and slammed it shut.

Max hated herself for crying. Loathed her very being.

She sat down in one of the chairs and squeezed her eyes closed. Every encounter with Perry reminded her of those days after Dr. Maxwell wouldn't prescribe any more oxycodone. He'd referred her to the pain clinic, and she had reluctantly gone. Gotten the spill on methadone. Even tried it out for a few weeks.

But she hadn't stopped taking oxy. She'd just found other sources for it . . . and done things she still couldn't comprehend in order to close the deal. She couldn't blame Thayer for divorcing her.

Your brain was sick.

That was what the doctors had told her at FRC. Such was the power of addiction that it could dominate your life. Make you abandon everyone and everything you cared about. The only thing that mattered was the next fix. And you'd do anything to get it.

Those days just before and after Thayer decided to end their marriage were the worst in her life. Mercifully, her memories of them were hazy.

But they came to her in her nightmares.

Three hard knocks on the door startled Max from the tortuous thoughts. "Come in," she managed.

"Hey," Amy said. "We're ready."

Max started to stand, but Amy held up her hands. "I'll just tell you in here." She plopped down in the chair across from Max. She started to say something but then stopped. "Are you OK?"

"Yes," Max lied. "Fine. What's the offer?"

"It's just. Your mascara is running. Here." She reached into her handbag, pulled out a tissue and a pocket mirror, and slid them across the desk.

Max took the Kleenex and opened the mirror. Sure enough, her makeup had smeared a tad just under her left eye. She dabbed at the spot, and a few seconds later, her face was clear. "Thank you," she said, pushing the mirror back across the desk. "My eyes have been watering some today. Allergies, I guess."

Amy blinked as if maybe she didn't buy that, but she didn't push it. "Our offer is 20K a month in alimony, ten million lump sum in cash, and Perry has to buy Stephanie's interest in the company and forfeit his percentage of the family partnership."

Max crossed her arms. "Why don't you ask him to throw in a testicle too?"

Amy groaned. "I know. I'm sorry. It's just . . ."

"Dagger," Max said.

"He's being unreasonable, and, you know, I get it. Perry was awful to his daughter and is on the verge of stealing his company. Dagger has a lot of pride."

"There's got to be something else," Max said.

"If there is, I'm not aware of it. Dagger is a very private man, and my role has been to represent Stephanie. Personally, I like your idea, and I think you're correct. The land is the more stable asset and has a greater link to the family legacy."

"But?"

"But Dagger is convinced that Perry is about to screw him."

"Then why doesn't Dagger talk to Perry? Flush him out. Hell, they're still part owners of the same company and will be regardless of how this divorce turns out."

"He's tried," Amy fired back. "He says Perry's been avoiding him since the divorce was filed."

Max crossed her legs. "Well, you can't blame Perry for that."

Amy flung her hands up in a *no shit*–type gesture. "It's an impossible situation."

Tell me about it, Max thought but didn't say. She was already dreading bringing this counteroffer in to Perry.

"You're doing a good job," Amy said. "Really, you are. I can't imagine any mediator doing much better. Stephanie likes you."

"She does?" Max was surprised. Especially after her tense encounter with Stephanie at CCI.

"Yep. She told me while Dagger was in the restroom. None of us were that nice to you yesterday morning . . . least of all me, but you haven't quit." Amy rose from her seat. "I'm sorry we don't have a better counter."

"I'll keep trying," Max said, also standing.

Amy turned for the door and looked at Max over her shoulder. "I'm sorry for being a bitch yesterday, but . . ." She shrugged and there was warmth in her smile. ". . . I kinda am a bitch."

Max couldn't help but laugh. "Apology accepted."

But as the door shut, Max's mood darkened. She took out her phone. It was now almost 11:00 a.m., and she could feel the clock ticking. There was a text from Thayer. How'd it go last night?

Thinking fast, Max thumbed the response she'd been mentally rehearsing. Great. We grabbed a pizza at Sam & Greg's and I think he enjoyed the adventure of being at the hotel. I met some of his castmates in the play, and they are nice. That Betty is a doll. Thank you again for letting me keep him.

Max pressed send and waited. She thought about her next move. Getting Amy and Stephanie on her side was huge. She was making progress. Unfortunately, the counter didn't reflect the momentum she felt she was gaining. Perry would be upset. He was an impatient narcissistic sociopath. Addicted to power and dominance as much or more than Max had been dependent on oxycodone.

Use that, she thought. *Don't fight the current . . . swim with it.*

Some of Ben Hedden's advice infiltrated her mind, though Ben could never have imagined the way she was considering using his training.

Her phone dinged, and Thayer had sent a thumbs-up emoji. She'd put him off for at least the rest of today.

Max grabbed her legal pad and took a deep breath. *Swim with the current,* she thought.

But as she reached for the door, she heard a scream from out in the hallway, followed by a loud bang as something hit a wall hard. "What the hell?"

Max grabbed the knob and turned. She peeked out her door and could barely believe her eyes.

34

If Dagger Richardson had an Achilles' heel, it was his temper.

Most of the time, he'd been able to get away with losing his cool. Money and power had a way of providing leeway in the self-control department. In fact, he almost felt at times like his reputation for blowing a fuse was an advantage. Business associates tended to tiptoe around him. Fear what might happen if they disappointed or angered him.

But there were those precious few who saw the trait for the weakness it was. And his son-in-law was one of them.

When Dagger opened the door to the men's room and saw Perry pissing at the urinal, he felt his adrenaline surge to the top of its meter. He knew a confrontation like this was unavoidable at the mediation, but he was still surprised at how quickly his anger funneled into a typhoon.

"You think I was born yesterday?" Dagger asked, grinding his teeth, but Perry didn't turn around. Then Dagger noticed the AirPods in his son-in-law's ears.

And just like that, the switch was flipped and months of resentment and hate boiled over inside him.

Dagger stepped forward, snatching one of the pods and flinging it across the room. "Hey, dipshit. I'm talking to you."

Perry's eyes darted toward him. "What the . . . ?"

Dagger grabbed Perry by the throat, and his son-in-law's pants dropped to his ankles. "You don't think I know what you're doing?"

"You're crazy." Perry barely got the words out. He was trying to push back, but he had no traction with his slacks down.

"Feel trapped?" Dagger asked. "Doesn't feel good, does it?" He released his grip, and Perry pulled up his pants.

"You can't win," Perry said. "And you know it."

Dagger felt adrenaline and anger pulsing through his veins. Even well past seventy, he was still a strong man, and he gripped Perry by the shirt collar and kicked the bathroom door open. Then he slung him as hard as he could into the wall.

As Perry slunk to the floor, Dagger towered over him. "You aren't man enough to destroy me. I crap bigger than you."

"Dagger, stop it." Max Ringo stepped in front of Dagger.

"Dad?" Now Stephanie was standing next to him. "What are you . . . oh, good Lord. Perry, are you all right?"

Perry struggled to his feet and pointed at Dagger. "You're going to jail."

"You'll be in hell before I get there," Dagger said, moving forward, but Max Ringo blocked his path.

"You need to back off, Dagger," Max said. Amy Dance had walked around him, and now both she and Max were in his way.

Perry was walking away. "You're all nuts," he said. Then he stopped and pointed at Max. "That SOB needs to leave. Right now. Otherwise, I'm gone, and we're done here."

"Then roll on, cat shit. Someone will come along and cover you up." Dagger spat his words. He'd lost all control. Hate and white-hot rage pulsed through his veins as he fought against the words that still leaped out of his mouth. "You're a liar and a thief. Cheat on my daughter. Destroy her life. Steal my company. My land. Who do you think you're messing with? I *am* this town."

Perry turned when he reached his conference room. "Not anymore." Then he pointed at Max. "Get him out."

35

Max's whole body tingled with a combination of adrenaline and fear. There were so many balls in the air right now that she was having a hard time focusing. Finally, self-preservation kicked in. She scowled at Dagger Richardson. "Leave. Now. Or I call the police."

"Not on your life."

"Yes, Dagger," Amy said. "You have to go."

Max bit her lip and took a step toward the older man, invading his space. "If you don't do as I say, I'm ending this mediation and calling the police." She took out her phone.

"Dad," Stephanie said. "Please. This isn't helping."

"Neither is this mediation," Dagger said. *"You?"* He held his ground and glared at Max. "How many cases have you mediated? Five?"

"Four," Max said, darting her eyes to Amy and holding up her phone. "I don't have a choice here."

"Do it, then," Amy fired back.

"No." Stephanie stepped between her father and Max and put her hands on the big man's shoulders. "Please go, Dad. Just keep your phone handy, OK? I won't make any offers without consulting you first."

He blinked his eyes, which were watery now. He took a step backward.

"Go home, Dagger," Max said, keeping her tone calm. "Listen to your daughter."

Dagger took another step back and then rubbed his neck. He looked at Stephanie. When he spoke, the anguish in his voice was palpable. "I'm just trying to protect you."

"I know," Stephanie said. "And I love you for it. But this isn't helping."

Dagger turned for the elevator. He took a few steps away and wheeled back around, peering at Max. "What I told you yesterday still holds true." He held up his fist, which was shaking.

"Go," Max said, but as the words left her mouth, she realized that her chances of ever settling this case might be leaving with him. A ripple of fear ran through her, but she kept her voice firm. *"Now."*

36

Nathan Ringo was exhausted.

He was also hungry. When he'd told his captors to fuck off after they'd asked for his cell phone code, Nathan thought he was being tough. Since then, though, they hadn't fed him anything but two delta-9 gummies.

Stupid, he thought. *I'm so stupid.*

But he still hadn't given up the code. He didn't want them going through his phone. He didn't care if they responded to texts as if they were him. His reasoning was more selfish.

There were pictures on the device that he didn't want anyone to see.

Nathan closed his eyes, feeling dizzy. He was so tired. And though it was cold in the barn, his forehead and hands were clammy, and his mouth was dry. *I'm going into withdrawal,* he thought.

He needed a meth fix, but how was he going to get one here? Trying not to panic, Nathan forced himself to think about Betty. He wondered if she was worried about him. He had thought more about her than about his own mother in the last day of his imprisonment. And why not? He'd spent a lot more time with Betty over the last two years than with Mom.

He visualized his last encounter with Betty. They were alone together in the dressing area of Lowe Mill after rehearsal. Everyone changed clothes in there. It was no big deal for him to see a girl in her underwear. But it was a big deal for Betty to sit next to him and put his hand on her breast.

How had it felt? he thought. How had it made him feel?

Scared.

Had he been aroused? He thought so. He'd had trouble breathing, and, while he hadn't gotten hard, he had leaked a little in his boxers. She'd wanted him to make a move. That was obvious. But he'd frozen.

What the hell is wrong with me? he wondered for about the thousandth time in the last few months. He thought again of the pictures on his phone. He was naked in all of them. In what he thought (hoped?) were provocative poses. Turned to show his butt. His chest. Bending over a table. Lying on a bed with his legs in the air. He'd created a profile on a gay dating app that didn't require a user to show proof of being eighteen. He'd shared his photographs with other men, who, in turn, sent him pictures. He'd seen their erect penises. Their asses. How had that made him feel?

Aroused? Maybe. Yes, if he were honest. But was it because he was doing something wrong?

He thought back to Betty's plump, perky breasts. He'd felt one. It was real. And he'd leaked. Felt warm all over. Scared to death in an excited way. That had to mean something.

Then why the urge to send naked pics of himself to men twice his age? How crazy was he? Here he was. Kidnapped. Facing possible death or dismemberment. On the verge of full-blown meth withdrawal. And what was he worried about the most?

Naked pictures on his damn phone.

I'm such a loser.

He opened his eyes, tired of the crazy thoughts that were no doubt loonier because of the THC that had flooded his system. He'd done this to himself yesterday. He'd wanted to get messed up. He'd planned to skip school and get on that dating app. Again. He'd been thinking of meeting one of the men, and he'd wanted to be high on THC and wired on meth for it. Instead, he was here. In this barn. Hands tied by a rope behind him.

At least they'd taken the duct tape off his mouth.

Again, he thought of Betty. He wondered what she looked like without her panties on. Did she have pubic hair? Shaved like him? Which would be hotter? Was that hot to him at all? He'd watched an old '80s movie a few weeks back called *Revenge of the Nerds*, and there was a scene where all these naked sorority girls were being secretly videoed by the nerds, and they all had manes of pubic hair.

Did that do it for him? He and his friends, including Betty, had laughed. He wondered if they'd been thinking the same thing.

Nathan moved his wrists back and forth behind him. Trying to rub them together to loosen the rope. It was working. A little. Or perhaps he was just high, and he was feeling something that wasn't there.

He knew his kidnapping had to be about his mom. His dad was boring. A pharmacist. Worked 8:00 a.m. to 5:00 p.m. Came home. Ate dinner. Watched a show on Netflix. Went to bed. His father was on a trip with his new girlfriend, who was a clerk at the pharmacy. Nathan had met her once, and she was just as boring. Asked a bunch of *just trying to be nice* questions that she didn't care about the answers to and gave him a big fake smile.

Nathan chuckled. Then laughed out loud. He was delirious. High. Hungry. Losing his grip.

Am I gay?

His mom was anything but boring. She'd been a lawyer. His friends all thought she was hot. Then the accident happened and everything got screwed up. That was almost three years ago, and Nathan had barely seen his mother in the last two. *To hell with her,* Nathan thought, then felt tears welling in his eyes.

She'd lived a dangerous life once she became addicted to drugs. *This has to be about her,* Nathan thought. *Some drug deal gone wrong and I'm caught in the middle.* He sighed, thinking of the arguments between his dad and mom before the divorce. They'd been awful, but at least his mom had been around.

The time without her had been surreal. *And now I'm a junkie just like her.* He'd been doing stronger stuff than delta-9 for a while. He'd been on meth for over a year, and he was hooked. And the irony was that it was his mother who'd provided his gateway to meth. Or rather, the stash he'd found in her car and decided to sample.

I need a hit, he thought, beginning to feel nauseated. "Hey!" he screamed.

But there was no response. He'd yelled a lot that morning, but since his refusal to turn over the code to his phone, they'd left him alone.

Am I gay? he wondered again. He watched gay and straight porn. He thought they were both hot. But watching porn wasn't the same as feeling a real live titty. He couldn't stop seeing it in his mind. The round shape. The pink nipple hardening to the touch. Her breath, sweet from gum. Her white panties. Had he wanted her?

Yes. He thought so. But he had been prepared to meet up with a man yesterday.

Nathan rubbed his wrist. *Is the rope getting looser?*

Or am I losing my mind?

37

"Are you kidding me?" Perry snapped after Max had rattled off Stephanie's counter. "I am not, under any circumstances, buying her out." He cocked his neck to each side in two swift motions, creating two audible pops, like he was resetting himself. "Max, what's the deal? Why aren't you getting anywhere?"

"The bad blood between you and Dagger is making it almost impossible."

"I trust he's gone now."

Max nodded.

"I figured you'd be able to make inroads with Stephanie. That was another reason I chose you. You're divorced. You've had health problems. I figured you would be the perfect instrument to bond with her . . . and help her to see things my way."

Max felt a tickle of unease. She'd forgotten about her call with Perry that morning at CCI, which had confirmed her suspicion that she was being followed. "Do you know why Stephanie was at the cancer center today?"

Perry said nothing.

"She was getting scans and then met with Dr. Maples for the results," Max continued. "I don't think they were what she was hoping for."

He moved his gaze to her. "Look, I'm sorry about Stephanie's illness. I really am. She was apparently diagnosed right after I filed. How could I know that was going to happen?"

"You couldn't. But, since you do know, you could have offered support. Maybe gone with her to an appointment. She was alone today. No family. No friends. Nobody."

"Why were you there, Max?"

"Because I'm desperate for an angle. Some way to reach her."

"Did you find it?"

"I think so," Max said. "I mean, her family's legacy . . . what she will leave her daughters when she dies . . . is the land. Not the company. Given the choice and all things being equal, which it appears they are very close to being, Stephanie would be better off taking the land and leaving you her interest in the company."

"Have you told her that?"

"Yes. And her lawyer. In Dagger's presence." Max then detailed her entire proposal while Perry listened and nodded along.

"I'd do that," he said. "In a New York minute."

Max felt a wave of relief. "Even the lump sum cash payout of ten million?"

"I might let you haggle with them a little." He grinned and rubbed his knee. "But yeah, that's a good settlement. I get what I want, and Stephanie is more than taken care of. On paper, she makes out with the better deal, and Dagger is able to save face."

"I agree," Max said.

"But Dagger wouldn't go for it?"

Max stood and walked to the window. She had lessened the space between them. *Play the game,* she told herself. "He thinks you're up to something. That you are hiding a material piece of information."

He put his feet on the table, raising his eyebrows at her. "What do you think?"

"That you are working an angle." She licked her lips. "Something big enough . . . or dangerous enough . . . to require the kidnapping of my son to guarantee that you get it." Max took the seat next to him. "And you need total control of Richardson Concepts to capitalize on whatever it is."

When he didn't respond, Max continued, her voice rising. "Perry, don't you *have* to tell Stephanie and Dagger about amazing opportunities? I was never a corporate lawyer, but I'm pretty sure we learned that in law school. You have a fiduciary duty to other shareholders and all that jazz. Aren't you worried about being sued?"

Perry studied her. "If you are correct . . . and there is some opportunity I'm chasing, do you think I'd be dumb enough not to cover my tracks? Sure, Dagger might sue me. Hell, I'd expect him to. But I've invested my money wisely, and he hasn't. I've got the high ground, and I'll destroy him if he or Stephanie comes after me."

"And if Stephanie dies of cancer, then all the better for you."

"I don't want that to happen. Contrary to popular belief, I'm not an animal. But that doesn't make what you just said any less true. Stephanie's death, while tragic, and Dagger's advancing age and poor financial decisions, while unfortunate for him and his daughter, have given me a considerable edge."

"Yet you still felt the need to kidnap my son. To blackmail me into pushing your agenda during this mediation. Why? Why not just let it play out? The arguments you make are sound for why the company should go to you. I would have believed them myself if you hadn't threatened me and my family. I think a judge might too. So why?"

"Because I am an impatient man." He pounded the table with his fist. "I want what I want when I want it."

Max felt her breath catch in her throat as he pointed his index finger at her. For the first time, she saw genuine anger and perhaps a twinge of fear in his expression. It scared her, but she kept her wits as her heart pounded. "You have a timing issue. And you've got to close the deal now or something awful is going to happen. Something as bad or worse as what you are planning for Nathan." They held eye contact. "I'm right, aren't I?" Max asked, her voice just above a whisper. "If you're in trouble, maybe I can help you."

Perry relaxed his shoulders. "The only way that you can help me . . . and save your son's life . . . is to settle this case on my terms." He pushed his chair back and walked to the window. *"Today."*

"You're a sociopath."

"All men and women of greatness are sociopaths, Max. We take what we want. Money. Power. Sex. That's the way it's always been." He turned back to the window. "That's the way it is now." He chuckled. "The irony in all this is that Dagger Richardson was the exact same as me. I learned from the master. No one screwed over more people in this town than Dagger. He took what he wanted and now he's being pushed out by someone stronger." He wheeled to face her. "Darwinism at work."

Max couldn't shake something he'd just said. "Have you considered the possibility that your master might already know about whatever it is you're doing?" She hesitated. "That *he* might be playing *you*? And everyone else too?"

"I consider all possibilities, Max. Now run along," Perry said, holding up his phone and glancing at it. "It's past noon." His eyes blazed with intensity. "You . . . and Nathan . . . are running out of time."

38

Max sat on the cold toilet and urinated for the first time since she'd left the hotel several hours ago. As with sleep and food, she hadn't thought about using the bathroom. Her brain had eliminated all concerns of food, pleasure, and her own physical needs. She had a one-track mind.

Nathan . . .

She took out her phone. She hadn't looked at it in a while and prayed that there was a message from Jason or Satch Tonidandel.

But there was nothing. She thumbed a quick text to her mentor. Jason, the day's half over. I'm making progress, but not fast enough. Have you heard from the colonel?

She cleaned herself up and thought of the gummies she'd bought last night and thrown into the back seat of her truck. They were still there. *Maybe a bite or a nibble just to ease the nerves?*

Max forced herself to take a couple of deep breaths. The bathroom smelled of air freshener, but she felt dirty. Her phone vibrated. She glanced at the screen and then hung her head. It was Jason.

> I haven't heard from him, and he isn't answering my calls or texts. I'm sorry. Hang in there.

Max peered at the time. It was 12:30 p.m. The mediation would be over at 5:00. What if the case didn't settle? They'd set two days aside for it. Would everyone come back tomorrow if they were close to an agreement? What would that mean for Nathan?

Is he still alive?

Max strode out of the stall. She took off her wrist sleeve and washed her hands.

As she exited the bathroom, her phone vibrated again. She walked down the hall, but when she saw the text, she froze. It was from the person who'd sent her the cryptic text last night. The one she'd responded to with the all-caps FU earlier today. She read the message and felt a wave of anger roll over her.

How does it feel to be a whore?

Max glared at the screen. She wouldn't respond this time. She didn't have time for petty text wars.

She paused at the defendant's door and steeled herself. If she was ever going to settle this case, it was now. Dagger was gone, and she'd made some gains with Stephanie and Amy. If she could convince Stephanie to relinquish her interest in Richardson Concepts, Max could lean on Dagger to sell out. Or maybe . . . just maybe that amount of progress would be good enough for Perry to let Nathan go. Perhaps Max could mediate her son's release on altered terms. *Is there something else I could give him?* Max let out a ragged breath and again checked her phone.

12:35 p.m.

Stephanie tensed as Max Ringo reentered the conference room. "All right," Max said, taking a seat across from her. Amy Dance sat with her elbows leaning on the table. Since Dagger's dramatic exit, Stephanie and her lawyer had barely spoken to each other. Stephanie had thought about telling Amy about her cancer diagnosis, but she just couldn't pull the trigger, coming to the same conclusion she came to each time she thought of telling her girls. Or her father.

What good would it do?

"Look," Max began. "As I'm sure you both expected, Perry didn't accept your offer. However, he asked me the same question y'all did. He inquired about what I thought, and I gave him the same proposal I ran by you."

"And?" Amy asked, a tiny glint of hopefulness in her voice. There had been precious little of that in this room since the mediation started yesterday.

"He was intrigued. He balked a little at the ten million lump sum payment, but not the alimony. He'll agree to trade his interest in the family partnership for Stephanie's in Richardson Concepts . . . and he'll buy out Dagger if your father will sell."

Stephanie looked at Amy, who met her eye. "I would advise that you not take a penny less than ten million on the lump sum cash amount. But if he'll agree to the rest . . . regardless of whether your father sells out . . ."

"It would be a good outcome for you," Max chimed in. "The value of your assets would be much more stable than his. Plus, the alimony award is as high as it can be, and you're getting the two homes you want." Max held out her palms. "I'm not sure I can do any better."

Stephanie leaned her arms on the table. "Dad is convinced that Perry has something up his sleeve."

"What if he does?" Max asked. "What if he's about to turn a sweet deal with the company and make a lot of money? He could lose it all within a few months. But the land . . . that's not going anywhere."

Stephanie stood. Her legs felt shaky. She needed to get out of there. Since leaving CCI, she hadn't eaten anything. "Can we break for lunch?"

"I'm sorry," Max said, shaking her head, looking embarrassed. "I forgot about lunch. Why don't you guys pull up a menu from Jimmy John's and tell me what you want. I'll order for everyone."

"No," Stephanie said. "Too late for that. I think I'm going to be sick." She walked toward the door.

"Stephanie, can we discuss a counter before you go?" Amy asked.

Stephanie tapped the door with her fist. "Offer the opposite to Perry," she said, looking at the mediator over her shoulder.

"The opposite?" Max asked.

"Yes. I give him my percentage of the family partnership, and he gives me his interest in the company. He still pays me 20K a month in alimony, but I'll pay him a lump sum cash payment." She coughed.

"He won't go for that," Max said. Stephanie darted her eyes to Amy, who was shaking her head.

"But you both were just telling me what a great deal it is. Great value and more stability. Does that only apply to me?"

"Stephanie—" Amy started.

"Enough!" Stephanie screamed, and both women jumped in their seats. "That's my counter."

When they were alone in the room, Max cleared her throat. "That outburst was . . . surprising."

"I know," Amy agreed.

"She's barely said a thing during this mediation."

"Under her dad's watchful eye," Amy said.

"Jesus," Max said, rubbing her eyes. "I practiced law for twelve years, and I don't ever remember seeing two lawyers come to blows like Dagger and Perry just did. Threats, yeah? But that was a full-on fight."

"It happened awful fast," Amy said. "And it was one-sided. Dagger was doing all the fighting. But still . . . crazy. I seem to recall making a few threats to you over the years during depositions."

Max snorted. "I'm sure I gave as good as I got."

"You did. We had some humdingers."

Max smiled, but her thoughts were on Stephanie. "She has a point, you know. Why is my proposal good for Stephanie to accept and not Perry?"

"Because Perry's ego is attached to the company. This whole damn mediation is a pissing contest between two narcissistic assholes." Amy sighed. "Want to grab lunch?"

Max was taken aback by the question. "Um, well . . ."

"Jimmy John's is good with me. Just something fast."

"I probably shouldn't," Max said. "I need to convey this offer to Perry. It's a doozy that he won't be expecting."

"Suit yourself. You want me to bring you something back?"

"Uh, yeah. If you don't mind. Maybe a turkey sandwich? Let me go get some—"

"Don't worry about it. You aren't charging enough for this mediation. It's on me."

Amy walked past her to the door.

"Thank you," Max called after her, and Amy waved without looking as the door closed behind her.

There's hope yet for humanity, Max thought.

Then, as she rose from her feet, she glanced at her phone and her hope dissipated. 1:15 p.m.

She had a little less than four hours left. The defendant and her lawyer had gone on a break, Perry's patience was wearing thin, and it was obvious that Stephanie would not do anything that went against her father's wishes.

"Damnit," Max whispered as she stepped out into the hallway. Hopefully, Dagger would stay in telephone contact. But, even if he did, how was Max ever going to break through that stubborn head of his and get him to see logic and reason?

I need help, she thought as she hesitated outside Perry's conference room, her body tensing.

I need a miracle.

39

The rifleman couldn't believe his luck.

It turned out that the Beasley Rogers law firm was right on the fringe of one of the sketchier areas of Huntsville. In fact, directly behind the building was a run-down convenience store called Mooty's that looked like the perfect place to close a drug deal. From that point west until the boundary of the Campus No. 805 social district was a blend of public housing, laundromats, and run-down shacks. Numerous homeless people and other rough-looking characters were walking the sidewalks and streets.

The rifleman fit right in with his cords, flannel shirt, and tattered jacket and cap. After buying a candy bar and a root beer from Mooty's, he began to walk down Seminole Drive, carrying an oversize duffel bag over his shoulder. No different from three other vagrants he'd seen thirty minutes earlier.

Without rushing but being careful to make sure he wasn't being watched, the man sneaked into a gap in the chain-link fence that separated the store and the Beasley Rogers parking lot. The only barrier between the lot and fence was some thick bushes, but they provided excellent cover for the man's intentions.

He found a spot with a clear view through the brush to the entrance and took a peek inside his bag. The sniper rifle was in there, as were several other goodies.

Then he again peered at the law firm building. The gun was good up to about a thousand yards, and the distance between where he was and the entrance couldn't be more than two hundred.

Perfect, he thought, rubbing his beard and sitting down on the cold mulch.

Now all he had to do was wait. He took out his binoculars and trained them on the front doors.

And watched.

40

Max stared at Perry. "You don't look angry." She'd just summarized Stephanie's counter to him.

"She was never short on surprises," Perry said. "I'm actually . . . impressed. She's calling my bluff."

Max cocked her head. "I think she's stalling, because she knows you won't take this offer, despite how good a deal it is on paper, and she's not sure what to do now that Dagger's gone."

"So we have a conundrum."

"Yes, we do. Stephanie will not sign off on a deal that Dagger doesn't approve."

Perry pushed his chair back and leaned his elbows on his knees. "What do we do?"

"I think you should call him."

"Me? He just attacked me. Are you crazy?"

"Desperate times call for desperate measures."

"You're the mediator, Max. If you think Dagger needs to be called, you do it."

Max stood and walked toward the door. "OK, I will." She hesitated. "Perry, how is Nathan?"

"He's alive."

"Please, is he OK?"

"My crew has punished him a little for not giving us his phone code."

Max felt her heart sink. "That was my idea. Please don't hurt my son for being a teenager."

"He's fine, Max. But the clock is ticking. It's almost one thirty."

She turned to him, feeling her heart beating fast. "I'm doing the best I can."

"Don't tell me that," Perry said, walking toward her. "That's what losers say after they fail."

Max gritted her teeth. "I'm not a loser. I just may need more time."

"You've got three and a half hours."

Once the door was shut, Perry took out his phone. He had three missed calls and two texts from Andrew Wick. The first message asked, How's it going? and the second was a series of question marks followed by an exclamation point.

Perry typed a quick response. Good. We are close.

He sent the message and then began to pace around the conference room table. The nature of mediation was being cooped up in a room all day, and he hated it. In his world, he needed to be on the move.

His phone chirped with a new message. It was Wick. You better not be shitting me.

"I'm not," Perry said out loud, before texting the same thing to his high-strung but well-meaning banker.

We are close, Perry thought. All in all, he thought things were going as well as could be expected. Max Ringo had done everything he'd hoped so far. Stephanie was at the breaking point. Amy Dance appeared to be sold. Dagger was the only holdout, but Perry had always known that the old man would be the hardest sell.

This was where it really didn't matter who the mediator was. Dagger had to conclude on his own that giving Stephanie's interest in the company to Perry was the right call. No one would be able to tell him the value of such a resolution.

The old man had to be manipulated. And while Perry was impressed with Max so far, he knew that there was only one person in Huntsville who'd consistently undermined Dagger Richardson.

Me.

Perry pulled up Dagger's contact info on his phone. He'd waited long enough. The old man was cracking. Dagger's physical ambush of Perry hadn't been a show of strength. It had been proof of weakness. Perry drafted his message, nodding as he tapped the screen.

> There's a rather obvious solution here Dagger. What did you always tell prospective clients? Let's make a deal. Come on, don't be a fool.

Perry smiled at his handiwork. Then he pressed send.

41

Max felt weird when she stepped off the elevator to the third floor. How long had it been? *Almost two years . . .*

Her last day at the firm was another recurring nightmare. The firm's longtime administrative staffer, Michael Waldrop, and two security officers in full uniform had escorted her out of the building. Leigh Ann had been crying as they passed her in the hallway. Max hadn't even been allowed any time to move out. They'd packed up her office and shipped her belongings to her. When she'd come home from Gainesville over a year later, all that was left of her time at Beasley Rogers fit in three cardboard boxes.

She'd been numb the day she was fired. The drug combination she was on made her feel like a spectator to her own destruction. So much of that last year before rehab was like that. How else could she have done the things she did?

Max had never thought she'd ever be here again. Walking inside the building was one thing. Even seeing Leigh Ann and Lori wasn't all that bad. But now, here, it all came back. There was no way she would have ever willingly come down here. But she was desperate for information and running out of time. When neither Amy nor Stephanie was back from lunch when she peeked inside the defendant's conference room, Max had made a knee-jerk decision and rung the receptionist to buzz Leigh Ann. A minute later, her old paralegal told her that she'd meet Max on three.

Good as her word, seconds after the elevator closed behind her, Leigh Ann came bustling out the double doors from the hallway. "Hey," she said. "How's it going?" Her voice was low. Conspiratorial. "And how's the wrist?" She pointed at the sleeve.

"Not bad on both counts. Wrist seems better . . . and I think we're close to settling the case. Thank you for letting me in." To get in the doors to the floor from the elevator area, you needed a security card. That was how it worked on all floors except five, which didn't require such protection because it was a mediation center, and no client files were kept up there.

"Ready?" Leigh Ann asked.

Max nodded. Then she followed Leigh Ann down the hallway of her past. The first door on the left was the medical malpractice war room. Max stopped for a second as they passed the place where she and Knox had spent countless hours prepping witnesses and getting ready for trials and depositions. The medical dictionaries and textbooks were still on the shelves, as was the newest edition of the leather-bound *Alabama Code*. Even the old whiteboard was still there, with the maxim "Standard of care = reasonable care under the circumstances" handwritten in big, bold black letters. The long rectangular table was mostly clear, with a few medical record notebooks stacked at one end.

They passed Max's old office, and she saw that the door was closed. The new name on the outside of it read "Lori Cannon."

As it should, Max thought, feeling both a tinge of regret and a surge of pride. Finally, they reached the corner office that had been occupied by Knox Rogers for at least twenty-five years. Leigh Ann knocked twice and then opened the door.

Knox was on his cell phone, but he gestured for them to come in.

As she'd done hundreds of times, Max took the seat across from Knox's desk. When her former partner hung up the phone, he stood and put his hands on his hips. "Maxine Christopherson Ringo."

She stared at him, struggling with her emotions. He still had the thick salt-and-pepper hair that receded a tad at the temples. Big glasses that she'd almost never seen him without. He wore faded jeans, a light-blue work shirt, and an old denim jacket that looked like it might be a relic from his high school days in Johnson City, Tennessee. It was Knox's casual-day getup, meaning she'd caught him on the rare occasion that he wasn't on the road meeting with witnesses or in a courthouse somewhere in Alabama.

"Knox Arnston Rogers." Max's voice cracked on the last name. "It is so good . . ." She trailed off and her lip trembled. She'd known she was going to be emotional when she saw him, but the circumstances of the Strassburg mediation had frayed her nerves to the point of exhaustion.

She covered her face with her hands, and seconds later, he was patting her shoulders. "Hey, now, cut that out. This is a happy moment."

"I . . . am . . . happy," Max said, and a part of her was. Unfortunately, the other part remained scared to death and frazzled. *The clock is ticking . . .*

Knox sat in the client chair next to the one she was in. "Leigh Ann, will you shut the door?"

Behind them, Max heard the paralegal say, "Sure."

"How's the mediation going?" Knox asked.

"Fine," Max lied. "I think we are close. It's hard to tell. You know the drill."

Knox groaned. "You, more than anyone, can appreciate how I feel about mediation."

"Not all that fond of the process, as I recall."

"Not hardly," Knox said, and his distaste was easy to understand. In the medical malpractice world, cases rarely settled. A doctor's reputation was everything, and settlements had to be reported to the medical board and the National Practitioner Data Bank. That created a record that even a confidentiality agreement couldn't prevent. So, unlike in a car wreck case, resolving a doctor's case short of trial didn't mean that the physician was done. The case might be over, but the hassle was, many times, just beginning. Hence, medical malpractice was one of the few areas in civil law where jury trials were still prevalent.

Which is exactly the reason I loved it.

"Thank you for letting me use the mediation center," Max said. She had already sent him an email of thanks but wanted him to hear it from her in person. "I'm sure that wasn't an easy sell within the firm."

Knox wrapped his arm around his chair. "Easier than you might think." He smiled, but there was no humor in his eyes. "I tend to get what I want around here."

"I remember."

"So, what's going on? Leigh Ann said you needed to talk with me." Knox pierced her with his crystal-blue eyes, and it was all she could do not to look away. Even dressed in double denim, the man had a smoldering intensity about him. A presence. When Knox Rogers was in the office, he was working, and you could bet there were at least ten files that needed his attention. He wasn't sentimental, and he didn't suffer fools or waste time.

Get on with it, Max thought, sucking in a breath. "Do you still keep up with Dagger?"

Knox blinked. "Not much. J.R. does more than me. I think they still hit the Voodoo Lounge once a week to tell war stories with the retired judges."

Max felt a warm sensation come over her. In her early days in the firm, the partners and associates would go somewhere for happy hour on Fridays, and the Voodoo Lounge, a basement bar on the south side of the courthouse square, was always a solid choice. In later years, and especially after COVID, that tradition died.

"He's been a problem during the mediation," Max said. "He isn't a party, but his daughter won't go against his wishes. And his relationship with Perry is toxic. They just got into a physical altercation, and I had to ask Dagger to leave."

"Good grief," Knox said. "You should have let us know. Dagger can be . . ." He trailed off.

"Is something going on with him?" Max dug. "He's been an unhinged bear the last two days."

"He can be volatile," Knox said, rubbing his chin. "Dagger usually keeps that side of himself in check, but with the divorce and all, I mean . . . we are talking about his daughter. When things get personal . . . they can get heated."

"I know that, but I was just wondering if he might be under some type of . . . additional pressure."

Knox squinted at her. "Spit it out, Max. What do you want to know?"

"Perry believes that Dagger is in dire financial straits. Are you aware of that? Also, is there a dispute or some type of conflict within Richardson Concepts that might be affecting things in this mediation?"

Knox crossed his arms, looking at the ground. "I can have Leigh Ann do an Alacourt search for any recent cases involving the company. I'm not aware of Dagger facing any financial crisis, but I can ask around and we can check the property records. What's your time frame?"

Max frowned. "The mediation is going to be over in three hours unless I can get them to extend until tomorrow, and I doubt y'all have the space here anyway."

"We don't," Knox said. "I'm sorry, but getting you two full days was—"

"I understand, and I hate to ask anything more of you. But I've been out of the game for a while, and if I could settle this one, it could be—"

"Huge," Knox said. "I get it, and I want you to succeed. I'm pulling for you."

"I know."

They stood at the same time, and Knox winked at her. "I really have missed you, Max. You were an excellent trial lawyer . . . and a good friend."

Max blushed. "I learned from the best."

"I'll get on the horn around here and I'll ask Leigh Ann to start digging. We'll be back in touch within the hour if not sooner."

"Thank you," Max said, striding to the door.

"Hey, Max," Knox called after her.

"Can I ask you something and not offend you?"

She tensed. "I don't know."

"Are you OK?"

She squinted. "That's a vague question, counselor. Can you be more specific?"

"Since rehab, have you stayed clean?"

Max felt as if she'd been punched. "Yes."

"That's good."

"Why would you ask that?"

"Truth?"

Max nodded.

"Because you seem . . . a tad off. Your eyes are red, and your hand . . . Leigh Ann said you weren't complaining of wrist pain when you arrived, but now you're wearing her sleeve." He held up his palms. "Don't shoot me. I'm just a little worried. It's not like you to be this . . . disheveled." He winced. "I'm sorry. I . . . was never very subtle."

Max forced a smirk. "You sure know how to make a girl feel good about herself." But that was Knox. He wasn't a backstabber. If he was going to hit you, he would punch you right between the eyes. She appreciated the candor.

For a split second, Max thought about telling him the truth. Knox was a lawyer the same as Jason Rich. She could pay Knox a dollar, and he, too, would have to keep whatever she told him a secret. *No. He's done enough.* And while Knox was a good man, his questions belied perhaps his greater concern.

He's worried I'm going to embarrass him.

"I'm nervous, Knox. I don't want to blow this opportunity." She clasped her hands together to keep them from shaking. "I haven't been in this type of environment in a long time, and it's overwhelming. Seeing my old friends. Walking this hall. Being here with you. It's surreal . . . and I feel ashamed. I guess I'm trying too hard. As for the eyes, I'm probably . . . definitely . . . sleep deprived." She bit her lip. "I won't embarrass you."

"I know that, Max. I would never think that you would."

You just did, Max thought as she turned and let herself out the door.

As she passed by her old paralegal's desk, she ripped off the compression sleeve on her wrist and tossed it to her. "Thanks for letting me use it."

Leigh Ann was typing and had to take her hands off the keyboard to catch the device. "Um . . . You're welcome. Sure you don't—?"

"I'm good, Leigh Ann. Thank you for your help." But Max didn't stop walking, keeping her eyes straight ahead. Her wrist throbbed, but she willed herself not to think about it. When she got on the elevator, she took out her phone. It was 2:23 p.m.

She started to send Jason another text but decided against it. If the colonel hadn't checked in by now, he wasn't going to be helpful to her.

As the elevator doors slid open on five, Max came to a humbling realization. Perhaps Knox and Leigh Ann would find something she could use to reach Dagger. But otherwise . . .

. . . *I'm on my own.*

42

"How's the boy doing?" Perry asked, hearing the agitation in his voice.

"Better now that he's eaten," Hicks said. "He passed out a couple hours ago. Those damn THC gummies are strong as hell, and we'd been withholding food because he was a little asshole about his phone code. But he seems stable for the moment. What's the plan, boss?"

"I'll let you know in a little over two hours," Perry said, feeling his heart rate thudding in his chest. Perry Strassburg rarely experienced panic, but he was on the verge. His son, Tru, still wasn't answering his phone. And Dagger hadn't responded to his text. "Do you have the fentanyl?"

"Affirmative. Already mixed into the meth." Another pause. "He'll be dead before he takes his second snort."

Perry closed his eyes. "OK," he managed. "Stand by." Then he clicked the phone dead.

"Mother . . . fucker," he hissed out loud, running his hands through his hair. He knew his plan contained a huge risk-reward delta. Of course, he'd had some help concocting it. He hesitated for a second and then made the call.

The phone didn't even ring once. *"What?"*

"I'm worried. We only have two and a half hours left."

"Have you ever had a high-stakes case reach a settlement at mediation until the bitter end?"

"No. But I've never been so personally invested in one either."

"Those are the breaks when you represent yourself."

"That was your recommendation, remember?"

"And it still holds true. A lawyer could not go along with . . . some of the things you've done."

"We've done," Perry corrected.

"You've," his coconspirator fired back. "Make no mistake, I'm untouchable here."

Perry thought about the recordings and videos he'd made. *I don't think so.* But he said nothing. "You still believe it's going to work?" he asked.

"Yes, I do. But . . . she may need more time."

"Time is a luxury I don't have," Perry said, the agitation making him itchy. "My own son isn't responding to calls or texts. I'm worried."

"You knew what you were getting into."

The line clicked dead before Perry could respond.

Damnit, he thought, pacing around the conference room. He'd walked so many circles since Max left that he was beginning to feel dizzy. He thought of his plan.

Was it my plan? He began to feel a cold sweat on his neck as he went over the call he'd just had and the events of the past few weeks. Then he thought about what Max had insinuated in one of their last caucuses.

Am I being played?

Perry again tried to reach Tru. His son was a ski instructor and a pothead. Staying in touch wasn't one of his strong suits, but he'd never ignored Perry for two straight days. Six rings. No answer.

Perry thumbed a text. "Tru, please call me when you have a moment. It is urgent." He sent the message and walked another circle around the table. Then he dialed Wick.

The call went straight to voicemail without ringing.

Perry felt the cold sweat on his neck again. In all the years he'd known Wick, had his friend ever been without use of his cell phone? There were times when Wick didn't answer, but those were rare. Perry never remembered a call going straight to voicemail. That would indicate the device was either turned off or the battery was dead.

Perry checked the time. 2:43 p.m.

He thought about calling Dagger, but he knew it would be a show of weakness. He'd made his play by sending the text. Better to wait the old man out. *If I follow up, he'll sense that I'm desperate.*

Perry tried Wick again. No rings. Straight to voicemail.

"Damnit," he whispered. When he heard three hard knocks on the door, Perry's body tensed. When Max didn't barge through, he cleared his throat. "Come in."

43

Stephanie peeked her head in first. Just a few inches. "Hey."

Perry gawked back at her with wide eyes. It was as if she'd caught him doing something he shouldn't be doing. She remembered a time when she'd walked in on him jerking off at work. She'd wanted to surprise him after hours and burst into his office.

And there he was. Sitting at his desk, pants down to his ankles, masturbating to porn. The look on his face then mirrored his expression now, and she couldn't help but smile.

"Hey," he said. He was already standing, and he took a tentative step toward her. "How are you?"

"Tired," Stephanie said. "Of being here. Of everything. I want it to be over."

"Me too," Perry said. She could tell he was fumbling for words. "How . . . are the girls?" he asked.

"Do you really give a damn?" Perry had been Mem and Ella's stepdad in name only, hardly ever coming to any of their activities.

"Why'd you come in here?" he asked, his fake empathy gone. Back to business.

"Thank you for not patronizing me anymore. I want this to be over. It is making me sick to my stomach." She hesitated. "It's worse than the side effects of chemo." She watched his face and could tell in an instant that he already knew. There was no surprise. No emotion. Just the blinking someone does when they are told something they already know and likely don't want to think about.

"I'm sorry," he said. "I never wanted to hurt you, Stephanie. Or to see you get hurt. I just—"

"Traded me in for a new model, though you've been pretty stealthy about showing her off."

"Not true."

"Yes, it is. Let me guess. She's more enthusiastic about your kinky sex games than I was? Or . . ." Stephanie felt her nostrils flare. ". . . perhaps you broke in someone even more prudish than me? I know you derive particular satisfaction from converting the innocent to your hedonistic ways." She snapped her fingers. "I've got one even better. You found someone more powerful than me after squeezing all the juice that I had."

Perry didn't even look angry. It was as if he were sizing up a peculiar bug he was about to step on. "I don't know what you're talking about. And . . . I would never call you 'prudish.'"

"Right. Well, I don't care anymore." She took a step toward him. "What do you want?"

"Shouldn't we let the mediator do her job?"

"I'm tired of waiting. *What do you fucking want?*"

There was a loud knock on the door and then Amy Dance burst inside. Followed by Max Ringo. "Stephanie, what are you doing?"

Stephanie's chest burned with anger. "Will you both just leave me alone?" She glared at her lawyer and the mediator over her shoulder. "I am trying . . ." Then she felt the nausea. Rolling up her esophagus. She covered her mouth and sensed the tears in the corners of her eyes.

"Stephanie, are you—?" Perry started, but Stephanie waved him off with both hands. She ran past the other two women and out the door. Then she stumbled into the bathroom and dropped to her knees without shutting the stall door.

The vomiting episode was violent, and she wasn't sure how long it would last. Tears streaked her face, and the smell of bile made her gag.

I'm so tired of this crap, she thought. *So . . . damn . . . tired.*

44

"Don't look at me," Perry said, his tone defensive. "She's the one who came in here."

Max shared a glance with Amy.

"What did she say?" Amy asked.

Perry coughed. He looked disturbed by what he'd just seen. "That she was tired and wanted everything to be over. She asked me what I wanted, and before I could say anything, you guys came in and she got sick."

"You know damn well that you aren't supposed to talk with Stephanie without me present." Amy was scowling, clearly flustered.

"She came in here of her own accord," he snapped. "I didn't seek her out. Maybe you should get control of your client, Amy." He turned his ire to Max. "And maybe you should take charge of this mediation. Unless you have a counter for me, Max, both of you can get the hell out of here."

"Gladly," Amy said, turning and slamming the door.

When Max didn't move, Perry strode toward her, eyes blazing. "Do you have a counter?"

"No."

"Well, go get one and stop wasting my time," he said.

As she grabbed the knob, he put his hand over hers. "Your son has about two hours of life left." He leaned forward, whispering into her ear. "Do you know how easy it is to lace methamphetamine with fentanyl?"

"Perry, please. This isn't my fault. Dagger is the problem."

"Well, you better figure it out. I'm getting—"

Two loud knocks on the door interrupted Perry, and he backed away. The door creaked open, and Leigh Ann peeked inside. "Hey, Max. I have a message for you."

"Thank you," Max managed. "I'll be right back, Perry. I need to see Stephanie."

"You do that," he said, turning his back on them.

Max followed Leigh Ann out of the conference room. It was all she could do not to cry.

Leigh Ann was carrying some documents under her arm. Once they were in the hallway, she handed them to Max. "This is everything Alacourt has on Richardson Concepts in the last few years. Nothing jumped out to Knox as being all that important. A couple of employee disputes. A workers' comp claim."

"Anything with Dagger against the company? Or Dagger versus Perry?"

"No," Leigh Ann said. "But . . ." She held up a manila folder. "There are at least seven mortgages recorded by Independent Commerce Bank on property owned by Richardson Farms, LLC." She licked her lips. "The loans total approximately $25 million, and they all appear to be several months past due."

Max's eyes widened. "Holy shit."

"That what you were looking for?" Leigh Ann asked with a wink.

"Yes. You are *the best.*"

"Knox also talked with J.R., and he said Dagger had not shown up at the Voodoo Lounge for their weekly booze fest in a long time and also had not returned J.R.'s last voice message about a mutual client. J.R. said he was worried about him. That Dagger wasn't acting like himself."

"Thank you, Leigh Ann. This helps so much."

Leigh Ann touched her shoulder. "Let me know if there's anything else."

"Will do." Max stepped into her mediation office and pulled out her phone. 3:15 p.m. She was losing her grip.

"Do you know how easy it is to lace methamphetamine with fentanyl?"

She wiped her eyes and stared at the table. *And Nathan is hooked on meth . . .*

Amy had put a to-go bag from Jimmy John's on it, but Max couldn't even imagine eating now. She thought she might be sick like Stephanie.

Finally, she fled the office. She needed to regroup. Freshen up. She went into the bathroom and ran water from the sink. She dabbed her eyes. Touched up her makeup and reapplied lipstick.

It wasn't until she turned the water off and was drying her hands that she heard the sniffles. They were coming from the far stall. She approached and smelled vomit.

"Are you OK in there?"

No response.

"Stephanie?"

"Go away."

Max leaned her back against the wall. She tried to think of something helpful or supportive to say, but the words wouldn't come. Instead, she spat out the facts. "He rejected your offer. You called his bluff."

A bitter scoff. "Well, whoop-de-freaking-doo. Is that a victory?"

"It is what it is," Max said. "Is there anything I can get you for the nausea? I think I might have some Zofran."

There was no response.

"Stephanie, I know we aren't friends or anything, but I'm here. I'll listen. I wasn't much of a listener before rehab, but maybe I'm a little better now." Max gazed across the bathroom at the tile wall. Mediation was a confidential process, but no one said you couldn't have a session in the bathroom. She took out her phone and texted Amy. I'm in the ladies' room with Stephanie. She's still sick. There shouldn't be any other visitors up here if you want to join.

She pressed send and sank to the floor. "I don't know what I was thinking becoming a mediator," Max said, still staring at the wall. "I loved being a trial lawyer. Was good at it. Enjoyed the confrontation. Going up against pricks like your soon-to-be ex-husband. Or legends like your father. I could hold my own until the accident."

The door to the bathroom creaked open, and Amy came inside. The lawyer raised her eyebrows when she saw Max sitting on the floor. The surface wasn't exactly dirty, but it was, after all, the bathroom. *I feel dirty anyway,* Max thought, knowing she probably looked like shit. She peered at Amy and put her index finger over her mouth. Her old rival nodded and crossed her arms, staying near the door.

"How did the accident happen?" Stephanie's voice was hoarse, dry.

"Was coming home from a concert at the VBC. My best friend and I had been to see Journey. She was the designated driver. Meanwhile, I had enjoyed a couple of cosmos. We'd flipped a coin to see who would drive." Max scoffed. "I won." She felt her eyes beginning to water. "We were singing 'Don't Stop Believin'' at the top of our lungs when we pulled out of the parking garage. We stopped at the Taco Bell drive-through and both got Nachos BellGrande that we were gonna take to my house." Max paid no attention to the tears that now fell down both sides of her face. "We were at the intersection of Drake and Whitesburg. Turning left. We'd just gotten the green arrow. Still singing. Her radio was up full blast, and we were belting out 'Faithfully.' She started to turn . . ." Max's lip trembled, and her nose began to run. The scent of vomit hung in the air, but Max was back in that car. A 3 Series BMW sedan. She could smell the Taco Bell. A place she would never go to ever again. That smell . . .

"Max?" Stephanie asked, her voice weak. Sad.

"The truck didn't have its lights on. It was a pickup. A teenage boy was driving. He was texting and he had a carload of other kids with him. I saw it at the last second. So did my friend. She blamed herself, but we were already in the intersection. There was nothing she could do. The truck never hit the brakes. Hit us going forty miles per hour, which was the speed limit. I guess we were all fortunate he wasn't speeding." Max could now taste the snot in her mouth, and she wiped her nose and face. "None of the teens were hurt too bad. And my friend was also fine. She didn't absorb much of the collision."

"You took it all," Amy offered.

Max nodded. "Broke my collarbone. Pelvis. The rotator cuff on my right shoulder was pulverized." Max bit down on her lip. "And I had a concussion." She gave her head a jerk. "When I woke up after surgery, the pain was unbearable, and they gave me oxycodone. After two procedures and almost a month in the hospital, I was discharged home. By then, my body was already dependent on the drug." Max stopped and stared down at the tile floor, which now glistened from her tears. For several seconds, the only sound in the bathroom was of their respective sniffles.

"How did you learn you had cancer?" Max asked.

Stephanie coughed, and for a moment, Max thought she was going to throw up again. Then, clearing her throat, Stephanie croaked out, "Pelvic pain. Started noticing it on my morning walks with Fredo. Went to see my OB and they did an ultrasound. Next thing you know I'm getting a full workup at CCI and being told that I have uterine cancer that's spread to the lymph nodes."

Max gazed at Amy Dance across the restroom, seeing the lawyer's face, which was streaked with tears, now turn pale.

"And what did the scans show today?" Max asked, talking to the closed stall.

"It's spread. To the liver and the bladder. It's in my bones."

Max winced. She looked at Amy, who had covered her mouth with her hand.

"A death sentence," Stephanie said. "It's just a matter of whether I want to prolong my life with poison so that I can spend a few more days like today. Trying not to puke my guts out and failing miserably."

The bathroom was silent for a long time. Max closed her eyes as tears again streamed down her cheeks. Crying for herself and for the woman in the stall. When she heard more sniffling that wasn't her own, she slid closer to the closed door. "Stephanie?" She reached under the door and extended her hand. "Don't do this alone."

Max saw Stephanie's feet shift forward and then heard the latch on the lock slide open.

Stephanie Strassburg was sitting with her back against the front of the toilet seat. Her face was streaked with tears, and a stream of snot poured out of her nose. The sleeves of her sweatshirt were covered with mucus and orangish-red bile. "I'm a mess," she managed. Max got on her knees and crawled into the stall. Then she wrapped her arms around the woman, feeling the tension in Stephanie's chest and shoulders relax.

The floodgates opened, and the woman began to sob. Beating her fist on Max's back. Finally letting go.

Max cried with her, and, at least for a few minutes, the world went away.

45

The gun was hidden in the glove compartment of the Tundra.

As she continued to hold Stephanie in her arms, Max began to think more and more of the old GLOCK 26 her father had stashed in the glove box for the last ten years of his life. When he couldn't drive anymore and gave Max the truck, he'd made her promise that she'd keep it in there. *It's a crazy world, Maxine.* She could hear his voice in her mind.

Even in his failing health, her father had taken her down to the range and trained her on how to use the weapon. Just as he'd taught her how to catch a softball when she was eight. How to drive a car at fifteen. And, maybe most importantly, how to keep believing in herself when she was in rehab. *We all make mistakes, Maxine. It's how we recover that defines us.* When everyone in her life deserted her, her dad stayed the course. He was dying of emphysema, but he drove the Tundra himself from Mentone to Gainesville to participate in the family workshop at the Florida Recovery Center. At the end of the program, the last event was the hardest. It was essentially an airing of grievances, where family members would tell the addict about all the ways the patient's addiction had hurt them while the other patients and families watched. It was agonizing but meant to clear the air and bring about ownership and healing. When it was her father's turn, he sat across from her in front of the group, and Max couldn't meet his eye. But instead of talking or complaining or venting, he just leaned forward and hugged her tight, just as Max was embracing Stephanie Strassburg now. Then he whispered into her ear: "*You're my girl, and I'll always be proud of you.*"

Nathan Elliott Christopherson was a man of few words and simple gestures. But without him, Max knew she would never have had the strength to come back.

Or to do what I have to do now, Max thought. She patted Stephanie's head and gritted her teeth. Then she peered at Amy, who was sitting next to them on the dirty floor. "What time is it?"

"Four oh eight," Amy said.

They'd been in the bathroom for over half an hour. Max let go and slid a couple inches away from Stephanie. She grabbed hold of the woman's hand and squeezed. "We've got around fifty minutes until close of business, Stephanie. I'm borrowing this office space for the mediation, so we'll need to leave then. Do you want to make one last offer?" Max asked. "We could make my proposal. We'd obviously have to leave out Dagger's interest, but dealing with his property is outside the scope of this divorce anyway."

"What are the terms again?" Stephanie's voice was weak.

Max cleared her throat. "Perry gives you his interest in the family partnership that owns the land. You give him your percentage of the company. Alimony stays at 20K a month to you. The house division is what we've previously agreed upon. Lump sum cash is ten million."

"Do you think he would agree?" Amy asked.

"He might counter on the lump sum," Max said. "But on the other terms, yes. I believe he would."

"It's a good deal, Stephanie," Amy said. "I recommend you make that offer with one change. Let's remove the alimony and bump up the lump sum to ten point five million. In the event of your death, alimony would cut off and not pass to your daughters, and given what happened at CCI today . . ." Amy trailed off and put her hand on Stephanie's shoulder. "It's time to be done with this mess. You have more pressing matters than screwing around with a divorce trial."

Stephanie wiped her eyes. "I can't make a deal without Dad's approval." She whistled through her teeth. "I'm not even sure I want to. Richardson Concepts means everything to him. He loves that damn company more than me. And so does Perry. Both of the men in my life love a business more than me."

"I don't think that's how your dad feels," Amy said, pushing herself to her feet and taking out her cell phone. "I'm going to call him." She clicked the phone. "When he answers, I'll put it on speaker."

But he didn't pick up. Six rings. No response.

Amy turned to Stephanie. "Can you try?"

Stephanie reached into her sweatpants and pulled out her phone. She pushed a button and looked at Max, then Amy. "I doubt he answers me either."

"He will," Amy said. "You're his daughter. This is the last day of mediation, and he has made it clear that he wants to be a part of every proposal you make."

But he didn't. Six more rings. Nothing.

"Damnit," Amy said.

They waited another minute, and each tried again. Still no answer. Then they both sent text messages, asking Dagger to call them.

"Why don't you try, Max?" Stephanie suggested.

Max got the old man's number and entered the digits on the keypad. Same result.

"He could be riding," Stephanie said. "Dad likes to go for a ride on his horse when he's stressed. But he never goes anywhere without his phone."

Max put her good left hand on the grimy floor and pushed herself to her knees and then her feet. Her legs felt wobbly, and one was half asleep, but she felt better than she had when she'd walked in here. Amy helped Stephanie to her feet, and then the women took turns washing their hands and cleaning up their faces.

As they walked out into the hall, Stephanie grabbed Max under the arm. "Thank you. For in there."

"You're welcome."

"I feel a little better."

"Max, I'll keep trying Dagger," Amy said, her tone frustrated. "I'm sorry."

"I'm sorry too," Stephanie said. "I ought to be able to make a decision without my father, but—"

"I understand," Max said. And she did. But it didn't make her predicament any less impossible. She headed for the elevators.

"What are you doing?" Amy called after her.

Max pushed the button going down. "There are a lot of lawyers in this firm who know Dagger. I'm going to keep trying."

"We'll do the same," Amy said.

The elevator bell rang, and the doors opened. Max climbed on, and she was grateful to be alone. She pushed "L" and looked at her phone. It was now 4:22 p.m. In the quiet confines of this moving box, she glanced at her reflection in the mirrored wall across from her. Despite her freshening up, her face was still puffy, and she fought the urge to look behind her to see if her skirt was now soiled from the bathroom floor. But instead of feeling vulnerable or self-conscious, she found that she didn't care.

Fuck it, Max thought, straightening her posture as the elevator door opened. She strode forward, walking fast and with a lean. Mercifully, there was no one milling about the lobby for her to have to chat with, and her old partner, Chris Ledyard, who was enjoying a smoke break under the breezeway, was on his phone with his back to her as she headed outside.

She'd parked in her customary spot, and she climbed into the front seat, not wanting to act unusual in any way. She leaned over, popped the glove box, and stared at the black steel pistol. On the handle were his initials: **NEC**.

It's a crazy world, Dad.

She grabbed the weapon and, for a second, panicked. *Where am I going to put it?* She hadn't brought her briefcase down with her. Then she remembered that this skirt suit had pockets. They weren't very deep, but she could stick the gun in the pocket and hold her hand over the handle, and it would be OK. Good enough to at least get through the lobby. *But not stealthy enough with Perry . . .*

She shut the door to the truck and walked toward the entrance. She didn't check the time, but she knew it had to be close to 4:30 p.m.

She stepped into the lobby, feigning embarrassment as she flagged the receptionist. "Do you have any duct tape?" Max pointed at her skirt, keeping her hand over the gun in her pocket and acting as if the skirt's waist had snapped. "I'm having a wardrobe malfunction."

"Let me see," Candace said, walking around the table to the back. Max waited, praying that she wouldn't see anyone she knew. Seconds later, Candace was back. "Here you go." She held the gray tape out to Max with a curious expression. "Would you rather have a bobby pin? That might work better. Tape is going to show."

Max blinked. *We're wasting time.* But she knew she couldn't arouse suspicion. "Do you have one handy?"

"Sure." Candace reached into her purse, fumbled for a second, and pulled one out. "Here you go."

Max took the pin and tape and made a beeline for the lobby bathroom. She went into a stall, sat on the toilet, and taped the GLOCK to her inner right thigh. In college, Max used to attach flasks of bourbon in this exact manner to be able to sneak liquor into the football games. A lot of her friends did the same, and the boys loved it. That had been fun and kinda sexy.

This scared her to death.

Max stood and went to the sink, splashing water on her face. She glanced at her phone again. It was 4:37 p.m.

It was time for her to make a rather unusual mediator's offer. As she walked out of the bathroom, she was pleased with her handiwork. The GLOCK was taped snug and secure, and she was confident no one could see it. Just like in the old days at Bryant–Denny Stadium.

Roll Tide, she thought as she pushed the elevator button.

46

Perry was in full panic mode. Wick's phone was still going to voicemail, and Tru had yet to respond to his texts or calls. Perry hadn't spoken to Tru's mother in years. Not since the boy had turned eighteen and the child support obligation ended. He'd supported his son since then, but he'd had nothing to do with Brandi, who had remarried a sales executive with the Space & Rocket Center. He pulled up her contact information and, after a second's hesitation, made the call.

She answered after four rings. "Well, this is a surprise." Her voice was a tad slurry.

"What are you doing?" Perry asked.

"Me and Scott are at Yellowhammer. Toasting the end of the day with a couple of craft beers."

"Are you drunk?"

"None of your business. What do you want?"

Perry closed his eyes. "Have you heard from Tru? I've been trying to reach him and he's not responding."

A scoff on the other end of the line. "Tru's never been all that good about answering his phone."

"I know that, but I've sent several texts asking him to call me, and he hasn't. That's unlike him. When was the last time you spoke to him?"

A pause and Perry heard a voice in the background—Scott, he presumed—ask, "Who the hell is that?"

"It's Perry," Brandi whispered to Scott. Then back into the phone mic. "We normally speak about once or twice a week. But come to think of it, I haven't talked to him this week. Is there anything going on that has you worried?"

"No. He just hasn't responded in a while, and even for him, it seems off."

"I'll call him right now and then buzz you back." Gone was the slur, and Brandi's voice was hyper. Before Perry could say OK, she ended the call.

Three minutes later, she called him back. "Yeah," Perry answered.

"OK, so now I'm worried. I rang him twice and got no answer. I also called his girlfriend?"

"Girlfriend? I didn't even know—"

"Shut up. Her name is Daphne and she's a stoner, like him, but a sweet girl. Daphne answered and said that she hasn't heard from him in three days. She has a key to his apartment, and she went over this morning and there's no sign of him."

Jesus Christ, Perry thought, remembering his lunch with Wick at J. Alexander's. The black Yukon that had followed him out of there. Wick had been worried and had consistently told him to check on Tru.

I should've been more diligent.

"Perry?" Brandi's voice was higher pitched. "What in the hell is going on?"

"I don't know," he said.

"Why did you need to talk with him? You almost never call him. I know, because Tru confides in me. He says other than visiting once a year and spending most of the time skiing, you hardly ever talk to him. Why now?"

Perry let out a ragged breath. "Brandi—"

"Have you done something to endanger our son?"

Before he could respond, three loud knocks reverberated through the room, and Max came inside.

"I have to go, Brandi. If you hear from him, call me."

"Perry, you can't just—"

He ended the call and gazed at the mediator. "Time's almost up, Max. Have you brought me the terms I need?"

"Not quite . . . but I think I have something that will be hard to refuse."

47

Something is wrong, Max thought.

Perry seemed off. Distracted. *Scared?*

"Max, do you have a counter?" he asked, and his tone didn't contain its usual arrogance.

"I have tentative confirmation from Stephanie that she will give her interest in Richardson Concepts to you in exchange for your percentage of the partnership. The house arrangement would remain as we've already discussed. In light of her terminal illness, she's dropped alimony but increased her lump sum cash demand to ten point five million."

"That works for me. What about Dagger's interest? And what do you mean by tentative confirmation?"

"Dagger hasn't approved the offer, and he's not answering his phone so I can't ask about his interest. Will you try to reach him?" Max fought to keep her voice steady. She felt the cold steel of the GLOCK taped to her thigh.

"Please," Max said. "If you get him, hand the phone to me."

Perry tapped on his phone. Then he put the device in front of him on the table. "It's on speaker," Perry said.

On the fourth ring, Dagger Richardson's gravelly voice responded. "What do you want?"

Max stepped closer to the table. "Dagger, it's Max Ringo. We almost have this case settled, but Stephanie won't do anything without your approval. She has agreed in principle with trading her interest in the company for Perry's in the family partnership with all the other terms the same and Perry paying a lump sum of ten million." Max swallowed. Her heart was racing. This was her last chance, and she heard the desperation in her voice.

"I'm assuming that the jackass in the room with you is fine and dandy with that arrangement."

"Perry has agreed to these terms . . . and he also wants to buy you out of Richardson Concepts for the current fair market value of $45 million." Max closed her eyes, her heart pounding fast as the seconds passed. "Dagger?" she pressed.

"I don't agree to any of that," Dagger said. *"And I never will."*

Then the line went dead.

For a long moment, Max studied the phone. The only thing she could hear was the thudding of her heartbeat.

"I really . . . thought you could do it," Perry said. She couldn't tell if he was mocking her or being sincere. His tone was monotone, as if he were thinking out loud.

Perry grabbed his phone and pressed something. He held the device to his ear, continuing to gaze at Max. He omitted any greeting when his call was answered.

"Is the fentanyl ready for the kid?"

"No," Max said, having trouble finding her voice. "No, Perry, please."

"Good," Perry said into the phone, ignoring her.

Max leaned over as if she were overcome with emotion. She moved her hands under her skirt and up her thigh until she reached the duct-taped gun. As Perry continued to talk on the phone, she began to unwrap the tape.

But just as she almost had the pistol off her thigh, an explosion boomed from outside the building that caused her to drop to her knees.

"What the hell?" Perry wheeled toward the window as another blast thundered from below. Then another. And another. It sounded like the building was being attacked.

"Oh my God," Perry said, his voice a whiny whisper. He rushed past Max and out the door.

Max reattached the duct tape and stumbled to the window. The scene outside was surreal.

Smoke and fire cascaded up from the ruined cars. Then the fire alarm rang out through the building and a voice came over some speakers out in the hall.

"Please evacuate the building. Take the stairs and exit as quickly as possible."

Jesus Christ, Max thought, running toward the door. Out in the hallway, the alarm was so loud she could barely think. She went into the mediation office, snatched her briefcase, and walked back out into the hall. She trotted toward the defendant's conference room, peeked inside, and saw that Amy and Stephanie were gone. Then the speakers blared again.

"Evacuate the building now."

"Good grief," Max whispered, but she couldn't hear her own words due to the sound of the alarm. Max ran back into Perry's conference room and again gazed out the window, but now there was so much smoke she couldn't see anything. *Has the fire reached the building?*

Max strode toward the stairs. As she reached the door, her phone vibrated. Max snatched it out of her pocket and looked at the screen as she began to descend the steps. The text almost made her fall.

You should have never come back.

Max felt the air leave her body as if she'd been sucker punched in the gut. It was the same message from yesterday. Max continued down the stairs as her ears rang with the blare of the alarm. As she reached the lobby, she saw fire trucks coming into the parking lot, and there were people crying outside in the breezeway. Max was in shock. Numb all over.

Is this about me?

She walked out the double doors, passing the panicked faces. She heard screams being drowned out by police and fire sirens. She took a few more steps but stopped dead still when she saw it.

No.

Max sank to her knees on the asphalt, not believing her eyes.

The Tundra was a ball of fire.

48

The rifleman had the target in his sights.

Perry Strassburg was standing on the sidewalk just to the right of the breezeway. He was on his cell phone, moving his head in every direction.

The man admired his handiwork. Five cars had been torched. Fire and smoke consumed the parking lot. It was complete chaos. And from his perch in the large bushes that blocked the view of Mooty's convenience store, he had a clear line of sight.

Strassburg was pacing. Still talking. *Stay still,* the man thought, hovering his finger over the trigger.

The target finally stopped moving. Distracted by something. He held his hands up as if to block a punch. He might as well be a statue now.

The shooter grinned.

Then he pulled the trigger.

49

Perry hung up with Hicks when he saw Max striding toward him.

"Max?" He put his palms out in front of him.

"Did you do this?" she hissed. "My truck just—"

Perry heard a whoosh and then the glass behind them shattered. *What the—*

Another crack. And more glass breaking, the fragments falling around them like rain pellets.

"Get down!" Max said, tackling him and covering his body.

Perry ran his hand through his hair, feeling the particles of glass. He was in shock.

Someone is trying to kill me.

He saw a black SUV swerving toward the sidewalk and remembered the Yukon that had followed him to the office after lunch yesterday. *The Syndicate . . .*

They'd lost patience with him.

He pushed Max off him and crawled to his feet. Before the vehicle even stopped, a woman was jumping out of it.

Perry's breath caught in his throat as he recognized her as part of his security detail.

"Get in, sir!" she yelled.

"Perry!" Max screamed from behind him.

He leaned down and spoke into her ear. "Say nothing to the police or Nathan's dead, you hear me?"

Then, as the blare of sirens drowned out her response, he was pulled into the waiting vehicle.

50

Max watched the black SUV speed out of the parking lot and turn right onto Clinton Avenue. Then she turned behind her, where the window of the first floor of the Beasley Rogers building had been shot out. She could see the conference room behind where the barrier had been, and her eyes locked on a tray of peppermints that now had a sheen of glass on top of them.

"Jesus Christ," Max whispered, crawling to her feet and taking cover behind one of the concrete columns. She'd heard the shots as they buzzed past her and Perry. Was he the intended target? Then she remembered the ominous text she'd received on her way down the stairs . . .

Did someone just try to kill me?

She tried to get her bearings. Her brain was scrambled, and she still couldn't quite believe what was happening. *My truck is gone. Dad's truck . . .*

Max took out her cell and gazed at the threatening message.

You should have never come back.

She tried to call the number, but it went straight to voicemail. Then she typed a quick reply text. Who is this?

Max put the phone back in her pocket. *What now?* she thought. She moved her eyes around the parking lot, seeing cars maneuvering around the emergency vehicles to leave. There were several police sedans on the scene, and fire trucks began to hose down the vehicles that had been targeted. The blare of sirens merged with the cries, screams, murmurs, and whimpers that surrounded Max.

It was a madhouse.

She peered around the column, scanning the parking lot and past it to the chain-link fence, seeing the Mooty's store in the background. The shots had come from that direction. With the police presence now, it seemed unlikely that the shooter would try again.

"Max?"

She turned toward the voice and saw Leigh Ann walking toward her. The tiny woman's eyes were wide with fear and shock. "Are you OK?"

"My truck . . ." Max pointed toward the lot.

"Oh no," Leigh Ann said. "Thank God you weren't in it."

"What about the other cars? Did anyone—?"

"No one was in them. One was J.R.'s Lexus." Leigh Ann let out a nervous chuckle. "But he seems more worried about a doctor's deposition he's late for than his car. Chris Ledyard's truck got hit too. He was out on his smoke break and saw the whole thing happen. He's pretty shook up."

"I bet. Me too."

"Max, my gosh." Leigh Ann hugged her. "Do you need anything? Your clothes are ruined. I have some workout stuff in my car, but none of it would fit you."

"I'm fine, Leigh Ann. Is Knox OK?"

"He wasn't here. Gone to Sheffield for some late meetings."

"Lori?"

"She's with him. They're fine. Lori left her car here, but it appears to be unscathed. It's a good thing the firm is so close to the fire department. Otherwise . . ." She trailed off, but Max didn't need her to finish the thought.

The whole building might have burned down.

"Do you need a lift somewhere?" Leigh Ann asked. "I'm getting out of here."

Max saw Amy Dance sitting on a bench under the breezeway. "Thank you, Leigh Ann, but I need to check on the parties to the mediation."

"OK. Good luck, girl. Do you still have my cell number saved in your phone?"

"Yes," Max said.

Leigh Ann put both of her hands on Max's shoulders. "Call me if you need anything. A place to stay tonight. A ride. Anything. You hear?"

Max felt tears welling in her eyes and she forced them back. She leaned down and hugged her former paralegal. "Thank you."

"I mean it," Leigh Ann said. "Anything." Then she walked around the back of the building.

Max turned and saw that Amy was still sitting on the bench. Max forced her feet to move forward. *I can't hide here forever.* She approached, her legs wobbly, and took a seat next to Amy. "Hey."

Amy said nothing. Max looked at the woman and saw that she had some soot on her cheek. "You look like shit," Max said, elbowing the other woman.

Amy peered at Max out of the corner of her eye. Her arms were crossed tight over her chest. "Speak for yourself."

Max managed a tired smile. "Is your car OK?"

"Fine. But I was standing right here when all hell broke loose."

"You weren't upstairs?"

Amy gave her head a jerk. "No. I'd ridden the elevator down with Stephanie. I was trying to get her to wait for you. While you were with Perry, Stephanie heard back from Dagger, and he told her that the mediation was over and to leave the building." Amy squinted at Max. "Is the mediation over?"

"No," Max said, trying not to sound desperate. She knew it wasn't up to her whether the mediation continued—either party could terminate the proceeding at a moment's notice—but Max couldn't quit. Not with her son's life hanging in the balance. She slowed her breathing and spoke above the sirens. "We're close, Amy.

Stephanie wants to make the deal. So does Perry." She groaned. "We just need a little more time for Dagger to come around."

"He won't budge, Max, and you know it. This case is going to trial."

Max shook her head and pushed herself off the bench. "Where's Stephanie?"

"Gone," Amy said. "She pulled out of the parking lot about two minutes before the bombs started going off. I was chatting with Chris Ledyard when the explosions happened. The force knocked me down on the bench . . . and I've been sitting here ever since."

"How do you know your car is undamaged?"

Amy snorted. "Because it's right there in the front. That dusty gray Honda Accord."

Max looked at it, and then down at the asphalt. She saw a police officer walking their way. *Here we go,* she thought.

"I bet we both have to give statements," Amy said.

"Yep," Max said, returning to her seat on the bench.

"Who do you think is behind this?"

Max thought of the sniper shots that had missed her and Perry. And the threatening texts she'd received. "I have no idea," she said.

"Well, Ringo, some things haven't changed," Amy said, her voice shaking a tad. *She's in shock,* Max thought. "Working with you has always been explosive."

Everything has changed, Max thought, but forced herself to play along. "Yep," she said again, squeezing Amy's shoulder as the police officer stopped in front of them.

51

Dagger Richardson was beside himself as he watched the news coverage of the bombing at the Beasley Rogers building. He was also drunk, having gotten into the bourbon just after noon. On his screen, firefighters were working to put out the blaze in the parking lot of the law firm. Then a reporter turned to the camera.

"We are live here at the Beasley Rogers building, and it appears that the damage has been contained. At approximately four fifty-seven p.m., five vehicles on this property exploded. According to eyewitnesses, the bombings happened about three to five seconds apart."

Dagger squinted at the screen. He saw his old friend and drinking buddy, J.R. Ford, talking to a police officer behind the reporter. J.R.'s face was red, and he looked pissed.

Dagger took a sip of bourbon and scanned his phone. He'd had no contact from General Zorn since this morning at the Blue Plate Cafe. *He said he had enough people to take out Perry . . .*

Had he succeeded? Was anyone else hurt? Dagger held his breath and called Stephanie.

"Hey." Her voice was tired and hoarse, but the sound of it sent a wave of relief through Dagger's body as he exhaled and then coughed.

"You OK?" he managed.

"I'm fine," she said. A dog was barking in the background. "Just got home. About to try to eat something and lie down for a while." When she didn't say anything about the bombing, Dagger decided not to mention it.

"Love you, honey."

"Love you too."

Dagger took another sip of bourbon and began to pace the downstairs floor of the farmhouse. He needed to think. He looked outside. There was probably an hour left of daylight. A ride might help him clear his thoughts, but he wasn't stable enough for that.

He plopped down on the couch and stared at the television. The news had moved on to something national, but Dagger was still thinking about the bombing.

He wanted to call the general, but he knew he couldn't risk it. *He'll reach out tonight. Micah is a man of his word.*

Still antsy, Dagger called J.R. Ford.

"Yeah," J.R. rasped, answering on the first ring.

"You all right? Just saw the news."

"Well, let's see. My car blew up, my law firm is a war zone of police cars, fire trucks, and news vehicles, and I had to cancel a deposition that's been rescheduled three times. How about you? Weren't you here for your daughter's mediation?"

"I was, but I left this morning. Couldn't stand it anymore. Is anyone hurt?"

"Not that I'm aware of, but several cars exploded, including mine. And a window was shot out with a high-powered rifle. Your son-in-law was almost hit."

Dagger felt his body tense, and his breathing slowed down. *Almost . . .* "Is he OK?"

"I think so," J.R. said. "Listen, I've got to go. The insurance company is buzzing me." The line clicked dead.

"Almost," Dagger whispered, again fighting the urge to call Zorn.

Dagger thought of his behavior earlier in the day. Losing his temper and attacking Perry. And the drinking. He ground his teeth together. *So stupid . . .*

Finally, he got up, poured out the bourbon, and started a pot of coffee.

He wanted to be sober when the police came calling.

52

While Amy Dance gave her eyewitness account of the bombing, Max walked inside the building and into the first floor restroom. Her heart was still beating fast, and she figured that she, like Amy, was suffering from shock. *A bombing in Huntsville, Alabama? An assassination attempt too?* "Good grief," Max whispered as she washed the soot off her face and hands, then went into a stall with her briefcase. After relieving herself, she undid the tape on her inner thigh and slipped the GLOCK into her briefcase under some documents and her legal pad. Then she smoothed out her skirt as best she could. After rewashing her hands and face at the sink, she assessed herself. Her blouse was still stained, but otherwise she looked and felt much better.

When she walked back outside, the officer was finishing up with Amy. As Max took the lawyer's seat on the bench, Amy got up and mouthed, "*I'll wait for you over here.*"

Surprised but grateful, Max nodded. Then, for the next ten minutes, Max answered the officer's questions.

There wasn't much to it. She hadn't seen the explosions, and she had no idea why anyone would target her or her vehicle for a terrorist act. She omitted the threatening texts she'd received from the random number, as she didn't want the police delving into her phone and seeing the other texts and calls from Perry. She couldn't take that chance. She also left out any mention of being shot at for the same reasons. Apparently, someone had seen the glass window shatter behind Perry, but with all the smoke from the explosions, the witness was not able to identify the woman standing next to him. Finally, she confirmed Amy's account that there had been a physical altercation between Dagger Richardson and Perry earlier that day and that Dagger had made threats toward Perry.

Max left her number for the officer to call if he had any further questions, and that was it. She asked about the truck, and the sergeant said that the crime scene technicians would be working with all the targeted vehicles for a few more hours and that he expected a wrecker would come and remove the remains. Someone in the department would call and tell her where it was taken.

"Thank you," Max said, as he turned and walked toward the Tundra. Max gazed at what remained of her father's truck and then down at the asphalt. *"You're my girl, and I'll always be proud of you . . ."* She squeezed her eyes closed, fighting the urge to cry. The Tundra had been a lifeline to her dad. She'd felt his presence inside the cab. Pulling for her. Urging her on. His scent lingering in the air as a reminder of who she once was . . . and could still be again.

Now, all she had left of him were the memories . . . *and his pistol.*

Max opened her eyes and gritted her teeth. She was about to look for Amy Dance when she felt her phone vibrating in her pocket.

She took it out, and the name of the caller sent a shiver of fear through her.

Caroline Parker.

The sight of Caroline's name on her screen used to be an almost-daily occurrence, but since Gainesville, it hadn't happened once.

Max let the phone ring four times before answering. "Hello."

There was a brief silence, then a throat clearing and a voice she hadn't heard in over a year. "Max?"

"Hey . . . Judge." She'd almost called her by her first name but then thought better of it. Once Caroline was elected to the bench, Max felt awkward calling her anything but "Judge" or "Your Honor" in public. Now, though, the awkwardness involved a lot more than titles.

"I heard about the bombing. Are you OK?"

"I'm fine. My truck . . . my dad's Tundra was one of the cars bombed, but I was inside the building." She paused, thinking of the police officer's questions. "After the bombings, someone tried to shoot Perry Strassburg."

"Was he—?"

"No. The shots missed and destroyed a window."

"Goodness gracious." There was a pause on the other end of the line. "Are the police still there?"

"Yes. They just interviewed me and Amy Dance. Amy's car wasn't hit, but she saw the whole thing."

"I can't believe it," Caroline said. "Odd that your truck was targeted. Is there any reason to think that the bombing is linked to the mediation?"

Max looked around the lot. She saw Amy Dance talking to Chris Ledyard, who was probably smoking his fourth pack of the day. "I don't know. The whole thing is crazy." She hesitated and then spat out what she was thinking. "Dagger Richardson has been a problem during the mediation. He attacked Perry earlier in the day, and I asked him to leave."

"You don't think Dagger—?"

"I don't know. I just can't think of anyone else with a motive, and it's obvious he hates Perry."

"But what would he have against you?"

Max sighed, tiring of the cross-examination. It reminded her of old times, but not in a good way. "I don't know, Caro—" She caught herself. "I don't know, Judge. He wasn't exactly thrilled that I was appointed to mediate the case."

For several seconds, neither woman spoke. Max felt uncomfortable, as if ants were on her.

"Is there anything I can do?" Caroline asked.

Max again looked at Amy Dance, who was now walking toward her. "As a matter of fact, there is."

"Name it."

"We need a place to continue the mediation tomorrow. I only had two days reserved here, and we're really close to a settlement."

"I see." She paused. "Max, can you hold on for a second?"

"Sure." Amy was now standing next to her.

"Who's that?" Amy whispered.

"Judge Parker," Max said. "I'm on hold."

Seconds later, Caroline was back on. "OK, I think I have an option for tomorrow. Judge Towry is out sick this week, so his courtroom on two is open. It's around the corner from me. You can put one party in the jury room, and the other can just be in the courtroom. Will that work?"

"Yes," Max said. Given what had just occurred, she was grateful to have an option that would require the parties to go through security.

"Is there anything else? Do you want me to intervene with Dagger? I don't mind entering an order prohibiting his attendance. I probably should, since he may be considered a suspect."

Max thought through the reality of this impossible situation. *Stephanie won't agree to anything without Dagger's approval.*

"Max?" Caroline pressed.

"No," Max said. "If you can help it, please don't do that. We need him present if the case is going to settle."

"All right then."

"Thank you, Your Honor."

"You're welcome," she said. "I feel bad, Max. I got you into this."

"You gave me an opportunity to mediate a challenging case, and I appreciate it very much."

"Regardless, I'm sorry about your dad's truck. I know he . . . and you . . . loved the Tundra. If you need anything else, don't hesitate to contact me."

Max closed her eyes. She missed her friend. "Thank you," Max said. "Can we start at ten a.m. tomorrow?"

"Of course," Caroline said. "I'll make sure everything is ready for you."

Before Max could express her gratitude again, Caroline ended the call.

"Well?" Amy asked. "What was that about?"

"We've got Judge Towry's courtroom tomorrow. Ten a.m. Are you up for a third day?"

"Yes, and I'm sure I can convince Stephanie to continue."

"Good. Let's check with Perry." Max clicked on his primary cell number and not the number he'd texted her on last night and this morning.

He answered on the third ring. "Do you have news?" he asked.

"I'm standing next to Amy Dance outside the Beasley Rogers building. Judge Parker just called, and she has offered Judge Towry's courtroom for us to continue the mediation in the morning. We'll start at ten. That work for you?" Max winked at Amy, but the gesture belied her nerves. Her heart was pounding. "We're so close, Perry. I think, and Amy agrees, that we ought to give it one more day."

Silence filled the air between them, and Max was almost at the point of panicking.

But after a few seconds that seemed like an eternity, Perry responded. "See you then."

53

Perry ended the call and gazed out the window of the Escalade. He'd asked his driver to travel up and down the parkway for a while. He needed to think, and he did that best on the move. He also wanted to know if he was being followed, and he asked the agent to be on the lookout for that too.

His plan had been to go to the farm once the mediation was over, hopefully with the good news that he was now 100 percent owner of the company. By the time he arrived, Hicks would have drugged the boy, but not too bad, and they could decide what to do with him. Perry's lean was to leave Nathan in a place where Max could pick him up. He would call her on the burner and give her the location, and that would be that. Hicks had a different take, believing it too risky to leave the boy alive.

But the bombing, the attempt on his life, and Dagger Richardson's stubborn stupidity had screwed his plans.

I could have Hicks take Dagger out.

He'd toyed with the idea of eliminating Dagger for several months, and he couldn't come up with a good way to do it that would leave him clean. Given the hostility between them, the sheriff's office would investigate Perry for any kind of professional-style hit, and, unlike with the Ringo kid, it was hard to think of a method to make Dagger's death appear to be an accident. There were ways . . . drugs that could be infused into the body to induce a heart attack or a stroke . . . but he'd been told that the CSI folks were now so good that it was almost impossible to make it look like an actual accident. And what if the bastard still pulled through?

We could make it look like a suicide . . .

Of all the possibilities, that was probably the best. Off Dagger like they'd done John Dutton on *Yellowstone*.

But Dagger had heavy video surveillance both at his home in town and at the farm in Toney. Getting in without being seen would be almost impossible. It wasn't worth the risk.

Perry rubbed his face and again went through in his head what he knew about the bombing and shooting, reaching the obvious conclusion.

I was targeted. The explosions were a diversion to get him outside, create chaos, and give the shooter a chance to kill him.

Except the bullets missed. *Was I lucky or is someone just trying to scare me?*

Perry rubbed his chin. The bombing smelled cold and calculating. Professional. Almost military in its precision.

The Syndicate, Perry thought. Dagger was also a possibility, but the old man didn't have the power he'd once wielded.

Perry glanced again in his rearview mirror but saw nothing suspicious. "Have you noticed anything?" he asked the driver.

"No, sir."

He looked at his phone and tried Tru again. On the third ring, he heard his son's voice.

"Hey, Dad."

Perry closed his eyes. "Where have you been?"

"I'm sorry. I went to Telluride for a few days to see some friends, and I left my phone in a bar. When I went back the next morning, it was gone. Anyway, I was able to get it replaced at no charge."

Perry shook his head at how classic the explanation was. "I was worried about you. So was your mom."

"Won't happen again."

"At least for the next few days, will you check in more often?" Perry asked.

"Sure," he said.

"And maybe when the first snow falls, I can come out there."

"Sounds great, Dad. Well . . ." This was the part where most kids would probably say *I love you*, or some dads would say it first.

"Take care, son." Perry ended the awkward silence. "Be sure to call your mom."

"I already have," he said.

Of course you have, Perry thought. A normal dad might feel sad or even guilty that he was an obvious and distant second behind Mom, but all Perry felt was relief. That was as good as it got for him. "Check in with me tomorrow, son." He thought about telling him to watch his back, but he knew that would just open up a can of worms that he didn't want to get into.

"Yes, sir. Bye."

Perry let out a deep breath and wiped sweat from his neck. "Take me to the apartment," he instructed the driver. Since filing for divorce from Stephanie, Perry had rented a two-bedroom penthouse unit at Belk Hudson Lofts downtown. On the way, he called Hicks and asked his security director to find a detail in Park City that could provide surveillance and security for Tru, at least for the next two weeks.

"And what about our boy here?" Hicks asked.

"We've got to keep him alive through tomorrow evening," Perry said. "The bombing today has delayed things."

"OK."

"Have you heard anything from your contacts in the sheriff's office about the attempt on my life?"

"No," Hicks said. "It's a bit of a shit show right now. Can't seem to get anyone on the phone."

"Keep trying," Perry said, ending the call. As the Escalade passed the Sea Salt oyster bar and Honest Coffee Roasters on Clinton Avenue, Perry tried Wick.

The call went straight to voicemail.

He sighed as the Escalade turned left onto Washington Street and, a few seconds later, pulled to a stop in front of the complex. The driver ran around the side of the SUV, opened the door, and ushered Perry inside. "Need anything else, sir?"

"Yeah," Perry said. He gave the agent the address of Wick's office and home. "Can you check them both out? Just a visual of the exteriors. Maybe ring the doorbell to the house if it looks like someone is there. Ask for Wick. Tell whoever answers that I've been trying to reach him on an urgent and time-sensitive business matter. If it's his wife, have her call me."

"Yes, sir," the driver said. Then he exited the building.

Perry decided to take the stairs. As he took them two at a time, he felt a burst of energy. Tru was OK. Perry hadn't been followed. He'd get the skinny on Wick from his driver.

As he entered the apartment, he started thinking forward. He'd still go to the farm tonight. Check in with Hicks. It would be good to get out of the chaos of downtown. Things were under c—

He stopped when he saw the man sitting in his den.

Andrew Wick's face was a purplish-red mess of bruises. Blood trickled down his chin. Duct tape covered his mouth, and his hands were tied behind his wrists.

"Oh my God," Perry whispered, taking a tentative step forward. "Wick?"

Wick's eyes glazed open. He was alive. Perry took another step into the room, and then his phone began to buzz in his pocket. He took it out and stared at the screen. The room felt colder and the hair on Perry's arms bristled with goose bumps. He blinked at the device to make sure he was reading the name correctly.

The caller was Andrew Wick. Perry scrutinized his friend's ruined face. Whoever had beaten him up must have taken his phone. Perry answered the call. "Who is this?"

"Mr. Strassburg." The voice was sharp and scratchy. "We were beginning to think you weren't coming home."

"Did you try to kill me?"

Perry saw Wick's eyebrows rise.

"I'll be asking the questions, Mr. Strassburg. Now . . . I want you to listen very carefully to what I'm about to tell you."

Perry exhaled a ragged breath. Then he did as he was told.

54

Amy Dance offered to drive Max to the hotel. She also asked if Max wanted to grab dinner, but Max said she wasn't hungry. She was still numb from the events of the day.

And dog tired.

Max opened the passenger side front door of the Honda and smiled when she saw the floorboard covered with files. *That looks familiar.* She moved them to the back seat, where there were more file jackets, a couple of legal pads, a gym bag, and some unopened mail. There were also a lot of empty Styrofoam coffee cups and water bottles.

"Sorry," Amy said. "My car is a moving trash can."

"Mine was the same way," Max said, though she'd done a better job with the Tundra than she had her previous cars. Of course, her responsibilities while driving the truck had been much less. "I remember the days of having a car full of files, kid stuff, and gym clothes."

"I wish I actually went to the gym. I can't remember the last time I made it to the Y. But having the bag in here makes me feel better."

Max chuckled as Amy maneuvered the car around the police and fire department vehicles and onto Clinton Avenue. She took a last look at what was left of the Tundra, still not quite believing that someone had planted a bomb in it.

"Where are you staying?" Amy asked.

"Courtyard by Marriott on University."

Amy tapped the steering wheel. "Didn't want to be in the hustle and bustle of downtown?"

"Too expensive," Max said. "And a little too close for comfort."

"What do you mean?"

"I don't know. It's been hard being back at the firm. Seeing old friends and colleagues from my prior life. The questions in their eyes. I couldn't avoid that for the mediation, but I wanted to stay somewhere I'd feel invisible." She sighed. "I guess that doesn't make much sense."

"I get it. I felt the same way after my divorce. My husband and I attended First Baptist Church with our kids. But when we split, I just couldn't go back there. Cy had grown up in that church, and I hadn't. The people were nice, and I knew they'd still accept me, but I could never pull the Band-Aid off."

"Where do you go now?"

"I don't," she said. "COVID wrecked everything for us. Our marriage fell apart with both of us home, and we lost the habit of going to church." She sighed. "We lost a lot of things."

"I can relate," Max said. "We survived COVID, but Thayer and I were pulling each other's hair out with us both home. Then after the accident . . . everything in my life went to shit."

"It's tough being a mother in our profession. It's just this revolving door of guilt. I need to be at work. I need to be at home." Amy sighed. "In a way, the divorce was good for me, because at least I don't have to feel guilty about being a poor wife anymore."

"I'm sure you were a good wife."

"No. I wasn't. I think switching to divorce work probably didn't help my marriage either. Seeing and hearing all the things that can go wrong on a daily basis is a recipe for paranoia."

"Why'd you switch?"

"I don't know. I was getting tired of the grind of PI work. The constant cold calls and initial meetings. Clients misrepresenting the facts and exaggerating their injuries. Don't get me wrong. Clients lying to you is a big part of domestic relations, too, but it hits different because the issues are more varied. At least they still are for me now. I'm sure I'll eventually burn out." She paused as she navigated the parkway off-ramp so that she could exit onto University Drive. "I was tired of car wrecks and especially done with med mal cases that were almost impossible to win and so expensive that even a victory didn't seem worth it."

"I can understand that," Max said, but her mind had drifted to Nathan. Were they feeding him? Was he still tied up? In withdrawal? *He has to be terrified . . .*

The adrenaline rush of dealing with the aftermath of the bombing had taken her mind off her son, but now that was all she could think about. *Will he survive another day? Is Perry lying to me? Is he going to kill Nathan anyway?* Max gritted her teeth as the questions tortured her mind.

"The thing is," Amy said. "Even after the damn explosions back there, did you see some of the lawyers? They were more worried about missed closings and depositions than they were about the fact that a terrorist act had just occurred."

"Ridiculous," Max said. "And sad."

"I just hope that's not me in thirty years."

"It won't be," Max said.

"You think?"

Max winked at her. "Amy, we fought like cats and dogs for almost a decade. In depositions, trials, hearings. You were probably my fiercest rival. And yet, you've been kind to me during this mediation."

"I was a bitch when it started."

Max chuckled. "OK, maybe, but . . ." She fumbled for the words.

"Go ahead, say it."

"You *are* a bitch!" Max screamed. "And so am I."

Amy laughed as she pulled her car to a stop under the covered breezeway of the hotel. Max grabbed her briefcase and hopped out. Then she knocked on the window. When it rolled down, she leaned on the sill. "Thank you again for the lift."

"Us bitches have to stick together," Amy said, holding out her fist, which Max nudged with her own.

Max took a step backward. Just as she was about to turn toward the entrance, Amy's voice stopped her.

"Hey, Ringo."

"What?"

Amy had cocked her head to the side, but her eyes blazed with intensity. "Is there anything else going on that you aren't telling me?"

Max squinted at her, feeling her heart rate speed up. "What do you mean?"

"I mean it's been a weird couple of days. I've been in a lot of mediations, and this one . . ."

"Has been crazy," Max agreed, but she knew Amy had more to say.

"It's just . . . I noticed you've been in there with Perry a good bit longer than us. Your eyes have been red a lot today, mascara running. You've seemed jittery at times . . . just not the Max Ringo I remember. I actually like this version better, but still . . ."

I don't have to explain myself, Max thought, staring at the ground as Amy trailed off. *Not under these or any other circumstances.* But when she looked up, she didn't see accusation in the lawyer's eyes. It was curiosity and concern. Max cleared her throat. "I was nervous for this mediation and haven't slept much the past few days. As for the extra time with Perry, it's been productive. He's not the one holding up a reasonable and fair settlement. Your client's fear of her father is."

Amy held up her hands. "Max, I'm sorry. I'm a lawyer and a bitch. What can I say?" She paused. "All that being said, I'm going to ask again. You're sure there's nothing else going on?"

Max put her hands on the windowsill. She leaned forward so that her face was only a few feet away from Amy's and looked her former foe dead in the eyes. "I'm sure," she said. "And tomorrow, we are going to settle this thing."

Max patted the side of the Honda and strode toward the entrance to the hotel. She thought she'd sold her lies as well as she could. But, as she passed through the electric sliding door, she glanced at her reflection and felt her stomach tighten.

Behind her, still parked in the drop-off zone, was Amy's Honda. The attorney hadn't moved and was still staring at her.

Not sold.

55

Perry stared at Wick across the dark living room. The call with the Syndicate operative had ended five minutes ago. Since then, neither Perry nor Wick had spoken. Finally, Perry broke the ice.

"I'm sorry."

Wick said nothing. The blood on his face had dried, but the bruises below his eyes were puffier. Perry started to tell him to go to the emergency room but stopped himself. Instead, he rose from the chair and stretched his arms overhead, feeling stiff. He'd sat for ten minutes while the woman on the phone gave her warning.

Perry went into the kitchen and grabbed a ziplock bag. He filled it with ice and gave it to Wick. "Here, you don't want your face to swell any more."

Wick glared at him but took the ice pack.

Perry started to pace a circle around the living area.

"You have to tell Dagger what's going on." Wick's voice was monotone. Numb sounding. "There's no other way."

Perry said nothing.

"If you don't, then I will." Wick's tone changed. From numb to defiant.

"That would be suicide for us both," Perry said. "Dagger is too volatile. Besides . . ." He trailed off.

"What?"

When Perry remained quiet, Wick stood on shaky legs and held up his index finger. "We are talking about $2.5 billion." He wiped blood from his cheek. "Not to mention *our lives*."

"Give me one more day, all right? If I don't have him and Stephanie out by early afternoon tomorrow, then I'll talk to him." Perry paused. "I sent him a text during the mediation suggesting that we make a deal. He'll come around. He knows he's out of options."

"Perry, are you listening to yourself?" Wick's exasperation was palpable. "I just got the hell beaten out of me. They broke into my office and then your apartment. We are in a desperate position, and you're acting like you've got the luxury of time. They warned us what would happen if we couldn't close this merger. The RFP on the missile receptors is rumored to be coming in the next thirty to sixty days. They prefer dealing with us, but they have other options, and they are not going to miss their window. If we can't get it done . . . you heard what she just said. *They will cover their tracks.* Perry, you know what that means? We are both dead men walking. Call Dagger *now*."

Perry was about to disagree when his phone buzzed in his pocket. He took it out. It was his driver. "Yeah?" he answered.

"Mr. Wick's residence was dark, and so was his office. Is there anything else you want me to check?"

Perry inspected Wick's beat-up face. "No, but I need you to come back to the apartment ASAP."

"Yes, sir."

Perry called Hicks next on his burner.

"Go ahead," the operative answered on the first ring.

"I arrived home this evening and found my banker, Andrew Wick, beaten to a pulp on my couch. Someone broke into my apartment and planted him here."

A pause as Hicks took it in. "Where was your driver?"

Perry grimaced. "Wasn't her fault. I dispatched her to do something. But she's going to need reinforcements. The Syndicate is getting antsy. Roughing up Wick is just the start."

"On the way."

"Hold for now," Perry said. "I'm coming out there. You can have them return with me."

"OK. Hey, boss, one more thing. We've lost contain on the mediator. We'd bugged her truck, but it hasn't moved since the—"

"Her truck was one of the vehicles that exploded."

Silence on the other end of the line.

"Hicks?"

Still no answer.

"Hicks?"

Finally, his chief of security grunted. "That's . . . weird. I was thinking whoever did this would've chosen random cars, but picking her vehicle doesn't seem as random."

"Could be a coincidence."

Hicks's silence let Perry know that he didn't necessarily agree.

"Were you able to reach any of your moles in the sheriff's department?" Perry asked.

"Yes, and they said the early reports are a clean job with the type of bomb and detonation device you'd see in a military operation. Definitely professional."

"And the rifle shots?"

"Nothing on that yet."

"What do you think, then?"

"Has to be either the Syndicate or Dagger. Both would have the means, motive, and opportunity. But . . ."

"But what?"

"Targeting Ringo's truck doesn't make sense. There were so many other cars in the lot. Could she have any enemies that might have done this? She was also standing next to you when the shots were fired." He hesitated. "It's possible that she might have been the target."

Perry rubbed his chin. "Could be. But who? And why?"

"I don't know, but I'd like to keep one of my team at the mediator's hotel. When the bug in her truck wasn't picking up anymore, I dispatched an agent there. Unless you instruct otherwise, I'd like him to stay."

"Why? Without access to a car, I doubt she'll be going too many places. Especially tonight."

"I agree. It's just . . ." Hicks's tone had a twang of curiosity in it.

"What?" Perry asked.

"I can't stop thinking about her truck. It's a puzzle piece that doesn't fit."

But Perry was thinking about his phone call with Max after the bombing. She'd sounded confident and had secured a courtroom for a third day of mediation.

Tomorrow, Perry thought. *Tomorrow is Judgment Day.*

For Max.

For Dagger and Stephanie.

For Andrew Wick.

Perry glanced at his bruised and battered friend, who was lying on the couch, applying the ice pack to his face.

Then he walked to the front door of the apartment and stared into the circular mirror on the far wall.

For me.

"Boss, is it OK for my agent to keep tabs on the mediator?" Hicks asked.

"That's fine."

56

The phone inside Max's hotel room was blinking when she stepped inside. She trudged across the worn carpet and sat on the king-size bed, sizing up the old telephone that still had a cord, an ancient relic from times gone by. She pushed the message button and heard an automated voice say that she needed to go to the front desk.

What now?

Before heading down, she took a shower. She was so tired, but the scalding water was revitalizing. Her swollen right wrist ached, but overall, she felt much better as she stepped out of the tub. She rubbed her left hand over the fogged-up mirror until she could see her reflection.

"I'm still here," she whispered. Then she changed into some joggers and a hoodie and headed downstairs. As she rode the elevator, her stomach growled, and she thought she might take an Uber down the road to Newk's or some other fast-food spot. When she reached the front desk, the clerk was reading a Georgina Cross paperback. Max hated to interrupt but cleared her throat.

"Can I help you?" the clerk asked, looking up from her bunny-eared copy of *Nanny Needed*.

"The phone in my room was blinking. I guess I have a message?"

"Room number?"

"It's 207."

The clerk reached under the desk and pulled out an envelope. On the front of it was Max's name in big, bold black letters.

MAX RINGO

There was no return address.

"Thank you," Max said, but the clerk's attention was already back on the novel.

Max walked into the sitting area in front of the bar and opened the envelope. The letter was handwritten and contained two sentences.

> Meet me at the dumpster behind the hotel if you want to see your son again.
>
> Tell no one.

Max felt her blood run cold. She thought about calling Perry and asking what he was up to, but that would violate the letter's instructions. Max closed her eyes. She was so tired, but the adrenaline was flowing again.

Max took the stairs back to her room. She stepped inside, hesitated for only a few seconds, and then went straight to her briefcase and pulled out the GLOCK 26, running her thumb over the initials, NEC. "It's a crazy world, Dad," she whispered. *Could things get any crazier?*

Max sighed and stuck the pistol in her pocket. "Let's find out."

57

The man assigned to Max Ringo was bored. He'd been at the hotel for over an hour and had seen Ringo be dropped off, and she had yet to exit the hotel. He'd backed his sedan into a space that was close to the dumpster in the rear of the parking lot. That gave him a good visual of the front door.

He was snacking on a bag of Doritos when the mediator came out the doors and began to head his way.

The man tensed. Since Ringo had no vehicle, why was she walking toward him? He started his car and was about to pull forward when he was startled by loud rapping on the driver's side window.

He turned and saw a man looking down at him. "Sir, can you please spare a few dollars?"

The agent waved his hand and shook his head at the beggar. "*No,*" he mouthed, still watching Ringo, who continued to walk a beeline straight for him.

"Shit," the agent whispered. He grabbed the gearshift to put the car in drive, but then his door opened. He scowled up at the homeless guy. "Damnit, I said—"

The butt end of a pistol came crashing down on his nose.

Max gripped tight to the gun in her pocket as she strode toward the dumpster in the back of the hotel. She could feel her heart pounding, and she was growing angrier by the step. She was tired of being a patsy and half hoped to see Perry Strassburg back here. Maybe it was time the prick saw the front end of a GLOCK 26. She heard rustling to her right and froze. A man was slamming the trunk shut on a sedan that had been backed into its space. Then he walked around the car and headed at an angle toward the dumpster.

Is that who I'm meeting? Max wondered, figuring it had to be. *Probably one of Perry's goons here to give me a warning.* She was fifteen feet away. Ten. Five. Max took the GLOCK out of her pocket.

"You won't need that." The gravelly voice cut through the air like a sharp-edged knife. "But I'm glad you were smart enough to bring it." The man lit a match near his face, and Max recognized the reptilian squint.

"Colonel?"

Satch Tonidandel stepped toward her. He wore a blue jean jacket, brown corduroy pants, and boots. His head was covered with a black cap. He held a pistol in his hand. "You aren't being followed anymore."

"How do you know?" Max stammered, still shocked to see him.

"Because I just put the guy tailing you into the trunk of his car. He's going to be taking a long—but not permanent—nap." He grinned. "And the bug on your truck was destroyed in the explosion."

Max opened her mouth and then closed it. "Was that—"

"Enjoy the fireworks?" Satch took a box of toothpicks out of his jacket pocket and slipped one into the side of his mouth.

"That was you?" Max's voice was wistful. Her legs felt shaky under her. "You blew up my dad's truck?"

"You're in a war, Max. We needed to buy some time. The truck was bugged. It was also old as shit. By making it a target, we ensured that no one would ever look at you as . . . being associated with the perpetrator. In fact, some might see you as the target. The rifle shots flew right over the heads of you and Strassburg."

Max was furious. "I tried all day long to reach you and heard nothing."

"I couldn't let you in on it," Satch said. "Also wanted to shake up this Strassburg prick. Since he didn't have a car on site, I went to plan B."

"And the other cars?"

"Random selection. I wanted it to feel like an act of terrorism."

Max crossed her arms. "Well, I think you succeeded."

"The building was close enough to the fire department that I knew there wouldn't be much chance of any collateral damage."

Max couldn't believe what she was hearing.

"Jason gave me updates throughout the day," Satch continued. "It sounded like you weren't going to be able to settle the case on the bastard's terms. So . . . I took action."

Max shook her head. "Good grief."

"You need to check out of here," Satch said. "Now."

"But—"

"Strassburg's security team will eventually come looking for their lost soldier. We have to go."

"Won't they blame me for that?"

"I know you're a skilled lawyer and mediator, Max, but how could you have gotten the jump on a security agent, knocked him out, and thrown him into the trunk of his own car? I suspect they'll think this was one of Strassburg's other enemies."

Max was still working through what Satch had done to the agent. "I'm glad you're here," she managed. "I guess."

"Listen, I've thought on it and I have some ideas. Are you hungry?" Satch asked.

"Yes."

The colonel pointed toward the front. "Good. Check out and I'll take you to the best Mexican joint in the free world."

Max couldn't help but crack a tiny smile. "Sounds wonderful."

58

Bandito Burrito was a hole-in-the-wall restaurant near the intersection of Governors Drive, Triana Boulevard, and Clinton Avenue. Parking was scarce, it was hard to get into, and the seating was limited.

But it was home to the famous green bean burrito, which might just be Max's favorite Mexican dish ever. She'd made a habit of eating at the establishment for lunch during her days at Beasley Rogers, because it was fast, close to the office, and consistently good. When the colonel put his blinker on as they approached her old haunt, Max clapped her approval.

The colonel turned his black Ford Raptor into the lot.

"Is this damn thing bulletproof?" she asked as they got out of the cab and she studied the truck. Nathan would have said it was "badass," and Max would have to agree.

"Yes, ma'am. It's a tank."

"Feels like it."

They ordered at the counter. Outside the window, Max saw the iconic sign saying that Bandito Burrito had been "serving up heartburn for forty years."

Five minutes later, she and the colonel sat in a booth with a basket of tortilla chips in front of them and two plastic containers of salsa. Both drank ice water out of Styrofoam cups. At 8:25 p.m., it was almost closing time, and they were the lone patrons.

"I'm sorry about your truck," Satch said. "I didn't realize it had been your father's."

Max popped a chip in her mouth. "If you had known that, would you have still—?"

"Yes," Satch said. "I hoped you could use the chaos as an excuse to postpone the mediation for a day." He took a sip of water. "Did it work?"

Max glared at him, not wanting to give him the satisfaction that his plan, crazy as it was, had, in fact, succeeded. "We are reconvening tomorrow morning at ten at the courthouse." She hesitated. "That was a hell of a gamble you took."

The colonel stared at the table. "I've had to make decisions like that my whole career, and I've learned to trust my instincts. You needed to shake things up. And you were also being followed both electronically with the bug and physically by an operative. We needed to flip the script and do it in a way that Strassburg wouldn't think you were behind it."

Max watched him as the waitress put their food in front of them. Satch Tonidandel was a strange man. What he'd done was reckless, dangerous, certifiably insane. And he scared Max with his perpetual squint and gravelly voice, but . . . there was also a rugged handsomeness to the colonel. And a warmth to his presence. He made her feel . . .

. . . safe.

Still, something was bothering her. "Listen, Colonel," she said. "I appreciate what you've done. I wish I could offer you some kind of compens—"

"Don't want money."

"Then why—?"

"Jason Rich is like family to me, and he cares about you. Jason had it bad when he got out of rehab. Didn't think he had much support among his fellow lawyers." Satch looked at his water. "I think you remind him a little of him."

"And what about you?"

"What about me?"

"Is Jason the only reason you got involved?"

Satch raised his head. "I'd do just about anything for Jason, but . . . no. I don't care much for bullies who think they're above playing by the rules. That's what this Strassburg bastard is." His voice grew lower. "He's playing God with people's lives. Ain't but one God, and he's not it."

"Amen," Max said. "And . . . thank you."

For the next few minutes, Max enjoyed her green bean burrito and thought about Dagger Richardson's financial struggles. *Why would Dagger want to hold up the deal? Why would he insist on Stephanie keeping her interest in the company?*

Max considered the mortgages on the real property. Dagger had already gotten loan money off his interest in the land and likely invested it in something else. *And the investment, whatever it was, is probably tanking . . .*

Still, though, Max didn't get it. Unless Dagger was planning to sell his and Stephanie's interest in the company, how would he be able to pay off the mortgages?

And what's the deal with Perry? Why does he need sole ownership of the company so bad that he kidnapped my son?

Finally, Max asked the question that had dogged her brain since her initial encounter with Perry Strassburg at the beginning of the mediation.

Why me? Why was I targeted?

"Penny for your thoughts?" Satch asked.

Max held her burrito in the air and gestured to Satch's plate, which was completely empty. He'd had three burritos to Max's one. "Good grief, you're already done?"

"In the army, we eat fast. Now tell me what you're thinking."

Max summarized her ideas to the colonel, who kept his reptilian squint aimed directly at her. It was almost unsettling how intense the man's gaze was.

Max concluded by asking what she'd been thinking a few moments earlier. "Why me? Perry Strassburg and Dagger Richardson could have had their pissing contest without involving me. I just don't get it."

The colonel sipped his water. "Been thinking on that, too, but . . ." He trailed off.

"What?"

"Nothing," Satch said. "You ready?" He stood and threw his water in the trash.

Max didn't have the energy to argue. She ate the last bite of her burrito, grabbed her water cup, and followed him out the door. "What now, then?" she asked, folding her arms. The night had gotten chilly.

"I reserved a room at the Embassy Suites downtown under my name. You need to get some sleep. I'm sure you're exhausted."

Max would never be able to rest until her son was safe, but she decided not to argue. "Then what?"

"I think the goal for you is the same."

"Settle the case," Max said, as they both climbed into the cab of the Raptor.

Satch turned the key, and the truck roared to life. "Affirmative."

"And you?" Max asked.

Satch studied her with his snakelike eyes. "I'm going to find your boy."

59

Nathan Ringo wasn't sure what day it was anymore. They'd taken him on Wednesday morning, but since then, he hadn't been outside, and there was no telling how many gummies they'd given him. Nathan had a healthy tolerance for THC, but he'd been high for so long that he was seeing things.

And despite being stoned out of his mind, he desperately needed a meth hit. His throat was so dry. Some of that was the gummies, but he figured a part of it was withdrawal too. He was also shaky and nauseated. Being bound with rope was driving him nuts.

He hadn't gone a day without methamphetamine for over a year. Since he'd stolen his mother's stash from the glove compartment of her car. By the time Nathan had snorted the last of that first baggie, he was hooked. His last fix had been Tuesday afternoon. He knew he couldn't go much longer. He was so thirsty.

Nathan tried to yell, but the only sound that came out was a muffled croak. The guard in the barn looked up from his phone, and Nathan raised his eyebrows and cried out again. It was maybe a little louder, but now he was out of breath.

The guard approached. "What's the word, kid?"

Nathan began to cough. He peered at the guard, who had a bored expression.

"What do you want?" the man asked.

"I-I-I'm a meth addict," Nathan said. "I can feel the w-w-withdrawals coming on. The shakes. Dry mouth. T-t-trouble breathing."

"Where do you expect us to get that?" the guard asked.

"P-p-please. If I don't have a hit, I could die. I'm not sure why I've been taken, but I doubt anyone wants me to die."

The guard frowned. "I'd be careful about making assumptions, kid."

Nathan struggled for breath. "Can I have some water too? Or anything to drink?"

"You're a demanding little bitch, aren't you?"

"Please. I've been here a long time, and I've barely had anything to eat or drink."

"Some of that's your own fault. You haven't eaten the food we've given you."

"That's because I haven't had my meth fix. My system's all out of whack. I usually take it after lunch right before play rehearsal. It gives me a boost. A pick-me-up. Without it . . . and with all the delta-9 y'all have been giving me, I feel like a zombie."

"I think that's probably the point."

Nathan swallowed. "I don't care about the gummies. I can be as stoned as you want me, but please let me have a meth fix. I can tell you where to get some."

The guard rubbed the back of his neck. "Let me go ask the boss. I wouldn't get my hopes up."

"Thank you."

Seconds later, Nathan was alone in the barn. There was a portable heater about ten feet away from him, but he was still a little cold. He was grateful to not have the rag in his mouth anymore. He breathed through his mouth quite a bit, and it had made him panicky to only be able to use his nose.

Please. Just one hit of meth. One snort of it to tide him over for a few hours.

He wondered what his mother was doing. Was she looking for him? Had she reported his absence to the police?

He gritted his teeth, trying to remember the way she'd been before the accident. *Badass . . .* He'd watched her once in court. In the seventh grade, his history class was studying some of the great legal battles of the twenty-first century. For extra credit, he'd shadowed his mother during a day of trial and then written a report on it. Her client had won, and she'd been awesome in the courtroom, but that was not what Nathan remembered most. There'd been an intense confrontation in the hallway between the lawyers, and one of the male attorneys on the other side had called her a bitch. She'd leaned toward him and held up her index finger, saying in a loud whisper, "That's the only thing you've gotten right this whole trial."

Badass, he thought again, wondering if he was losing his mind.

"I'm sorry, kid, but no can do on the meth." The guard was back, but Nathan could barely see him. His words sounded like they were being spoken through a paper bag.

Nathan swallowed, and his throat felt like sandpaper. The room began to spin. Before he passed out, the inevitability of his situation dawned on him.

I'm going to die.

60

Stephanie Strassburg woke up on the tile floor of her bathroom. Fredo was barking from somewhere in the house, and her phone was ringing next to her. The lights were on. She must have passed out hugging the porcelain god. She'd done that a few times in college and once after the Symphony Ball a couple of years ago. On those occasions, the culprit had been Southern Comfort.

She much preferred that poison to chemotherapy. She reached for the phone and pulled it to her, not wanting to lift her head yet. It was Perry.

Odd.

She couldn't remember the last time he'd called her on the phone. Even texts had been a rarity in the past few months, and, since filing for divorce, he had been radio silent. She let the phone ring until it cut off. The screen said she'd missed four calls.

Now she was curious. She lifted her head off the tile and leaned her back against the toilet. She blinked at the screen.

All four of the calls had been from Perry. She checked the top right of the phone. It was 8:38 p.m.

Kinda late . . . and he never calls anymore.

She'd started to call him back when the phone began to ring again.

The screen read "Perry."

"Hello," she answered, hearing the scratchiness in her voice.

"Steph, I'm sorry to call so late, but do you have a minute? We need to talk."

"No," she said. "I told you everything I wanted to say this afternoon."

"Please, honey. I'm in the driveway. I only need five minutes."

Stephanie felt a jolt of anger run through her that gave her some energy. "Are you kidding me? First, don't *ever* call me honey again. Second, my attorney has told me not to talk with you about anything dealing with our divorce."

"You didn't follow that advice today when you barged into my conference room. Come on. Five minutes. You don't even have to let me in."

Stephanie ended the call. When her phone started ringing again, she put it on silent and trudged into the bedroom. She wore pajama bottoms and a sweat-streaked T-shirt. She slipped on a robe and some house shoes and walked into the kitchen. She grabbed a bottled water and headed to the dining room, where Fredo was barking at the window, disturbed by the headlights coming from outside. Stephanie peeked through the blinds to the driveway and saw the black Escalade. As her cell began to vibrate in her robe pocket, she sighed and went into the kitchen. She found a rawhide for Fredo, and, after a few seconds' hesitation, the French bulldog took the bone and disappeared into the kitchen.

Then she shuffled back to the front door and unlocked it.

She stepped out on the porch and waved at him to come toward her. Seconds later, he hopped out of the passenger seat of the SUV and strode toward the home they both still co-owned, but which he hadn't set foot inside in over three months.

And the porch is as far as he gets today. I don't care how cold it is out here. And it was chilly, having dropped into the fifties after the sun went down. She sat in the swing and gestured toward the wicker chair adjacent to her. She felt like an old woman.

Meanwhile, Perry was still dressed in the suit he'd worn during the mediation. His hair was a tad disheveled, but he looked healthy and handsome.

And I resemble a clammy version of pure-grain dog shit.

"Hi," he said, taking his seat and spreading his legs as wide as they would go.

Stephanie fought the urge to kick him in the groin. "What do you want?" she asked.

He ignored the question and clasped his hands around his head, yawning. Stephanie remembered times early in their marriage when they'd gone on walks to Honest Coffee in the morning or Oshi Poke for sushi at night. The house was an easy stroll to downtown, and Stephanie enjoyed that time with him. Occasionally, after their walk, they'd sit on the porch, sipping coffee or wine and talking about the day or week ahead. Stephanie wondered if any of those moments were authentic or if Perry had just been using her the whole time. Or if he even knew the difference . . .

"Crazy day," he said. "I trust you got out of the parking lot before the bombings?"

Stephanie crossed her arms, trying not to shiver. She'd seen the coverage of the explosions on television when she'd gotten home and couldn't believe it. She'd called Amy, who'd filled her in on what happened. "I heard you were shot at."

Perry nodded. "Did you hire a hit man?"

"If I had, you'd be dead."

"And what about your father? Did Dagger try to take me out?"

"If *he* had, you'd definitely be dead." Stephanie shook her head. Any good feelings from her memories of past walks with him were gone. "What in the hell have you gotten into? This has to be about you, right? Bombings? Sniper fire? Dad is convinced you are up to something. What is it?"

Perry ignored the questions and sighed. "Stephanie, I want to be done. To settle our case and have it all be over."

"And I'm sure you're here to tell me what I have to do to make that happen. Sorry, asshole, but Dad's not budging. I can't get him to move, and I'm not sure I want to. Why should you end up with the company he founded?"

"Do you want him to end up broke?" Perry's voice was calm and matter of fact.

Stephanie cocked her head. "What?"

"You heard me."

"That's crazy, Perry. Dad—"

"Has mortgaged a lot of the land. He did it without our consent to finance an investment into cryptocurrency, and . . ." He snapped his fingers. "He got conned."

Stephanie stared at the brick floor of the porch.

"Look, Stephanie, like I told you this afternoon, I do care. About you and, believe it or not, Dagger too. I don't want either of you to get hurt. I hate it that you are sick, and I can tell you've had an awful night, and it breaks my heart."

"Go to hell," Stephanie said. "I don't believe a word that comes out of your mouth. All you care about, Perry, is *you*. What's best for *you*. And currently, that means trying to get control over Richardson Concepts. I'm sure if our land was sitting on an oil fortune, you'd prefer the property over the company. You're a narcissist and a chameleon and I want you to get off my property."

"*Our* property. At least for the time being." He stood and walked down the steps. He turned back to her and stuck his hands in his pockets. "You need to talk to him, Steph. The great Dagger Richardson can die a rich man, much wealthier than he was when he inherited the family dynasty. Or . . . he can blow up the whole thing and die a pauper. What legacy do you want him to have?"

Before she could answer, he started walking away.

Stephanie felt a surge of anger. "Don't you worry about my dad's legacy!" she yelled after him. "Dagger Richardson is Huntsville. *And you?* You're just a bloodsucking tick that's buried in his skin, and you need to be picked out and flushed down the toilet."

At the door to the SUV, Perry looked back at her. Stephanie was expecting some type of arrogant comeback, but he surprised her. "Have you told Dagger about the cancer?"

She fumbled for words, but none would come.

"He deserves to know, and . . . it might change his thinking."

Stephanie spoke through clenched teeth. "You must not know my dad very well."

"I think I do, Stephanie." He looked down at the ground and back up. "But if you won't tell him, I will."

"Don't you dare threaten me."

"I'll see you in the morning." He pointed his index finger at her. "Think about what I said." He moved the digit in a circle. "All of it." Then he climbed into the SUV.

As the vehicle backed out of the driveway, Stephanie extended her own finger. The middle one. But as she walked back into the house, she took out her phone.

And called her dad.

61

Dagger was talking to the police when he heard his phone vibrating in his pocket. He took it out, saw that the call was from Stephanie, and decided not to answer it. He peered at the two officers sitting across from him. "Look, I'm sorry not to be of more help, but I don't know anything about this bombing or shooting. Yes, I got mad at my son-in-law earlier today and we did get into an argument, but I'm not crazy. And even if I was a raving lunatic, I don't have access to explosive devices."

"Do you know anyone with that kind of access?"

Dagger scowled with exasperation at the detective. Monica Beech was a no-nonsense detective with straight black hair and fierce green eyes. During his years as county attorney, he'd gotten to know her pretty well and, a few times, had suggested that they could be more than coworkers. A proposition that Monica, happily married to a local dentist, always refused. Now in her fifties, Monica was still an attractive woman.

And smart as hell. It bothered Dagger that she'd been assigned the case. "For the love of God, Monica." He held out his arms. "I'm not a terrorist."

"You are a powerful man with powerful friends. You also have a strong motive."

"I had nothing to do with this. Now, unless you plan to arrest me, I'd like you to leave."

"Did you put your hands on Mr. Strassburg at any time during your argument with him?"

"I'll take the Fifth on that one, Detective. *Again.* If that sonofabitch wants to press charges, then arrest me. Otherwise, I'm tired and want to go to bed."

Monica peeked at her cohort, a man with a military haircut, at least ten years her junior. He shook his head.

"OK. That's all we have for now."

Dagger smirked. "Do you really think the DA is going to file assault charges against me?"

"Just doing our job," Monica said.

"Well, do it better. There's apparently a terrorist on the loose, and you're spending the county's tax dollars harassing a broken-down old man who couldn't possibly have done it."

Monica grinned. "I've never heard anybody in this town or county describe you as 'broken-down.' Quite the contrary, actually." She paused. "Here's my card."

Dagger ignored her outstretched hand. "I remember your number."

The detective's nostrils flared, but she didn't take the bait. She set the card on the coffee table in front of them. "We'll be in touch."

Once they were gone, Dagger collapsed into his rocker in front of the fire. He thought about calling Stephanie back, but he didn't want to hear about why he should approve Perry's last offer at mediation.

Dagger poured a trickle of Jack Daniel's into his coffee. Then he took a small sip, feeling the burn. He felt better. More himself. He'd handled the sheriff's deputies well, and the interaction had given him energy.

As had his call with General Zorn, which had come in an hour earlier from a burner phone.

They had a plan, and it was time to implement it. Dagger grabbed his cell and pulled up his last text from Perry. He sipped the whiskey-laced coffee and gritted his teeth. Then he thumbed his response.

I'm ready to make a deal.

After sending the message, he strode to the master bathroom and took an ice-cold shower, feeling his heart pounding in his chest. Relishing the pain of the cold as it shocked and then massaged his worn-out muscles. Afterward, feeling awake, alert, and focused, he dressed in a new suit, shirt, and tie. He grabbed his car keys and headed for the front door, stopping for a few seconds in his study and staring at the case filled with guns. He unlocked the mahogany cabinet and pulled out his SIG Sauer concealed carry nine-millimeter pistol. He stuck the weapon in his front pocket and let out a deep breath.

My final act, he thought, turning to leave.

He walked out on the porch and gazed at his family's land. A white glow glimmered over the crops of corn from the quarter moon above. He heard his phone ding with a new text. Dagger snatched the device out of his pocket and studied the screen.

Glad you came to your senses. Do you want to sign the documents in the morning at mediation?

Dagger's thumb was shaking but he managed to respond. No. I don't want my girl to see. Let's do it tonight.

When Perry replied with a thumbs-up emoji, Dagger couldn't help but grin.

Seconds later, he was in his car and pulling out onto Douglas Richardson Road. B.D. had insisted that the county name the damn road that abutted the farm after . . . who else? Himself.

But Dagger felt that the designation fit, as it was also his name. He sat up straight and gripped tight to the wheel.

My name.

My road.

My land.

My company.

Dagger Richardson took another deep breath and exhaled. He rolled the window down, and the chilly air was refreshing on his face.

"*My final act,*" he whispered under his breath, turning onto Highway 53.

Headed south toward Huntsville.

62

Satch Tonidandel was living on borrowed time. He'd made choices in his life that he couldn't take back. Choices that he'd felt at the time were the right call and, sometimes, the only call. Still . . . men had died because of his decisions.

My brother died because of me.

Satch couldn't shake the guilt. It was his constant companion. He saw the soldiers he'd sent into battle in his dreams. Mostly, though, especially since the end of the Sand Mountain war, he saw Mickey.

The mischievous grin, the smart-ass comments, the girlfriend he'd left behind. All those visions swirled in Satch's mind. For almost a decade after Afghanistan, Satch had lived with his brothers in their childhood home, nursing PTSD like it was a beer. For a while, he'd seen a doctor for it at the VA hospital, but it didn't do any good. He could've stayed in the army and been a lifer, but he didn't want to work at a desk and make decisions at ten thousand feet.

The field of battle was where he belonged. And until Jason Rich asked him for help in his conflict with the Sand Mountain meth ring, he'd been a ship without a compass.

For a few years, he'd felt alive again. Jason needed him and his set of skills. And he'd done the best he could. He couldn't fault the decisions he'd made. It was more in the execution that he'd failed his brother.

For the past five years, he'd been drifting. He and Jason were still close, and he loved him like a brother. Jason had moved on, and Satch was proud of him for that. Satch was also proud of his brother Chuck, who had put the past behind and was using his gifts to serve the Lord.

But Satch was still in the war. The battles were long over, but Satch refought them every day. Trying to come up with a scenario where Mickey didn't die.

I should have died too.

That was life, Satch knew. The good ones, like Mickey and their parents, died first. *And the ornery cusses like me have to bury them . . . and live on . . .*

. . . for what? Why?

Satch thought he'd found his why last night in front of the fire. He'd seen something in Max Ringo. Felt her desperation. She'd made mistakes too. And she was being bullied by a psychopath.

But was that really why he'd decided to lend his expertise? To be some kind of hero? Had he told her the complete truth?

No.

Satch liked Max and wanted to help her. And he loved Jason Rich. And, of course, he'd loved Chuck and Mickey and their parents.

But what Satch Tonidandel loved most . . . what he lived for . . . was something that most men ran from like scared kittens.

War, Satch thought, as he drove past the Beasley Rogers building, where the parking lot was still covered with police vehicles investigating the outcome of the decisions Satch had made just a few hours ago.

Satch had woken early this morning and driven down to the gun range he and his brother, Chuck, still operated in the Honeycomb area of Lake Guntersville. In a storage room in the back was where he'd found the explosives.

Sometimes, when a unit faced a larger and more formidable foe, the best defense was a good offense. Max was outnumbered and in a vulnerable position with her son being taken. But Satch was confident that Perry Strassburg wasn't counting on Max having a friend like him.

The bombing and rifle shots hadn't flipped the script, but they had given Max some breathing room. And Satch some time to develop the second part of his plan . . .

He pulled the Raptor to the curb a block from Strassburg's apartment. Satch had tailed Strassburg home from the Beasley Rogers building, and knew the bastard lived in the Belk Hudson Lofts. He'd staked the place out for a couple hours and managed to place a GPS device on the hubcap of the passenger side rear wheel of Strassburg's black Escalade. Since such time, the vehicle had made only a couple of short trips around town.

Satch rolled down his window and breathed in the cool October air. At almost 9:00 p.m. on a Thursday night, downtown Huntsville was dead. Satch heard music blaring from the Martin Bar & Bistro up the street, but there were few people on the sidewalks. The radio continued to report on the bombing a few hours earlier, and Satch assumed that folks had decided to stay home tonight. He took out his binoculars and saw the Escalade parked out in front of the complex with Strassburg's driver standing guard outside it.

For the next thirty minutes, Satch sat behind the wheel and waited. He knew it was a long shot that Strassburg might go to wherever Nathan Ringo was being held tonight. But he also figured that following the bastard was his best chance to find the boy. *He'll want to check on his investment,* Satch thought, trusting his instincts. *Especially after the events of the past few hours . . .*

If the colonel had to guess, Nathan was being held at a warehouse in town . . . or a farm in the county. In either scenario, there would likely be a ton more security there than Perry had with him now.

Reflexively, Satch glanced behind him and thought about the arsenal he had in the covered bed of the truck. An oversize duffel bag contained five hand grenades, two pistols, and an old but trusty M249 SAW machine gun, a relic from his army days. Next to the bag, in their respective covers, were a sawed-off twelve-gauge shotgun and the sniper rifle he'd used a few hours ago to send shots over Strassburg's and Max's heads. If and when the battle came, he'd be ready.

Satch returned his attention to the driver, who was now on the move. The colonel felt a flutter of excitement as the guard held the front door of the apartment complex open and Perry Strassburg strode out and hopped into the passenger seat of the Escalade. Seconds later, the SUV was heading west on Clinton Avenue. Satch put the Raptor in gear and followed from a safe distance behind.

Adrenaline began to tingle in his veins.

63

As the light from a quarter moon fell over the farm in New Market, Hicks lit a cigarette. He was growing tired of this assignment. They'd had the boy for more than thirty-six hours now and would likely have to hold him for at least twenty-four more and possibly the weekend.

Hick hated surprises, and the extra time was not part of the plan.

Neither was the bombing . . . or the attempt on Perry's life.

Hicks inhaled and blew a smoke cloud into the air. The incident at the Beasley Rogers building bothered him for obvious reasons.

My fault, Hicks thought. It didn't matter that he'd had an agent monitoring the building. In fact, that made it worse.

Perry Strassburg was Hicks's responsibility. *My detail.* And someone had been able to infiltrate their perimeter and somehow detonate five bombs while setting up in a position to take two sniper shots. Hicks knew the police were likely reviewing security footage right now, trying to get some angle on who did it. But most of the time, even with good surveillance cameras, you couldn't capture everything. Based on the reconnaissance that Hicks's operatives had already done, he doubted that the footage would show much. And even if it did reveal the culprit, what would that give them? Likely a shadowy figure and nothing more. The bombs were probably planted under the backs of the cars and could have been attached in less than a minute by a person skilled with explosives.

But who?

Hicks took another drag on the cigarette as he saw the Escalade pulling into the driveway off Winchester Road. The only illumination over the fields of cotton was the approaching headlights and the moon above.

The mediator's involvement was the one fact that didn't add up. If either the Syndicate or Dagger was trying to make a statement, then why was Max Ringo's truck blown up? Hicks didn't believe in coincidences. The mediator's white Toyota Tundra exploding seemed to be one. So did her presence next to Perry when the shots were fired. Or, at least, they had until the phone call he'd received just a few moments ago.

As the Escalade pulled to a stop in the driveway, Hicks dropped the cigarette and stomped it out. Then he walked toward the SUV. He beat Perry's driver to the door and opened it for him.

"I have some disturbing news," Hicks said, forgoing any greeting.

"Take me to the kid first," Perry said, striding past him without looking, a man on a mission.

"Yes, sir," Hicks said, following him toward the barn. Two minutes later, they were staring at Nathan Ringo's pale, sweaty face. The boy's neck was jerking, his legs shaking. His eyes were shut tight, and he appeared to be humming.

"What's wrong with him?" Perry snapped.

"He's been begging for meth. He looks like he's in pretty bad withdrawal."

"Good grief," Perry said, rubbing the back of his neck. "What should we do?"

"Nothing," Hicks said. "A death caused by withdrawal from illegal drugs is about as good as an overdose. Right?"

Perry studied Nathan. "I guess. Not as easy to control. I'd prefer an OD, but . . . I see and agree with your point."

"When do you want to dispose of him?"

Perry began to walk out of the barn and Hicks hustled to keep up with him. "Let's hold off until morning. With what happened to Wick tonight and the bombing . . ." Perry sighed.

"We have to get rid of him," Hicks said, completing the thought. "There's no way around it."

"Let's wait until morning and talk then," Perry said, moving toward the house.

"Are you staying the night?"

"No. Just for an hour. I have a meeting later tonight in town, and I'll be at the apartment afterward. I'll call you at first light."

Hicks cocked his head. "*A meeting?* Boss, after what's already happened today—"

"I have no choice," Perry said.

"How many agents will you need?"

"Just my driver and maybe two guards in another car to follow." Perry trotted up the steps to the porch but came to an abrupt stop. He turned toward Hicks. "You said you had disturbing news."

Hicks squinted up at Perry. "The operative assigned to the mediator went off the grid a couple hours ago. I had to dispatch someone to find him."

Perry blinked his eyes, confused. "Did they . . . ?"

Hicks nodded. "In the trunk of his car."

"Jesus Christ. Dead?"

"No. He had a bruise on his forehead. Apparently, while he was watching Ringo, a man started knocking on his door. The man had a beard and raggedy clothes. Assuming he was homeless, my agent rolled down the window and got clocked."

Perry rubbed his chin. "What do you think?"

Hicks took out another cigarette from his pocket but didn't light it. "Could be the Syndicate or Dagger staking out my team. Trying to weaken our forces. I don't know, but one thing is for sure. Because of the bombing and my agent being attacked at the hotel, we don't have any clue where the mediator is or what she's doing."

"So what? I wasn't even sold on having her followed. I chose Max to be the mediator for a reason. She's brilliant, but she's also broken and alone, and she has burned all her bridges in Huntsville and, as far as I know, everywhere else. She's my bitch, and if we can't find her, that probably means that she's working like hell trying to settle this case."

Hicks lit the cancer stick and pressed it to his lips, taking a long drag. "OK."

"You don't believe me."

"It's not adding up," Hicks said. "Her truck being targeted and now this. Doesn't smell like the Syndicate or Dagger to me."

"What does it smell like?"

He squinted at his boss. "Like maybe the mediator has a friend out there."

64

MoonPie John's Mercantile was an old-fashioned general store off Walker Lane in New Market, Alabama. Along with offering every kind of moon pie and moon pie accessory a person could hope to find, the store had a hell of a good café.

But at 10:35 p.m., the store was long since closed. Satch Tonidandel pulled into a parking spot to the side of the building and checked the GPS app on his phone.

Still at the farm, the colonel thought, eyeing the screen. Then he scrolled through his contacts, found the name he wanted, and fired off a quick text.

Need you to check out a property for me. Satch typed out the address for the farm on Winchester Road, which was about six and a half miles from MoonPie John's. Then he opened the door to the Raptor and stepped outside. The air was at least five degrees cooler than it had been an hour ago in downtown Huntsville, and it felt even chillier than that. He lowered the tailgate on the Raptor. He sat down and gazed up at the sky.

Satch had driven by the farm twice in the last half hour and seen no markings that made the property stand out. Just a gate and a gravel driveway leading somewhere that couldn't be seen from the highway.

Which made it perfect for hiding the Ringo kid. It was twenty minutes outside town. Discreet. And Satch guessed that the ownership would have no direct connection to Perry Strassburg.

The colonel couldn't call for backup. At least not yet. Too much risk for the kid. Satch figured that Max was being played. That Strassburg had no intention of letting Nathan off that farm alive.

He hoped he was wrong.

But I'm not . . .

Satch took out a wadded-up pack of Big League Chew from his pocket and put a chaw in his mouth, savoring the bubble gum taste he'd loved since he was a kid and the instant shot of sugar. Then he sent Max a quick text.

Do you know anyone who owns property off Winchester Road in New Market?

He sent the message and focused on the GPS app, which showed Perry Strassburg's Escalade on the move.

Satch wouldn't be following the SOB back into town.

The boy is at the farm.

Satch peered up at the stars, thinking of his brothers but glad they weren't here with him.

He'd never put his family in danger again.

As for himself . . . he'd blown up five cars earlier today, but hell, that was just showing off. At some point in the next few hours, he'd launch a full-scale attack.

He didn't know his enemy's forces yet, and there was no way to be sure what Strassburg had until Satch infiltrated the farm. Once he did that, there'd be no going back.

Until then, he'd gather as much information and reconnaissance as he could.

The person he'd texted about the property ownership would come through. He always did. And Max was a resourceful woman. A lot stronger than she thought she was. Satch figured she'd provide something that would help too. But at the end of the day . . .

This is a solo mission.

Satch grinned and squinted up at the quarter moon above.

I wouldn't have it any other way.

65

Max stared at the bedside alarm clock. It was 10:42 p.m., and she had been pacing the floor of the hotel room for the past hour. Unable to sleep. Wired on the events of the day and what might lie ahead.

The colonel's text sent a wave of adrenaline and hope through her. *Winchester Road? New Market? Is that where Nathan is?*

She wanted to be with Satch. She needed to do something. Anything that might be helpful.

She forced herself to concentrate on what she could control. *Do my job,* she thought, remembering Jason Rich's advice. There was one monstrous roadblock between her and a settlement on Perry Strassburg's terms.

Dagger . . .

She grabbed her phone, knowing there was one final move to play with the old man. She brought up the number Amy had given her for Dagger and clicked it. When he didn't answer, she left a voice message for him to call her. Undeterred, she decided to send a text.

Under different circumstances, she might have tried to be subtle, but she didn't have time for that now.

> Dagger, this is Max Ringo. Please call me. Stephanie is keeping something very important from you that could affect the mediation. She's sick, Dagger. Very sick. Please call.

She pressed send and began to pace again.

Less than a minute later, her phone began to ring. She answered, and before she could say anything, Dagger asked, "What do you mean? Sick?"

"I don't want to do this over the phone. What's your address? I'll meet you—"

"I'm in town. I have a late meeting. What hotel are you staying in?"

Max almost said "Embassy Suites," but she could sense the colonel protesting in her thoughts. "The AC downtown." A very short walk from Embassy Suites.

"All right. Meet you in the bar in ten minutes?"

"Yes, sir," Max said, closing her eyes and saying a silent prayer of thanks. "See you there."

Fifteen minutes later, they were sitting under a couple of portable heaters on the outside patio of the AC Hotel. The spot had a beautiful view of Big Spring Park, and Max was struck by the peacefulness of the picture. Moonlight glistened over the pond and illuminated the red Japanese bridge. To the right was the white-columned Huntsville Museum of Art. Ducks were waddling along the water's edge, and a young couple was holding hands as they hustled past on the sidewalk.

The scene could be a postcard.

Max studied the old man sitting across from her. She'd just told Dagger Richardson that his only daughter had terminal cancer. At first, Dagger had protested, saying that couldn't be true. Now, though, she saw resignation on his pale face and in his bloodshot eyes.

"I'm sorry," Max said. "I just . . . thought you should know. This whole mediation rides on your approval of the settlement. I think . . . *I know* . . . I've come up with a proposal that Perry and Stephanie are both agreeable with. But Stephanie insists on having your blessing."

Dagger stared at the pond. He wore a charcoal pinstripe suit, a white shirt, and a red tie. He looked ready to try a lawsuit in court or preside over a board meeting.

Or attend a funeral . . .

Max stood and placed a tentative hand on his shoulder. "If you're going to be the ultimate decision-maker, you need to have all the facts." She hesitated and lowered her voice to just above a whisper. "This isn't about you, Dagger. Or Perry. Or the company. This is about Stephanie."

Dagger Richardson put his face in his hands. "All I'm trying to do is what's best for her."

Max leaned forward and whispered into his ear. "Then do it."

66

Dagger ordered a shot of Jack Daniel's from the bar after Max left the patio. Then a second one. And, finally, a third. He paid and stumbled out into the night.

Numb. Both in body and in soul.

He had another meeting to attend. Perhaps the most important one of his long life. *My final act,* he thought and then spat on the sidewalk.

As if any of it mattered anymore. He trudged toward a park bench and found that he was struggling to breathe. He sat down and punched the palm of his left hand with his right fist and then pointed his index finger at the sky. *"First Judy and now Stephanie."* He spat again and glared at the moon. *"Fuck you! Do you hear me, you sanctimonious bastard? Fuck . . . you."*

Dagger pushed himself off the bench, anger and hate pulsing through his veins. He needed to get to his next meeting. Again, he scowled at the sky.

I'm not going to quit.

Dagger gritted his teeth and continued to walk through the park. Past the museum of art, where Stephanie and Perry's wedding reception had occurred over a decade ago. That had been such a fun night. Their union had held such promise.

Dagger strode on, glancing at Pane e Vino, his favorite Italian restaurant, and then crossing Church Street and walking toward the Big Spring. Hearing the soft hum of the waterfall mix with the murmurs of passing cars above. He trudged up the steps leading from the spring to the west side of the courthouse square, feeling every bit of his seventy-seven years. By the time he reached the top, he was out of breath and nauseated. Still, he forced his legs to move.

"*One more meeting,*" Dagger said, moving his gaze around the square and feeling the cold steel of the SIG Sauer in his pocket.

"My final act."

67

Catacomb 435 was Huntsville's premier speakeasy bar. To receive entry to this hidden gem on Jefferson Street, you had to push the bell button on a red fire call box on the front of a building between two retail stores. A person would be given access if he or she knew the password, which was provided by the bar when someone made a reservation. Then the patron would enter the building through two nondescript glass doors, walk down a windy staircase, and enter an unmarked door . . .

. . . and step right into the 1920s. The quaint room smelled of smoke from the bourbon concoctions the bartenders would conjure up. There were a few round tables and chairs, a couple of couches, and a small bar with four stools. Because it was underground, there were pipes that ran along the ceiling and several places where the wall was simply brick. A '50s-era television set hung on one wall, playing *Ozzie and Harriet* reruns with no sound. Underneath the ancient relic was a gold throne that could seat two people. There were a couple of almost-hidden tables tucked in the right and left corners of the room.

Perry saw his quarry planted in one of those now. He peeked at his watch. Dagger had said to meet him here at eleven thirty, and Perry was a few minutes late.

Perry felt his stomach lurch as he took a tentative step forward. All his plans would likely depend on the outcome of the next few minutes.

"Fall guy," Perry said as he grinned at the other man from across the room. "Cool password. Is that what I am tonight?"

General Micah Winfield Zorn pointed his pistol at Perry, who took another step forward.

"What, no bartenders?" Perry asked. "The best thing about this place is the cocktails."

"I had Sheila make you one," Zorn said, gesturing for Perry to take a seat in front of an untouched drink. "It's my favorite . . . and she's my favorite."

"Don't mind if I do," Perry said, grabbing the glass and taking a short pull from it. He didn't sit. "Smooth," he said. "Sweet at first and then the bourbon grabs you. So . . . are you going to kill me?"

Zorn kept the gun pointed at Perry as he crossed his legs. "I'll say this for you, Strassburg. You've got brass balls. I could shoot you right now, have you taken out with the trash, and dispose of the body, and no one would ever know what happened to the great Perry Strassburg."

"You could," Perry said. "I'm a dead man walking . . . if you value your friendship with Dagger Richardson over $100 million."

"Why are you doing this?" Zorn asked.

"Because, as I've been telling you for weeks, my partners in the Syndicate think it would be incredibly valuable to have you as a silent partner." Perry watched the other man, aware of the dangerous game he had played to get to this point. The pistol remained pointed at his chest. "With your connections in and out of the army, your contributions to the newly merged company would be invaluable, particularly in obtaining government approval of the HSR report. It's a perfect fit financially . . . and for the other reasons the Syndicate wants this deal."

"And if I don't join you? If I blow your brains out right here, run your body through a meat grinder, and feed the scraps to my dogs, then where are we?"

"Then you've passed on generational wealth because of some stupid loyalty to a man we both know would cut you from neck to nuts if it benefited him."

"You're asking me to commit high treason against my country. And to betray my oldest and best friend." The general kept his voice neutral.

"Oh, please. You've been double dealing on your *oldest and best friend* for weeks. Telling him one thing, playing along with his ridiculous scheme to take me out, lying to him about having me watched, all the while getting the complete skinny on what I'm doing . . . and who I'm doing it with." Perry paused. "General, men like you, Dagger, and I don't have friends. We have partners. We have business colleagues. We have people we use for sex. But we don't have friends." Perry took the seat across from Zorn. "As for the country . . . the Syndicate is coming whether you or I join them or not. They have too many operatives here, and they are persistent as hell. Wouldn't you rather have some control over what they're doing . . . and what they see?"

Zorn took a sip of his drink, saying nothing.

"I'm offering you the far superior deal, General," Perry pressed. "If you're like me, you already have trouble sleeping at night because of the choices you've made." He paused. "Might as well be uber rich."

Zorn blinked but kept the gun steady. "A hundred and fifty million," he said.

Perry grinned. "Changing the terms of the deal at the last minute to squeeze me?" He bowed his head. "One thirty-five."

Zorn leered at Perry for several seconds, continuing to train the gun on Perry's face.

"Don't be a fool," Perry said. "If you kill me, Dagger is going to do this same deal with the Syndicate."

The general blinked.

"You know I'm right," Perry said, sipping from his own drink. "How else is he going to pay off his loans?" Perry paced a couple of steps to his left, as if he might be giving a closing argument in front of a jury. Then he grinned at Zorn. "To reach my level, General, you have to understand the other man's game. This is Dagger's opus. He'll have you take me out, and then he'll cut his own deal with the Syndicate."

Perry smiled at the barrel of the GLOCK. "But, unlike me, your old buddy has no plans to cut you in."

Zorn held Perry's glare. "You're good," he said.

"I'm right," Perry corrected. "And you know it."

For several seconds, the room was silent. Finally, the general set the pistol down and extended his hand. "One thirty-five it is."

Perry grinned and shook the other man's hand. "I think this is the beginning of a beautiful friendship," he said.

"I thought you didn't believe in friends."

As the clock behind them struck midnight, Perry Strassburg winked and took a sip of his bourbon. "I don't."

DAY THREE

68

At 2:00 a.m. on Friday, the lights to the Voodoo Lounge popped on, and Dagger Richardson blinked to adjust to the brightness.

He was supposed to meet General Zorn here an hour and a half ago, but Zorn never showed. Nor had his old friend called or even texted.

Dagger had been ghosted, as he'd heard his granddaughters call it. But it was more than that. Dagger was old and stubborn, but he wasn't stupid.

I've been played.

He took out his phone and stared at the one text he had received. It was from Stephanie, just after midnight. She wanted to meet early this morning. Had something she needed to tell him. Dagger grimaced. Max Ringo had given him a sneak preview of what was likely coming, but he still dreaded hearing his daughter confirm the worst. But he'd been too tired to argue or protest. His reply instructed her to meet him at the farm at six thirty, and they could watch the sunrise together.

Dagger put up the phone and wiped his eyes, which were wet and tired. Then he gazed around the basement bar, which he'd spent many a Friday afternoon telling war stories in, and then up at the bartender. Earl Little was wiping a glass with a paper towel.

"I called you an Uber," Earl said. "The driver's outside waiting in a red Chevy Malibu."

Dagger smirked. "Only the best for me, huh, Earl?"

The bartender cracked a grin. "You know it."

Earl and his younger brother, Vance, were longtime friends and clients of Dagger's, and their father, Buck, a retired circuit judge, was a regular drinking buddy of Dagger's. Zorn and Dagger had spent many an evening tying one on here, and that was why the bar was the perfect cover. After Zorn took out Perry at Catacomb 435, the general and Dagger were supposed to meet here to go over damage control and next steps. Zorn had said he'd paid off a waitress at Catacomb 435 to be ready to swear that she saw Perry leave the speakeasy alone at just past twelve thirty—the same time that Earl could say Zorn and Dagger were at the Voodoo, tossing back longnecks. Given the assassination attempt on Perry earlier in the day and his rumored involvement with the Syndicate, there were a lot of potential suspects who couldn't be accounted for, and Dagger and Zorn would have a concrete alibi. It was a good plan, and it would've worked. Alas . . .

I was played.

"You OK, boss?" Earl asked.

"I'm not drunk, if that's what you mean. I haven't had anything but Sprite since I got here."

"I know . . . and that's not what I mean."

"Then why'd you arrange a ride for me?"

"Because I've known you a long time, and I've never seen you sit at the bar alone and drink nothing but soda. Your mind seems a million miles away, and it's really late. Figured you could use a lift."

"Well, thank you. Actually, my car is a nice hike from here." Dagger eased himself off the stool. "You're a good friend, Earl. Give Vance my regards and tell your daddy that we need to get together soon." Dagger started to walk toward the staircase.

"Is something wrong, sir?" The concern in Earl's voice was evident, and Dagger didn't have the energy to lie.

"Yeah, son." But before Earl Little could respond, Dagger was halfway up the steps.

Something is very wrong.

69

Max was in the front seat of a car. It was a BMW 5 Series. Tan interior. Familiar, both to the eye and to the nose. His hands were in her clothes, up under her skirt, probing her panties, slowly pulling them off. She wanted to scream, but she didn't. She felt his rough face on her cheek. The whiskers of his five-o'clock shadow digging into her neck. Then his mouth and teeth on the same spots. His breath wasn't awful, but it wasn't pleasant either. Coffee covered up by mouthwash.

She felt like she was watching it happen. As if she were outside the car, cocking her head at this awful sight. They were parked at the overlook on Cecil Ashburn. Not exactly the stealthiest place for this transaction, but Max didn't care. That was the thing. *She did not care.* She was out of oxycodone, and getting more was the only thing that mattered. She felt her blouse being pulled off, and now his whiskers were on her breasts. She was so numb her nipples didn't even harden. She watched him undo his belt and slide down his khakis, felt herself being pulled toward him, and then her face was in his lap.

She felt and then saw him stiffen. She did what was expected, and he asked her to look at him while she did it. He kept saying things. Telling her how good it felt. How sexy she was. But she heard nothing. Felt nothing.

She did not care.

Then she saw headlights flashing bright into the car. And the man's expression changed from greedy satisfaction to fear as he gaped out the windshield. He'd put his hands out in front of him, as if he were being held at gunpoint. Max raised her head. Saw what he saw.

Then she started to scream . . .

Max was pulling at her hair and yelling at the top of her lungs. She rolled over and off the bed, still stuck in the car from her dream. The recurring nightmare. Hearing the voice from outside the vehicle. The anguished cry. Max hadn't felt anything then, but she did now.

She felt it all.

She held her knees, which were shaking. Then she stood from the hard floor on stiff legs and appraised herself in the bathroom mirror. She looked like death warmed over. Hair a rat's nest. Face pale as that of the priest in *Poltergeist II*. She was wearing a faded blue Journey T-shirt with a hole near the belly button and Iron Man pajama pants that were actually a hand-me-down from Nathan. She'd taken them to rehab so she had something to remind her of him. They made her feel wholesome, but they looked ridiculous. *What time is it?* she wondered, peering at the clock on the nightstand.

4:59 a.m.

She'd slept all of five hours.

Sighing, Max made a cup of coffee in the hotel room Keurig and checked her phone. She'd sent a preemptive text to Thayer last night, saying she'd had a great time with Nathan and that he was ready for school in the morning. In response, she'd gotten a thumbs-up. The only other message she'd received was from the colonel, and it chilled her to the bone. It was a location pin followed by these instructions: Going in here. I'll have your boy before the sun rises. If you don't hear from me by seven am tomorrow, call Jason. He'll know what to do. Left the Raptor behind an abandoned barn a quarter mile west from this pin. Keys are in the floorboard.

He'd sent the text just after midnight.

Now, at 5:02 a.m., only a few hours from the start of the third and final day of mediation, Max knew she couldn't sit here and wait.

After ordering an Uber ride, she took a quick shower and dressed in her only casual outfit. Jeans, a beige blouse, and boots. Then she slipped on her jacket and grabbed her briefcase. Before leaving the hotel room, she took her father's GLOCK 26 pistol out of the bottom drawer of the bedside table and stuck it in her jacket pocket.

She rode the elevator down to the lobby and then walked out the exit doors to where her car was waiting.

They were sixteen miles and twenty-three minutes away. It was 5:17 a.m. If she knew the colonel, and she thought she did even though they'd barely met, he'd be declaring war on a farm in New Market in the very near future.

If he hasn't already.

70

They were holding the boy in the barn.

That much was obvious to Satch. For the past four hours, there'd been two guards at the entry to it, and one man who came in and out a few times. The colonel had seen at least three other guards at one point or another. So there were a minimum of six armed agents watching the barn, the house, and its perimeter.

Which I'm just on the edge of.

Satch was hidden in a nestle of trees approximately three hundred yards away. He'd been camped out here for most of the night, and what he'd seen so far wasn't terribly encouraging. *Six guards . . .*

And there could be more. Strassburg had a small army out here. He wondered if there was anything else in play at this farm other than the boy.

Satch figured that this property was likely Strassburg's headquarters when he needed to be stealthy. Or when he was plotting something that involved criminal activity.

Or both, Satch thought.

The colonel had spent the early morning doing reconnaissance, and there were few openings. He'd been able to strap an explosive on a tractor about eighty yards from the barn, but he couldn't get close enough to any of the other vehicles without being seen. Would that be enough of a diversion? He had the grenades, and they would help, but he'd hoped to set at least three devices similar to what he'd used on the law firm building.

One will have to be enough, he thought, knowing it might not be. Satch wasn't a bullshitter, and he damned sure wasn't going to bullshit himself.

He could get inside the barn and probably find the kid.

But getting out?

Shit, he thought, watching the house. He could kill at least one of the guards with his rifle. Then push the detonator on the bomb on the tractor. That would be two diversions. Still . . . what if he missed? And if he didn't miss, how could he escape with Nathan Ringo and not get both of them killed?

He suspected Nathan would be weak if not passed out, which meant Satch would have to carry him, and then he'd have to steal one of the SUVs and take it at least as far as his Raptor. It would be impossible for him and the kid to escape by foot.

Satch could think of only one way he could accomplish his objective, and it was the Rambo solution. He gnawed the toothpick down to where there was nothing left and spat the remains on the ground.

I'll just kill them all first.

The only problem with that plan, other than the slim chance it would work, was the possibility, however faint, that Nathan Ringo wasn't here. That Satch was wrong.

The colonel brought his phone up under his jacket so the light from the screen wouldn't show. It was 5:59 a.m. The sun would rise in a little over thirty minutes.

As a leader, Satch Tonidandel was decisive. He wasn't right every time, and he and his soldiers didn't always execute perfectly. But he never doubted his plan.

And he wouldn't be starting now.

He scanned the perimeter and made his decision. He'd detonate the explosive on the tractor. Then he'd run in the opposite direction around the flank of the barn.

And kill anyone that gets in my way.

"Time to unleash hell," he whispered, moving into the open.

71

"I think we need to kill the boy," Hicks said, his voice sharp on the other end of the line. "Hell, he's almost dead already."

Perry rubbed the sleep out of his eyes and gazed at his phone. It was 6:05 a.m.

"What do you mean?"

"I mean the withdrawals are much worse now. Foaming at the mouth. He's knocked over his chair a couple of times and almost choked to death. It won't be long. Killing him now would be like putting a dog out of its misery." He paused. "Only problem is I'm not sure we can use drugs anymore. He may not be able to snort the meth."

"What will you do, then?"

"Not much choice. We'll have to shoot him."

"No. Force-feed the fentanyl to him if you have to, but you can't execute him. My plan doesn't work if he's shot. He has to die from an overdose, or like we discussed last night, death related to withdrawal would be acceptable. Then you can drive the body to someplace where drug deals are cut or perhaps way out in the woods if he dies from withdrawal, and the police will draw the obvious conclusion. That was always the—"

A huge boom sounded from the other end of the line.

"Hicks?" Perry asked.

No response, but there was a rustling as if his chief operative was moving.

"Hicks!"

"We've got a problem, b—"

But his words were cut off by another loud crash.

Good grief, Perry thought, feeling adrenaline pulse through his body. He began to pace the floor of his bedroom.

"Hicks!"

"Jesus Christ," Hicks hissed in a loud whisper.

Then the line went dead.

Perry held the phone out from him. He started to dial the agent back but thought better of it.

What the hell just happened?

He strode into the kitchen and poured himself a glass of ice water. Had General Zorn double-crossed him?

Or was it the Syndicate? He scanned the den, where Andrew Wick had been sitting, his face ruined, the previous evening.

Are they making another statement?

"Damnit," Perry whispered, taking a long sip of water. The Syndicate operative had told him they'd give him until the end of today. Why in the world would they attack the farm? But if not them or Zorn, who?

Perry gritted his teeth and then shook his head twice. *Control what you can control,* he told himself.

He had Zorn on board. Dagger had to be nearing the end of his rope. The case would settle today, and he'd have majority control of Richardson Concepts.

He walked back to the bathroom and turned on the shower. *Hicks will call in a few minutes,* he thought. *He'll call and there will be some damage. Just like there was yesterday. This has to be another warning from the Syndicate that time is of the essence.*

He stepped under the hot water, looking at his phone on the counter. "Hicks will call," Perry said out loud, forcing his tone to remain calm.

But for the first time in as long as he could remember, Perry Strassburg was scared.

72

The explosion almost caused Max to fall. She'd been leaning against the fence, trying to figure out what to do. On the Uber ride out there, they'd passed the abandoned barn, and Max had seen the outline of the Raptor behind it. Then, about a quarter mile later, they'd come to the pinned location, which was nothing more than a grassy spot off Winchester Road that abutted a fence. She'd thanked the driver and assured him that she was fine. That her family was thinking of buying this property and that she was meeting the owner out here early for a sunrise tour. That seemed to satisfy his mild curiosity, and seconds later, she was alone.

All she could see on both sides of the highway was farmland.

For about twenty minutes, Max thought about what she could do. She'd brought her GLOCK, and she could climb through the opening in the fence that the colonel must have created.

Then what?

It was not like she was a soldier or even a trained marksman. She had gone to the range a few times with her dad, but she wasn't a great shot, and it had been years since she'd fired the pistol.

Besides, even if she was a good shot and did have some military training, where the hell would she go? It was pitch dark, and this farm had to be well over two hundred acres.

Stupid, Max thought, cursing the impulse that had brought her here at this ungodly hour but then shaking it off.

She might not be a soldier or a marksman, but she was a mother.

And my son is in there.

She decided to wait for a sign. If the colonel had entered here, the odds were he'd come out here too. But, after almost a half hour, she was getting antsy.

Just before the force of the explosion almost knocked her to the ground, she'd been about to say *fuck it* and go through the fence anyway.

Now, as her heart pounded in her chest, she saw smoke plumes rising over the farm where the blast must have occurred. *My son is in there.*

Max took a step forward, and then it dawned on her that, because of the smoke, she knew exactly where to go.

She couldn't shoot a gun worth a crap, and she wasn't a soldier.

But there's one thing I know how to do pretty damn well. Max took two steps backward.

Then she turned . . . and started to run.

73

Satch Tonidandel felt like he was back in Afghanistan. He hadn't been in any type of combat since the end of the Sand Mountain war five years ago, and, as rough as that business was, it paled in comparison to this. There, he'd had his brothers.

Here, he was all alone. One versus at least six and maybe more.

Bring it, he thought, tossing another grenade in the direction of the tractor, which had exploded thirty seconds earlier. He ran around the side of the barn, thinking as he moved. That was how it always had been for Satch in war. When others were losing their minds, unable to process the information that was coming at them at Mach 1, Satch was at his absolute best. The world slowed down.

He saw the field.

Four agents had run toward the tractor. That left two guards, and Satch bet at least one was in the barn. He slid through a side door to the structure and was immediately hit with the sour smell of puke.

He's here, Satch thought, moving his back along a wall through a hallway before he reached an opening. He saw no one, but he still removed the sawed-off shotgun from inside his jacket and held his pistol in the other hand. Crouched but moving, Satch edged past several horse stalls before he came to a shut door, which must be an office of some sort.

He opened it fast and turned to his left as gunfire erupted from a semiautomatic weapon. When it stopped, Satch held his ground.

He wore his night vision goggles and sensed movement. The guard in the room was getting closer. He peeked at the opening and saw in his peripheral vision a boot. Satch fired at the foot with his pistol and heard a scream and then a crash and more gunfire. When it stopped, he heard another yelp, and he stepped into the opening and noticed the soldier on the ground.

Satch fired his sawed-off shotgun without hesitation, and the man's head splintered into a canoe as he fell to the ground dead.

Satch darted his eyes around the room, which reeked of vomit. The boy had been here, but he wasn't now. He turned and heard a sound coming from one of the stalls. He crouched, moving as fast as he could while flashing his eyes in every direction.

As he reached the third stall after the office, he saw a chair toppled to the side and a boy with his cheek hugging the hay.

"Nathan?" Satch asked, stepping into the area, gagging on the smell of vomit and seeing a puddle of it on the ground by the boy's head.

Satch knelt and took out a knife, cutting the rope that bound the kid's hands. Satch shook his shoulders, and foam oozed from Nathan Ringo's lips and down his neck. The boy's eyes rolled up into their sockets.

"Nathan!" Satch hissed into the kid's ear in a loud whisper. The boy's pupils adjusted, but Satch knew that Nathan was not only in shock but also in severe withdrawal from methamphetamine.

"Can you walk?" Satch asked.

Nathan blinked his eyes and then sank to his knees, vomiting. Satch looked behind him. He heard sounds from outside. Voices. Getting closer. The farm, which was a good two miles from the nearest property, was far enough into the country and off Winchester Road that he doubted any police would be notified of the gunfire or the tractor explosion.

Satch stuck the shotgun and pistol back into his jacket and undid the strap carrying his M249. He laid the automatic rifle against the side of the stall and draped the boy over his shoulder. Then he snatched the machine gun and headed toward the side door where he'd entered.

There were screams and shouts from outside and they were getting closer. Coming toward the barn.

Bring it, Satch thought again, dropping to one knee and easing Nathan to the ground. He placed him a few feet away and then returned to his position, one knee on the ground, rifle at his shoulder, with a clear view of the front entrance. "This is going to jar the hell out of your ears, boy, but there's no way around it."

As the agents came running into the barn, Satch waited until the last possible moment, counting their number. One. Two. Three.

That would have to be good enough.

"What the hell is going on?" one of them asked. "Renfroe?! Are you in here?!"

Renfroe's in hell, Satch thought as he tapped the trigger, knowing they couldn't see him in his crouched position in the dark barn.

As one of the operatives reached for the light switch, another one screamed for him to stop. *Security guards,* Satch thought. *Not soldiers.*

The lights flicked on and then off, and a fourth operative entered the barn. When he did, Satch Tonidandel pulled the trigger on the machine gun.

And the inside of the barn lit up like the Fourth of July.

74

Hicks's first instinct was that the Syndicate operatives who had attacked Andrew Wick yesterday and who likely were behind the bombing and shooting at Beasley Rogers were making another statement. But as gunfire erupted in the barn, he knew that was wrong. *The Syndicate agents meant to scare. Not kill.*

This was something different entirely.

Hicks thought back to the incident at the law office yesterday, which had never added up.

Now, as the shooting stopped, Hicks had no idea what or who they were dealing with as he scoped the perimeter of the barn, using hand signals to communicate with his remaining men. There were four in there and another three out here, including him. That made seven total operatives.

Against who? Hicks thought. *Or what?*

More gunfire to the side of the barn. Coming from the outside. *Shit,* Hicks thought. He'd sent the team inside to snuff things out and keep the enemy contained.

So much for that. Hicks moved to the opposite side of the barn, walking backward, his assault rifle pointed in the direction of the last shots.

Then static blared from the handheld walkie-talkie attached to his waist. "Sir, I'm shot. We didn't see wh-wh-where it was co—" And then the patter of gunfire blared through the receiver.

Hicks turned to the house, where there was an agent, and then behind him to the flames of the tractor. Another operative was over there. *We're dropping like flies . . .*

"What in the hell is—?"

He cut off when he saw the man circling the other end of the barn, machine gun at his hip, firing at will. Hicks dove for cover as bullets whizzed past him. He rolled and returned fire. Then he heard footsteps and gunfire from behind him.

Hicks gasped for breath and struggled to his feet.

"He went back in the barn!" the agent behind him yelled. Another of his team came around the same side of the structure as Hicks was on. Eyes wide. "We've got four confirmed dead in there, sir."

"Is it just one man?" Hicks couldn't believe it.

"Yes, sir. He caught them coming in the front entrance after the explosion, and it was easy pickings."

"All right. He's contained now." Hicks blinked his eyes and made his decision in an instant. "Light it," he ordered.

"What, sir?" one of them asked.

"*Light the barn,*" Hicks barked.

—

Satch scrambled for his breath. *There's just too many of them.* He pulled Nathan near him and peeked out the window above the front door. He didn't see anyone, but he knew that was on purpose. *They want me to come out . . .*

Satch glanced at the floor. The kid was fading fast, barely conscious. The colonel had just a base knowledge regarding drug reactions and withdrawal, but it was obvious that Nathan needed immediate medical attention.

Damnit, Satch thought. He figured their remaining numbers were around three to five. *They'll box me in. And then they'll attack.*

Satch could hide the boy and then himself and pick them off one by one. But charging into the barn wasn't the best strategy for Strassburg's team. The better play, if they didn't care about the building . . .

He had the thought as soon as he heard the crash of flares through the side windows.

. . . is to light it.

Satch saw the fire moving across the walls of the barn like a bright-orange snake. *Jesus, God.* The barn began to fill with smoke. He peeked back out the window. He could break it and start shooting, but that would be futile.

"Give it up, motherfucker." A voice from the outside. Deep and firm. Commanding.

Satch said nothing, peeking through the glass. He could see one agent. He figured each of the side doors was being guarded and they'd lit the roof. Then he glanced down at Nathan. Foam was coming out of the boy's mouth again.

If I attack and die, they'll pull him out. They won't kill him until after the mediation.

Satch ground his teeth, thinking of Mickey. Then Chuck and Jason. He had at least a hundred rounds left on the M249's belt, and he planned to use them all.

It's tough being brothers.

Then he burst out the doors of the barn.

—

Hicks could barely believe his eyes as the man came barreling out of the barn's entrance. He had a beard and wore a dark cap, but there were no other discerning features other than his size, which was mammoth.

"Fire!" Hicks screamed, rolling to the ground as the man continued to press forward, shooting at will, as he went around the side of the barn.

"*Damnit,*" Hicks hissed. "Kill the SOB."

"He's hit," a voice said over his handheld.

"Is he dead?" Hicks asked, glancing at the barn, which was engulfed in flames. Thinking of the kid. His men. *How in the hell do we cover all this up?* He moved toward the entrance to the barn, but then his feet were lit up with bullets and he dove to his left. *Not dead.*

"All right, let's close in," Hicks said. "He's trapped and he knows it."

"Yes, sir. Flanking from the west."

"East," another voice said.

"I'll cover you," Hicks said. Then he blared out his order. "GO!"

As the men moved toward their target, Hicks caught a flash of something out of the corner of his eye. He glanced, and his stomach clenched. *Headlights.*

"Someone's coming," Hicks said. "Abort and hold your position."

Hicks watched the road, then realized that this vehicle wasn't on the road. It was coming right down the damn cotton field.

"Sir, do you see—!"

"Yes, damnit!" The knot in Hicks's abdomen tightened. He felt paralyzed.

"Sir, that car's not slowing down!"

Hicks took a step closer as the headlights drew nearer. *Mother of God,* he thought.

That was no car.

Satch was hit. The bulletproof vest had stopped the shots to his chest and abdomen, but his right hip had taken a couple slugs. He leaned against the side of the barn, but he couldn't stay here long. The smoke from the fire was growing, making it harder to breathe.

This is the end, he thought. *If I don't kill them all . . . or sacrifice myself, Nathan is going to burn up in that fire.* Satch touched his hip and looked at his fingers.

Blood. He was running on adrenaline. He knew the pain would kick in soon, but now he felt nothing. He leaned forward and peered around the edge of the barn. There was an operative with a machine gun pointed in his direction, but the agent wasn't focused on Satch but instead staring out at the farm.

Satch peered in that direction, too, blinking to make sure he wasn't dreaming.

"I'll be damned," he whispered.

It was the Raptor. And he didn't have to guess who was behind the wheel.

Satch coughed as the smoke from the barn infiltrated his lungs. He watched the Raptor's approach. Three hundred yards. Two hundred. At a hundred yards, the truck began to take machine-gun fire from Strassburg's team.

But she kept coming, just as Satch knew she would. He heard screams and more machine-gun patter. And, above them, the roar of the Raptor. When the truck was approximately fifty yards away, Satch let out a deep breath and stepped around the edge of the barn. He saw three agents pointing their weapons at the runaway pickup. Satch reached into his jacket for his pistol. Then, he strode toward them, firing the GLOCK in his left hand and emptying the belt on the M249 with his right.

"Hoo-rah!" he screamed.

75

Max didn't flinch when the bullets crackled against the windshield of the Raptor like hail. *Nothing's getting in here,* she thought, adrenaline and anger raging through her body. Truth was, she could barely hear the gunfire.

In addition to being bulletproof, the truck had a hell of a stereo system, and she had "Lunatic Fringe" blaring full blast from the playlist on her phone.

The whole world had gotten very simple.

These bastards had her son, and she was going to get him back if she had to kill every last one of them. As she got closer to the light, she saw two sets of flames. A smaller patch to the left that looked like a piece of machinery, maybe a tractor. And then, straight ahead, a barn.

Please don't be in there, she thought, gritting her teeth and seeing fire and smoke billowing out of the roof of the barn. She saw the men shooting at her. Two to the left of the building and one dead center. And then she noticed them turning, pointing their guns away from her. The one in the center went down, and Max saw the reason why.

A man was coming around the right edge of the barn, firing with what looked to be two guns. *The colonel . . .*

Max's heart leaped, but she kept her wits. She turned the truck hard to the left toward the two agents returning the colonel's fire.

They scattered in either direction as the Raptor closed in, but they'd underestimated her speed. Max pushed the pedal to the floor and ran up behind one of the agents and then over him. She turned the wheel sharp to the left and sprayed grass and dirt and spun around. She saw the man she'd hit, and he was on his stomach and not moving. *Where did Satch go?* she thought, circling the barn. When she saw him, she felt it like a punch to the stomach.

He was lying on his back. A man was standing over him holding some type of machine gun. Max screamed and again floored the Raptor, and the man was trapped. The barn was to his right, so he had to move left. When he did, he wasn't fast enough. Max screamed as the Raptor ran over the agent and trampled him.

She again spun the truck in a circle and drove back toward Satch, cutting the music and hopping out of the truck with the engine running.

"Colonel! Are you all right?"

Satch was holding his right leg. "Nathan's in the barn. Front door."

Max took out her GLOCK and ran. Her heart was in her mouth, but she felt like a superhero. She passed the bodies of a man and woman on the ground, who both looked dead. Then she stepped through the open doors of the barn.

When Max saw her son, she let out an audible sob. Nathan was on his knees, coughing. Behind him was a wall of fire and smoke that was closing in.

Max knelt by her son and grabbed him by his shoulders, lifting him to his feet. He opened his green eyes.

"Mom?"

"It's me," Max said, ruffling his sweaty hair. "Can you walk?"

He fell into her and his legs gave way. There was her answer. She stuck her gun in the front of her pants, bent her knees, and picked Nathan up around his legs and waist as if she were carrying him like a princess. She used to pick him up like this when he was a baby and spin him around until they both were dizzy.

The heat was now on her face, and her eyes were burning. Smoke filled her lungs, and she coughed, but she was able to back out of the barn. But when she turned, a man was blocking her path holding some kind of pistol. Max recognized him. It was the operative she'd seen on the surveillance video at Sleazy's. The man in black who'd followed her son out of the convenience store. Who'd kidnapped Nathan and brought him here. Max glared at the man. Hate burned in her chest.

The man took a walkie-talkie out of his jacket and spoke into it while continuing to point his gun at Max. "This is Hicks. Anyone copy?" But there was only static in response. He took a step forward, visibly limping. "Ms. Ringo?" he asked.

"That's right," Max said. She started to place Nathan on the grass, but Hicks's voice stopped her.

"No. You just hold on to him. I want you to bring him in the house."

"He's too big," Max lied. She could have carried him to Huntsville if she needed to.

"I think you'll manage," Hicks said.

"Cops will be here soon."

The man laughed. "Out here? You must not have spent much time in New Market. I'll have this cleaned up by—"

His voice was cut off by the sound of a blast. Hicks fell to the ground, writhing in pain. His kneecap was hanging off his leg, destroyed. Max turned toward the sound, setting Nathan down and covering him.

The colonel was limping toward them, holding a sawed-off shotgun with both hands.

Hicks rose to his knees, pointing his gun at Satch.

Max didn't even think. She pulled the GLOCK out of her waistband and fired.

Her bullet hit his chest just as Satch's connected with his throat, and he toppled over. Dead.

Max dropped the gun and gazed around the farm, which was lit by the fire from the barn and the flames from the nearby tractor. She counted three dead bodies.

"Oh my God."

"There are four more in the barn," Satch said. "Come on. Nathan's in bad shape. He needs medical attention as soon as possible."

Max snapped back into it, looking at Satch's blood-streaked leg. "So do you," she said, running to her son and picking him up just as she had before. She carried him to the truck and put him in the back seat while Satch crawled through after him.

Max jumped into the driver's side and grabbed the wheel of the still-running Raptor. As she floored the accelerator, she heard retching from the back. She turned and saw foam coming out of Nathan's mouth, and his eyes had rolled back in his head.

"Hang on, son."

Max sped down the driveway and turned right onto Winchester Road. As she did, she turned her playlist back on. In the rearview mirror, she could see a faint plume of smoke in the sky, but the farmhouse was too far off the highway to observe anything else. Then she moved her gaze from Nathan to Satch. "Colonel?"

He didn't answer.

"Colonel!"

"I'm here," he said, but his voice was weak. "What in God's name is this music?"

A hysterical laugh escaped Max's mouth, followed by a sob and a cough. She tasted the smoke in her lungs. Her son was close to an overdose and possibly suffering from smoke inhalation, and the colonel had been shot multiple times in the leg.

Don't die, Max thought as she entered Huntsville Hospital into the GPS and focused on the road ahead.

Don't you dare fucking die.

76

They met at the family cemetery on the south end of the farm. The sun was rising a brilliant orange over the rows of cotton to the east.

Dagger was already there when Stephanie arrived.

A gravel road ran through the property, and Stephanie parked her Range Rover to the side of it. Her father's horse, Saban, was tied to a fence post behind the grave markers.

Stephanie got out of the SUV, feeling stronger than she had in a long time. After an awful night, the morning hadn't been terrible so far. Perhaps it was Perry's surprise visit to the house that had fired her up, but she felt motivated for the first time in a while.

She knew what she had to do. In truth, she'd known for a while.

When she reached her father, she followed his gaze downward to the headstone that marked her mother's final resting place.

JUDY PRICE RICHARDSON. 1.6.1945–2.5.2023

Her dad had wanted to meet here, which seemed appropriate for the conversation that they were about to have. *Does he know?* Dagger was a smart, intuitive man, but she didn't think he had any idea.

Unless someone's told him . . . Stephanie thought back to her conversation with Perry last night. "*If you don't tell him, I will,*" he'd threatened.

"You already know, don't you?" Stephanie asked.

Dagger kept his head bowed. He grabbed Stephanie's hand, his grip strong. But also desperate. The way someone holds you when they're afraid of losing you.

"Cancer," Dagger said.

"Yes," Stephanie said. "Who told you?"

"Doesn't matter. What kind is it?"

"Uterine that's metastasized. Same as Mom."

"Did the doctors give you a . . ." He trailed off, and Stephanie's heart ached. They might have their differences, but she loved her dad, and she knew that he loved her.

"No. Could be three months. Might be two years. You know the drill."

"They don't have a clue," Dagger said. "Have you been doing treatment?"

"Chemo and radiation." She began to walk around the small cemetery that housed the last remains of every Richardson since after the Civil War. "But it hasn't worked to stop the spread yet. Only made me sick as a dog."

Dagger grimaced. "I'm assuming the girls don't know yet."

"No, they don't. And I'd rather them not until the very end. I'm sure you understand."

He turned away from the grave and rubbed the back of his neck. "What can I do, sweetie? I'll . . ." His voice shook with emotion. "I'll do anything you want."

"Let me settle with Perry for the deal that was on the table yesterday."

"Honey—"

"This isn't a game to me, Dad. I want it over. Today. Then I want you to pay off the mortgages we owe, and we'll be out of this crisis."

Dagger stared hard at her. "You know about those?"

"Perry told me yesterday."

"That sonofabitch."

"He is and then some. But I believe him when he says he doesn't want to see us in foreclosure. That would be so unnecessary." Stephanie fought to not say the word "stupid." She would not disrespect her father. Even now, even sick, that was a line she wouldn't cross.

"Honey, I wish you would stay out of it. I'm actually working on something, and . . ." He trailed off, and his shoulders slumped. "I know what I'm doing."

Again, Stephanie fought with her words, not wanting to hurt him but needing to emphasize that enough was enough. She approached him and took both of his hands in her own. She rose on her tiptoes and kissed his cheek. "Then do it," she whispered.

Dagger stayed in the cemetery until the sun had fully risen. It wasn't much over forty degrees, and his bones were as cold as his heart. He tried to spit on the ground, but his throat was too dry and nothing came out. He wiped his mouth and squatted in front of his dead wife's grave. He kissed his hand and touched the stone, running his fingers over the engraved letters. "It's not fair," he whispered. "For you to be here . . . for Stephanie to be about to join you . . . and for me . . ." He rose to his feet.

Dagger put his hand in his pocket and felt the cold steel of the pistol. He was still wearing the suit he'd put on last night. After he'd driven home from the Voodoo Lounge, he'd sat in front of the fire the rest of the night. Tired but unable to sleep.

Weak . . . but not done yet.

Yes, he knew what he had to do. He wouldn't be burying Stephanie. He couldn't endure that kind of pain. Nor was he going to leave her and his granddaughters in financial ruin.

Dagger again felt inside his pocket for the SIG Sauer handgun. Then he strode toward his horse and climbed into the saddle, taking one last look at Judy's grave and all the other Richardson headstones.

His family's legacy would be changed forever today.

He'd give Stephanie what she wanted. He'd actually be giving her a bit more than that. Just in a different . . . more *volatile* manner.

I know what I'm doing, Dagger thought as he kicked the side of the horse and it jumped forward. As he pulled on the reins, he heard his daughter's voice in his mind, echoing what Max Ringo had told him last night.

Then do it.

77

Max paced the lobby of the emergency room waiting area of Huntsville Hospital. It was hard to believe she'd been here a day and a half ago for her right wrist. She looked at her hand, which was still a tad swollen. Either it was healing or she'd forgotten about the pain.

Her son and the colonel had both been taken to the back. When they'd arrived, Satch had told her to go inside with Nathan and that he would park the truck. "Just tell them that he'd been missing for a couple of days and you found him in this condition near a campfire on Monte Sano. Be sparse on the details."

"What are you going to say?"

"That I own a shooting range and had an accident with an assault rifle being dropped and the trigger getting jammed." Despite the obvious pain he was in, Satch managed a wink. "I was the only casualty."

"Colonel?"

"How can we afford to tell the truth, Max? There are seven dead bodies out at that farm, and no witnesses to the boy being kidnapped. It's still your word against Strassburg's."

"But I've got you. You're my witness."

"I'm a crazy ex-soldier suffering from PTSD who's been in a lot of extracurricular trouble in Marshall County. I have just as much credibility in this town as you. Maybe less."

"But—"

"Trust me, Max. Sometimes going to the law doesn't help. We've already delivered justice out there."

"But not to the man who deserves it."

"He'll get his too."

By then, they were pulling into the ER entrance, and Max didn't have time to think about it anymore. Now, though, as she paced the lobby over an hour and a half later, she had thought about it quite a bit, and she saw the wisdom of the colonel's logic.

Nathan was here. With her. She couldn't be blackmailed anymore. And almost all the people who had done it were dead.

Except one . . .

Max ground her teeth together as a physician came out the double doors and headed her way. "Ms. Ringo?"

Max's stomach twisted into a knot. "Yes. Is my son OK?"

"Follow me," he said, going back through the doors with Max on his heels. Once they were in a small treatment room, he closed the door and peered at her. "Nathan is severely dehydrated and in full-blown withdrawal from something. Do you know what he was taking?"

"Meth," she said. "When he went missing, his friend, Betty, told me he was hooked on it."

"That was my suspicion."

"Is he going to be all right?"

The physician's face was grim, but he nodded. "He's stable. If you'd found him any later, he might have suffered an anoxic injury, but he should be fine." He paused. "But your son clearly has an addiction, and it's going to be a long road from here. I'm going to recommend a transfer to a treatment facility."

Max felt hot tears running out of her eyes. "Whatever he needs, but . . ." She held her arms out. ". . . he's going to live?"

The doctor grabbed her hands and squeezed gently. "Yes, ma'am, he is."

78

At 9:15 a.m., Dagger Richardson walked through the doors of the Jones & Butler law firm downtown. For over thirty years, Dagger had practiced law in this very building, and he was still of counsel to the firm. The conference room was right off the reception area, and his old friend was waiting for him.

"Dagger." J.R. Ford extended his hand and Dagger shook it.

Then Dagger peered at the receptionist, a young woman with dark-brown hair and blue eyes. "I'm Dagger Richardson," he said.

"I know," she said, pointing to the framed photograph on the far wall. It had been taken a few months after this branch was opened. Dagger's proud mug was front and center.

"We're just going to use this room for a few minutes. I didn't think there'd be any problem."

"None at all, sir. It's an honor."

Dagger smiled, seeing the blush on her face. On another day, he might have flirted with the young woman, but his heart wasn't in it today. "Come on," he said, nodding at J.R. and holding the conference room door open for him. Then he shut it behind them.

The room was typical with its long rectangular table, three leather chairs on each side, and two more at the ends. Dagger stood with his back against the far wall. "Thank you for coming on such short notice and especially after everything that happened yesterday."

"You'd do the same for me."

"Do you have what I asked for?"

J.R. opened his briefcase and pulled out three pages that had been stapled together. "Here it is," he said, furrowing his brow as he placed the document on the table. "You sure about this?"

"You ever known me not to be confident of a decision?"

J.R. chuckled and ran a hand through his thick silver hair. He took off his glasses. "I've never known you to relinquish control either."

Dagger peered at his old friend, who was clearly worried about him. "It's time, J.R."

"All right then," the lawyer said, walking to the door. "You're sure?" he asked again.

"As shit," Dagger said. "We need two witnesses."

J.R. frowned. "I'll be right back."

79

Judge Towry's courtroom was on the second floor of the Madison County Courthouse. Stephanie Strassburg saw Amy Dance waiting for her at the top of the wide staircase.

"Good morning," Amy said.

"Morning. Have you seen my father?"

Amy shook her head. "I haven't seen anyone yet. Judge Towry is out today, and Judge Parker's clerk met me here and showed me where everyone will be. But Perry hasn't arrived, and I haven't seen Dagger either."

"What about Max?"

"No."

Stephanie took out her phone. She had no missed calls or texts, and it was 9:53 a.m. "I figured I'd be the last one here."

"And you're the first. Come on. Let me show you where we will be."

Stephanie followed her through the doors and into Judge Warren Towry's courtroom. There was a gallery with two columns and five rows of eight chairs each. Beyond that was an enclosed area that Stephanie assumed was the jury box. Then two tables on either side of the courtroom, and the judge's bench.

Amy walked down the corridor between the gallery columns and around the jury box to the left. Behind one of the counsel tables was a door, and Amy led Stephanie through it. They passed a bathroom and then entered the second door on the left, which was a rather big room with a long table and at least six chairs on either side.

"This is the jury room," Amy said. "We'll be here today, which is preferable because of the privacy. Perry will be out in the courtroom."

"Gotcha," Stephanie said.

"Need anything? Water? Snacks?"

"I have everything I need in my purse." She paused. "I doubt I'll be eating much."

"Well . . . if you feel sick, you saw the bathroom."

"I did, and I'm good. For now."

"OK," Amy said, crossing her arms. "Were you able to talk with your father last night or this morning?"

Stephanie nodded.

"And?"

"And . . . we'll find out in a few minutes."

80

Dagger walked up the steps of the courthouse at 9:57 a.m. It had been a while, at least three years, since he'd been inside this L-shaped archive of mid-1960s architecture. He was old enough to remember the courthouse the way it had looked before 1966, and he had never thought the "modern" version was an improvement, despite the fact that it was much larger. Bigger usually meant better, but not in this case.

Not that anyone gave a damn about his opinion anymore. As he walked through the doors, he passed around the security area, flashing his courthouse badge to the officer in charge. The guard nodded without so much as a second look.

Some lawyers in Madison County could bypass the metal detector if they underwent a rigorous background check, showed that they had reason to be in the courthouse on a regular basis, and applied for and purchased a badge. Dagger, as the former longtime county attorney, was issued a badge years ago and had been lucky to find it this morning.

As he ascended the stairs, he felt the pistol in his pocket. He'd worn an overcoat today, which was suitable for the temperature outside, a cold and dry fifty-four degrees. If it had been much warmer, the coat might have stood out, but today he fit right in. Several other people had on heavy jackets and sweaters. Just before ten in the morning was a busy time at the courthouse, as lawyers were hustling to hearings.

Dagger had already recognized several faces, but he just nodded without stopping. As he reached the second floor, he saw Amy Dance standing outside Judge Towry's courtroom. "Where is Stephanie?"

"Jury room," she said.

"And what about the asshole?"

"He hasn't arrived yet, but Max said he'll be stationed out in the courtroom."

"Is the mediator here?"

"No."

Dagger grimaced. "All right. I'm going to see my daughter."

"Dagger—"

He looked at her over his shoulder. "Don't you worry. It'll end today." He gritted his teeth and entered the courtroom. *In more ways than one . . .*

81

When Jason Rich knocked on the treatment room door, Max ran to him. They hugged and she tried to hold it together. "Thank you for coming."

"Of course. How's Nathan?"

"He's gonna make it."

"And the colonel?"

"Just out of surgery but should be fine." She pursed her lips. "He said he had an accident at his shooting range."

"Was that the colonel's idea?"

"Yes, but I think he was right. What happened out at that farm . . ." She trailed off and her lip trembled. She hadn't had much time to think about those moments in and out of the Raptor when she'd taken her son. ". . . would be hard to explain."

Jason said nothing, but his grave expression let her know that he understood. "How can I help?"

"Can you stay here? Nathan is back in the detox area and probably will be for several hours. There's really nothing for me to do but wait, and the mediation was supposed to resume at ten." She paused and glanced at her phone. She had three text messages from Amy Dance asking where she was. "And I'm already a few minutes late."

"Of course. I'll need to stay for the colonel anyway."

"Are you sure?"

"Go," Jason said, pointing to the door.

Max started for the exit.

"Hey, Max."

She turned.

"What are you going to do?"

"What you told me to do from the beginning. My job."

82

Dagger knocked on the door and then entered without waiting for a response. Stephanie was sitting down, scrolling through her phone. She glanced up at him.

"Hey," she said.

Dagger walked toward her, pulling the document he'd signed almost an hour earlier out of his overcoat pocket. He unfolded the paper and placed it in front of her.

"What's this?" She took it. "Oh, Dad. No."

"Yes," he said. "I thought about it most of the night. I can't sell out to that sonofabitch. I just . . . can't do it. But you can. And now that you're my power of attorney you can sell my interest in Richardson Concepts to him."

"Daddy, no."

Dagger couldn't help but smile in spite of the pain he felt in his heart. "You haven't called me that in a while."

"I can't let you do this."

He stepped away from her. "Too late," he said. "I've done it. Paragraph nineteen gives you the right to sell property and business interests on my behalf."

She stood and approached him. "You still don't approve."

Dagger felt his eyes growing hot. "Doesn't matter what I think anymore." He turned to leave.

"Daddy?"

He stopped but didn't turn.

"Thank you."

Dagger Richardson looked at her over his shoulder, seeing not the cancer-stricken forty-something-year-old in front of him but the pig-tailed girl of ten who used to ride shotgun in his pickup truck over their land, peppering him with questions. "I love you, honey. Don't you ever forget it."

"Dad, we—"

But Dagger opened the door and closed it before she could get the rest out.

He strode down the tight hallway, feeling sick to his stomach. Which was amplified tenfold by what he saw in the courtroom.

"Well, well, well," Perry said.

Dagger stared at him across the courtroom, which was otherwise empty. *Fitting,* he thought, feeling the cold steel of the nine-millimeter pistol in his pocket. *In a court of law . . . and I'm about to take justice into my own hands.*

"I'm curious," Perry said, a fake grin plastered to his face. He wore a charcoal suit and a conservative maroon tie. "Have you heard from your buddy General Zorn lately?"

Dagger felt his pulse quicken. He began to walk toward Perry. He kept his hands in his pockets, his right holding tight to the weapon, the overcoat blocking the front of his pants from view. "No, I haven't."

"Really?" Perry said, wrinkling up his face. "I have."

Dagger nodded. Everything made sense now. Micah hadn't been watching Perry for him. The general was never going to take out Perry.

Micah Zorn had sold out to the higher bidder.

I was played, Dagger knew. Just as he'd known earlier that morning at the Voodoo Lounge.

"Cut him in, did you?" Dagger asked. His voice was steady. Instead of feeling angry, he felt cold. "I taught you well."

"You ready to sell out?" Perry asked. "Your loans are being called today. You need cash, Dagger. I'm sorry . . . but what can I say?" He held his arms out wide. "I win."

Dagger had walked around the counsel table and was now in the corridor of the gallery, just a few feet away from him.

"Come on," Perry said. "It's OK. You did teach me well, sir. Let's make a deal, so that you can save face." He extended his right hand for Dagger to shake.

Dagger Richardson took a step forward. He extended his hand but didn't shake with Perry. Instead, he stuck the barrel of the pistol against Perry's forehead. "Does it feel like you've won now?"

Perry's eyes went wide.

"Does it?" Dagger's index finger hovered over the trigger as he stared at the object of all his pain.

"He's not worth it."

Dagger tensed at the sound of the voice but didn't move or even look at the person who'd just entered the courtroom.

"Put the gun down, Dagger. *Now.*"

Dagger held the pistol steady. "This is the only way to make him pay."

"No, it's not. All shooting him in the head will do is give him a merciful and quick death. He won't feel any pain. You will not accomplish your objective."

Dagger blinked his eyes, as if awakening from a trance. He glanced at the doors, and Max Ringo was standing in front of them. She wore jeans, boots, and a light-colored blouse. Her jeans had grass and dirt stains on the knees. The picture didn't fit, and he was starting to get dizzy. His arm began to shake.

"Please, Dagger," Perry said. "This is cra—"

"Shut up," Dagger said, slapping him with his free hand across the face. Dagger blinked and looked at Max.

"He's not worth it," she said again, her tone as fierce as her green eyes. "Go, Dagger. I've got this."

Dagger finally returned the pistol to his pocket. He walked toward the exit, feeling as if everything was happening in slow motion, stopping when he reached Max. "Make sure my girl gets a fair deal."

"I will," Max said. "She'll get more than that."

Dagger touched Max's shoulder, just as she'd done with him last night on the patio of the AC Hotel.

Then he strode out of the courtroom.

83

Before Perry Strassburg could get a single word out of his mouth, Max had grabbed him by the balls.

Literally.

"You piece of shit."

Perry grimaced and then yelped, but Max kept her grip steady. "I'd think hard on what you're doing," he said. "You wouldn't want your boy—"

"My son is at the hospital," Max whispered. "He's messed up, but he's going to make it." She squeezed his scrotum. "No thanks to you."

Perry's eyes went wide.

"It's a real mess out there, Perry. I suspect the fire is raging by now. I ought to turn you in."

He swallowed. "But you won't, because you know that everything I said at the beginning of this mediation still holds true. That farm isn't mine. There's no connection that can be traced between any of the people out there and me." He gasped, struggling to talk with his testicles being clutched. "It will simply be your word against mine."

She gritted her teeth. "No. The odds are actually a lot better for me now, but an investigation after everything that happened before could destroy any second chances I might have with my son and career. I won't let you do that to me, and you're in fantasyland if you think an investigation of you won't sting. It might even cost you whatever you've been working on that's made getting control of Richardson Concepts important enough to kidnap my son." She squeezed again and felt his legs give. "I own you."

She let go of his crotch and he sank to the ground, writhing in pain. "I'll be back with an offer from Stephanie." She knelt and spoke in a low voice. "I plan to settle this case today. The irony . . . is that you're probably still going to get what you want."

84

In the recovery room, Satch Tonidandel blinked his eyes up at the ceiling. He was coming back to consciousness, remembering the last thing he'd done before going into surgery. He was a retired colonel in the US Army, and there was one box that he knew needed to be checked after any battle or skirmish. Since he couldn't do it himself, he'd sent a quick text to someone he trusted.

He glanced at a nurse with green scrubs. "Can you do me a favor?" he asked.

"Sure."

"My phone is in the front pocket of my jeans. Can you get it for me?"

"You need to be resting, sir. It's too—"

"Please," he said. "This is very important."

She blinked but then walked away.

A couple minutes later—he wasn't sure of the time, as he was still woozy—the nurse returned with his phone. "I'll have to take it right back from you."

He pulled up the screen and saw that he had one message that was all of two words. It was a response to his request. Satch grinned as he read the cryptic text.

On it.

85

Max reviewed the power of attorney document and then peered at Amy. "Seems legitimate to me." Max turned to the back page and saw the typical language at the end of real estate and business documents: "This instrument was prepared by J.R. Ford," she read out loud. "Guess we might want to check with J.R."

"I already have," Amy said. "Dagger signed the POA this morning in front of J.R. and the two witnesses listed. His signature was also notarized by a third witness. All three are paralegals at Jones & Butler."

Max took a deep breath and exhaled. *Belt and suspenders,* she thought, a saying of Knox's when you wanted to make damn sure you accomplished the goal. Then she looked at Stephanie. "You ready for this to be over?"

"Yes," she managed, wiping tears from her eyes. She'd been almost inconsolable since Max had entered the room. Not able to grasp that her father would give it all to her.

In a calm voice, Max went over the offer she thought Stephanie should make. Then she looked at Amy, who nodded.

Max grabbed the POA and looked at Amy. "He'll want to see this."

"Of course."

Max looked down at Stephanie, who met her eye.

"Do it," Stephanie said.

—

Two minutes later, Perry peered up at Max after reviewing the POA. "I don't believe it."

"I didn't either," Max said. "But Amy has verified with J.R. Ford that the document is, in fact, legitimate and was signed this morning by Dagger in front of J.R. and three witnesses, one of whom, as you can see, is a notary."

Perry whistled through his teeth. They were seated across from each other at one of the counsel tables in the courtroom. Perry squinted at Max. "Well, what's the offer?"

"Residential property remains the same as the last few offers."

"Obviously."

"Lump sum payment to Stephanie increases to fifteen million, with five of it being put in trust for her two daughters."

"Tell me about the part that matters," Perry said.

Max kept her voice even. "You give Stephanie all your interest in the real property, and she will give you her forty percent of Richardson Concepts."

Perry slammed his hands down on the table and closed his eyes.

"And . . ." Max began, and Perry's eyes flashed open. "Dagger will sell his thirty percent interest in Richardson Concepts to you for $45 million." She bit her lip. "According to your own business valuation expert, that's exactly the fair market value of Dagger's interest."

Perry cocked his head at her, and then, after several seconds, he grinned. He began to slow clap, '80s-movie-style.

"Do we have a deal?" Max spoke through clenched teeth.

"You're one hell of a mediator, Ringo," he said.

"Do we have a deal?" Max repeated the question.

Perry stopped clapping. "Yes, I believe we do."

86

Amy Dance offered to draft the settlement agreement, and Max was grateful to relinquish that task. Once she had all the provisions inserted, first Stephanie and then Perry reviewed it. After they both had approved, Amy and Stephanie signed for the defendant, Stephanie also signed as power of attorney for Dagger, and Perry executed his name for the plaintiff. A time period of thirty days was agreed upon to formalize the land and company transactions, but Perry assured them that he would have the documents prepared and sent for their review on Monday. "We'll have this thing closed early next week," he told Amy in Max's presence.

"Sounds good," Amy said. As Perry and Amy discussed logistics, Max peeked her head into the jury room where Stephanie Strassburg was still seated, gazing aimlessly at the wall across from her.

"You OK?" Max asked.

Stephanie wiped her nose. "I wanted this," she said. "I did. I wanted it to be over." She turned to Max, and her eyes were red. "Thank you. I thought I'd be happy or . . . at least relieved."

"How do you feel?" Max asked.

"It's weird," Stephanie said. "Today went better than I could have ever expected. My dad actually chose *me*. Over the company he founded and his own ego and pride. He *picked me*." She let out a sob. "I should feel good about that, right?" Again, she looked at Max. "Right?"

"Yes," Max said.

She sighed and rubbed her face with both hands. "Then why do I feel guilty?"

Max opened her mouth, but the words wouldn't come. Sometimes, there were no answers. She'd learned that painful lesson in rehab. All a person could do was move on.

Stephanie shook her head as another sob escaped her lips. *"Why do I feel so damn guilty?"*

87

Dagger rode Saban to the cemetery, wearing the same clothes he'd worn to the courthouse. The temperature had dropped ten degrees since the morning.

"Winter's coming," he said, sliding off the saddle and patting the animal behind the ears. He trudged toward the graves of his ancestors, feeling each step. Feeling all the steps of his seventy-seven years. When he reached Judy's spot, he winced. "Well, hon, it's all hers now. I'm done making mistakes that cost this family." He turned in a circle, taking a few moments and examining each headstone, maybe more than a few at his father's.

He thought he'd feel ashamed, but he didn't. He felt free.

His gaze fell on his horse, and he chuckled. *You forgetful sonofabitch,* he thought, walking toward the light-gray stallion. Almost as old in horse years as Dagger was in human. He approached the animal and kissed his wet nose. Then he untied him from the fence post. "All right, Saban, you glorious bastard. Fight on." He slapped him on the ass, and the horse took off across the pasture.

Dagger wiped his eyes and walked back to Judy. The phone in his left pocket was vibrating, and he took it out. The call was from Stephanie. He touched the screen, but he didn't answer it. Instead, he dropped the phone and reached into his other pocket.

He pulled out the pistol and admired the farmland that had been in his family for over a hundred years. Because of his actions today, it would stay with his daughter, where it belonged. As for the company he'd founded . . . his legacy . . . his life . . .

Dagger focused on Saban, who was looking right at him from one hundred yards away. The animal's gray coat bristled with the wind coming off the pine trees to the north. *What a beautiful ride it's been, old boy.*

Then he stuck the barrel of the gun against his temple.

And pulled the trigger.

88

Max walked out of the courthouse with Amy Dance. She was exhausted and wanted nothing more than to sleep for about twenty hours. But she knew she couldn't rest until she had an update on Nathan. And she wondered if she'd ever be able to fall asleep again after the events that morning in New Market. Still, even with all that, winning was better than losing. She'd settled the case. That was a win for a mediator.

But given how happy Perry Strassburg had been when the mediation concluded, it felt like a hollow victory.

"You did a great job, Max," Amy said, as they reached the bottom of the steps. "By the way, why were you late this morning? And why are you dressed casual?"

Max was a bit thrown off by the questions, but she recovered quickly. "My son was sick last night, and I had to take him to the ER. I just threw on some clothes and didn't have time to go back to the hotel."

"Oh my God. What happened? Is he OK?"

"He will be," Max said, but she wasn't going to be giving any more specifics. "I enjoyed working with you, Amy. You did a great job, and the settlement for Stephanie is very fair."

"It's more than that," Amy said. "By any measure, Stephanie made out better than Perry, but . . ."

"But what?" Max asked.

"I just can't get over how giddy Perry seemed in there. He wasn't doing much to hide his excitement."

Max chuckled. "Oh, I'm sure the bastard feels like he's won in some toxically masculine way. He beat Dagger down. Won the pissing contest, and now he owns the whole company. That was worth it to Perry, and it almost didn't matter the cost."

"I guess." She sighed. "I can't help but think that Dagger was right. That the prick's got something cooking that's going to make us all feel stupid."

Max gazed up the stairs. Perry still hadn't come out, and she figured he was probably waiting for her to be long gone. He would be feeling her squeeze in his nether regions for a while. "Maybe," Max said. "But all we can do is our jobs."

Amy held out her fist and Max nudged it with her own. "You're my new go-to mediator, Ringo. You'll be hearing from my office."

"You mean that?"

"Hell yes. No one could have settled this case but you. *No one.*" She took a step backward. "Need a ride?"

"No, I'm good. Thank you, Amy. I mean it."

Amy smiled, her eyes warm. "Thank you, Max. *I* mean it."

The walk from the courthouse to the Embassy Suites was less than a mile, and it did Max some good to move. It was a cold, brisk day, and Max sensed that winter was on the way. It felt good to think about something as mundane as the weather. As Max crossed Church Street and passed the Cozy Cow restaurant into Big Spring Park, she called Jason.

"So?" he asked.

"The case settled."

"Well, that deserves a Ric Flair WOOOOOOO!" Jason screamed. "Congratulations. I knew you could do it."

"How's Nathan?"

"No change. The nurse came in a few minutes ago, and said he was still getting fluids, and that his condition was stable. He continues to drift in and out of consciousness." Jason paused. "And he's been asking for you."

Max felt heat behind her eyes. "And the colonel?"

"Out of surgery and ornery as ever."

Max laughed through her tears. "He's quite a man. I've . . . never known anyone like him."

"That makes two of us."

"I'll be there in a few minutes," Max said. "Gonna check out of the hotel and get an Uber to the hospital."

"Max, are you OK? The colonel hasn't told me what happened, but I know you must have gone out to that farm and brought him and Nathan to the hospital, and the colonel's leg was shot up pretty good. Then you had to go right into the mediation. It's . . ." He whistled. ". . . a lot."

Max walked over the red Japanese bridge, seeing a dead duck floating on the water next to a group of chicks. She felt a chill come over her that had nothing to do with the temperature and her lack of a jacket. "I don't know," she said. "It just feels wrong. It was a fair settlement. In fact, if anything, it slanted Stephanie's way. But . . ." She trailed off, looking over her shoulder at the dead duck. Its brown body and similarly colored feathers. Beak face down in the dark water.

"But what?"

"He got what he wanted, Jason. He kidnapped and almost killed my son. Probably would have killed him if the colonel hadn't found that farm. He should be in prison or dead. But when I left the courthouse, he was happy as a clam." Anger pulsed through Max's body. "That's not right."

"No, it's not, but you can't control everything, Max."

"I know that, but I just don't think I can let him get away with it."

Silence on the other end of the line.

"You don't agree?" Max asked.

"I think the time to turn him in was this morning, Max. I obviously don't know all the details, but you and the colonel made a decision. I agree with it, but still . . . I think it's too late."

"Maybe for involving the police."

"Max, just come to the hospital, OK?"

Max crossed Monroe Street. She'd reached the parking lot of the Embassy Suites. She ignored his question. "There was something else, Jason."

"What?"

"Stephanie should have at least felt relieved, but she didn't. She looked like a truck had run over her."

"Max, you know as well as I do that lawsuits take their toll on people in different ways. She's probably just numb."

"Could be," Max said, but she wasn't buying that as she strode through the entrance to the hotel. "Listen, Jason, I've got to go."

"Max, you're coming to the hospital, right?"

But Max couldn't hear him anymore. She was back at the farm in New Market. In the bulletproof Raptor, machine-gun fire pattering the windshield like hail, running over two operatives and then shooting the man in black. And then Nathan, weak and foaming at the mouth, the blare of "Lunatic Fringe" in the cab of the truck as she sped down Winchester Road.

Her thoughts moved to the courtroom. Visions of Dagger, Amy, and Stephanie. And finally, the grin on the face of the man who'd blackmailed her. Who'd taken her son and almost killed him. Who still thought he was God.

Who got everything he wanted . . . because of me.

"Max?" Jason's voice sounded far away.

"I'll see you in a few," Max said, ending the call and striding toward the elevator. As she rode up to her floor, she began to feel the same thing that had permeated Stephanie Strassburg's soul at the close of the mediation.

Guilt.

89

Stephanie knew something was wrong. She knew it the minute her father didn't answer his phone as she was leaving the mediation.

But when she saw his horse riding free across the pasture as she drove up the path to the farmhouse, she knew it in her bones.

Truth was, she'd felt something the minute he'd dropped the power of attorney document on the table in the jury room. That look in his eyes. Was it defeat?

Or surrender?

Stephanie wasn't sure, but she'd never seen her dad look so vulnerable. In another setting, she might have embraced it. But in the courthouse where he'd begun his prestigious legal career, everything felt wrong.

She parked her Range Rover and got out of the vehicle without shutting the door, running toward Saban. "Hey, boy. Where's Daddy?"

The horse whinnied, and Stephanie climbed into the saddle. Gone were any thoughts of her sickness or condition. Adrenaline, anger, and fear fueled her now. And, of course, guilt. *He chose me . . .*

Stephanie had a haunting sensation that she knew exactly where her father had gone. She pulled on the reins and the horse moved forward.

She didn't even have to guide or steer the animal. "Take me there, boy."

When they reached the cemetery, Stephanie was relieved at first. All she saw were the grave markers. She eased off the horse and opened the gate to the small set of burial plots.

She was three steps in when she saw his hand. Lying outstretched on the ground, his body blocked by the headstone of her great-aunt Pamela Richardson. For a moment, Stephanie was paralyzed. She didn't want to know, but she had to know. Finally, she whimpered and took a tentative step around her great-aunt's grave.

The scream started in her chest.

By the time it reached her lips, her legs had given way, and she dropped to her knees.

Behind her, Saban whinnied, but she paid the horse no mind. She crawled along the cold ground toward her father's limp body. Blood oozed from the side of his head. She started to say "Dad" but stopped herself. She reached for his shoulder, but her hand didn't quite make it. Her whole body shook.

He chose me . . .

Stephanie yelled again, but it came out like a repressed sob. Spittle oozed from the corner of her mouth. She felt nauseated, but she steeled herself, squeezing her fists together. Then she screamed once more, and her voice was stronger. But wild like an animal's. She looked behind her, and Saban was running in a circle around the cemetery.

Stephanie was losing steam. She fell forward and caught herself with her hands. All she wanted to do was die next to her father.

This is my fault.

She started to lie down.

But then she saw the gun. A couple feet from her father's outstretched right hand.

She grabbed the pistol and pressed her other hand to the ground, pushing herself to her feet. She stood on shaky legs as guilt, sadness, and anger battled for her soul.

She put the gun to her own head, just as Dagger must have done a few hours earlier. Stephanie blinked her eyes and gazed at her mother's headstone. Then down at her dead father's corpse. She clenched her teeth as her finger hovered over the trigger.

Seconds later, Saban stood on his hind legs and squealed.

As a single gunshot rang out over the cemetery.

90

The hospital room was dark, the only light coming from the fluorescent bulb in the bathroom. Max watched her son breathe. As Nathan's chest moved up and down, she closed her eyes, thanking God for the thousandth time that he was OK. She held his hand, then kissed it. As she turned to exit, she heard his voice.

"Hey, M-M-Mom."

"Hey," Max said, her voice shaky.

"I'm sorry," he said.

She stepped toward him and leaned close to his ear. "Me too. For everything." Then she kissed his cheek. "Get some rest. I love you."

Max walked toward the door. There were no visitors allowed on the detox unit, but they'd made an exception for her because she'd represented the director of the ER in a malpractice suit a few years ago. She'd been given ten minutes, but her time was now up.

"Hey, Mom."

Max looked over her shoulder at him. "Yeah."

"Thank you."

A half hour later, Max stepped off the elevator on four, which was the med-surg floor. She carried a steaming bag of Burger King with her and two drinks. A special order from the patient. She strode down the hallway toward his room, thinking about how long the day had seemed. After checking out of the hotel, she'd come straight to the hospital. Jason had been happy and relieved to see her, and she'd apologized for the weirdness during their phone call. She knew she was likely suffering from some kind of PTSD, but the crisis wasn't quite over. Until Nathan was discharged from the hospital, she told herself she had to stay focused. Once the colonel was placed in his room, Jason came to see her, and she volunteered to hold the fort for the night, with Jason promising to be back in the morning to take Satch home. Despite the colonel's protests, the hospital recommended a one-night stay. "I'll watch out for him," Max had said, hugging her mentor tight. "Thank you for being there for me, Jason. I don't know what I would have done without you . . . and the colonel."

He'd squeezed her shoulders. "You would have figured out another way. You're a survivor. And if you hadn't come out to that farm this morning, I'm not sure the colonel or Nathan . . ." He trailed off. "Thank *you*, Max. You hear me?"

She'd wiped tears from her face. "I hear you."

Now, as she reached her destination, she set the drinks on the floor and rapped her knuckles on the door.

"Come in," he growled.

Max propped the door open with her foot, grabbed the drinks, and then brought everything in.

The patient was sitting upright and holding a remote control in his right hand. He squinted at her with his reptilelike eyes. "You get it?"

"Whopper meal with large fries and a large Coca-Cola."

"Hoo-rah," he muttered.

She set the food and drinks down on the roller table in front of him. Then she removed a Whopper Jr. from the sack, grabbed her Diet Coke, and sat in the visitor's recliner.

For several minutes, they ate in silence. Eventually, Satch wadded up the paper his burger came in. "Ain't nothing on TV. Not one damn thing worth a crap to watch."

"You need to sleep."

"So do you."

She patted the recliner. "And I plan to do it right here."

"Aw, now that's not necessary," Satch grumbled.

"I know, but I want to. I can't leave Nathan, and they won't let me stay in his room. So . . ." She shrugged. "You're stuck with me."

He looked at her and flung up his palms as if to say "Whatever." After a few seconds, he peered at her. "Can I ask you something?"

"Sure?"

"What made you come out there this morning?"

"You gave me the location pin. I hadn't heard from you, and I was worried."

"It was foolish. Things could have played out different."

"But they didn't." Then she scowled at him. "Are you really going to fuss at me for saving your ass?"

He scoffed and looked away. "No . . . I'm not. Just pointing out that it was dumb."

"Well, I don't follow your orders, Colonel. I trust my instincts. When you sent that pin, you told me where my son was. I couldn't stay away. I'm his mother. You understand that, don't you?"

Satch said nothing, and Max was growing annoyed by the conversation. She stood and started to snatch the remote control from his table, but Satch grabbed her hand.

Max winced, as it was her sprained wrist, and Satch immediately let go. "I'm sorry. I just—"

"It's OK," Max said, hesitating for a moment. "Hold this one." She extended her left hand. Satch squinted at her and then took hold of her fingers as she sat on the edge of his cot.

"You saved my life today," he said. "It was foolish, but it was also brave. When I saw the Raptor coming over that cotton field . . ." He whistled. "I can't think of many times in my military career when I've been . . ." He trailed off, as if searching for the word or unwilling to say it.

"Rescued?"

"Yeah," Satch said.

For a long moment, the only sound in the room was their breathing and the occasional beeping of his IV.

"How's Nathan?" he asked.

"He's OK, but he's going to need to go to rehab." Max paused. "Once he's out of detox, they are going to transport him to Bradford in Madison, where he'll be for at least a couple of months."

"You tell his father yet?"

"I called Thayer when I got back to the hospital after the mediation. I told him that I received a call from one of Nathan's friends that he hadn't gone to school this morning. I went looking for him and found him passed out by a campfire on the mountain."

"Not bad," Satch said. "You're a good liar, Ringo."

"Shut up. Figured I needed to stay consistent with the story we told the hospital."

"How'd he take it?"

"Upset at first, but overall, pretty well. Thayer was always even keeled. He admitted that he had suspicions that Nathan was hooked on something and that he should have said something." Max paused. "He's on his way home and should be here tomorrow morning."

"Well . . . that's good, I guess. Are you going to tell him the truth?"

Max had been avoiding that question since returning to the hospital, but she knew she couldn't ignore it forever. Thayer had a right to know, and if she didn't tell him, Nathan certainly should have the right to. She sighed. "I haven't decided." She'd think about that one tomorrow. Another question was bothering her more right now. "Do you think we should go to the police?"

"No," Satch said, without hesitation. "Too much to explain. Cops and sheriff's deputies look for easy solutions, and there isn't one here. It's complicated, and justice would never be served on Perry Strassburg. The only direct witness to his misdeeds is you. There is no connection between him and that farm in New Market. All we'd do by going to the police now is bring trouble on ourselves."

Max nodded along with him. She knew his thinking was sound, and her instincts this morning after arriving at the hospital had been the same as the colonel's.

He squeezed her fingers. "The way this works out . . . it's a big success for you, right?"

Max remembered what Amy Dance had said. *You're my new go-to mediator, Ringo.* And Caroline would likely still keep sending her referrals. "Perhaps."

"You did your job, Max. And you did what had to be done to get your son back."

Max returned the colonel's squeeze. "I couldn't have done it without you."

He winked at her. "We fight till the battle's won."

Max stared into his intense blue eyes and then stood from the cot, turning toward the window. The sky was full of clouds. She couldn't see the moon or even any stars. It was pitch dark.

"You OK?" the colonel asked.

Has the battle been won? Max thought, clenching her fists and thinking of Perry Strassburg's arrogant grin.

"Max?"

"Fine," she said, staring into the darkness.

91

Perry drove himself to the farm. He didn't want to risk any witnesses to whatever he'd find. He took the Escalade and gave his driver the night off.

"Sir, I haven't heard from Mr. Hicks today. Is everything OK?" the agent had asked when she gave Perry the keys.

"It's fine," Perry said. "Hicks may be taking a leave of absence, but you'll still have a job with me."

The driver had raised her eyebrows but said nothing more.

Now, as Perry turned off Winchester Road and pulled up the long gravel drive to the house, he tried to remind himself that the day had been a success. He'd won. The company was his and his alone. He'd called Wick immediately after the settlement paperwork was signed, and he'd thought his old friend was going to hyperventilate with happiness and relief.

"We'll have it all done by the end of the day Monday," Perry said. "I can sign with the Syndicate as early as Wednesday."

"Two point five billion dollars." Wick had whispered the words, but Perry now screamed them from the front seat of the Escalade.

"Two point five billion dollars!"

But as he made the final turn and saw the house in the distance, the good vibes dissipated in an instant. Perry blinked his eyes, making sure they weren't deceiving him.

The barn was gone. All that was left was a pile of charred wood. Perry stopped the SUV and climbed out of the front seat, surveying the damage. To the left were the remains of what looked like a tractor. There were wheel tracks everywhere, as if someone had cut doughnuts in the grassy area between the barn and house.

Perry took out his burner phone, but he didn't call Hicks. *He's gone . . .* Perry walked to the edge of what remained of the barn. There had been seven agents stationed at the farm, including Hicks, and he saw no evidence that any of them were here. He focused on the ruins, wondering if he was looking at his security team's final resting place. Then he made the call.

"It's a mess out here," he said.

"You should have seen it this morning."

Perry swallowed. "You . . . were here."

"Did you get it done?"

Perry peered around the dark farm. With the house and barn being so far from the nearest road and more than two miles from the closest farm, the fire and skirmish had gone unnoticed.

As if they'd never happened.

"Perry?"

"Yeah," he said. "It's done."

"You must feel good about yourself."

But before Perry could respond, the line went dead.

"Well?"

The voice came from behind him, and he wheeled toward it. He gasped when he saw who it was.

"How long have you been out here?"

The woman ignored him, stepping closer. They were ten feet apart. "Well?"

"Well, what?"

"How do you feel?"

"Fine," he managed. "I—" But his words cut off when he saw the gun pointed at him.

Perry started to say something else, but three loud pops rang out. He felt a sharp, searing pain in his chest, and he touched his sternum, seeing blood on his fingers. "I don't . . ." He dropped to his knees as the words trailed off. He was dizzy. Losing consciousness. He collapsed on his back, staring up at the cloud-filled sky.

Then she was standing over him, pointing the pistol at his face.

"But . . . I did it," he said.

They were the last words of Perry Strassburg's life.

A few minutes later, the remaining wood in what was left of the barn was burning again. Logs from the pile to the side of the house had been placed on top, and more would be needed.

As flames lit up the otherwise-dark farm, the woman watched the fire. She walked forward and threw a few sticks on the blaze.

It was going to be a long night.

EPILOGUE

Mentone, Alabama, November 27, 2025

Thanksgiving Day on the mountain dawned frigid and clear. Max awoke as morning's light peeked through the blinds in her bedroom window. She put on her sweats, a hoodie, and a toboggan and walked to the kitchen. After drinking a huge glass of ice water, she peeked into the cabin's only other bedroom.

Nathan was sleeping. His chest rising and falling. The slightest of snores escaping his mouth.

Max said a silent prayer of thanks and then slid out the back door of the cabin. After walking the first quarter mile or so, she began to jog. Then, a minute later, she hit her running pace, which was about a nine-minute mile. Not fast by any stretch, but she was improving.

It had taken her almost two weeks to recover from the Strassburg mediation. Physically, she'd been exhausted, and spending a few nights in the hospital while Nathan went through detox hadn't helped much in that regard. But she'd also been drained mentally and emotionally, as the people who had dominated her life for three days monopolized the news.

Dagger Richardson had committed suicide hours after the mediation. Meanwhile, Perry Strassburg had disappeared and was presumed dead after the remains of his severed hands turned up in a dumpster on North Parkway. The last person known to have had any contact with him was his friend Andrew Wick, who had spoken to Perry over the phone around 7:30 p.m. on October 24. The banker said Perry was "in great spirits."

Max had been interviewed several times in connection with both Perry's disappearance and the bombing at the Beasley Rogers building during the mediation, and the mental stress of those interrogations took their toll. But she stayed the course and said nothing.

Most of the news coverage had centered on Stephanie Richardson Strassburg's role in discovering Dagger's body at the family cemetery, after which she claimed to have shot her father's gun once into the air before passing out next to his corpse. Rumors persisted that Stephanie might have actually murdered both her father and her not-quite ex-husband, as their respective deaths resulted in a phenomenal windfall to her. These spoils included the imminent merger between Richardson Concepts and an international private equity group estimated to be worth billions. So far, while an investigation of both deaths was ongoing, no arrests had been made.

Unbelievable, Max thought, smiling at the irony. The person who cared the least about the land and the company—the two chips that the whole mediation had centered on—might end up with all of it.

At the two-and-a-half-mile point, Max reached the edge of Lookout Mountain. She stopped and peered out at nature's canvas. The sun was rising a majestic yellowish red over the pine trees and the valley below. Max wiped sweat from her brow with a towel and drank several sips of water from her carry bottle.

As Satch had predicted, Max's career had taken off since the Strassburg mediation. She'd handled two mediations for Amy Dance, both successful, and one car wreck case for J.R. Ford, which she'd resolved. Caroline had also appointed her to mediate three additional matters, and she'd already settled one of them.

I'm rolling, she thought, feeling hopeful for the first time in a while. Later today, she'd host a Thanksgiving feast at the cabin in Mentone, and she was grateful that Thayer had agreed to let her have Nathan for the first two days of the holiday. It was Nathan's first break from

Bradford, and he'd been so excited to see her yesterday at pickup. Someone else had promised to come for lunch today as well . . .

Max felt a flutter in her heart. It was good to be looking forward to the future. But, before she could walk into the light, she needed closure from the darkness. To have that, she knew there was one more thing she must do.

Monday, she thought, nodding at the view and turning to run home.

When she arrived back at the cabin, the smell of bacon filled her nostrils. As she walked into the kitchen, she saw her son standing in his pajamas in front of the stove, stirring eggs in a skillet. She looked at the counter, where at least six strips of crisp bacon had already been made and were lying on top of a paper plate.

"My roommate at Bradford says the eggs are better if you cook them in the bacon grease," Nathan said, looking over his shoulder at Max. His long hair was unkempt, but his eyes were clear. Sobriety looked good on him. *One day at a time,* Max thought. *For him and for me. Hell . . . for everyone.*

"I can't wait to try them," Max said.

Nine hours later, as the sun began its descent behind the mountain, Max heard a knock at the door. She sighed, thinking that Nathan must have forgotten his key. He and Betty had gone for a walk. While Max was a little nervous about letting her son out of her sight, she'd become close to Betty since the mediation and had agreed to Nathan's request to invite her to Thanksgiving. She knew her son needed friends, too, and Betty had promised not to do gummies or anything else around him. *One day at a time,* Max thought again, hoping she wasn't being naive.

She strode to the door and peeked through the keyhole. When she saw him, she felt gooseflesh on her arms. She undid the latch and opened the door.

Colonel Satch Tonidandel wore a faded leather jacket with a patch of an eagle with its mouth open on the side. A black button-down shirt, dark jeans, and boots rounded out the ensemble. He'd trimmed his beard, and it looked like he'd tried to run a comb through his hair, but it was still as disheveled as ever. He took off his aviators and squinted at her.

"I'm sorry I'm late."

Max put her hands on her hips. The colonel had promised he'd be there for lunch at 1:00 p.m., and it was now past four. "What happened?"

"I guess I was having second thoughts."

"Oh. Well . . . do you want to come in?"

"No," Satch said. "I mean . . . I can't. There's something I need to show you first." He pulled a manila envelope out of his jacket.

"Colonel, what's this about?"

He gripped tight to the package. "Before I had my surgery, I asked my friend Albert Hooper, an investigator that Jason has used many times, to monitor that farm and photograph anyone that came out there. It was a military tactic. You never want to leave a battlefield without taking stock." He paused. "Hooper saw something." Satch tried to hand her the envelope, but Max took a step backward and stared at it like it was a poisonous snake.

"Just tell me what it shows," Max said.

"You need to see for yourself." The front door was connected to a porch, and Satch stepped to his left and placed the envelope on a wrought iron coffee table. "There's a summary of the property ownership in there too. Turns out the two brothers who owned the land died six months ago, but the farm hasn't been used by them in years. Instead, the person who inherited it has been running things. Hooper dug around New Market and was able to obtain the name of the current owner." Satch pointed at the envelope. "It's all in there."

"How long have you had this information?" Max asked.

"A couple of weeks."

She took a few steps closer to him. "Why haven't you told me?"

"Because I don't want to hurt you."

"Why now, then? On Thanksgiving, for God's sake?"

"There was never going to be a good time. With what you told me you were planning to do Monday, I just had to come clean on what I knew."

She started to argue but stopped when he leaned forward and kissed her cheek. "I'm sorry," he whispered.

"You guys need a room?" Nathan's singsong voice came from the driveway, and Max pulled back from Satch. The boy was grinning wide at them, as was Betty next to him. They were holding hands.

"Nathan," Satch said.

"Glad you could make it," Nathan said.

The colonel managed a smile. "I won't be staying long. I'm happy to see you, son."

"Same here," Nathan said, and he and Betty ran up the steps and into the cabin.

Max gazed at Satch, still feeling his whiskers on her cheek. "Please stay."

"I'll see you soon," he said, touching her cheek with his thumb. "But you're going to need some time to process that . . ." He nodded at the envelope. ". . . alone."

Huntsville, Alabama, Monday . . .

Max arrived at the Dallas Mill Deli first. She ordered a Diet Coke but couldn't stomach any food, not even the strawberry pretzel salad. When she saw Caroline enter the restaurant, her jaw tightened. Her old friend wore a stylish royal blue suit, while Max was in jeans, boots, and a pullover.

"Hey," Caroline said. "You not eating?"

"Sit down," Max said, gesturing at the seat across from her. They were in the far right corner. The exact table where they'd eaten hundreds of meals together. The same spot where Max had dined alone the first afternoon of the Strassburg mediation.

Caroline blinked her eyes but took her seat.

"Why'd you do it?" Max asked.

"Do what?"

Max took out the photograph that had been in the envelope the colonel had given her. She slid it across the table and turned it so that Caroline could see.

"I'd like to give you the benefit of the doubt," Max said, speaking through clenched teeth. She'd had a lot of time to rehearse this speech but found her emotions getting the better of her. "Was Perry blackmailing you too? Is that why you appointed me as mediator? Did he force you to make your land in New Market available? You know, the property you inherited from your uncles, the Carpenter brothers? I'm just spitballing here, but let me guess. He was screwing you, and it was *very* stealth. Not even savvy Amy Dance or all Dagger Richardson's sources could figure out who Perry was having the affair with. Surely, none of them would think it was prim, proper, perfect Captain Prude, Caroline Parker. I'm sorry . . . *the Honorable* Caroline Parker."

Caroline said nothing. Her face was beet red, but she remained silent, moving her eyes around the small café.

"So what was the deal?" Max continued, growing angrier in response to her old friend's silence. "Did Perry have a video of you and him in the throes of passion? Or am I giving him too much credit? Was this whole damn thing orchestrated by you? Do you have the ultimate God complex? Were you using your power to make me feel the same pain that you did when you found out that I accepted your husband's offer and blew him in exchange for oxycodone? Is that why you sent me those cryptic texts during the mediation, calling me a whore and warning me that I should have never come back? Which is it, C—?"

"*You're out of your mind, Max,*" Caroline interrupted, her voice low and reeking with contempt. "Have you been using again? I should have you arrested for making such baseless accusations."

"Oh, fuck off, *Your Honor*. Free speech isn't a crime. Besides, I think the police would love to hear my theory." She leaned her elbows on the table. "And I'm stone sober, bitch." Now, Max's voice shook with emotion. "I set up this lunch because I wanted closure. I wanted to apologize for what I did. I know it was awful. Bruce was . . . *is* . . . a predator, and I'm sure I wasn't the only patient he abused. Regardless . . . I'm sorry, Caroline. You were my friend, and I shouldn't have done what I did. I have nightmares about being in that car with Bruce almost every night. All I can say is that I was out of my mind, lost in the abyss of addiction." She paused. Tears streaked her cheeks, but she made no move to wipe them. "But I got help. I'm better now. I'm seeing things clearly."

"What do you see?" Caroline asked.

"A shell of the woman who used to be my friend." Max stood from the table, fighting the urge to fling her Diet Coke at Caroline. Instead, she leaned over until her face was just an inch from the judge's. "You know, I never blamed you for the accident. You were the one driving. If you had been a second quicker, you might have avoided that truck. Some folks might argue that you ruined my life."

"Oh, come on, Max."

"But you did hold a grudge, didn't you?" She stuck her index finger into Caroline's chest. "Well, we're even now. Stay away from me and my family . . ." She pointed at the photograph. ". . . or I'm going to make trouble for you."

Max strode to the door. She'd done what she came here to do. As she climbed up into the passenger side of the Raptor, the colonel peered at her.

"You OK?"

She nodded, but the tears wouldn't stop falling. "Will you play that song that you like so much? The one that reminds you of your brother."

Satch fiddled with his playlist.

Seconds later, the beginning of "Spotless" by Zach Bryan and the Lumineers piped out of the speakers. Max wiped her eyes and looked out the windshield at the restaurant.

Caroline Parker was standing in the far corner, just as she'd been doing the Wednesday afternoon of the mediation.

Staring right at her.

Max held eye contact for several seconds, feeling a door closing on the past, as the colonel backed out of the parking space.

A few minutes later, as the Raptor roared onto I-565 East, Max turned the volume up full blast, gazing at the skyline of downtown Huntsville.

"*One day at a time,*" she whispered. Then she reached for the colonel's hand.

Caroline Parker didn't look at the photograph until she was back in her chambers. Before closing and locking the door, she told her judicial assistant to cancel her afternoon hearing docket. "I'm not feeling well," she said.

Now she sat in her high-backed burgundy chair and examined the picture. It was grainy, and she could certainly argue that the photo was AI generated or even that it wasn't her.

But Caroline knew the truth. *It is me.*

In the photograph, she was standing in front of the ruined barn.

On its face, the picture proved nothing. But the time and date of the photograph was another story. October 24, 2025. 2:34 p.m.

About five hours before I killed Perry Strassburg . . .

Max had come close with her two theories, but the truth lay in the middle. Perry hadn't overtly blackmailed Caroline, but he had implied that she needed to play along. A man like him could survive a scandal, but a judge? Prim and proper Caroline Parker?

Captain Prude, Caroline thought, smirking at the photograph.

But Perry hadn't owned her. On the contrary, she'd used him. She'd wanted revenge, and Perry had given her the means to accomplish it.

It had been her idea for Max to mediate the Strassburg divorce. And further, it had been her plan for Nathan to be kidnapped and Max to be blackmailed. She'd even volunteered the farm for Perry's operations, as it was a remote location and not easily connected to her.

But since she did, in fact, own the farm, she'd felt like she had to cover her tracks once Max made a mess of things out there. If someone dug hard enough, they'd eventually link the land in New Market to her. Just as Max had.

But if they never had a reason to dig . . .

No, Perry wasn't pulling the strings. *I was,* Caroline thought.

And I still am . . .

She put the photograph in her briefcase. *It proves nothing,* she thought.

The farm was clean now. There was no trace of the barn that used to stand a hundred yards from the house. It was gone. As were the bones of the people who had died there.

Except for Perry's hands, which she'd severed with an axe a couple minutes after killing him. She thought that was a fitting touch, given the vile things he'd done with them.

Caroline walked to the window, thinking of Max striding out of the Dallas Mill Deli like some kind of conquering hero. She scoffed.

Backstabbing bitch, more like it.

Caroline took out her phone and pulled up the deleted video. Every twenty-nine days, she had to recover this footage and then delete it again, and there were twenty-four days left in this cycle.

She clicked play and saw the BMW come into view. Her best friend, Max Ringo, in the front seat. Kissing Bruce. Then her head disappearing into his lap . . .

Caroline pressed pause and glared at her husband's puffy red face.

She would never forget taking the video. Standing in front of that damn car and hearing Max's screams. Seeing the fear in Bruce's eyes.

The night her life was forever ruined. When she'd lost her husband and her best friend in one fell swoop.

Now, almost two years later, Caroline still felt the rage boil within her. She thought about what Max had said at the deli before leaving. *"We're even now."*

Caroline Parker squeezed her hands into fists.

No, Caroline thought. *Not today. Not tomorrow.*

"Not ever," she whispered, staring down at the paused image on the screen.

ACKNOWLEDGMENTS

My wife, Dixie, has been my rock of encouragement, love, and support. She's also my first editor. None of this happens without her.

Our children, Jimmy, Bobby, and Allie, inspire me every day.

My mom, Beth Bailey, is always my first reader and greatest supporter.

My agent, Liza Fleissig, continues to guide my career with persistence, loyalty, and grit. She is a fierce advocate and a trusted friend.

My developmental editor, Clarence Haynes, offered advice and suggestions that improved this story. His encouragement helped me push this novel past the finish line.

Megha Parekh, my longtime editor and friend, provided insights that were instrumental in helping me find my vision for this novel.

Erin Mitchell has been a lifeline to connect me with readers, fans, and bookstores. I appreciate her help so much.

Thank you once again to my friends Steve Shamesm, Bill Fowler, and Rick Onkey, who provided early reads of this story and have been with me from the beginning.

My brother, Bo Bailey, is my sounding board for almost everything I do, and his encouragement and wisdom helped me decide to start mediating cases again . . . and assisted with this story.

George Smith and Brad English, my colleagues and friends, both lent their expertise in government contracting law and answered every question that I had.

Jonathan Lusk, my good friend and a divorce law specialist, provided great insights on domestic relations law.

Ben Rice, the dean of mediators in Madison County for years, gave me stories, advice, and expertise that helped this story. I hope you enjoy your retirement, Ben. There is an Easter egg in this novel for you!

Dr. Henry Everitt and his lovely wife, Patricia, took me to an impromptu dinner after a book event in Houston, and have been such wonderful supporters of my career.

Allen Schreiber, Phillip McCallum, and Gaynor St. John are fantastic mediators and have become great friends. Watching each of you work and participating in our group's phone calls have helped me as a mediator and also informed this story. I am so proud to be a mediator with Schreiber ADR.

Joe and Foncie Bullard continue to support my career, and our annual visits with them on the Gulf Coast are something I cherish.

My father-in-law, Dr. Jim Davis, provided an early read, and his encouragement and wise counsel have been invaluable to my career.

Mark Wittschen, to whom I dedicated this novel, has supported my dream of being a writer since our days as roommates at Davidson College. Always one of my first readers, Mark has offered incredible insights not just for *The Mediator* but for all my stories. Thank you, roomie!

ABOUT THE AUTHOR

Photo © 2019 Erin Cobb

Robert Bailey is the *Wall Street Journal* bestselling author of *The Boomerang* as well as the Jason Rich series (*Rich Justice*, *Rich Waters*, and *Rich Blood*), the Bocephus Haynes series (*The Wrong Side* and *Legacy of Lies*), and the award-winning McMurtrie and Drake legal thriller series (*The Final Reckoning*, *The Last Trial*, *Between Black and White*, and *The Professor*). He also wrote the inspirational novel *The Golfer's Carol*. *The Mediator* is his twelfth novel.

A retired attorney and registered mediator, Bailey lives in Huntsville, Alabama, with his wife, Dixie. They are the proud parents of three children, two dogs, and two cats. For more information, please visit the author's website at www.robertbaileybooks.com.